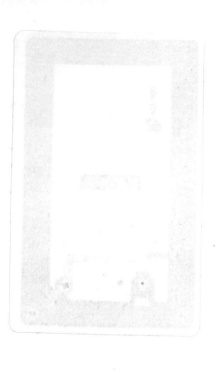

Romancing the Throne

Romancing the Throne

NADINE JOLIE COURTNEY

 KATHERINE TEGEN BOOKS
An Imprint of HarperCollins Publishers

Katherine Tegen Books is an imprint of HarperCollins Publishers.

Library of Congress Control Number: 2016950153
ISBN 978-0-06-240662-0

Typography by Torborg Davern
17 18 19 20 21   PC/LSCH   10 9 8 7 6 5 4 3 2 1

First Edition

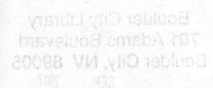

For Erik and Aurelia.
You are my everything.

one

My serve has been my secret weapon ever since I mastered it at Wimbledon junior tennis camp two years ago. The moment I arch my back and feel my racket make contact with the ball, I know Libby is done for.

She runs for it, almost tripping over herself in her haste to get to the corner. The ball slices right and smashes into the hedges. She's not fast enough.

Game, set, match.

"Damn!" She stops at the net, her chest rising and falling heavily from the sprint. There's a ring of frizz around the crown of her curly brown hair. "You never practice—it's not fair you're so good!" She tucks her racket between her knees as she wipes her brow with her forearm. The morning sun is unusually harsh, even for August.

"If you got it, you got it," I say, grinning. "Don't feel bad, Libs! You'll catch up with me someday."

The joke is my sister has no reason to feel insecure. She's an academic rock star, just like Dad was at school, but at least I inherited Mum's sport gene.

And it's nice to know there are still things I can beat my big sister at.

She pulls down her scraggly ponytail, the hair falling around her slim shoulders. "Let's play again. I know I can beat you."

"Dream on."

"Scared you'll mess up your makeup?"

"I'm not falling for that trash talk. I need to get ready for the party, so I *am* worried I'll mess up my makeup, as a matter of fact. I guess you'll just have to survive knowing you're second best," I tease.

Libby bounces the ball on the other side of the court. "C'mon . . . one more set. We'll be done in ten minutes. That's all I need to beat you," she says, smiling.

"Tempting, but no." I shake my head and swat a ball across the net. It sails into nothingness, making a satisfying *whomp* as it hits a wall draped in lilac-colored wisteria. "My train leaves at one thirty and it's going to take me at least an hour to get ready. Thank God I'm already packed. Although I would kill for a quick dip in the pool." My parents have been doing renovations little by little since buying this house, and the Olympic-sized swimming pool—my mother's dream ever since she was a girl—was finally finished at the beginning of the summer.

"All you do is lie out by the pool and play with that damn beauty app," she sighs. "We've only played tennis twice this summer." Libby starts walking around the court, gathering the scattered balls.

"Hey, my tan's not going to top up by itself," I say, adopting a more serious tone when I see her disappointed face. "But I'm sorry. We should have played more."

"Nah, I'm not angry. I've been distracted, too." She bops her racket against her heel, anxiety creasing her delicate features.

"Greene House?" I ask.

"Yeah." Over the summer, rumors started that Libby's headmaster had been taking bribes from parents in exchange for high marks. Libby made me promise not to tell Mum and Dad. If the rumors turn into something real, it could ruin Libby's last year—universities might look at all the top students coming out of Greene House as suspect.

I try to distract her by making light of it, gathering balls and dumping them in the hopper. "I never understood why you wanted to go to an all-girls school in the first place. No man candy? Cringe!"

"What a novel concept," she says, smiling. "Picking a school for the academics. What *was* I thinking?" She walks around the net and smacks me on the bum with the face of her racket.

"Whatever." I make a big show of looking exasperated. "Sussex Park is just as good as Greene House. We're fifteen-time field hockey champions."

"We send more women to Oxbridge universities than any other school in England."

"Our graphic design program smokes yours."

"The prime minister's wife and the Queen of Jordan went to mine."

"Oh, yeah? Well, *Prince Edward* goes to mine. Boom." I make a mic drop gesture with a tennis ball and we both start giggling. "I wish we'd gone to the same school from the beginning. If the Greene House stuff gets really bad, you should transfer to Sussex Park."

"It's not that easy." Libby looks around the court, which is now empty. "I think we're done here." We turn and start to make our way across the court and through the gate, turning up the wide, sloping lawn toward our house. We've been living here for four years—not only do we have a tennis court and a pool, but we have acres and acres of fields, and the house itself is gorgeous. It's a three-story Tudor with brick, stone, and wood half-timbering and a gabled roof. I only spend the summers and holidays here, when I'm home from boarding school, but I still can't believe this is ours.

It's so smart that it even has a *name*: Wisteria.

"It's exactly that easy. Sussex Park loves sibling legacies—double the tuition. Mum makes a few phone calls, writes a check, and voilà!"

"In my last year of school?"

I shrug. "Why not?"

Libby shakes her head as we walk up the low stone steps leading to the pool and back garden. "I *like* Greene House. All my friends are there. I'm already signed up for all my A levels. Hopefully everything will be fine and I won't have to worry about it. New subject. Excited for the party tonight?"

"*Obviously.* India's house makes Downton Abbey look like a cottage. They even have a garden maze."

"Sounds terribly smart."

"You could act a little more sincere. Be happy for me!"

Libby laughs. "What do you want from me, Lotte? That's *amazing*! I am positively *astounded*! This party is guaranteed to change your life—*forever*!" She raises an eyebrow. "Is that better?"

Libby keeps her sarcastic side hidden from most people, but I secretly love seeing it. "Fine. But I'm super excited. Did you know India's grandfather is the Duke of Exeter?"

"You don't say. I only heard you telling Mum *and* Nana *and* whoever you were chatting on the phone to earlier."

"Oh, stop pretending you're above it." I lean down as we walk by the pool, splashing a little water on her. She squeals.

"Your friend's grandfather could be the Duke of America for all I care. It's not like we don't know people with titles and nice houses. Both of our schools are full of them. And Wisteria is hardly a shack."

"Yeah, but this is different. You've never met India. She's *amazing*."

"Preparing to be amazed."

I roll my eyes at her. "Besides, she's good friends with Prince Edward."

"That's two mentions in two minutes. Somebody's got him on the brain," she teases.

"I do not."

"India's a regular girl, and Edward's a regular boy. There's nothing special about either of them."

"So wrong."

"You know it's not important what people like that think of you, no matter how posh they are, right? What matters is how you see

5

yourself. You've got to be comfortable with you," she says, her face turning serious.

"Okay, Dr. Freud."

"You're too preoccupied with money and status, Lotte."

"Oh, come on. You know how kids at our schools work. There's *no* money," I say, holding my hand palm-down near the waist of my tennis shorts, "and there's *new* money"—I gesture at our massive garden, full of roses and jasmine and hyacinths, as we walk through it toward the indoor terrace—"and then finally there's *old* money." I raise my cupped hand above my head to signal the upper limit. "You can pretend all you like that that stuff doesn't exist. But it does."

"That stuff isn't as important as it used to be."

"That stuff is *always* important. We've got to work twice as hard to prove ourselves to the kids with old money—while pretending we totally don't care."

Libby shakes her head. "I hope you're exaggerating. I have no interest in proving myself to anybody—it sounds exhausting."

I shrug.

"All I'm saying is, everybody loves you. You're smart, you're kind, and you're gorgeous. I know you'd be just as happy hanging out with normal people as with royalty. And they'd *all* be lucky to have you. Don't forget that."

"Well, Prince Edward is royalty *and* he's normal. So it's a double bonus," I say, butterflies working my stomach as I think about the possibility of hanging out with Prince Edward tonight. "But thank you. You should bottle that praise and release a motivational app. I'll play it whenever I need a boost." My eyes widen as I adopt a creepy voice and raise my arms like a zombie. "You're *smaaart* . . . you're *gooorgeous* . . . everybody *looooves* you . . ."

She laughs. "I'll miss you when we go back to school."

"Me, too."

As we walk through the terrace and then inside the French doors leading to the sitting room, I think for the millionth time how nice it would be to have something lining the walls or dotting the bookshelves showing *my* success. Instead, the wood-paneled room is a shrine to my sister's academic perfection, with her certificates, badges, and trophies on conspicuous display:

First Place, Year Ten Science Carnival.

National Achievement Award in Writing: Year Eleven.

Greene House Student Merit Award.

Libby Weston for the win!

Mum obviously realized at some point that turning our house into the Libby Weston Fan Club was a little weird, and earlier this summer two framed photos of me competing in field hockey and athletics suddenly materialized atop the baby grand piano by the brick fireplace.

Hey, at least they're trying.

"Race you to the kitchen!" I say.

"Not if I get there first!"

We elbow each other while running into the kitchen, laughing as we try to beat each other to the fridge. The kitchen was last summer's upgrade project; Mum had it gutted and remodeled to look like the prime minister's kitchen, which was featured in *House Beautiful* magazine. The showpieces are the island, with a white marble countertop, and the huge Aga stove—two other things she's been fantasizing about for years and finally was able to get after her business took off.

"Careful, you two!" Mum's at the kitchen table, typing on her laptop with a buffet of documents laid out in front of her. A glass of white wine sits next to the computer. "I've been working on these all morning."

"What's the latest?" I ask, chugging water and standing at the counter while scrolling through my favorite beauty app, Viewty. I heart a photo of dip-dyed fringe, and then bookmark a picture of purple-and-silver smoky eyes, making a plan to try the look myself later. Libby pulls a chair out and sits next to our mother.

"We have a big order shipping next week. I've been reviewing the stock to make sure everything is organized." She points a manicured finger at the screen. "See that? Not a bad day's work for your ol' mum, huh?"

I look up momentarily from scrolling through the photo feed, peeking over her shoulder before looking down at my phone again. "Holy crap! Harrods ordered your shoes? That's sick! Way to go, Mum!"

"Thank you, Charlotte, but will you please put your phone away? You're glued to it."

"She's on that app *again*," says Libby. "I don't know why you use it so much if you're always complaining about how buggy it is."

"Sorry," I say. "But there's nothing better out there." I leave my phone on the counter, grab a banana from the fruit bowl, and sit down opposite her. Outside the picture windows, the sun blazes over the fields surrounding our home. When we first moved here, I didn't like the thought of being so secluded out in the country, but now I love it. "You going to miss me tonight? Throwing a big party while I'm gone?"

"Dad is picking up a curry."

"Do you think he knew when you got married that you'd never cook a day in your life?" I ask between bites of banana.

"I cook! Sometimes . . ."

"Well, why should women be expected to cook anyway, right?" I say. "So sexist. So antiquated."

Libby laughs. "So says the girl who's dying to become a princess."

"I'd be a *totally* modern princess," I say, raising my chin in mock haughtiness. "The royal family wouldn't know what had hit them."

"You'd throw Buckingham Palace's first garden-party electronica concert."

"And Snapchat from the balcony."

"And Instagram photos of your outfits with the hashtag 'princess pose.'"

"Ooh, look at you! Libby knows what a hashtag is! Somebody's been brushing up on her social media." The only thing Libby regularly uses is Twitter, so she can keep up with breaking news. As for me, Instagram is my drug of choice—I have over ten thousand followers, which thrills me—though I wish the number were even larger. Thanks to Mum's shoe business, Soles, my collection is massive and my "shoes of the day" posts get hundreds of likes. "I wish you'd join Instagram, Libs. You're such a great photographer—you'd love it."

"Who'd want to see my boring photos?" she says. Mum and Dad

bought Libby a professional DSLR last year—finally responding to years of subtle hints. True to form, however, Libby doesn't like doing anything unless she can excel at it, and she's too shy to share her photography attempts—even though I think they're amazing.

"Um, earth to Libby. Boring people with your photos is the entire *point* of social media." We giggle.

"None of my friends are on Instagram, anyway."

"Ugh, Greene House. Lame. You really should move."

We exchange a panicked look as I remember that Mum doesn't know about the scandal yet. I quickly change the subject.

"I should probably start getting ready for India's party. Can't go looking like *this*." I point to myself and pull a face.

"You're beautiful without makeup, honey," says Mum. "I wish you knew that."

The first time I applied makeup, I felt transformed. I'm sure it had more to do with my age—thirteen—than my actual self-esteem, but I was going through a rough acne patch and felt like a total ugly duckling.

Mum had started Soles the year before, and it took off like a rocket. Suddenly, we were rolling in money. We moved from a small two-bedroom town house in Guildford—where Libby and I shared a bedroom—to a *six*-bedroom house in Midhurst, a quaint town dotted with Tudor architecture. Overnight, we upgraded not just our house but our lives: now we could afford vacations, new clothes instead of hand-me-downs from cousins, a car for each parent, and, of course, boarding school. Not everybody was happy about the transition. Even though I invited my old friends over for sleepovers all the time, they dropped me soon after we moved. I think they were jealous of the fact that we suddenly had money, but they said I was up my own bum. I cried every night for two months—Libby came home from school three weekends in a row her first year at Greene House just to comfort me. While it was hurtful and confusing, it also made me determined to surround myself with people who admired success, instead of resenting it.

To cheer me up, Mum let me tag along on her first Soles photo shoot. The makeup artist showed me some tricks, and everybody agreed I looked a million times better after she plucked my brows and applied mascara and lip gloss. Even my dad said I looked pretty when Mum and I got home from the shoot—and he *never* focuses on looks. Soon after, Mum bought me all the makeup that the artist recommended, and I left for my first day at Sussex Park a few months later fully made up: armor on.

I've never forgotten that lesson. People say it's what's on the inside that counts—but you're fooling yourself if you think they ignore the outside, too.

"You're certain Prince Edward will be there?"

Libby groans. "Not you, too, Mum."

"It's very exciting!" Mum says defensively, taking a sip of wine. "Your father and I have spoiled you both. Sending you to top schools has paid off. You don't know how lucky you are. Not everybody is a classmate of the future king. Most people will never run in those circles."

"He's just—"

"—a boy," I say, finishing my sister's sentence. "We know, we know. But come *on*, Libby. Has that all-girls school turned you to stone? Even *your* feminist heart has to beat a little faster thinking of a prince as hot as Edward."

She smiles. "I never said he wasn't hot."

"Thank you! That's all I ask. Just a little acknowledgment that your sister has made it to the big leagues."

"How many people are expected at India's?" Mum asks.

"From what I heard, her parties are small. Only about twenty people." I don't tell my mum that India's parties are also notorious for teenage debauchery. Last year, the entire Sussex Park campus was abuzz for weeks with talk of Flossie Spencer-Dunhill's drunken skinny-dip with Tarquin Sykes in the Huntshire pool.

I know Libby's right: it's kind of embarrassing that I'm *this* excited about gaining India's friendship. Even with my self-esteem at an all-time low when I was younger, I've never been a wallflower, and I have a ton of acquaintances at Sussex Park. But my old friends—mostly hockey teammates—graduated last year, and after India's best friend, Byrdie Swan-Grover, graduated, India tapped *me* for friendship. Being part of India's group is a stamp of approval that guarantees major social access—the kind of approval I've been dreaming about ever since leaving my old school. I'm cool with India's friend Flossie, who plays hockey, and with Alice Hicks, who's in a few of my classes. And, of course, India and I have been friendly since we sat next to each other in English class my first year and instantly bonded when we realized we both thought manufactured pop groups were totally lame. But the rest of her clique is a mystery. India's small circle is the best of not just Sussex Park but of English society in general—and

Prince Edward is smack dab in the center of it.

Why *wouldn't* you want in on that?

"So, do you really think India means to set you two up?" Mum asks. "Surely she was joking."

"I don't know." I shrug, trying to play it cool. I'm trying to keep my hopes in check, since boys like Edward tend to only date girls like India—the upper-class kids like to swim in the same pond, recycling the same few options over and over. "I guess we'll find out."

"It's incredibly exciting," Libby says magnanimously, reaching over to squeeze my hand.

I poke Libby in the ribs playfully before picking up my phone again. "Right? It's huge. He's very private. Not just anybody gets to hang out with him."

"Nana's going to lose her mind. Have you told her, Mum?"

"I may have mentioned in passing that you were going to a house party he would be at . . ."

"Ha! I bet the two of you had a forty-five-minute conversation all about it," Libby says. "Where she immediately decided they would become a couple, started daydreaming about a spring wedding, and plotted out exactly what she'd say to the King and Queen when she met them."

"Ugh," I say. "No pressure or anything."

Mum laughs. "Guilty." The wineglass rapidly empties. "Nana kept repeating the importance of her rules."

"Oh, God, Nana's Rules for Dating," I groan. "How many times did you have to hear that when you were growing up?"

"You're better off not knowing."

"*Rule Number One,*" repeats Libby. "*Never let a boy know you like him.*"

"*Rule Number Two,*" I say. "*Always play hard to get.*"

"*Rule Number Three. Let him see you surrounded by other gentlemen,*" she counters.

"*Rule Number Four. Don't give away the milk for free,*" I laugh.

"Because women are cows, and barnyard metaphors are so progressive," Libby says, shaking her head. "She's *so* special."

"She's truly from a different time," Mum says. "Can you imagine what a nightmare it was trying to date with all that rubbish in my head?"

"As long as Lotte doesn't compromise her goals," says Libby, suddenly serious. She looks at me. "This is a big year for you. You need to keep your marks up and focus on hockey, too. You're so great at it—you could get a scholarship! Don't get distracted by boys."

"Oh ye of little faith. Like I can't juggle boys and books?"

"Yeah, but he's not a normal boy—he's a prince."

"Whatever. Tom-ay-to, tom-ah-to."

She rolls her eyes, smiling at me. "Well, then, promise me one thing: Treat him like any other guy, okay?"

"Relax," I say. "I'm a big girl. I can handle myself just fine."

"I know you can." She's silent for a second, and then breaks out into a grin. "And if you can't, your big sister will be your attack dog."

"Atta girl!"

We each kiss our index finger twice, holding them out until they touch.

"Are you two still doing that?" Mum asks, looking amused. "I haven't seen you do that in *years*."

When Libby and I were little, our absolute favorite movie was *E.T.* We'd re-create the scene where Elliott and E.T. bike through town, with Libby wearing one of Dad's red zip-up sweatshirts and me sitting in a milk crate on the floor of our cramped living room or our shared bedroom. We loved the scene when E.T. touched Elliott with his glowing finger, and over the years, it morphed into our own private thing. Whenever we do it, it's an instant code reminding us that we always have each other's backs.

"Sisters forever," we say together.

Mum beams with pride. "My little girls. You've grown up so fast."

two

"I'm so chuffed you're here, Lotte," India says, hugging me as I get off the train in Gloucestershire. She holds me at arm's length, looking me up and down. "You look wonderful. You've clearly been in the sun."

India is tall and willowy, with the sort of quiet confidence I can only dream of. I've tried to mimic her graceful, glacial movements, and I end up feeling like a stiff robot. But somehow, on India, all the poise and maturity totally works. She has the bearing of an old-world empress trapped in an English teenager's body.

"Here, let me help with that." India reaches out and grabs my mum's Louis Vuitton duffel bag, carrying it to her dusty VW Golf. "We're going to have *the* best time tonight. Flossie, Alice, and Tarquin are already here, and there's another group driving in from Tetbury before dinner. Mummy and Daddy are in Honkers, and my grandparents have promised to make themselves disappear. We'll have the place to ourselves." Her low voice is always scratchy, husky—as if she's smoked an entire pack of cigarettes.

"Honkers?"

After three years at Sussex Park, surrounded by kids from the wealthiest families in the world, there are times when I still feel like a stranger in a strange land. The sharpening of my observation skills while at boarding school would put any private investigator to shame.

"Hong Kong, darls. You should come next time we go. You'll love it." India swishes her waist-length blond hair as she tosses my luggage into the boot of her car. I wince as Mum's new Louis Vuitton duffel brushes up against a dirty pair of riding boots and a mud-caked saddle.

This is something I've noticed with India's set. Unlike what you'd expect, new and gleaming is bad. The older, dirtier, and more worn-in something is, the fonder they are of it. It's not like India's running around in rags, of course. She favors J Brand skinny jeans, skintight tank tops in every color of the rainbow (which she buys in bulk during London shopping trips to Harrods and Harvey Nichols), and has an arm crowded with trendy bangles, charms, rubber bands, strings, and candy-colored concert wristbands. But during winter, I've caught her more than once wearing a cashmere jumper with tiny holes in the elbows or on the collar. My mother would worry about people thinking she was common—when it comes to clothing, the newer and more expensive, the better. India and her friends seem to wear their grandmothers' ancient hand-me-downs as a badge of pride.

They're a paradox, those old-money aristocrats.

At Sussex Park, money is everywhere—although nobody talks about it for fear of being branded tacky—but only a handful of students are true aristocracy. Boundaries and barriers are almost impossible to cross in the draconian English class system, which fascinates me. India's set have a certain air about them: a worldly knowingness. They're courteous and friendly, and they might not call you out for your protocol mistakes—but believe me, they notice.

After all, only people who know the rules in the first place are allowed to break them.

Even I think the prospect of Edward dating a regular, non-titled girl like me is very unlikely. Like clings to like—everybody in his crowd is the earl of this or the viscount of that.

Luckily, India doesn't seem to care about all that. But still, I have to try harder to fit in—a lot harder.

"Hong Kong sounds awesome. Although I don't know how keen my parents will be."

"Parents are a damn nuisance," India says, waving her hands in contempt as she starts the car and sets off toward Huntshire.

"You're lucky," I say. "Your parents never bother you—they're not a nuisance at all. Mine are always up in my business." India's parents rarely come to campus, and when they do, they're aloof and uninterested. They seem happy to let her run the show.

"The less involved parents are, the better. They don't understand us. You have to train them. It's like boys, really."

I laugh. "Speaking of boys . . . who's coming tonight?"

She raises an eyebrow at me and smiles. "Plotting your conquests already? Tarquin's here—although everything out of his mouth is bound to be a *complete* disaster, as always. Oliver's on his way as we speak. There's a group of Eton boys arriving after dinner. And, of course, Edward."

"Oh, yeah? Nice."

"You're as transparent as a plastic bag," she laughs. "Don't try to play it cool."

I blush. "Fine, you caught me."

The first time I ever saw Prince Edward, it was three days into my first year at Sussex Park, when I literally bumped smack into him on the quad while texting Libby.

"Oh! Are you all right?" he asked.

I looked up, ready to start offering my apologies. Then I realized the tall boy whose bony chest my forehead had just made contact with was Prince Edward. *The* Prince Edward.

Sussex Park had its fair share of royalty and nobility, but most of the princes and princesses were from faraway countries you'd never heard of and couldn't pronounce—like Djibouti or Tuvalu. Going to school with the future king of England (and Scotland, Northern Ireland, Wales, and the Commonwealth), though, was a *very* big deal. Edward sightings were still rare on campus. It was rumored that he mostly stayed in his dormitory, only coming out to eat and attend classes.

"Oh my God!" I said. "It's you!" The second the words tumbled out of my mouth, I wanted to take them back.

"Last time I checked," he said, looking down at his forearm and pulling on the sleeve of his rugby shirt. He was wearing a rucksack and faded trainers. "Yep. Still me." He smiled at me before continuing on. "Have a great day—see you around!"

As soon as he'd passed through the stone arches at the south end of the quad, I whipped my phone back out and called Libby. "Oh. My. God. You are not going to *believe* what just happened."

Students tended to stick with classmates in their own year, and like India, Edward was a year older than I was, so our paths rarely crossed. Sometimes he'd smile at me, but I wasn't convinced he didn't smile at everybody.

Of course, now that I'm about to encounter him again today, I can't help but get excited. It's three years later, I'm about to turn seventeen, and I've got my flirting down to a fine art.

There will only be a handful of us here tonight—so he *has* to notice me.

"Edward will be here in time for dinner. He's driving in from Cedar Hall."

I nod, recognizing the name of his family home from my mum's issues of *Hello!* "What's for dinner tonight?"

"Nothing special. My grandmother Pidge arranged pizza for us in the garden. Her chefs are off for the night."

As we zoom down the narrow A433, I think how, to an untrained eye, these country roads might look similar to the roads near our house in West Sussex. But there's more of a hush here; the leafy trees shading the road seem greener somehow. It's as if the scenery knows that the people who live in this part of England expect a higher level of privacy.

We drive though unspoiled medieval towns, with stone houses dating back hundreds of years. We cross over a shallow river, which trickles through an impossibly quaint village surrounded by thatched cottages. India points out the oldest tree in England, a two-thousand-year-old oak nestled in the grounds of a small church.

After miles of winding country lanes, we turn off onto a narrow cobbled path where I notice a brown sign. There's a small house-shaped icon, and the word "Huntshire" painted on it in white letters. We pull up to a back gate. Recognition dawns on a security guard's face as he waves India through.

It's a magnificent place. A narrow brook curves around a muddy building made out of wood. The smooth grass runs alongside a circular lake, where a mirror of still water is lined by a copse of trees.

We pass the stables and make a sharp right, turning onto a paved driveway leading to the largest house I've ever seen.

I see three sprawling levels of gray stone tethered to the earth in front of us as we pull right up to the front entrance.

I try to remember all the rules I've learned as I've slowly made my way into India's circle.

I think of Nana: *Don't look too impressed.*

Screw that.

This is by far *the* most majestic house I've ever seen. The word *house* doesn't begin to do it justice.

"Nice," I say casually.

"Yeah." She shrugs. "It's home. Well, it's home until Grandfather dies and Uncle John inherits it and kicks us out."

Ah, the peculiarities of the English class system.

The huge portico on the north front of the house resembles the entrance to a pantheon rather than a family home. I'm expecting an army of butlers and housekeepers to come outside and take our bags, like on *Downton Abbey*, but India pops the boot open, and the two of us sling our bags over our arms. She walks up to the front door and saunters in like she owns the place.

"It's never locked," she says. "If you make it past the gate, you're meant to be here."

The wide, cavernous entrance hall is decorated with gold paneling everywhere, featuring black-and-white checkered marble floors and several thrusting marble pillars flanking each side. The ceiling is breathtaking, with water lilies carved into the plaster and gold skirting the edges. To the left of the entrance hall is a huge, dusty fireplace. There are a dozen or so lavish-looking hall chairs and a substantial number of ancient-looking artifacts. While the house looks like a hotel on the inside, it's empty and quiet: No servants bustling around. No reception desk. No one but India and me.

There's an imposing oak staircase leading up to the first-floor picture gallery. Tapestries of various sizes depicting medieval kings and queens line the walls, and Romanesque busts on marble columns stand next to each window.

India trudges up the sweeping staircase and turns left, where large portraits hang proudly. The faded gilt on the frames has the telltale patina of centuries of age—unlike the faux-aged frames my mother is fond of buying. "My ancestors," she says by way of explanation, gesturing toward canvases as we pass down the hallway. "An assortment of silly Frasers through the years. The first duke, who fought alongside Henry the Fifth in the Battle of Agincourt . . . the fourth duke, who fled to France during the Restoration by posing as a woman under cover of night . . . the ninth duke, who tried to convince the king that American independence would be a fad . . . my great-grandfather, the eleventh duke, who died on the *Lusitania* a year after inheriting . . . my grandfather, the current duke, who was born in India and still calls Mumbai Bombay." She makes a frustrated noise. "I don't know *what* my family was thinking naming me. Talk about cultural appropriation."

"Have you ever thought about changing it?"

She rolls her eyes. "It's not worth the grief they'll give me. My parents are old school, to say the least. I'm still surprised my dad took the lesbian thing on the chin." India came out to them this summer, texting me furious updates for weeks. "But, you know, they roll with the punches. Keep calm and all that."

"Speaking of, where's your dad's portrait?"

"Dad's the younger son: he doesn't matter. Uncle John's portrait will go up after he inherits. He's panicking over it—claims he doesn't want the bloody thing and all the pressure that goes with it."

"Why doesn't he just give it up?"

"He'd need to go to court, it would be a whole *thing*. Nobody wants that, not even him. Well, maybe my dad, but he's the only one."

"You don't want your dad to inherit?"

India squints, looking thoughtful. "Then he'd be on the hook for the whole bloody estate. The pressure of financial upkeep, the stress of letting down generations if you fail—it's a nightmare. It's much more trouble than it's worth."

We walk down another passageway wide enough to drive a truck through, where the floor is covered in an ancient-looking maroon, blue, and gold weave. Dusty gilt-edged mirrors and battered wooden console tables are placed against the sides. The hallway has the musty smell of an old-age home.

As we turn right into yet another endless hallway, I can't help myself. "Bloody hell, this place is massive."

India laughs. "There are a hundred and fifty-six rooms. My grandfather rents part of it out for weddings most summer weekends. Brings in good income to keep the place going." She starts pointing at door after door. "Those are guest quarters . . . more guest quarters . . . that's a room that hasn't been used since the 1700s . . . that's just a loo . . . that's a staff staircase leading back downstairs."

We make another right turn and encounter a parallel hallway in the back of the house. "I used to ride my bike down these hallways. Drove my nanny bonkers," India says. "That's a drawing room . . . that's a staff door leading up to the third floor. This staircase goes down to the kitchen, another one mainly for the staff . . . I don't know *what* that room is used for, I think it used to be a ballroom . . . my bedroom is just around that corner."

"What about all the rooms on the other side of the house?" I ask.

"More living quarters. Staff quarters on the third floor of the west wing, some larger guest rooms and a study where my grandfather keeps all his maps and war memorabilia, drawing rooms with pianos, stuff like that. And, of course, their private living quarters back in the east wing." She points to another door. "That's Pummy's room."

"Pummy?"

"My older brother, Andrew. Everybody's called him Pummy since he was a baby—I can't remember why it stuck." The upper classes love to call their children ridiculous nicknames that sound like something from a children's nursery rhyme. No doubt India will someday be proud mother to a baby Moony or Smush or Flopsie.

India stops in front of a door that looks just like every other one. "This one is yours: the Oak Room."

There are several portraits on the walls and a gigantic four-poster bed that dominates the room. On the bed is a green velvet cover with gold embroidered stitching. The room is adorned with heavy tapestries hanging from the tall, wood-paneled ceiling, and two large windows look out onto Huntshire's rolling hills. The walls are decorated in muted shades of green and salmon . . . and is that a hand-painted mural? Next to a stone fireplace, framed by an enormous gold mirror and two French taper candelabras, is an elegant wooden armoire. On a low marble table, there's a pot of tea, a tray of digestive biscuits, and the latest issue of *Elle* with a black-and-white picture of Emma Watson on the cover. The room has clearly been renovated for guests—from what I've read in *Hello!* and Julian Fellowes books, most guest bedrooms at grand old country houses are sterile, drafty cubicles. By contrast, this room feels like the Ritz. I wish Libby were here to see this.

"It's fabulous," I say, looking around and realizing there's no en suite bathroom. "Um, but where is . . ."

India smiles. "The loo is down the hall, remember? People think it's so glamorous living in a house like this, but they don't realize I grew up with coal heating, it took ten minutes to walk to breakfast, and you share the lav with ten other people." She turns to leave. "Everybody's probably out back by the pool, so I'd take advantage of the privacy and get ready now if I were you. Come down whenever you like, but dinner's at seven sharp. Meet beforehand in the Smoking Room."

With three hours until dinner, I have time to kill. If Libby were here, she'd explore the grounds, walk through the gardens, maybe take an excursion down to the stables or peruse the library before the rest of the troops arrive. Me? I pull out a hair dryer and the massive makeup bag from my duffel. I'm going to use every single moment to make myself look perfect.

I spend forty-minute minutes trying on outfit combinations before settling on an "effortlessly"—ha!—casual look for tonight: flowing white top, black shorts that hit mid-thigh, and gold sandals. After a relaxing hot shower, I blow-dry my long hair slowly and carefully, adding little braids to the sides so it looks bohemian and artfully messy.

I pad down the hallway from the bathroom back to my room. One of the hanging portraits, of a studious young man holding a book, makes me think about Libby. What if the scandal at her boarding school taints all the hard work she's done? It wouldn't *really* affect her chances at getting into a good university, would it? I couldn't care less where I attend. University isn't for well over two years—it's a lifetime away. But Libby's had a single-minded pursuit of St. Andrews, Dad's alma mater, since she was young. I hope my sister isn't screwed over by something that she has nothing to do with.

Eventually, I decide to put her troubles on hold. I have enough to worry about in my own life. Libby's smart. She'll figure it all out.

Makeup is another endeavor: after forty-five minutes applying waterproof mascara, eye shadow, eyeliner, tinted moisturizer, foundation, bronzer, blush, shimmer highlighter, and lip gloss, I'm satisfied. The trick is to *look* like you're not wearing any makeup, which—like the "this old thing?" outfit—is harder than it sounds. I spritz on a waterproof finishing spray, to keep anything from running or smudging if we go into the pool, and then text Libby to get her opinion.

ME: What do you think? Is the makeup too much?

LIBBY: Maybe a little less lipstick

LIBBY: But I love the braids—you look amazing!

ME: K, thx, love u!!

ME: Heading down to dinner now

LIBBY: Love you, good luck! You're going to do great!

I wipe off my lip gloss, swiping on clear ChapStick instead. Libby's right: it looks even more natural. I check myself from every angle in the dusty gold mirror opposite the armoire, marveling at the dappled evening light streaming through the picture windows. It's better than any Instagram filter. I snap a selfie, tagging Huntshire's location and captioning it "Dinnertime! #countrylife #magichour," and then do a quick ten-second Snapchat video, showing off the view from my window with a timestamp filter.

I check my phone again: it's already a quarter to seven. I walk down the long hallways, feeling like an outsider as I make my way back downstairs.

Stop it. You were invited. You belong here.

The entrance smells like cinnamon. I walk downstairs, stopping by a tall gold clock and trying to remember which way India said I should go.

To the right of the entrance is a green hallway full of portraits, leading to the other wing of the house. To the left is a massive library.

I feel like I'm in a Choose Your Own Adventure novel from my childhood. On one side: coziness, familiarity, and warmth. On the other: uncertainty, danger, and intrigue. Which to choose?

I move toward the library, peeking inside.

It's a cavernous two-story hall with paneled ceilings and amber walls, looking more like the lobby of a grand old resort than a single room. Square oriental tapestries cover the vast length of the hall, polished wood peeking out every twenty feet. A chandelier the size of a helicopter hangs from the paneled ceiling way down in the middle of the hall, and there's a giant organ taking up an entire wall at the far end. There must be twenty thousand books in here. This room alone must take an army of staff to maintain—if you can even call it a room.

"Looking for the Smoking Room, miss?"

I jump, feeling guilty.

An older man in a black suit comes and stands behind me, carrying a tray.

"Yes, thank God you came along! This place is enormous."

"Follow me, please," he says, leading me toward the green

28

hallway. I check out all the old portraits of Frasers on horseback and in uniform and clutching flowers and wearing jewels, wondering how many bloody portraits one family can take over the centuries. We pass by a study, and then finally arrive at the Smoking Room.

Outside the room, there's a gruff-looking man in a navy suit and yellow tie. He takes a step toward me as I approach, as if to block my entry.

"Um . . . the Smoking Room?" I point toward the door, barely recognizing the timidity in my voice.

He nods, taking a step back.

The room is gorgeous, but it's less grand than I expected—especially compared with the library. There are a few overstuffed sofas and ancient chairs, a piano in the corner, a fireplace in the center of the room, and a colossal floor-to-ceiling war tableau covering half of the wall opposite the door. The floor is covered in a red-and-gold antique rug. On top of the piano, there's a framed photo of an old man with the King and Queen. With the exception of the truck-sized painting and the royal photo, it's pretty damn similar to my parents' drawing room at home in Sussex.

And on a hideous floral sofa nearest the fireplace, with his head buried in his iPhone, is Prince Edward. A golden retriever is curled up into a ball next to him, its massive head leaning on Prince Edward's thigh.

I walk in, clearing my throat. "Hiya!"

He looks up from his phone, his face breaking into a warm smile. "Hi! Charlotte, right?" At Edward's voice, the dog lifts its head, looking at me lazily.

Prince Edward knows me. Holy crap.

"Yep, Charlotte Weston. India's friend."

"She mentioned you were coming. You're from Midhurst?"

Remember what Libby said: treat him like any other guy.

"Have you got a dossier on me or something?"

He laughs. "Something like that."

"Where is everybody else?"

"They're never on time."

"Scary guy standing watch outside the door."

"Oh, that's just Simon. Ignore him." Recognition dawns—it must be his bodyguard.

As if sensing my thoughts, the dog jumps off the sofa and rearranges itself on the floor. I will myself to walk over and sit next to Edward on the sofa. "I like your kicks." He's wearing a pair of blue-and-red trainers with his jeans and rugby shirt. Up close, I notice how wide his shoulders are. I picture myself snuggling into him by a roaring fire at Kensington Palace, his arms wrapping around me as we make out during adverts of *Britain's Got Talent.* I have to snap myself back to reality, otherwise I'll start blushing.

"Thanks!" He puts his phone down and swings his arm around the back of the sofa, crossing one leg over the other and jiggling a heel up and down. "So, you're a forward on the hockey team?"

"Seriously, how do you know all this? My stalkers are normally *way* less up front about it."

"I have MI6 on my side," he says, stone-faced. It takes me a second to realize that he's joking.

"Undercover. Nice."

We hear a din out in the hallway, and Flossie, Alice, and India walk in.

"There you are," India says. She's wearing a flowing white caftan with gold embroidery, looking perfect as always. "I knocked on your door. But I see you were otherwise occupied." She smiles, inclining her head toward Edward, and I blush. The two of us stand to greet everybody.

"Hi, Charlotte," Flossie says, looking back and forth between Edward and me.

"Hi, Flossie! Good to see you!"

She smiles. "You, too."

Flossie and I have been hockey teammates for two years now, though it was only after India took me under her wing late last year that Flossie started acknowledging my existence.

"Eds! We missed you by the pool today. You would have *loved* the new diving board." She opens her arms wide and kisses him on both cheeks. "He does a mean backflip," she says to me.

"Two weeks in Paris with your family and suddenly you're double-cheek kissing?" India says to Flossie before giving Edward a hug.

Flossie glares at her, but India doesn't notice. She's already turned her back.

"Hi, kids, big kisses," Alice says distractedly to Edward and me, walking around the near edge of the room by the fireplace. Her wild red hair floats around her thin face in a fuzzy halo. "Where's the booze cart? I desperately need a drink. I've had the worst day."

"Oh, no," I say. "What's wrong?"

"My parents just phoned to say my pet ferret, Mr. Moose, died."

For a second, I think Alice is joking. But then I remember last year in our English class when Alice gave an impassioned speech about how plants have souls, and another time when she declared that she intended to spend her Christmas holiday using sonar equipment in Scotland to see if there was anything large in Loch Ness. She's an eccentric one.

"I'm so sorry. Is he your only pet?"

"Oh, we have a menagerie. Horses, dogs, cats, goats, a donkey, the most *wonderful* llamas, you name it. My brother Hamish collects snakes—mostly ball pythons, of course. But the loss of one of your children always stings."

I nod, wanting to show support but not really sure how to respond. "Of course."

Flossie points to my legs. "You're covered in dog hair."

I look down at my black shorts, which—sure enough—have a thin layer of golden retriever hair all over them. I try to appear cool as I calmly dust my hands over my thighs and bum, letting the hair fall to the floor. Inside, though, I'm cringing.

I mean—I like dogs, my mum likes dogs, everybody likes dogs. But the bloody upper classes are *obsessed* with them.

"Did I get it all?" I ask Edward.

He glances down at my legs nervously, as if worried he'll get yelled at for checking me out. "Looks good to me."

Oliver and Tarquin walk in, each holding a six-pack of beer.

"Beer? You must be joking." India points to the drinks cart in the corner, partially hidden behind a tall plant by the fireplace. "There are like fifteen bottles of gin over there."

"Gin is for mums. I want beer," says Tarquin. Even though he's as posh as it gets, he has a faint Cockney accent, which amuses me—India says it's because of his childhood nanny. His brown hair is still wet, and his round cheeks are fire-engine red, as always. He grabs her, planting a wet, sloppy kiss on her cheek.

India ignores the kiss, plucking a beer bottle from his pack and holding it between her fingers. She inspects the label, wrinkling her nose. "Stella?"

"Didn't seem to bother you ten beers in at Arthur's last weekend," says Oliver, his dimples popping. He removes the top and looks for a place to put it. Tarquin grabs it from him and tosses it in the corner.

"Let's not *completely* trash the joint," India says. "My father isn't heir. They could kick us out of here at any time."

"Oh, please—you have loads of servants. It'll be pristine by morning." Tarquin looks at me but doesn't bother coming over. He nods in greeting. "Hey, Edward. Hey, Charlotte."

Oliver approaches us both, slapping hands and body-slamming shoulders with Edward and then giving me a polite hug.

I watch all the commotion, looking over at Edward to gauge his reaction. He seems amused, settling back into the sofa cushions as Flossie comes over again.

"Eds, are you thirsty? Beer? Wine? G and T?"

"A beer would be great, thanks."

"I'll take one, too, please, Flossie!" I call after her. I lower my voice, muttering to Edward, "I mean, might as well take advantage of her scurrying around after you." Normally I'd be more deferential to Flossie, but I'm taking a risk that Edward will be amused.

He raises an eyebrow. "India told me you were a bit of a firecracker."

"Did she?"

"Among other things."

"*Really?* What other things?"

"It'll only make you blush."

"Try me!"

"She said you were gorgeous, for one," he says, holding up his hands and ticking off fingers. "She also said you were smart, a great athlete, and had excellent taste in men. So far I know she got three out of four right."

The corners of his mouth hook upward, and his eyes dance back and forth between mine. His eyes are dark blue, like my favorite J.Crew jumper. I find myself fighting the urge to lean forward and kiss him.

We're off to a very good start.

three

The full party has arrived, and twenty of us are lounging by the swimming pool as the stars twinkle and fireflies buzz. Huntshire backs up onto one of the most spectacular gardens in England—a vast expanse of hedges, greenery, flowers, and a Hampton Court–inspired maze.

I walk over to the edge of the pool, where it slopes down a green incline leading to the maze, and plop myself next to Oliver on a crumbling stone fence. He's tall and handsome but not at all my type: very buttoned up, with close-cropped reddish-blond hair and a stiff, slightly awkward manner. His father is one of the top bigwigs in the British army—like a general or something.

"What are you drinking?" I ask. His plastic cup is full of a brownish liquid.

"Whiskey. Want a sip?"

"Sure, I love whiskey!" I've never tasted it before, but I've heard it's revolting. I steel myself as I take a small sip, swirling it around the way I've seen my father do at family dinners with my uncle. I swallow gingerly, willing myself to have a poker face as the burning liquid hits my throat. "Good stuff."

"I'm impressed," he says. "Most girls can't handle whiskey."

"Don't be sexist. You don't have to be a boy to drink," I say, poking him in the ribs. I take another sip, this time slightly bigger, before handing the cup back to him.

As I expected, Edward soon comes over to join us. Seconds later, Flossie appears, too.

"What's going on?" Edward asks. He sits down on the fence next to me.

"We're getting our whiskey on," I say.

"Charlotte's a tough old bird," says Oliver approvingly.

"Is she?" Edward asks. He looks at me. "What did you do this time?"

"That's between Oliver and me," I say coyly, hoping a little competition will spur Edward on rather than scare him away.

"Hey, Oliver! Flossie! I need your help!" India calls from across the pool. She's carrying a tray of cupcakes with one hand and a bottle of vodka with the other.

"Duty calls," says Oliver, marching across the lawn.

"What does she need *now*?" Flossie sighs, following behind him.

"And then there were two," I say, leaning back and letting my hair fall over my shoulder.

He meets my gaze and we smile at each other. I'm doing my best to appear cool, but my heart is beating double-time. God, but he's *so* cute.

"Can I tell you a secret?" I ask, scanning the situation and taking another risk.

He leans forward. "I'm all ears."

"Oliver thinks I'm a rock star because I had a sip of whiskey, but I hated it. It tastes like jet fuel."

Edward laughs. "I know what you mean—I don't have a taste for anything but beer and cheap wine. When people serve me expensive wine at dinner, it's such a waste. I have to gulp it down and pretend I know the difference."

"I'll keep your secret if you keep mine," I say, raising my cup.

We lock eyes.

"Oh, but you're almost out," Edward says. "Can I get you something?"

"Whatever you're having," I say. "Beer is just fine."

This must be the first time in his life that Prince Edward has been dispatched to get a drink.

He chuckles. "One bottle of Belgium's finest, coming right up."

He makes his way over to the icebox and pulls out two bottles of Stella, holding them aloft triumphantly as he returns. He skillfully removes the tops using the ledge of a wall as an opener, banging his palm down over the metal caps.

"Somebody's been around the block."

"If you had spent time with my friends growing up, you'd know how to open a beer bottle in three seconds flat, too."

I do my best to look dainty as I take my first sip. I'm not used to drinking very much at all—whether it's whiskey *or* beer.

I notice that Edward is already halfway through his beer, whereas I've taken only two small sips. I wonder if he burns through girls as fast.

"What are you two whispering about?" India calls from the side of the pool.

"We're talking smack about you, obviously," says Edward.

"Good. As long as I'm at the center of all your thoughts," India says before turning toward a member of staff trying to get her attention. Flossie stands next to her, holding the tray of cupcakes and looking bored. She and I lock eyes for a second before Flossie smiles at me.

"Is it my imagination, or does Flossie keep giving me weird looks?" I ask in a low voice. He starts to crane his neck and I put my hand on his arm to stop him. "No! Too obvious!"

Edward turns his head and makes a quick sweep of the balcony. "Oh, yes, she obviously hates you. Daggers. I'd lock your door tonight if I were you."

"You're terrible," I say, nudging him with my shoulder, which only serves to push us even closer together. "I've known her for a couple of years, but I feel like she's being kind of weird tonight."

He cocks his head to the side. "I don't think she's being especially weird with you—that's just Floss. But if I had to guess, I'd say she's jealous."

"Jealous? Of me?"

"Why wouldn't she be?"

"Hmm, that's true. I *am* pretty amazing."

He crooks up an eyebrow in amusement. "Humble, too."

"I'm just joking."

He shakes his head. "No, you're not. And that's why you *are* amazing." He looks back at Flossie discreetly. She's followed India to the far corner of the garden, where India's holding court with Oliver, Tarquin, and a few people I don't know. "I've known her since we were infants. Our parents are close friends."

"Did you two ever date? Is that why she's jealous?"

"Nah," he says. "We kissed once when we were like twelve, but it was during a game. She's had a crush on me ever since."

"Now *you're* the humble one."

He laughs.

"Technically, we're related," he says. "Our great-great-great-grand-whatevers were siblings, so I think we're fourth cousins."

"You snogged your cousin? Gross!"

For some reason, Edward finds my reaction hilarious. "Not quite that . . . but sure."

"So, she's just not your type?"

"Not even a little bit." His eyes crinkle.

"I see," I say, taking a sip.

"You didn't ask me your question."

"What question?"

"What my type *is.*"

The edges of my lips curve into my sexiest smile. I look him full in the face, my pulse racing as I say boldly, "Oh, I think I know exactly what your type is."

I reach out to brush an imaginary something off his shoulder, letting my hand linger a moment too long. Really, I just want another excuse to touch him.

Across the pool, India whips off her flowing white dress to reveal a gold bikini on a body to die for. "Edward, stop chatting up my friend and get over here! You, too, Lotte. It's time we all got wet." With that, India dives headfirst into the pool.

"With an invitation like that, how can we resist?" I say.

"After you," Edward says, offering me a hand. I clean the gravel off my bum and follow him to the pool.

The large, rectangular pool is surrounded by solid beech hedges, which have been cut into pillars and shaped into arcs. I remove my shoes and throw my clothes on a nearby chair. Underneath, I'm wearing my red bikini.

I catch Edward looking at me, but he glances away when he notices me looking. He pulls off his shirt and we stand in front of each other shyly.

"So . . . are you just going to stare at me all night?" I ask.

Edward takes me by the hand, pulls me after him, and the next thing I feel is a blast of cold water as we plunge clumsily into the pool.

As we laugh and splash around in the cold turquoise water, I jump on his back and try to dunk him. We begin grabbing at limbs and climbing all over each other like puppies. He lifts me up slightly and I realize that my cleavage is now at his eye level.

"Not quite so high!" I squeak, feeling a flash of self-consciousness.

My bikini top is so ludicrously padded, I might as well have towels stuffed in my bra.

He slides me lower down his torso. Now we're eye to eye. "Is this better?"

With our bodies pressed together, I can feel his heart racing just like mine.

"Much."

I close my eyes briefly, willing him to lean in and kiss me.

Instead, he just grins and sinks down to the bottom of the pool, pulling me under with him.

Before I know it, it's two a.m. and we're all drunk as farts, running around Huntshire's expansive grounds in our wet bathing suits. Somebody's found an old Polaroid, and we all mug for the camera. After a series of silly photos of just the two of us—Edward holding me in his arms, me jumping on his back, the two of us hamming it up with beer bottles—Edward and I play hide-and-seek in the maze, which has over a thousand yew trees and a single path leading to the center. It's all so romantic I don't know how this could end with anything *but* a kiss.

I finally find Edward in the center of the maze, a narrow, enclosed space. Edward leans in, and our faces are mere inches away from each other.

I'm in a maze with a handsome prince.

"I caught you," he says. He's so close I can see a faint freckle on his right cheek. I can pick out the flecks of gold in his blue eyes.

"I caught *you*," I say, shivering as much from the cold night air as from his steady gaze. I can feel his warm breath, sweet with the faint smell of fermented hops, as he leans forward and rests his lips on mine.

As our lips meet, I feel a frisson of energy and excitement and triumph shimmy down my spine. He leans into me hungrily, and I push my body back into his, acutely aware of the bare skin of my stomach grazing against his.

I've been fantasizing about this moment for so long, but I never believed it would actually happen. I mean, who snogs the future king?

I've kissed only a handful of boys, but I suspect I'm not a bad kisser. And the way Edward is running his hands over my back right now, not to mention nibbling gently at my tongue, makes me suspect this isn't the worst five minutes of his life, either.

"God, Charlotte, you're a hell of a kisser."

"You're not so bad yourself."

As he leans down again, he starts kissing the side of my neck, sending waves of pleasure through my body. I let out an involuntary little moan, and he grins at me. "Ah, you like that, do you?"

In response, I pull him onto the ground and then roll us over onto his back, so I'm now on top. I saw a woman in one of my dad's favorite James Bond movies do that once, and it looked so cool.

"And *you* like *this*," I laugh.

"Guilty."

I feel more comfortable and confident being in control. I'm willing to bet Edward isn't used to girls taking the lead, either.

I giggle, leaning down and meeting his lips again. As our lips and tongues touch, I try to stop myself from laughing, but a wave of involuntary giggles comes over me. Every time I try to get serious, I succeed for only a few seconds before the giggles rise up again.

"I'm that bad, huh?"

"No!" I laugh. "I don't know what's gotten into me. Happiness. Or nerves."

"I don't believe you've been nervous a day in your life."

"I have!" I protest, leaning forward so that my elbows are on either side of his head and my forearms are resting on his chest. "I get nervous. All the time."

"I'll believe that one when I see it."

"What about you? Surely nothing makes *you* nervous."

"Oh, plenty makes me nervous. I just do a good job of hiding it."

I shift on top of him and suddenly realize that a bulge is poking through his bathing suit.

"Hi there," I giggle.

He blushes. "See? Nerves."

"That is *not* what nerves feel like."

We both start giggling, and before I know it, we're kissing again, Edward's hands running all through my hair, down the length of my back, up the sides of my legs.

Suddenly, the mood shifts from light and sexy to heavy and expectant, and I realize that I'm standing on a precipice. Is this the moment? I'm not sure I'm ready. Scratch that—I *know* I'm not ready.

I like Edward, but my first time having sex isn't going to be on the grass in the back of somebody's garden—prince or no prince.

I put my hand lightly on his chest, sitting up slightly. "This is the most fun I've had in a long time. But I should go to bed."

He looks concerned, sitting up, too. "Are you feeling all right?"

"I'm feeling fine. I just . . ."

"I understand," he says, nodding. "At least, I think I do." He holds my gaze, blushing a little. "You're kind of amazing."

"Oh, go on." I pause and then say, "No, but seriously, go on."

He laughs, standing and offering his hand to pick me up.

"You're not transferring away from Sussex Park, are you?"

"No, why?"

"Good. Then this won't be the last time I see you." He gathers my face in his hands, leaning down to give me one single, sweet kiss.

"Should we say good night to everybody?"

"I'm going to stay awake. But I'll walk you back to your room."

"No need," I say. "Let's say good night here."

I lean up on my tiptoes to give him one last kiss, then turn on my heel, running out of the maze and back into the house.

I'm not surprised in the least when, on the train back home to West Sussex the next day, I pull my buzzing phone out of my pocket to find a text from Edward waiting for me.

EDWARD: I can't wait to see you again. Xx

four

Once I get home from Huntshire, I have only three weeks of summer left until school starts. The time crawls by at a snail's pace. Even though Libby and I spend loads of bonding time together—she's ecstatic because she finally manages to beat me at tennis—I can't wait to get back to school so I can see Edward.

I don't tell Libby that, of course.

On the first day of school, Dad drives Libby and me the fifteen minutes to the Haslemere station, lugging our bags onto the train and then giving us each hugs. Mum's in London for the day on Soles business.

"Make good choices," Dad says from the platform. "I'm too young to be a grandfather." I can't tell if he's joking or being serious.

Even though I'm convinced my father was born an old man, every once in a while he comes out of left field with a zinger that reminds me he's a human being. Like Libby, he's serious but can have a surprisingly wicked sense of humor.

"No promises," says Libby.

I wave him off. "Tell Mum we love her!"

We ride to the Guildford station, giggling together while watching *Unbreakable Kimmy Schmidt* on my iPad.

When the train arrives at Guildford, Libby and I hop off to transfer. She helps me with my giant suitcases. They were too big for the spaces above my seat—after all, I had to pack enough clothes, accessories, hair products, and makeup to get through the term until Christmas.

"Promise you'll text me when you get to school," she says.

"Don't worry about it, Mum! You text *me* with the latest about Greene House, okay?"

"Deal. Love you!"

"Love you more!"

Soon, the town of Little Bookham looms through the train window as we pull into the station. I spot a gray, crumbling church spire in the distance, but the rest of the town is hidden under a thick canopy of trees. As the train pulls to a stop, I head to the gangway to retrieve my bags. A shuttle bus is waiting in the car park. Twenty minutes later, the bus drives through the massive wrought-iron Sussex Park gates, and I feel a flurry of excitement in my stomach. Home for another year—and *this* year is bound to be epic.

After everybody has arrived, checked into their dorms, and

unpacked, the whole campus convenes at the chapel in the late afternoon for welcome remarks from Master Kent.

A long, narrow building from the 1700s, the chapel has magnificent Gothic arches, and red, blue, and gold stained-glass windows depicting scenes from the Bible. There's a tranquil stillness inside, even when the building is packed to capacity with all eight hundred students and one hundred and seventy-five teachers. On each side, there are six graduated rows of pews, divided into sections for each year. The first years sit at the front of the chapel, under the watchful eye of their dormitory heads and prefects. The sixth form gets to file in last, taking up the pews at the very back.

Like students at most of the top boarding schools, we're required to wear uniforms: navy suits with green-and-white ties for the boys, navy blazers or jumpers and pleated green-and-white tartan skirts for the girls. It's meant to keep clothing from being a distraction—but, of course, some students look better in the uniform than others. I do my best to make my uniform more fun through the small details: shiny black ballet flats or high-heeled Mary Janes, the tightest jumper I can get away with, and smoky eyes or cool nail art I've discovered on YouTube or Viewty.

Even though I already did my hair and makeup at home this morning, I spend another forty-five minutes getting ready before chapel—I want to look extra hot when Edward sees me for the first time. It's been almost a month of daily contact, and I can't remember the last time I went to bed without a "good night and I can't wait to see you" text from Edward loaded with Xs.

But once we see each other again in person, will the spell be broken?

As Master Kent strides to the lectern in the center of the stage, he flashes his thousand-watt smile at all of us. *Donation bait*, my mother once termed his Hollywood grin.

"Each year brings with it a sense of promise. It's not just a new chapter. It's an entirely new book, with the pages blank. It's up to you to create your story," the headmaster booms in his plummy tones. "What will you write this year? What symphony will you conduct? Which opus will you bring to life?"

I scroll through Instagram as the master talks, waiting for the welcome remarks to finish so I can meet up with India. Flossie has posted one of her yoga photos, so I like it, commenting: OMG! You're so flexible!!

"Hi!" India says when I exit the chapel afterward. She gives me a big hug. "You look bloody fantastic. How was the rest of your summer? Your Snaps from Devon looked brill."

I'm about to respond when my heart skips a beat. Standing behind India, looking edible, is Edward.

"Hi, Charlotte," he says shyly. His cheeks have a faint pink tinge to them. Is he *blushing*?

"Hi, Edward," I say, my own face feeling hot.

We step toward each other tentatively, embracing awkwardly. I brush my lips against his cheek.

As we stand in front of each other, India looks amused.

"You look great," Edward murmurs.

"This?" I say in disbelief, gesturing down to my pleated skirt. I've tried to hike it up a little to show off my legs—I'm proud of how toned they are from all my sport. "I look like a Mennonite."

He laughs. "It suits you."

"Oh, stop playing coy," India says, sliding her arm through mine and motioning for Edward to follow us. "You look gorgeous in the uniform, and you know it."

The three of us head to the dining hall for dinner, walking down the long row between all the tables, known as the Catwalk. Two minutes later, the rest of India's friends have shown up: Flossie, Alice, Tarquin, and Oliver from the party over the summer; their short, pasty friend David, who has a reputation as the sixth-form class clown; and a pretty, delicate-looking American named Georgie.

Prince Edward is in the center of the long wooden table— relaxed, laughing, and holding court. And I'm there on his left, his hand resting on my thigh under the table.

Is this really my life?

India and her friends always sit at the back table, underneath one of the three massive brass chandeliers that dominate the room's gold ceiling and mahogany walls. I just hope they all still like me after they get to know me better. What's that phrase? Familiarity breeds contempt.

I get a text from Libby soon after we've sat down to eat.

LIBBY: So? How's it going?

ME: We're getting married.

LIBBY: Yay! That good?

ME: It's unreal. I'll call you tonight after dinner xxx

"So, how was everybody's break?" India says, leaning forward and clasping her hands together. Her voice imitates a parental tone.

"Amazing," says Flossie, taking a spoonful of frozen yogurt. "We went all over France. A week in Paris, a week in Saint-Tropez, and some time at Dad's cousin's place in Normandy. And then we went back to Denmark, of course, to visit Mummy's family. We stayed at Amalienborg a few days and then went up to Gråsten for a couple weeks."

India told me once that Flossie's mother is basically Danish royalty—her grandfather was the youngest son of a king, or something like that. Whenever Flossie travels to Copenhagen, they stay at one of the palaces—Amalienborg is where the king and queen as well as the crown prince and princess all live. Plus, Flossie's double trouble: not only is her lineage impeccable, but she's also from one of the richest families in England. Britain's archaic succession laws mean, as an only child, her father's title will go to her uncle. But even with the succession bypassing her, Flossie will still inherit millions.

"Girl, that sounds incredible," I say.

"Thanks! It was."

"What was the total?" Tarquin asks Flossie.

"Total?"

"Number of guys you snogged?"

She looks offended, taking two more bites before swallowing and answering. "None of your business."

"Aww, c'mon, Floss. Give us the dirt—we want a bit of juicy gossip. We know you had some fun."

Edward takes his hand off my knee and picks up a piece of bread, throwing it at Tarquin. It bounces off his freckled nose and falls on the black-and-white checkered floor. "Hey. Knobhead. You're being a prat."

Flossie brightens while Tarquin's pale skin turns red.

"What about you, Oliver?" India asks, ignoring Tarquin's wounded look. "I saw some great Snaps from you over the summer."

"Oh, yeah!" Oliver says, his cheeks dimpling. "Mum has this major conference every year in San Fran, so we talked Dad into letting me go with her. I hit up the Mission, smoked a ton of ganja in the Haight, made friends with this old hippie dude who was in Vietnam. It was major."

The idea of Oliver, the son of an army general, smoking weed in a park with an old hippie makes me giggle.

"*You* were in the Haight?" Georgie says in her flat California drawl.

"Yeah? Why?"

"I mean, isn't it obvious?" she says, gesturing to the way he's sitting. His back is ramrod straight, perfect posture, no doubt drilled into him by his stiff father. "You look like you've got a stick jammed up your ass."

Surprisingly, he doesn't look offended.

I laugh. "Looks like the American can say things the rest of us can't."

"It's the only reason they keep me around," she says. "I'm Georgie, by the way."

"I'm Charlotte." I look her up and down. Georgie's face is open, her smile easy. I decide I like her. "Where are you from?"

"America. Or *the States*, as you Brits like to say."

"Yes, but where in *the States*?"

She grins at my exaggerated voice. "LA."

"From Hollywood," says Alice, looking impressed. "Her dad is Omar Rogers."

"Like, the film director?"

"Guilty," Georgie says.

"Wow. That's cool!" I hope I'm not too effusive—but it *is* cool. Omar Rogers has two Academy Awards, one for Best Screenplay and one for Best Director. Georgie's mum must be Prudie Phillips—they look like twins, with the same creamy mocha skin and high cheekbones. Her on-again, off-again romance with Omar has been in all the tabloids for decades.

"Georgie's dad and my mum are old friends," says Edward. "We've known each other for years."

"'Old friends,' is that what we're calling them?" Georgie quips.

Pink spots appear on Edward's cheeks. "Okay, they dated. Before Mum met Dad."

"Madeline—Queen Madeline, whatever you call her now—was always the one that got away, Dad says." Georgie mimes sticking a finger down her throat. "*Believe me*, you do not want to hear your sixty-five-year-old father waxing poetic about the glory days of his sexual prime—especially not with somebody who's now queen. Gross." Everybody laughs, even Edward.

"He dodged a bullet," Edward says. "Mum's a handful." I've never heard Edward talk about his family before. "And what about you?" Edward says, turning to me.

"I spent all summer in Midhurst. Hippies in the Haight would have been a major improvement."

"We did some damage together in London, though," India says. "Especially at Selfridges."

"Yeah, my dad wasn't too pleased about that. He had a fit when he got the credit card bill." Mum had to convince him that my six new dresses and several tops were "necessary" for school.

"Why?" says Flossie. "It's not like he can't afford it."

"Um, right. But my dad is a bit old-fashioned. He's proud of his background, wants us to understand the value of a pound—all that."

She rolls her eyes. "Parents are so weird."

"I don't think that's weird," Edward says. "I understand wanting to instill values in your children. It's nice, really." He smiles at me and puts his hand back on my knee, squeezing it.

"If you say so," Flossie says, looking glum.

The kitchen staff comes around to clear our tables, and Edward turns to me. "Want to go for a walk?"

I nod eagerly. He slips his fingers through mine and helps me stand up.

"Okay, guys. See you all later," he says.

As he leads me through the dining hall, walking down the center aisle between the rows of tables, heads swivel. I haven't been *invisible* to the Sussex Park campus, but walking hand in hand with Prince Edward at the height of the dining hall rush hour might as well be a coming out party.

On the way out of the dorm, a tall brown-haired guy I recognize from one of my classes last year smiles at us. "Hi, Edward. Hi, Charlotte," he says in a northern accent.

"Hi!" I say, embarrassed I don't remember his name. I read somewhere that people like you more when you say their name—it makes them feel recognized. I hope he doesn't notice that I haven't remembered his.

"Hey, Robert," Edward says, as if reading my mind.

He's cute. Not as cute as Edward, though—and his accent is a dead giveaway that he probably didn't grow up playing polo and taking ski holidays in Switzerland.

"See you back at Stuart," Robert says, giving us a wave as we exit.

"Friend of yours?" I ask.

"He's the Stuart Hall prefect. Really decent guy. I like him a lot."

We walk hand in hand through campus, the lampposts lighting our way as we cut around the back of the chapel and tread over the grassy hill sloping down to the hockey field. It's warm for a September evening. The campus is always at its quietest during mealtime, and it's easy to pretend we have the whole place to ourselves.

"My home away from home," I joke as we walk across the hockey field.

My heart pounds as I realize we're walking to the Oaks: the most remote, private, and dimly lit area of campus. Also known as Snog Point.

"So you're really into hockey, huh?"

"I love it. I've played it since I was a kid."

"Are you any good?"

I could go one of two ways: false modesty or confidence. Something tells me Edward's secure enough to appreciate the latter.

"I'm the best player on the team."

He breaks into a wide grin. "I love how you just say the truth, no hiding it."

"It gets me in trouble sometimes," I confess.

"Like when?"

"Like when I'm angry."

"I'd better not make you angry, then."

"You'd better not," I tease.

We settle on a large boulder next to a strapping oak tree. In the distance, barely visible in the darkness, I see Edward's personal protection officer, Simon, lurking discreetly. He's so good at blending into the background that I forget he's there 99 percent of the time.

"I must admit, I wouldn't have pegged you as a hockey player."

"No? Why not?"

"Look at you—you're like a supermodel!"

"Oh, stop," I say lightly, my pulse quickening.

"You know it, too. You're gorgeous *and* sporty—it's like the total package."

"Even after I got into makeup and clothes, I never stopped loving hockey. It's a great workout—but more importantly, it's just fun."

"Tell me more. Why do you love hockey so much?"

"It's nonstop," I say. "It's hard to score, so each goal actually *means* something. It's not like lacrosse, where the score can be a zillion to a zillion. I love how when you're racing across the field, you have the destiny of the entire team in your hands. Even if you're good on your own, you're still dependent on everybody else." I shrug. "I joined a team for the first time when I was ten, and I was hooked. My dad set up a net in the back garden and played goalie while I tried to score on him for hours at a time." I poke around in the grass, plucking out a dandelion weed and running my finger over the white spores, suddenly feeling shy.

He puts his arm around me, pulling me close to him. "I love hearing you talk about it. There's so much passion in your voice. It's really cute. I like it."

"Cute?" I ask, looking up at him through my lashes and frowning. "Puppies are cute. Toddlers are cute."

"Not cute. Sexy. Very, very sexy."

He tips my chin up with his finger and brings my mouth to his. Kissing him again is just as electric as I remembered. As we kiss, I can feel the steam rising up around the two of us and curling around our bodies. I fit perfectly into the crook of Edward's arm. We melt into each other.

I don't make it back to Colvin Hall for two hours.

Outside Colvin, Edward and I grin at each other, our fingers locked as we lob good-bye kisses back and forth. Finally, I break away.

"I really need to go! I'll get into trouble!"

He looks at his watch, our fingers still entwined. "It's only nine fifty-five."

"Yeah, and curfew is in five minutes. I already missed tonight's dorm meeting in the common room." Suddenly, I realize I forgot to call Libby. Whatever, I'll call her tomorrow. It's not like we won't be texting fifteen times a day.

"But you have McGuire. She's probably not even doing bed checks."

I laugh. "Is that going to be the theme of this year? I have McGuire, so I can get away with anything?" Old Mistress McGuire is the dorm head, and she's been practically blind and deaf since the nineties, so Colvin Hall is *the* dormitory of choice for sixth-form students.

"Yep. That—and me, being addicted to you." He cups his hands around my face, kissing me again. "Your cheeks are hot."

We kiss for another five minutes before I finally manage to tear myself away, running inside and letting the main door of Colvin slam behind me. I turn around to peek before I run up the steps, and I can see Edward through the double doors, still standing there, grinning at me.

Once I'm back in my room, sneaking past McGuire's closed door, I give myself a long stare in the mirror. I look an absolute mess—my makeup is smeared, my lips are swollen, and my nose is bright red from a serious make-out session—but I can't remember ever feeling prettier.

It's literally the happiest I've been in my entire life.

five

Two days later, I'm on the hockey field, about to start practice. As the team run their drills, I realize I've left my mouth guard in my bag and I race to the sidelines as Coach Wilkinson blows her whistle at me.

"Come on, Weston!" she bellows at me in her American accent. "We don't have all day!"

I run over to my bag, rummaging through it while looking for my zipper pouch with the mouth guard.

My iPhone vibrates and I reflexively pick it up, hoping it's Edward. It's Mum calling.

I press divert. I'll call her back later.

I'm still rooting around the bottom of my bag when the phone vibrates again. Now Libby is calling. Why is my family being so needy all of a sudden?

"Libs?" I whisper into the phone, trying to angle my body so that Coach Wilkinson can't see me. She'll have a total meltdown if she sees me chatting on the phone while the rest of the team waits. "What's up?"

"Are you busy? I have something to tell you!"

My heart starts pounding. "Are you okay? Is everything all right?"

"Everything's more than all right—it's the most amazing news. I'm transferring to Sussex Park!"

"Okay, the coast is clear," I say. "Make a run for it!"

I grab Edward by the hand and together the two of us sprint up the stairs of Colvin, turning down the hallway and trying to keep from laughing as we burst into my room. I close the door behind us, grinning at him. My chest is rising and falling heavily, as much from running as from the excitement of not getting caught by Arabella Whiteley, our head of house, or McGuire.

The group had a long and leisurely dinner together, everybody still enjoying the temporary novelty of being back at school and surrounded by friends 24/7. It felt like ages before Edward and I could sneak off together without getting called out for being party poopers.

He looks around my room. I've finally finished decorating it, with white fairy lights strung up on one wall, a blue-and-white tapestry laid at the foot of my bed over the cream-colored comforter, and mismatched frames covering the wall opposite my bed, full of photos of my family and friends. I've neatly organized all my clothes by color and category in the wardrobe by the door, but I know better than to expect my system to last. It'll be a cluttered disaster by the end of the month, like always.

Whatever—it's the intention that counts, right?

"So, this is where the magic happens, huh?" Edward says.

"You'd better believe it." I put my iPhone onto my music dock, pulling up Spotify and opening my favorite nighttime playlist.

"Who's this?" he asks.

I look at him as if he has two heads. "Are you serious?"

"Um, yeah."

"It's Tegan and Sara."

"Oh, okay. I'm not really into EDM."

I start laughing. "They're not EDM! What do you like?"

He looks embarrassed. "I don't want to tell you."

"Well, now I *have* to know. Celine Dion? Barry Manilow? ABBA? What's your dirty little secret?"

"ABBA does have some good songs," he says. "But I kind of like . . . um—" He mutters something under his breath I can barely hear.

"What?"

"Katy Perry."

I groan. "*Katy Perry?* That's so cheesy. I don't know if I can be seen with you now."

"C'mon! Her songs are awesome!"

"You're worse than my dad."

"Don't hold it against me."

"Oh, I definitely will," I say, grinning at him. "Is this better?" I change the music to a poppy sixties French playlist: lots of Françoise Hardy and Serge Gainsbourg. Perfect make-out music.

"I don't know it, but I like it."

I gesture to my bed, and he plops down on it. "Wine? It's cheap, I promise."

"Sure," he says, laughing.

I unscrew a bottle of Chianti that I bought from the Tesco on the high street—they never ask for ID.

"Here," he says. "Let me, please."

"Ooh, you're *so* chivalrous," I say, teasing. He pours us two small glasses in Sussex Park coffee mugs. I look down at the inch of wine, frowning. "Are you this stingy with everybody? My ten-year-old cousin drinks more wine than that."

He laughs. "Okay, alkie."

"Hardly. Gotta make sure you're liquored up. How else are we going to tolerate each other's *horrible* company?" We both take sips, grinning at each other.

"I don't know—I think we could find something to do," he says, standing up, touching my hand with his, and pulling me toward him. We start kissing, and even though his lips are soft and his hands are roaming all over my back and I should totally be losing myself in this moment, I can't stop thinking:

OH MY GOD, EDWARD AND I ARE KISSING.

At some point, we tumble onto the bed together, and eventually I lose myself in the feeling of his lips and fingers on my skin. It feels like ages before we break apart. His nose and cheeks are red, and I'm sure my hair is a tangled rat's mess.

"You look like a disaster," I say.

"Totally worth it."

I pull out my phone to take a selfie of the two of us, but Edward puts his hand on my arm gently.

"No photos, okay?"

"Huh?" I put the phone down.

"I don't like . . . it's just . . . I know it sounds weird, but I don't like taking selfies, okay?"

I feel stung. "Okay."

"It's not personal," he says, all in a rush. "It's just that—you know how the press is, right?"

"Yeah."

"Hackers have gotten really good. They can break into your iCloud storage. They can steal your photos and download your voice mails. I just don't like too much private information about me floating around." His voice is shaky but his gaze is firm.

"It's not information, it's just a silly photo," I say in what I hope is a light voice. "I'm not going to post it to Instagram."

"I get that—but I'd still rather maintain my privacy, if it's all right with you." He sounds a little icier than I'm used to.

"Okay, that's cool. No worries. Um. So . . ." I put the phone away, changing gears. "Oh, how crazy is this? My sister Libby is transferring to Sussex Park tomorrow."

He looks grateful for the diversion. "Oh, yeah? After the year's already started? Why?"

I explain last week's phone call with Libby. The day after she started back at Greene House, the board discovered proof that the headmaster had definitely been taking bribes, and they ousted him. Word spread like wildfire through Greene House that the head-master had been sleeping with one of the parents, too, although I haven't seen that tidbit hit the papers yet. Once the writing was on the wall, Libby knew she couldn't risk staying and ruining her university chances. Mum and Dad have already put the wheels in motion, and Libby should be here tomorrow morning. I'm *beyond* excited.

"That's awful," he says. "I'm surprised more people aren't talking about that."

I look at him weirdly. *"Everybody's* talking about it. It's in all the papers."

"I don't really read the papers."

"Ah. Right. Of course."

We look at each other awkwardly. Somehow, the night has gone from fabulous to flat in an instant.

He looks at his watch. "Well, you'll probably want to get a good night's sleep if your sister will be here tomorrow. It's getting late any-way."

I peek at my phone. It's already way past midnight. "Holy shit, it *is* late." We spent about three hours kissing and three minutes talk-ing. "Get out!" I say, shooing him toward the door as we both laugh.

"See you tomorrow?" he asks.

"You know it."

We exchange a quick kiss and then Edward leaves, sneaking back down the hallway.

✿ ✿ ✿

I pace outside the master's office, my black heels making little scuff marks on the shiny marble floor. I wonder what's taking them so long. They've been in there for an hour.

Behind the large oak doors, Libby and my mother are having a meeting with Master Kent, discussing the details of Libby's transfer from Greene House. It's been just over a week since Libby called me.

I figured the meeting with the master would be a quick formality and offered to go along and wait outside. But after pacing the halls of the administration building hundreds of times waiting for them to come out, I'm beginning to regret my decision.

I slump in an uncomfortable leather-and-wood chair across from the door, pulling my pleated skirt down as I open Viewty on my phone. I scroll through the looks, hearting my favorite nail art and bookmarking a cool braids tutorial I want to try myself later. Once I've tapped out the latest looks on my feed, I open Instagram and start scrolling.

Flossie's posted a selfie holding her field hockey stick in front of a mirror. I like the photo, hoping she's not still upset that Edward picked me over her. India's assured me that she'll get over it.

India's most recent picture aims down at her boots on the grass, her arm bangles and rings visible as she holds a Starbucks iced coffee. I make a mental note of the rings she's wearing; I'll have to pick some up like that.

Georgie rarely posts on Instagram, preferring Snapchat, but I see that she's posted a photo of Oliver by the Oaks. I wonder what that means. Are they hanging out now?

I've been so preoccupied with Libby's arrival that it's been a full day since I've posted anything. I scroll through my photo album, looking for an appropriate photo.

I could post one of me in the dining hall—David grabbed my phone and snapped it as I stuffed my checks with bread rolls while the group died with laughter—but I look like I have seven chins. Nope. Everybody knows you post unflattering or self-deprecating photos of yourself only if they're at least semi-cute.

I wish I had just *one* photo of me and Eds. I get his privacy thing, I guess—but I still think he's being a little paranoid. *Obviously* I'd never post anything of him, and I sincerely doubt the press is going to be hacking into student phones.

Still, it's a good reminder that dating a royal isn't the same as dating a normal guy. There are *actual* rules—not just silly made-up ones like Nana believes in.

I rub my temples, feeling both emotionally and physically exhausted. Mum and Libby arrived on campus at eight a.m., and I'm absolutely shattered. What I wouldn't give for a venti latte right now.

The door opens and I look up, startled. Mum and Libby come out, both looking pleased.

I stand up. "How'd it go?"

Mum answers. "Good. We're all sorted. She's enrolled; we have her dormitory assignment; the master made sure she was in all the right classes. It's going to be great."

"Libby?"

She nods, a wide grin from ear to ear. "All sorted!"

"Yay!"

Mum pats her on the back. "Honey, didn't you say you needed to use the lavatory? Why don't Charlotte and I wait for you outside?"

As Libby walks away, Mum and I watch her go. It's only when she's exited through the heavy wooden doors that Mum whips back around.

"Did you know all that nonsense was going on at Greene House?"

I blink, surprised by the irritation in Mum's voice. "Um, yeah . . ."

"Charlotte, you can't imagine the nightmare this has been. It's cost your father and me a lot of money."

I frown. "Is that all? Money?"

"No, of course that's not all. Money is no object when it comes to you girls. But it infuriates me to think she was heading back to that horrible school and nobody knew. It could have ruined her chances at getting into St. Andrews."

We exit under the portico onto the wide green lawn. It's sunny but cold—a typical early autumn day in Sussex.

Mum shakes her head. "How did I miss this?"

"You've been busy with Soles, and you've been traveling nonstop the past few weeks. Plus, it was summer." I shrug. "It doesn't mean you're a terrible mother or anything. You were distracted."

Mum sighs. "You'll take her under your wing, won't you? Show her the ropes."

"Of course I will. You don't even need to say it."

"They've put her in your dormitory. She'll be one floor above you."

"Please stop worrying. I have it covered. My friends here are super nice," I say. "Libby will be with me; I'll make sure she fits in and makes friends, and everything will be *just fine*."

"Thank you, honey. It's always been easier for you socially. Poor Libby." She crosses and uncrosses her arms anxiously. "Speaking of your friends, how is everything going"—she lowers her voice—"with Edward?"

I brighten up. "Amazing. He's the best."

"And?"

"And nothing. Everything's going great. I couldn't be happier. I'm pinching myself daily."

"Good. You'll let me know if you have any problems, won't you?"

"Problems? Like what?"

"I don't know—maybe he'll pressure you to do something you're not quite ready for—"

I roll my eyes. "Or maybe I'll pressure *him* to do something *he's* not ready for."

Mum sighs. "Sure. That, too." My mother is progressive enough, as far as parents go, but when certain issues, like sex, come up, I'm reminded of how differently our generations see things. At least she's light-years ahead of Nana.

Libby exits the building, walking over to the imposing oak tree Mum and I are standing underneath. "I always found this place gorgeous."

"Greene House was pretty, too."

"Yeah, but not like this. It's like a catalog."

"What time is your first class?" I ask.

She pulls a piece of paper out of the blue Sussex Park folder she's been clutching like a security blanket. "I've already missed my first class for today. I have a two-hour free period and then lunch. My next class is this afternoon."

"Perfect. You're coming with me," I say, tugging on the hem of her floral maxi dress. She follows me up the hill toward Colvin. "We'll get you into your uniform, have lunch, and then I'll walk you to class."

"What about your classes?" she asks. "Don't you have things planned for today?"

"Who cares? My French seminar will survive without me for one day. You're much more important."

"Aww, thanks, Lots."

"Her bags?" Mum asks.

"Right. Where's the car?"

Mum points to the car park behind the administration building. "How many bags have you got, Libs?"

"One."

"*One bag?* Of course you do. Well, that makes it easy. Mum, you know where Colvin is, right?"

"Yep." She starts walking toward the car at a brisk pace, calling over her shoulder. "Room thirty-eight, right? I'll meet you girls there in ten minutes!"

Libby and I turn and walk up the quad. First period is still in session, so campus is quiet, the few students not at class tucked in their dorms studying or sleeping. She looks impressed by the columned brick building as we approach Colvin. "This is where you live?"

"This is where *we* live. Pretty, right?"

Colvin is on the far end of campus, nestled at the edge of a field of lush oaks and perfectly situated for privacy. The ivy-covered brick and wide, columned entryway make it look like a beautiful manor. With the exception of the library and main hall, it's by far the prettiest building on campus.

She nods. "It's gorgeous. Sussex Park is much grander than Greene House. It's like a university campus."

"You're going to love it. I know you miss your friends, but everybody here is friendly, I promise." I hold the front door open for Libby and then lead her left down the hall toward the sterile ground-floor sitting room. "This is the Colvin common room. It's pretty much open all the time, although you can only watch the telly from five p.m. until ten p.m. Good luck getting a seat on the sofa Friday nights when *Gogglebox* is on; it's always packed. Boys are allowed as long as the door stays open and three feet are on the floor at all times."

"Three feet?"

"Two of yours and one of his," I explain, shrugging. "Or vice versa. It's one of those dumb rules nobody questions and everybody ignores. And use the microwave at your own risk: it hasn't been cleaned since the nineties."

I lead us out of the common room, back down the hall, and then up the stairs. "Which room are you in again?"

"Thirty-eight."

"Want to see my room?" We stop on the second floor, where I push my door open. "Voilà."

"You leave your door open?" she asks.

"Yes—and you should, too. People who close their doors all the time are weird."

"But what if somebody steals your stuff?"

"Nobody's going to steal your stuff!"

"Yeah, but how do you know?"

"Oh my God, I just do, okay?"

I look around my room, feeling proud. I might not be able to cook to save my life, but I pride myself on my eye for design. Libby thinks it's ironic that I'm into do-it-yourself design, since my tastes are way more expensive than hers, but I love the feeling of taking chaos and clutter and creating something beautiful. I've downloaded a few new DIY apps recently and got inspiration for both a lampshade and a photo collage that I want to make soon.

"It looks fantastic! You're so talented, Charlotte." Libby keeps trying to push me into doing design professionally, but I wouldn't even know where to begin. I still have years to worry about things like a career.

I put my hand on Libby's back and gently usher her up another flight of stairs and down the hall toward her room. The inside of Colvin is just as majestic as the outside—wide hallways, vaulted ceilings, a marble floor covered with an expensive though ancient navy carpet—but the cluttered walls make it clear that teenagers live here. They're covered in tacked-up notices, drawings, sport flyers, wrinkled sheets of paper with emergency phone numbers and email addresses, and lists of rules and regulations long ago faded yellow. Room thirty-eight is the last one at the end of the hall: it's cold and empty. I wonder who used to live here and then remember: it was Indira Bhatti, the Bollywood teen pop star. She left school unexpectedly in the first week because of a TV show in Mumbai.

Rumor is she's being homeschooled.

There's a stripped single bed, empty shelves, and a view of the quad in the distance.

"It needs a little bit of love," I say. The bed lets out a loud squeak when I sit on it.

She settles next to me on the bed. We sit in silence for a few moments, and I realize that Libby is doing that thing where she retreats inside herself. It's been her way of coping with stress since we were little. She starts chewing on her cuticle, and I reach over and gently swat her hand away from her mouth.

"You're going to do great, Libs," I say, knocking her foot gently with my own. "I've got your back."

"Thanks, Lotte. Do you think this was a mistake?"

"It was *not* a mistake," I say firmly. "I know it's scary, but it's a good change. We're together the way we always should have been."

She smiles, leaning her head on my shoulder. "I agree. Thank God you didn't follow me to Greene House, otherwise we'd *both* be up the river."

"See?" I joke. "You should always just do exactly what I do."

My phone vibrates: it's a text from Edward. I hold the phone up so Libby can see it. "I still can't get over it," I confess to her. "Me and Prince Edward. Beyond, right?"

"Completely beyond. How are things going with him?"

"Good. He lives across campus, in one of the senior boy dorms. Stuart Hall."

"No complaints so far?"

"Mmm, not really."

"Not really, or none?"

"I mean, maybe just *one*. He's private. Like, really private."

Libby looks at me blankly, as if she's waiting for me to continue. When I don't, she says, "That's all?"

"Yeah . . . why?"

"What were you expecting, Lotte?" she asks, laughing. "Did you think he'd start Snapchatting your dates?"

"Ha."

"Instagramming your meals? Live-tweeting your jokes during *Strictly Come Dancing*?"

"You're hilarious. Keep it up."

"Okay, so other than the famously private guy you're dating not taking out a full-page ad in the *Guardian* about the two of you, how is everything else going?"

"Well, Ms. Smart-Arse, I'll have you know we eat all our meals together every day, and he comes over after dinner every night. Last night, he was here until almost one in the morning."

Libby's eyebrows widen. *"One in the morning?"*

"Yup."

"Are boys allowed in the rooms? And don't you have bed check?"

"We're supposed to, but our head of residence is about ninety years old and has been here for decades. She did one official bed check the first day of school, but that's it. She hasn't seen the inside of my room once. And no, boys aren't allowed in."

"What about the head of house?"

"Arabella? She doesn't care. She only took the job to get a better room."

"That's surprising. My residence head at Greene House knocks on each door one by one every night and talks to every girl."

"Kind of pointless, when you consider that it's an all-girls school—and no more talking about Greene House!"

"Ugh, sorry, bad habit. What was Edward doing here at one in the morning?"

"What do you think? We weren't *talking.*"

"Charlotte! Are you sleeping with him?"

"No, no, no. Nothing like that. I mean, *something* like that, but . . . we just snog. Fool around a little bit. He's barely seen me with my shirt off."

"Are you going to sleep with him?"

"Maybe. I don't know."

"*How* old is he?" she asks.

"Seventeen. Eighteen in the spring. His birthday's the week before yours, actually." Unlike most students in her year, Libby is already eighteen. My dad was transferred by BP to Germany for a year when I was two and Libby was four. When we returned, my parents decided to hold her back a year in school.

She nods. "Be careful. We had three pregnancies at Greene House last year."

"At Greene House? Who were they sleeping with?"

"Campbell Hall was down the road. All boys. Maybe you should go on the pill," she says. "Or an IUD—just in case."

"In case I'm *so* overwhelmed by princely passion that I simply can't bear it, throw him to the ground, and spontaneously have my way with him?"

She giggles. "Something like that. Plus it'll help regulate your periods. Win-win."

"Maybe you're right. I can get some at the infirmary here."

"Would they have to call Mum and Dad?" she asks, looking alarmed.

"Shit. I didn't think of that. I don't know. I'll have to ask around." I pause. "But wouldn't that be crazy? To lose my virginity to *Prince Edward*? Do you think there's a big fanfare when he has an orgasm? Duh-duh-duhhh! Presenting . . . the royal load!"

She clasps her hands over her mouth, pulling a disgusted face even as she laughs. "Too much! You're so gross!"

"Aren't you supposed to be the big sister?"

We giggle.

After a few seconds, she says, "Just don't sleep with him *only* because he's a prince, okay? And definitely don't sleep with him without protection."

"Libby, come *on*. Cut me a little bit of slack. I'm not an idiot."

Of course I've wondered what it would be like to lose my virginity to Edward, but I'm not ready yet. I don't know what I'm waiting for, but I imagine I'll know it when I feel it.

Mum pushes the door open. "Here we go!" She rolls Libby's suitcase into the room. "Isn't this cozy! You'll be able to decorate this room nicely, Libby."

Libby and I shoot each other panicked looks. Judging by Mum's cheery manner, she didn't hear us talking about sex. Now *that* would be awkward.

"Thanks, Mum," I say, standing up and giving her a hug. "We'll call you later tonight. Have a great drive home, okay?"

Her face falls, but she quickly smiles. "I guess I should leave you be."

Libby stands up, giving Mum a bear hug. They embrace for several seconds. I pull my phone out of my bag, glancing at the time. We have at least two hours before lunch—plenty of time for me to work some magic on my sister.

Finally, Mum pulls away. She's still clutching the sleeve of Libby's favorite olive-green army jacket—she's had it for so long, I'm half expecting the damn thing to grow legs and start walking around on its own. "Call me, day or night—if *either* of you needs me, okay?"

"We'll be fine, Mummy! Love you!"

"Love you, Mum," Libby says.

After a few more pained glances, Mum leaves, her heels making muffled clicks on the hardwood floor as she walks down the hallway.

Libby plops back down on the bed. "What's next?"

I'm already unzipping Libby's suitcase, throwing clothes onto the bed next to her.

"You're going to wrinkle everything!"

"You really care if *this* gets wrinkled?" I ask, holding up a frayed flannel shirt. "No offense, Libby, but most of your clothes are a disaster." Her face falls, which makes me feel horrible. "I mean, you look super cute *right now*, of course," I say, rushing to soothe any hurt feelings.

The girls at Greene House didn't have to wear uniforms. Libby's always been more relaxed and bohemian in her clothing choices: she wears lots of long, flowy dresses and pairs her oversized army jacket and combat boots with just about everything. I don't think I've ever seen her in a pair of high heels. She's kind of like an absentminded professor—too focused on her studies to worry about silly stuff like fashion.

I don't think it's silly, of course.

"No offense, Charlotte, but I don't feel the need to impress anybody."

"Oh, please. People *like* to be impressed. It's polite. It makes them feel like you care what they think." I hold up my hand. "And don't say you don't care what they think. Of course you do. There's nothing wrong with that."

She raises an eyebrow. "When did my little sister get so wise?"

"I've always been a total genius, you just never noticed." I rummage through her clothes, separating them into two piles: keep and donate. The donate pile outpaces the keep pile five to one.

Libby watches me work. "Am I to gather that all of *those*"—she points at the rapidly expanding pile of concert T-shirts and stretched-out jumpers—"are clothes you're not going to let me wear anymore?"

"There's a charity center in town on the high street. We'll go this weekend, donate all these grungy old clothes, and then buy you new ones. In the meantime, you can borrow some of mine. You and I are the same size—and mine will actually *fit*. Lucky you!"

"It's pointless to resist, huh?"

I nod firmly. "This is all for your own good. We're going to get you started on the right foot here at Sussex Park."

Operation Libby has officially begun.

six

L ibby can't stop fretting as we walk to lunch.

"Are you sure I look okay?" she asks, biting her thumbnail as she looks down at her uniform.

I scan her critically. The pleated green-and-white tartan skirt looks juvenile on almost everybody, but since Libby is absurdly tall, it falls above her knee and somehow manages to look chic. "You look great." She's wearing the rest of the standard-issue uniform—fitted white button-down shirt and V-neck navy jumper—paired with her favorite black combat boots. I'm dying to get her into a pair of ankle booties, but I know better than to rip the plaster off. With Libby, it's all about baby steps, and I don't want her to feel uncomfortable.

As we walk down the quad, other students smile at the two of us, a few piping up with "Hey, Charlotte!" as I wave and greet them.

"You're popular."

"I'm friendly," I correct her.

"I can't wait to finally meet all your friends. I feel like I know them with how much you won't shut up about them," Libby says. I roll my eyes, but I'm happy to see her back in a teasing mood.

As we walk into the dining hall, Libby's eyebrows rise. "Holy hell."

It's easy to become immune to the grandeur after spending three years here, but the Sussex Park dining hall is a truly spectacular place. I try to see it through her eyes. The ceiling is tall and vaulted. There are four massive gold-and-brass chandeliers. The hall is long and narrow, and at the far end, there are stained-glass windows. It's an impressive space.

"Follow me," I say, winding through the tables as more students greet me. "Over there are the hot foods. That's the salad bar." I point to an ice cream station. "The dessert runs out by the end of the night, so you'll be disappointed if you get here too late."

My group sits at the very back of the room at their usual circular table. "Hey! Meet my sister. This is Libby."

They look at her curiously.

"We've been waiting for you," says Flossie. "Seems like we've been hearing about this famous sister *forever*."

"Or at least for a week," says Georgie, smiling.

India stands up, her waist-length blond hair engulfing my sister as she hugs her. "Libby. Welcome to Sussex Park." She looks at Alice and Flossie, who stand up and walk over to Libby, embracing her one by one in a receiving line.

"You have a perfect nose," Alice says to Libby solemnly. "Is it real?"

Libby looks alarmed. "Um, yes?"

"I'm Georgie! Nice to meet you!" Georgie gives Libby a warm hug.

"Didn't know you had a sister, Weston," says Tarquin, staring at her legs.

"I've only mentioned it a billion times," I say, rolling my eyes at him. "Thanks for listening."

"You're welcome."

"You're visiting?" asks David. There's a smudge of mustard on his chin, and I discreetly motion toward it. He runs his hands across his face, smearing it further.

"I just transferred in."

"From which school?" Flossie asks.

"Greene House? In Surrey?"

"One of my cousins went there," Flossie says. "Thank *God* you escaped."

India pulls out the wooden chair next to her, patting it. "Here, Libby. Sit next to me."

"Have you seen Eds?" I ask, pulling up a chair from a nearby table. "I want him to meet Libby. He texted me an hour ago."

Everybody shrugs. "I haven't seen him all day," India says, taking a sip of her tea.

As the group talks, tossing around jokes and insults, Libby is quiet. She looks around the room a lot, taking everything in and occasionally nibbling on her thumb cuticle. I know her well enough to realize that she's probably getting overwhelmed.

After forty minutes, Edward is still a no-show. I text him as we leave.

ME: Where r u?

A few minutes later, a response:

EDWARD: Sry, family stuff. Talk later.

I frown. "We should head out," I say to Libby. She obeys, standing up to leave the dining hall.

"Bye, Libby," India says. "See you tonight at dinner."

"Bye!" she says cheerily. "It was nice to meet you all!" Her voice probably sounds normal to everybody else, but it's higher than usual, which means she's definitely stressed.

"Watch out for the campus ghost!" Alice calls after her. "His name is Francis. He haunts the library!"

"Is she serious?" Libby mutters to me.

I shrug. "You never bloody know with Alice."

I lead Libby out the doors and toward Powers Hall, the humanities building. It's a three-story redbrick behemoth with white trim, white windows, and Greek Doric columns outside the entrance.

"Looks like you're not going to meet Edward for a while," I say.

"That's okay. I'll meet him soon."

"You'll love him, Libs, I promise."

"Cool. Can't wait." She seems distracted. Her excitement from earlier in the day seems to be slipping away as reality sets in.

I lead Libby inside the doors, smiling and responding briefly to people who say hello. We climb the marble steps to the first floor, where I stop her outside the class. "Are you sure you're okay?"

"I'm sure."

"Do you want me to pick you up after class?"

She pauses. "I appreciate it, Charlotte, but you don't have to worry about me so much. I'll be okay. I promise."

"Suit yourself. I'll see you later this afternoon, okay? Text me when you're ready and we'll meet up. Sound good?"

She waves me off, and I walk upstairs one more floor to history class.

After class, Edward texts me to meet up outside Powers Hall. He engulfs me in a hug, his arms warm. "Sorry. I've had a hell of a day." Around us, I see students shooting us curious glances. I'd be curious, too, if I saw Prince Edward hanging on some girl.

"Me, too," I say, throwing my bag over my shoulder. "Let's head into town—just hang on one sec so I can text my sister." I pull out my phone and tell her to meet us by the front gates in five minutes.

We walk through campus, exiting the brass gates at the end of the sloping driveway.

"So she's finally here? How's she doing?"

"Good! A little overwhelmed, but she'll manage."

"It's a lot, I'm sure—transferring into a new school your last year, leaving all your friends, having to adjust to a new place. She's lucky to have you here."

"Thanks. I just want her to fit in. We're kind of different."

"What do you mean?"

Libby's fifty feet away, standing beyond the brass gates looking at us. She's still wearing her uniform, but she's thrown her favorite army jacket over it, slouching with her arms folded across her chest. Her hair is pulled back into a loose bun, a pen stabbed through the topknot to hold it in place.

"Is that her?" he asks.

"Yep."

"I see what you mean. She seems quieter."

"Yeah. She doesn't let her hair down right away. But she's hilarious once you get to know her, I promise."

"Cool."

"You two will love each other," I say, raising my voice as I call out, "Hey, Libs! Hope you weren't waiting too long."

"It's all good! I came here right after class."

"How'd it go?"

"Not bad. Decent teachers, interesting class discussion, lots of student engagement—two thumbs up." She looks back and forth between Edward and me. "Hi," she says, smiling and sticking her hand out. "I'm Libby."

He smiles at her, shaking it. "Hi back. I'm Edward."

I have to restrain myself from saying, "Yeah, I think she knows who you are."

"Well!" I clap my hands together. "Now that we're all acquainted. Ice cream?"

We turn right and walk up the high street, passing boutiques, cafés, and restaurants while making our way toward the ice cream shop.

"How are you finding Sussex Park?" Edward asks her.

"Too soon to tell," she says, "but so far, everybody seems nice."

"*Everybody?*" I say. "Even Tarquin?"

Edward starts laughing. Libby smiles as she looks back and forth between the two of us. "Was that the guy with the floppy hair at lunch?"

"That'd be the one," I confirm.

"Tarquin," Edward says, shaking his head, more to himself than to us.

We walk into the ice cream shop and place our orders. There's an awkward silence while we each collect our cones and then pay.

"That looks delicious," Edward says, lamely attempting small talk while gesturing toward Libby's cone.

"Would you like a bite?" she asks, offering it to him.

"More of a choc man myself."

She gestures to the cone in his hand. The chocolate is beginning to run down the side of the cone. "I see."

"But thank you so much."

"Well, this conversation is *riveting*," I joke. "Shall we go outside and debate the merits of sprinkles versus fudge?"

We exit the ice cream shop, walking to the end of the high street and sitting on the edge of a fountain. A few tourists notice Edward and begin gesturing excitedly.

"I think you've been spotted," Libby says.

He reaches into his knapsack and pulls out a white baseball cap with a giant maroon *D* emblazoned across the front.

"That must be so weird," she says. "Always being recognized."

I look up at her in alarm. We're not supposed to talk about the elephant in the room. Edward's friends have an unspoken agreement that we pretend to ignore who he is. Libby's just being her normal, straightforward self, but I'd assumed she would cool it with Edward.

He scratches his head before pulling on the cap. "Yeah. It is." He pauses, adjusting the cap low so that his eyes are hidden. "I'm used to it by now."

"That's good," she says.

"But it still sucks."

"I'm sorry to hear it." She takes another small bite of her ice cream. "But it's the trade-off, I guess."

"Trade-off?"

"Your bargain. You get more than others, so it's only fair that you have to give something up in return, like your privacy. Don't you think? And you can actually do something good and meaningful with your life—unlike most people. You're lucky, but not for the reasons that everybody thinks. That's all just shiny stuff. It doesn't matter in the end, and you're not really better than anybody else because of it."

Crap. This is not how I wanted things to go down.

"I'm getting hot," I say, pointing across the street. "Let's go over there in the shade." I stand up, dusting off my skirt. I look back and forth between the two of them in alarm, not sure how Edward will react to Libby's bluntness. I've never heard anybody talk like that to him before. I wonder if he has, either.

He looks her full in the face. "I never said I was better than anybody else. And I certainly don't think it."

"Good," she says, nodding emphatically. "Charlotte would never be with somebody arrogant. I knew there must be more to you than meets the eye."

"One hopes," he says, standing up. "I might still let you down. But I'll do my best." He chomps into the cone.

My eyebrows are practically at my hairline. I can't believe Edward is taking this so good-naturedly.

We finish our ice cream and walk back to campus. Edward's phone rings and he excuses himself, walking a few feet away to take the call. I hear him say, "Yes, Mum," and realize he's talking to Queen Madeline.

"Are you having a brain aneurysm?" I hiss.

"What?" she asks.

"Maybe you can wait a full hour after meeting him before going on the offensive with the insults."

"I wasn't being insulting."

"Are you serious? You called him arrogant. You said he wasn't impressive at first glance. You said he wasn't better than anybody else and implied he's stuck-up. *Jesus*, Libby. People skills. Learn them."

Her face reddens. "I didn't mean anything by it, Lotte. I wasn't trying to insult him, honestly."

She looks over at Edward, who is listening intently and nodding, saying, "Yes . . . Yes . . . I understand . . . You don't need to remind me . . . I'll be there . . . Of course," over and over.

"It must be stressful being him. He seems kind. I feel sorry for him, actually."

"You feel sorry for *Edward*?" I snort. "Now you've officially lost your marbles. Shh, he's coming back."

He walks back to us, smiling tightly. "Sorry for that. Shall we?"

"Everything okay?" I ask him.

"Mmm-hmm," he says. I'm not convinced but don't want to press him further.

Suddenly, Libby stops. She pivots on one heel and says sharply, "Edward. Charlotte. Follow me *right now.*"

We follow her, looking at each other wide-eyed as she whips around the corner and then turns into a village shop.

"Have you lost it?" I ask her. "What's with all the MI6 stuff?"

"There was a photographer," she says. "Hiding behind the fountain in the town square." As she's talking, a heavyset balding man rushes by, looking frantically right and left while holding a camera. He passes by the shop without spotting us.

Edward lets out a sharp puff of breath. "I didn't even see him. Thank you so much. I hate the bloody paparazzi."

"I figured," she says.

As we walk back through the campus gates, I feel a pebble in my shoe. My leg is a bit sore from hockey practice, so I stop walking, hopping on one leg to excavate the piece of gravel from my ballet flat. I look ahead, about to catch up with Libby and Edward, when I stop in my tracks.

They're walking side by side, their steps in sync. While I'm always racing to catch up with Edward's long strides, Libby's three extra inches of height help her walk smoothly, calmly, unhurriedly next to him.

Libby looks back, realizes I'm behind them, and stops, putting her hand lightly on Edward's shoulder to halt him. They both turn to face me, waiting for me to hurry and catch up.

After dinner with the group, Libby and I head back to Colvin to watch the telly together. The common room is empty, so we spread out on either side of the sofa, our legs and feet draped over each other. It reminds me of how we used to watch television together when we were little: jammed against each other like conjoined twins, despite the entirety of the rest of the large sofa.

"You survived!" I say. In the background, a *Friends* rerun flickers— one of our favorites.

"I survived," she repeats, sounding exhausted.

"Thoughts? Concerns? Questions?"

"To answer all three: no, yes, and a billion."

We laugh, eventually lapsing into silence as a car advert comes on showing two sisters driving in an Audi together.

"This is cool, isn't it?" I say. "You and me together during the school year."

"It feels like summer," she nods, smiling. "Except with way more homework."

"Ugh, don't get me started on homework. I need to figure out what I'm going to do for my graphic design project." The only two classes I enjoy are graphic design and history. Graphic design is basically an hour of playing around on the computer, and history is just stories and old gossip, really. "I love that class, but man is it a ton of work. We're doing mobile design now. I want to create something fab."

"Why don't you create that app you're always talking about?"

I love Viewty, but their search functionality is terrible. I've been looking for an app that combines beauty with design DIY, and what few things I've found are equally lame. Libby has been on my case for over a year to create it myself.

"Like that's even possible."

"It *is*," she insists. "You're so talented. And it's not like your professor expects you to get it perfect. But start small, do your best, and take it from there. You never know."

I pull out my iPhone, quickly scrolling through Viewty. I couldn't do anything, like, *professional*, but I could probably make something decent for class. I close the app again, setting the phone down on my stomach.

"So young," I say. "But so wise." We giggle.

After another half an hour of *Friends* reruns, Libby starts yawning. "Do you mind if I go to bed?" she asks. "I'm sorry, but I'm knackered, Lots."

Her yawn is contagious. "No worries. Let's go up."

I turn off the television and the common room lights, and together the two of us walk down the hall and up the stairs.

"Hey," she says. "Want to have a little slumber party tonight? Like old times?"

I grin. "Do you even have to ask?"

After stopping by the bathroom, Libby borrows a T-shirt, and together the two of us slide under my covers.

"Remember the day Mum got that huge Soles order?" I say, feeling nostalgic.

"I do. From Selfridges."

"It was just a day like any other. We woke up, and we had lunch, and we went to the community pool—"

"—oh, God, that place was so gross—"

"—and suddenly our lives changed forever."

"Except it wasn't exactly sudden," she points out. "Mum and Dad had been working for years to get to that moment. It seemed overnight, but in reality, it was ages of effort."

"That's true." I pull the covers up to my chin, snuggling in closer to Libby. "It feels like a million years ago."

"Well, so much has changed."

"Like us, finally together! I'm so happy you're here, Libs."

"Me, too. I can't believe we didn't go to the same school from the beginning." She yawns again.

"Part of me thinks the reason I never applied to Greene House was because I was scared I wouldn't get in," I say, leaning my head over toward her shoulder. I've never admitted this out loud.

"You're so talented, Lotte. You just have to believe in yourself like I do," she says, her voice getting heavy with sleep as she contorts her arm to scratch the top of my head. "You're so smart, but you don't give yourself enough credit."

"Thanks, Libs," I whisper into the dark. "It's nice to hear that."

"Okay." She yawns again. "Sleepy time."

"Love you, Bug," she says, using my childhood nickname.

"Love you, Button," I say, turning over and falling asleep.

seven

Like many boarding schools, Sussex Park has a small coterie of day students. They're included in pretty much everything except Friday afternoon house meetings—the last thing after classes standing between us and weekend freedom.

Officially, the head of house is supposed to review complaints about the communal facilities, update the students on campus events, and provide a safe atmosphere for grievances or concerns. In reality, it's just a pointless ten minutes where everybody yawns and buries their head in their phone as Arabella munches on crackers and lazily reads off a handwritten list provided by McGuire.

This week's announcements include a reminder to turn off the TV and lights after using the common room, a plea to stop using up all the hot water in the showers, and fair warning that McGuire will be conducting a "surprise" bed check tonight for the girls who haven't already submitted paperwork for weekend leave.

After we all file out of the common room, Flossie and Alice blow us air kisses and head upstairs to get their overnight bags. Flossie's parents are back in the UK and have invited her and Alice to spend the night with them at their country place nearby. Georgie rushes off, muttering that she'll see us at dinner. She's wearing makeup, which is rare.

That leaves Libby, India, and me.

"Come by mine," says India.

"I shouldn't." Libby looks upstairs apprehensively. "I'm drowning in homework since I started the school year late. It's going to take me weeks to catch up."

"You know the teachers will totally cut you a break. They don't expect you to do all the assignments." I don't even know why I'm saying it. I know better than to argue with Libby over schoolwork.

"I need letters of recommendation and these teachers hardly know me yet. Universities are going to be looking *hard* at my marks this year. I can't be a slacker."

"You? A slacker? That's hilarious," I say.

"How about I study for an hour or two, but then I'll come meet you guys later tonight after dinner?" Libby says. "I have a stash of cookies I picked up in town."

"White chocolate chip?" I ask.

"What else?"

"You are dismissed." I nod. "Go. Be free. Study until you have attained enlightenment, young grasshopper."

Libby smiles at us, rushing upstairs gratefully. India and I follow behind, climbing the stairs at a snail's pace.

"I swear, she's the only person I know who thinks an A-minus is a failure."

"Bless her," India says. "It's sweet. At least *one* of us is doing her homework."

We walk into her room and sit on her bed. There's a single framed photo on the bedside table: India, her parents, and her four brothers, smiling prettily into the camera on a gray beach. The setting sun pokes through the window, bouncing off the gold signet ring on the pinkie finger of her left hand.

"She's a rock star—academically, at least. Although she's always on my case about university."

"Already? But it's not for ages," India says.

"You're preaching to the choir."

"I always wanted a sister. Are you two close?"

"Very. Even after she went away to boarding school, we texted each other every single day. I missed her like *crazy* that first year. Now we mostly only see each other in summer, though." I'm quiet for a second, suddenly feeling sad for all the time lost.

"You think she's enjoying it here?"

"Definitely."

"Good."

"Well . . . mostly."

"Mostly?"

"She's finding her rhythm."

"That takes time. She transferred schools in her last year, left all her friends, has her little sister looking over her shoulder—it's a lot."

"True."

"But it's kind of you to worry about her," says India. "You're a good sister."

"I just want her to fit in. Greene House was so different."

"How so?"

I think back to the times I visited the campus with my parents. "It was so serious—*much* more regimented. The girls put pressure on themselves like you wouldn't believe. They have an amazing humanities program, and everybody gets into great universities, but it always seemed like such a miserable grind to me. I wanted to be at the same school as Libby, but after I toured it, I realized you couldn't have paid me enough to go there."

"She does seem rather tightly wound," India says.

"Nah, she's not that bad. And she wasn't like that when we were kids—I mean, yeah, she was always less outgoing than me, but when she's comfortable, she can be really silly and just *funny*. Greene House wasn't the right place for her."

"Why don't you have a girls' day out tomorrow, just the two of you? You're always around us, around Edward—maybe she just needs a little quality Charlotte time."

"The world needs more Charlotte time," I say, laughing. "That's a good idea." I think back to Edward talking with his mother and how tight-lipped he was being, changing the subject. "Random question, but speaking of Edward—do you think he's been weird recently?"

India considers the question. "I wouldn't call it weird, exactly—he's just off in the clouds again. He's been like this since we were kids. Every once in a while, he gets overwhelmed by life and just . . . disappears."

"Huh."

"He skipped dinner twice this week, remember?" she points out. "His life is hard. Most people don't understand that."

I think back to Libby telling me she felt sorry for Edward. "I shouldn't take it personally, right?"

"No. But he needs somebody understanding. He's under a lot of pressure, especially now."

"Why now?" I feel like I don't know him at all. It *has* only been a few weeks that we've been dating.

India turns away, reaching for the pack of Camel Blues she keeps in the jeweled case next to her bed. "Close the door, will you?"

As I close the door to the hallway, she opens the window, lighting up a cigarette.

"Don't take it personally," she repeats. "He's got stuff going on."

I roll my eyes. "We've all got stuff going on."

"*Family* stuff."

"Oh."

"He turns eighteen this year," she says, as if this explains everything.

"Which means . . . ?"

"It means our little caterpillar is about to become a butterfly, and he's freaking out about it," she says. "You guys don't talk about this at *all*?"

When Edward and I hang out, we don't do much talking—we're either watching TV, making out, or absentmindedly scrolling through our phones.

Suddenly, I feel like a terrible girlfriend. *Am* I his girlfriend? Or am I just some girl he's dating?

I shrug. "Not really."

"Don't feel bad," she continues. "You've got a lot going on, too. It's not up to you to fix everybody's problems for them. Just give him some space and he'll come around."

"You're right. Good idea."

She collapses back on her bed, her mermaid hair floating on her pillow around her as she takes a deep drag of the cigarette. "I'm full of 'em."

Later that night, Edward and I are in the Colvin Hall common room, snuggling together on the sofa while watching telly. I invited Libby to come watch television after dinner, but she begged off to keep doing homework. Even though she's only a couple of weeks behind schedule, she's panicking about catching up.

It's been warm for October, but suddenly the weather has turned freezing, the wind whistling outside the window. I snuggle closer to Eds for warmth and lay my head on his chest. Neither of us is paying attention to the TV: I'm hopping between Viewty and Snapchat, and he's texting somebody.

"Everything okay?" I ask. "You've been frowning at that thing for the past ten minutes."

"I'm sorry. Just texting with my dad."

This makes my eyes go wide. "I'm sorry. You're *texting* with your father?"

He chuckles, looking up from his phone. "I guess that does sound a bit bizarre. Yes, my father texts occasionally. The King knows how to text."

"I heard you on the phone with your mum before—the day you met Libby. You seemed tense. I mean, even before the whole photographer thing."

"Yeah. I'm sorry. There's a lot of family stuff going on right now."

I look at him expectantly, but he doesn't say any more.

Three Colvin girls from the third floor—Sara, Henrietta, and Violet—walk into the common room. "Hey, Charlotte. Oh! Edward! Hi!" says Henrietta.

"Hi," he says, smiling. He clicks off his phone, sliding it into his pocket. "You ready for *Gogglebox*?"

Violet stands in the doorway, looking uncomfortable. "Um, we can go watch it in Trinity Hall, if you want."

Edward opens his mouth, but I beat him to it. "It's fine! We're leaving soon anyway."

"We are?" Edward asks.

"India texted me. She's at Snog Point with Georgie, Oliver, David, and Tarquin. We can go after the advert." I'll go upstairs before leaving and force Libby to join us. Twenty minutes of fun won't kill her.

"I don't know," he says. In the corner, Henrietta puts a bag of popcorn in the microwave, the smell wafting through the common room as the kernels pop. "That popcorn smells good."

"You can have some!" she says, looking elated.

"But they've got snacks, too—Georgie's mum sent her a care package with homemade cookies. Plus, India has a bottle of wine."

"It's cold outside." He puts his arms around me, pulling me closer to him. "I'd rather stay inside with you."

I know I should find this sweet, but it only makes me feel grumpy. My idea of the perfect Friday night is hanging out with all our friends and sneaking off for kisses, not sitting on a stained sofa with three girls I barely know.

"Fine," I say, deciding I'll try to make the best of it. "Hey, Henrietta—mind if I have a little of that popcorn?"

Two campus shuttles take students to and from London twice a week, on Wednesdays and Saturdays. On Libby's second Saturday at Sussex Park, we plan to catch the morning shuttle into London for a girls' day out, but I'm so knackered from a week of early field hockey practices that I skip breakfast in favor of more sleep. I wake to find Libby standing over my head, asking when we're leaving.

I look at the time on my phone. "Damn it! The bus left three minutes ago."

"It's okay," Libby says. "Aren't there a bunch of shops and restaurants in town?"

"Yeah, but the ones in London are better."

"Why? A Topshop is a Topshop. A café is a café. We'll be fine."

I roll over, burrowing under the covers. "Okay. Wake me in another hour."

"Come *on*, Charlotte. You're the one who suggested it!"

"And now I have a new suggestion: sleep."

She flings the covers off me as I shriek in response to the blast of cold air on my legs. "You have half an hour! I'm going to go upstairs and do some homework in the meantime."

I pull the covers back on top of me, yawning. "How about forty-five minutes?"

She smiles at me. "Fine. But I'm coming back for you in *exactly* forty-five minutes—and you'd better be ready."

"Whatever you say, Mum," I say, rolling over to sneak in a few extra minutes of sleep.

It's an easy ten-minute walk to the far end of the high street, where all the chain clothing stores are. We hit up Topshop first, me pulling clothes off the racks and handing shirts, dresses, jumpers, and trousers to a shop assistant who finds us a changing room.

I've decided that Libby needs better clothes. I know what she wants: loose and low-key. But she needs to look like she belongs with India's crowd, not like she's a refugee from the 1990s. The wrong clothing will immediately mark you as an outsider.

When I was younger, it's not like I spent time thinking about the clothing choices of upper-class girls. In the town we grew up in, discount clothing from Marks & Spencer was the norm—fashion wasn't even a little on my radar until we suddenly had money and I realized I needed to fit in. But if I *had* thought about it earlier, I would have assumed posh girls wore tweed and riding boots and tailored red jackets: really serious, horsey stuff. India and the rest of the girls occasionally wear stuff like that, but more often than not they're dressed in jeans, cable-knit jumpers, and scruffy trainers, like regular teenagers. I've spent years studying every little detail of how they dress, and luckily I have a sharp enough eye to pull it off. If I'm being charitable, it's not really *that* different from how Libby dresses, except she wears the same few clothes over and over again. She prefers to divert her monthly allowance into a savings account.

Me, I spend mine. Life is short, and it's made for actually living, right?

"What is *that*?" Libby asks, pointing to a sparkly blue skirt.

"A skirt. I thought it would be good for nights when we go into London."

"Why would we go into London?"

"You'll need something to wear dancing."

"Won't we get in trouble? How will we get there? Won't the clubs turn us out for being too young?"

"Oh my God, relax! I've got it covered."

"It looks like a headband," she says, taking the skirt from me and holding it gingerly, like it might explode.

"Your style is all over the place. Clothes like that"—I point to her oversized flannel shirt and boot-cut jeans—"mean you'll still be a virgin when you're forty. Why are you wearing those jeans anyway? I lent you a ton of clothes. There were some J Brands in there."

"I love these jeans. And they weren't cheap. I got them at Selfridges."

"They look like mum jeans."

"They're comfy. I can wear my favorite boots with them."

"Nowadays, in *the future*, we humans wear skinny jeans, and we wear our boots *over* the jeans," I say slowly, exaggerating my words as if Libby is an alien.

"Skinny jeans look weird on me."

"Then you just haven't found the right pair."

"I'm not comfortable showing off my body like you are."

"I don't know *why*—your body is sick. Keep your nineties jeans, if you insist. But there has to be a middle ground between miniskirts and muumuus."

She laughs. "Fine. I'll try on a pair. Dress me, fashion Yoda. I'll help you with your homework in return."

"Ew. Pass."

"I'll bake you white chocolate chip cookies?"

"Now you're talking!"

I grab another dress, sending Libby into the changing room.

The minutes tick by. Finally, I go in. "Well? What's the holdup?"

She pokes her head out from behind the door. "I look silly."

"Out with it. Let me see."

Libby steps into the hall, her eyes downward. She's wearing a fitted bright blue dress that shows off her waist to perfection. It's longer than anything I'd wear, but knowing Libby, she probably considers it a miniskirt.

"Hot stuff!" I whistle. "You look banging."

She blushes. "You don't think it's a little tight?"

"Libs, that's kind of the point. It's a dinner dress. Do you like it?"

She turns around, inspecting herself from multiple angles in the mirrors. "I do . . . but what about the chest? You don't think it's too low-cut?"

"We have professors that wear dresses more revealing than that. It's perfect. It shows off your body without making you look slutty."

She frowns. "Don't objectify women like that. Slapping labels on females because of their sexual choices—"

"Okay, jeez, I'm sorry." I hold up my hands in surrender. "It shows off your body while still making you look like a strong woman who knows her mind. Is that better?" She rolls her eyes at me. "I think it's a winner. You look seriously hot."

Libby stares at herself in the mirror for several long seconds. Her face relaxes slightly and she looks pleased.

"You're allowed to think you're pretty," I tease her. "I won't tell." She blushes.

"So that dress goes in the yes pile. Try on the red one."

Each of the next few dresses is rejected for being over the top, but after a solid forty-five minutes of trying on clothes, we have a respectable pile of dresses, blouses, and trousers. I even manage to get her into a pair of skinny jeans and ankle booties.

"This is too much stuff," Libby says, carrying an armful of clothing to the cash register. "How are we going to buy all this? My allowance won't cover it."

"Credit cards, duh."

"Dad made it clear our cards are for emergencies only."

"You're having your first Saturday night dinner with the group tonight and you have nothing to wear. This totally qualifies as an emergency."

She plunks her card down, looking doubtful.

"Now we need to get you some fitted jumpers. Yours are too baggy."

"We can't buy *more*. Mum and Dad will kill us!"

"They'll get over it."

We hit several more shops, buying choice pieces at each until I'm satisfied with Libby's bounty.

"I feel like that makeover montage in *Pretty Woman*," Libby says.

"Minus the prostitution." I gently steer her by the elbow toward a hair salon across the street.

"Is this the part where I walk in as an ugly duckling and emerge a swan?"

"Something like that."

I come to the salon once a month for a trim: the irony of having long hair is that you have to cut it all the time to maintain it, otherwise it turns into a shapeless mess. India turned me onto this salon, coming here to maintain her own crazy-long hair in between her trips to London.

Libby and I sit quietly in the reception area. I grab a copy of *Hello!* from the coffee table and start flipping through it. A few pages in, my eyes widen at a photo of Edward at home at Cedar Hall in Gloucestershire over the summer. He's playing polo, sitting confidently astride a horse with a mallet slung over his shoulder. I love the fierce look in his eyes.

"Hey, Libs. Look. The guy I'm dating is in *Hello!*"

She nods, smiling a little. "Surreal."

The receptionist calls her name and escorts Libby to a stylist's chair. I follow with her.

"So, what are we doing today?" he asks, running his fingers through her hair. He's a skinny man with bleached hair, black eyebrows, and thick black-rimmed glasses.

"Not too much," she says. "Just a trim."

The stylist and I exchange a look.

"She doesn't need much," I say. "She's low maintenance, so just a good hairstyle she can work with. But I want her to start blowing it out. Maybe you can show her some straightening techniques, too. And add a few layers. And maybe a tiny bit of fringe. Should we do highlights?"

"Just a trim," Libby repeats firmly.

The stylist spends nearly an hour painstakingly pulling on Libby's curly chestnut hair with a round brush, running the blow dryer down the hair shaft over and over. It falls in thick waves, cascading over her shoulders.

"You have so much more hair than I do," I say. "I'm jealous."

"Jealous? Of *this* mess?"

"Most of my clients would kill for hair like yours," the stylist says, pulling on a tender section of Libby's scalp and causing her to yelp. "Sorry. No pain, no gain." She shoots him a dark look.

When he's done, we stand back and admire his handiwork. Libby's hair is normally a little frizzy and pulled back, but now it falls in loose waves around her face. He's given her a few easy layers, but nothing over-the-top. She looks both naturally beautiful and sleek— a million times better.

"You look *gorgeous*, Libby. Absolute stunner."

"Wow," she says. She touches her hair and sits forward in the chair, staring at herself in the mirror. "It's so soft. How?"

"Loads of conditioner—and some serious elbow grease."

"We're going to a dinner tonight," I say. "Can you make sure it lasts until then?" Libby's hair turns into a frizzy pouf-ball at the merest hint of moisture in the air.

The stylist pulls out a big can of hair spray, spraying Libby's hair until it's well lacquered.

"This must be some fabulous dinner the two of you are going to."

"Just to Donatella with some friends." Our friends meet in town most Saturday nights for dinner at Donatella, an Italian hole-in-the wall famous for a lax student-drinking policy.

"All this fuss for Donatella?"

I bristle. "I want her to feel pretty. Are we all done here?"

At the checkout counter, I pull out my wallet. "I'll pay for this," I say magnanimously. "My treat."

Libby bursts out laughing. "Your treat? You're putting it on Mum and Dad's credit card!"

My cheeks redden. "It's the thought that counts."

"Thank you for a wonderful day, Bug," she says. She throws her arms around me, pulling me toward her as I sign the receipt and shove the credit card back into my wallet. She plants a big, sloppy kiss on my cheek. "You're the best sister ever."

"And don't you forget it," I say huffily, leading her out of the salon. I pretend to be irritated, making a big show of wiping my cheek, but I'm pleased.

Once we're back in my room, I play music on my iPhone and scatter Libby's new clothes all over the floor.

"Charlotte! You're going to wrinkle everything!"

"Calm down. We need to figure out what you're wearing tonight.

You can Marie Kondo everything when we're done." I pull the blue dress out of the bag. It looks even more stunning in soft lighting. "What about this one?"

"Okay. But what if I'm cold? It's not very heavy."

I rummage around my top drawer, pulling out a pair of opaque black tights. "That's what these are for. We'll pair it with the new booties and the new black coat—the faux fur collar is major. It's all going to look beyond."

"You're sure I won't be overdressed?"

"Libby. Relax. Do you trust me?"

She nods. "Yes."

"Good. Now sit down so I can put makeup on you."

I spend the next half hour painting on foundation, applying contour, shading her brows, and patting blush on her cheeks.

"Orgasm?" she asks, looking at the blush compact.

"It's the best. Goes with almost every complexion."

I reach into my lipstick drawer, pulling out two shades of lipstick, a lip liner, and a light pink gloss.

"That's all for me?"

"Yeah." I apply a succession of lip liner, lipstick, and gloss. "Okay, now your eyes. I do them last, 'cause it's the most important part of the look. There are YouTube gurus who would disagree with me, but . . ." I shrug. "Whatever works, right?"

She starts giggling. "Remember when you got sent home from school for putting on too much makeup?"

My cheeks redden at the memory. I stole some makeup from Mum's bag and applied it in the bathroom of our primary school. My teacher called the nurse, who thought I'd come down with a fever—my face was covered in splotchy blush and bronzer.

"Not my finest hour. Mum and Dad couldn't stop laughing!"

"You've always been such a beauty genius. You can tell that story after you make your first million and are giving the keynote speech at—what's a beauty conference?"

"Hmm. CEW?" Cosmetic Executive Women is one of the leading organizations for beauty executives. My favorite blogs report on its awards each year.

"There you go. At CEW."

"Stop talking," I say, grinning. "You're going to look like a Picasso if you keep moving your face."

I hold my wrist to steady it while I apply a thin line of eyeliner. Next, I buff on several shades of eye shadow, blending until her eyes are smoky.

I lean back to inspect my handiwork. "Now this is what I'm talking about." Libby looks fantastic.

She examines herself critically in the full-length mirror next to my wardrobe. Several seconds of silence pass. Finally, she says, "You did a really good job."

"Thank you! I just cleaned you up a bit." I pull out my phone. "Hold still. I want to take a Snap."

She smiles widely for the camera, reminding me of a little kid.

"That's going on my Insta," I say, saving the Snap to my camera roll and then uploading it to Instagram. "I want to break twenty thousand followers by the end of the school year." I look at my phone again. I've spent so much time getting Libby ready for the party that

I've completely neglected myself. "We only have forty-five minutes left, and I need to get myself ready. Can I leave you by yourself?"

"Charlotte, I might be inept with makeup, but I'm not a toddler."

"Okay, chill, no need to get all snappy."

I rush down the hall to the shared bathroom, bringing my shower caddy. I already washed my hair this morning, so all I need to do is suds up my body and apply some makeup.

While in the shower, I start daydreaming about my friends' reactions to Libby. They're going to be blown away when they see her.

But when I return to the room wrapped in a towel, I find that Libby has rubbed off half my work.

"What did you do?"

She looks sheepish. "I was hoping you wouldn't notice."

"Wouldn't notice? You've rubbed everything off!" The eye shadow is practically gone and her lips are almost bare.

"I'm not used to wearing all that makeup—I felt like a clown!"

"You looked bomb."

"Well . . . I'm wearing the dress you wanted. And my hair is nice and sleek. And I still have on *way* more makeup than normal. Isn't that enough?" She looks hopeful.

"Fine. I just want everything to go great. I want you to fit in." I look at Libby with a hard eye. "Actually . . . you still look amazing. Less is more, and it suits you better, anyway." Suddenly, I feel a little bit guilty for trying to bend Libby to my will. I need to do a better job of accepting her for who *she* is, not who I want her to be.

She visibly relaxes. "Thank you."

"Natural beauty is totally in, so you're on point."

"I appreciate the effort. It means *so* much to me, Charlotte."

"You're my sister, silly. I'd do anything for you."

"Anything?"

"Anything. Here," I say, tossing her the latest issue of *Tatler* magazine. "Read this while I get ready."

She wrinkles her nose. "This magazine is so silly—I never understood why you and Mum are obsessed with it."

I gasp. "You did not just say that."

"It's so boring!"

"How do we come from the same family? Sorry, but I don't have any issues of the *Economist* lying around."

She laughs. "I don't read the *Economist*. But thanks for the vote of confidence."

"Whatever. You're like a thirty-year-old. We need to make you young again."

She looks at me wryly. "Was I ever young?"

"Yeah, good point." I grab one of the old issues of *Elle* from the floor of my closet. It's hidden underneath a pile of dirty clothes that I keep meaning to send out for the school's laundry service. "Read this instead," I say, tossing her the issue. "It's fashion *and* feminism. Give it a chance: you'll love it."

"How did I ever survive without you?" she says teasingly.

I shake my head. "I genuinely don't know."

eight

Even though all I have to do is apply party makeup and put on my clothes, it still takes me over an hour to get ready. By the time I'm finished applying my eyeliner, brushing out my hair, and putting on my clothes, Libby and I are dead late. I still take five seconds to Snap myself and post an Instagram of my shoes before leaving. Five seconds won't kill anybody.

At least I've chosen a relatively simple outfit: gray tunic over black leggings, thick black cashmere scarf, gray stiletto boots, and my favorite black bomber jacket. I don't want to steal attention from Libby tonight.

When we walk into the back room at Donatella fifteen minutes later, our cheeks pink from the wind, heads turn. As Libby shyly takes off her coat, however, nobody's looking at me.

"Damn!" says David, whistling.

Oliver grins. "Looking good, Libs."

"I would hit it," Tarquin says to nobody in particular. "Definitely."

As the boys look at her with interest, India gives Libby the once-over, nodding approvingly. "Your hair looks nice like that."

Next to Oliver, Georgie grins at Libby, shooting her a thumbs-up. Even Flossie looks impressed.

I look at Edward, hoping to see a big smile, but his reaction is neutral. He looks at me, patting the seat next to him.

"Oh, but where will Libby sit?" There's an open seat at the end of the table, between Tarquin and David. "I'll sit there," I say. "Libby, why don't you sit here next to Edward?"

Libby does as she's told. I plop down at the opposite end of the table and Tarquin immediately turns to me.

"Weston," he says, "your sister is a right fittie."

"She is?"

"Yeah. She's hot. I'd do that."

"Vomit. Don't be a wanker."

He responds by reaching over and filling my empty wineglass. I notice that there are already several empty bottles of the house red, a bitter swill that might as well be vinegar. "You've got catching up to do. Drink up."

The fireplace warms the small room, which otherwise has no heating. I keep my jacket on, leaning back to let the fire warm me. The English aristocracy seem to think suffering is glamorous. How else to explain the addiction to everything cold and drafty? I think it must be a throwback to their ancestors, who had titles but not the money to back it up. Of course, with the current interest in all things royal, those days are over—if you've got a title and a country estate, you're milking it for all it's worth.

My phone pings with a text.

INDIA: Job well done. She looks bloody fantastic.

ME: Thx! Did major damage on parents' cc today, ha!

INDIA: Worth every penny.

I look up from my phone to smile at India, and Edward catches my eye. He blows me a kiss.

"What took you two so long?" asks Flossie across the table.

"We were shopping," I explain.

"Did you buy anything good?" she asks, turning to Libby.

"I don't think there are any clothes left in town! Dresses, shirts, trousers—everything."

"Libby hasn't gone shopping in a *long* time," I say.

"Charlotte has demanded I donate my jeans to an old-age home and burn all my flannel shirts," she says.

"I don't know, flannel is kind of retro," says Flossie. "Like, in a good way."

"Right?" says Libby, turning to me and smiling. "*See?* I wasn't a fashion disaster, I was *fashion forward*. Everything old is new again."

"You looked lovely then and you look lovely now," India says kindly. Libby gives a small smile, blushing and looking pleased.

"She's shy, eh?" Tarquin says as India leads the conversation on the other end of the table.

"Yeah, we have a loud family. She fades into the background and lets us all tear each other to bits like a pack of wolves. Plus, she's self-conscious."

"I have no bloody idea why," he says, taking a gulp of wine as if it were water. "Put in a good word for me? I'm going to try my luck."

"Ha! You'll need it."

I make a show of playing along with Tarquin and ribbing him good-naturedly, but in actuality, I find him a boor. He's the worst type of aristocrat: entitled, smarmy, and convinced that everything coming out of his mouth is brilliant. Luckily, he mistakes insults for flirting.

He cocks his head, looking at Libby thoughtfully. She's quietly sitting at the end of the table, taking tiny sips of her wine and watching India, Flossie, and Edward as if observing a tennis match.

"Yeah, I'm going to hit that."

"You're a pig." He thinks I'm joking. I'm not.

"What about you?" He leans in closer. "You and Eds? A little side helping of dessert?"

"Jesus, Tarkie, you're on fire tonight. Have you got *any* shame?"

"C'mon!"

"It's none of your damn business—but, no, if you must know."

"Really? Surprising. Hoping to lock him down first?"

I'm tempted to throw my drink in his face. I ignore him.

"So, Edward," I call from across the table. "You and Libby are in the same maths class, yeah? How's old Jonesy?" Professor Jones is only in his forties, but he carries himself like he's a thousand years old, wearing thick spectacles and using a walking stick. His hair is already completely gray.

"Still impossible. That man is a proper sadist."

"Libs, you should tutor Edward. Libby is an absolute whiz at maths," I explain.

She blushes. "I'd hardly call myself a whiz."

"Stop being so modest—you're a genius. I *dread* that class next year."

"Are you having problems in maths?" Libby asks Edward.

"Always," he laughs.

"I'd be happy to help you, if you like?" She looks over at me, as if for affirmation, and I nod at her, smiling. I know she's drowning in homework, but she's still willing to take time out of her schedule to help others—I love this about her.

"I wouldn't want to trouble you," he says, refilling his wine and then offering it to Libby. She accepts half a glass.

"It wouldn't be any trouble," she says.

"There!" I say. "It's settled!"

The waiter arrives to take our orders. He's an older Italian man with a suffocatingly thick accent—somebody I've never seen before. It leads to a comedy of errors: lots of pantomiming and raised voices.

"If they don't speak English, shouting at them isn't going to help," I say to Tarquin.

"Bloody foreigners."

"I'm sorry, isn't your family German?"

"The King is German. *Everybody* is German."

"I see," I say, trying to stop myself from rolling my eyes.

When the waiter gets to Edward, he does a double take.

"Prince!" he exclaims. "Eduardo!"

Edward flushes a little bit. A mild flash of annoyance skitters across his face, but in an instant, it's gone, replaced by a wry smile. "*Sí, sí,*" he says. "Eduardo. That's me."

After he walks away, Libby leans over to Edward, quietly saying something I can't hear. He gives her a grateful look and nods. "It is. Thank you."

She smiles back. Victory! They're getting along.

I feel like Libby is finally enjoying herself, which helps me relax in turn. I spend the rest of the meal laughing with my side of the table—drinking wine, uploading Snaps of my food, and inhaling my pasta carbonara. One of the major advantages of field hockey practice five times a week: I can eat boatloads of pasta—my favorite—without it affecting me. While I hate waking up early, that perk alone is worth the price of admission.

After dessert, I push away my half-eaten plate of tiramisu. I haven't even thought about Libby in over an hour, after angling my chair away from her to joke with David. I look back and see her and Edward deep in quiet conversation, their chairs turned toward each other and their heads leaning down. Libby is ticking things off her fingers one by one. I strain my ears and catch her saying the words "Pareto principle." They must be talking about study habits.

If you walked in the room and looked at them, you'd have no idea that tonight was the first proper conversation they'd ever had.

I smile, happy they're bonding—even if it's over something as boring as their studies.

"Why are you grinning like a maniac?" David asks.

"Am I? No reason."

Everything's proceeding exactly as planned.

A few hours and several glasses of wine later, we all walk back to campus together.

India, Edward, Libby, and I hang back from the rest of the group. David and Tarquin run around like drunken fools, chasing up behind Flossie and Alice and hoisting them over their shoulders. Georgie and Oliver are ahead of everybody, walking arm in arm. I'm not sure if they've hooked up yet, but it's clearly heading in that direction, which makes me smile. Sometimes opposites just attract.

The sexual tensions in our group are always shifting. It seems everybody has a crush on somebody else from week to week: one week it's David lusting after Alice; the next, he has his sights set on Flossie. Now that Flossie seems resigned to the fact that she'll never have Edward, her radar has turned back toward Tarquin; she's constantly laughing at his inane jokes. They've already made out a few times, and they're perfect for each other—they're both convinced they're the most wonderful people on the planet and that everybody else is beneath them.

Everybody—girls and boys alike—is a little bit in love with India, although she only dates girls, of course. I don't know anybody who isn't attracted to that sort of burning confidence. It doesn't hurt that she's gorgeous *and* nice.

As we make our way back onto campus, the group immediately settles down and starts to break apart, everybody blowing kisses and quietly saying their good-byes as they tiptoe back to their halls of residence. I notice Georgie and Oliver sneaking off together toward Snog Point.

Now it's just Edward, Libby, and me.

"Tarquin fancies you," I say.

"Does he?" she giggles. The wine seems to have gone to her head. She winds her arm through mine as we walk down the sloping hill toward Colvin. "Should I be interested?"

"No," Edward says firmly. "He's fun for a laugh, but I'd never date him."

"Yeah, he's a total wanker," I say. "And thank goodness. I'd be *so* embarrassed if you dumped me for Tarquin."

Edward laughs.

"Then why are you all friends with him?" Libby asks.

Edward shrugs. "I've known him since we were kids. We grew up together with India and Flossie. If I were just meeting him now, I don't think we'd be mates." The Gloucestershire set is nothing if not tight-knit: just a few titled families running in the same circles over and over.

We walk back through campus. The oak trees look gauzy in the moonlight.

"What was that Indian restaurant you were talking about at dinner, Edward?" Libby asks.

"Maharajah."

"I love a good curry."

"Yeah, that place is one of our favorites," I say.

"Why don't we all go next week?" Libby says. "I'm dying for some popadams."

"How about Tuesday?" I say.

Edward nods. "Works for me!"

"It's a date!" Libby says.

The three of us reach the crest of the hill and say our good-byes. Edward hugs Libby and then gives me a quick peck on the lips.

"Bye!" Libby waves at him, reminding me of a happy toddler waving bye-bye.

She links her arm through mine again as we walk to our residence hall.

"You're right, Charlotte," she says. "He's lovely!"

"I knew you'd get along! You just needed to give him a chance. What'd you talk about?"

"Mostly polo—I had no idea it was such a dangerous sport. Did you know that people die every year?"

I nod. "Those horses go almost fifty miles an hour, I think. It's crazy."

Libby shakes her head in wonder. "It sounds a bit strange, considering we grew up in the shadow of Cowdray, but I've never paid much attention to polo."

"Because you were too busy being a nerd," I say, poking her in the ribs playfully.

She swats my hand away. "He said that we could go see a game with him soon, if you want to. He's very passionate about it."

"Sure." I shrug. "That sounds like fun."

"You don't mind if I tag along, do you?"

"Of course not."

"It'll be fun," she giggles.

"You're smashed!"

"Maybe a little. I only had two glasses of wine. Barely that. But I'm not used to drinking."

As we enter the residence hall, closing the front door gingerly behind us, I put my finger to my lips.

"We need to be quiet," she says loudly. Her voice reverberates off the marble.

"Shh!" I whisper in a panic. "Don't . . . say . . . *anything.*"

We tiptoe up the stairs. When we reach the second floor, Libby accidentally stumbles, calling out "Damn!" as she trips.

I grab her by the hand and pull her after me, sprinting down the hall to my bedroom and shutting the door. In the hallway, I hear McGuire's door open. It's several seconds before it closes again.

"That was close," I say, my heart pounding. "You should sleep here tonight."

"It's only one floor. I can make it."

"You smell like a wine cellar. It's not worth it. Let's have another slumber party."

"Ooh!" She smiles. "Let's do that!"

We start getting ready for bed.

"How do you wear all that makeup all night?" she groans. "I'm dying to get this slop off my face."

"Try these." I toss her a packet of makeup remover wipes. "Perfect when you can't be bothered to wash your face."

She rubs the wipe all over her face.

"You look like a Jackson Pollock painting. Here." I take another wipe and gently tissue the eyeliner, mascara, and foundation residue off her cheeks. "Much better."

"Thanks, Lotte," she murmurs, pulling the covers down and crawling into bed. She scooches next to the wall.

"You're still in your clothes! Aren't you going to change?"

But Libby is already snoring lightly.

I smile at my drunken sister, changing into a T-shirt and boxers before climbing into bed.

nine

"Weston!" Coach Wilkinson blows her whistle. "Get your ass over here!"

I run over to the sidelines, sweating through my jersey.

It's a bright, clear Tuesday in late October: the type of blustery day where it's warm in the sun but freezing in the shade. Running all over the field during practice has exhausted me. I started the practice with several layers this morning at six thirty a.m. Now, I'm in only a T-shirt and shorts, and I'm boiling.

She places her hands on her hips. "Do you think I'm an idiot?"

Coach Wilkinson comes from America. She married a Brit she met while backpacking through Europe after college, and then she stayed. I've seen enough American telly to know that her accent must have softened over the years: it's not as harsh and flat to my ears as most American accents. She kind of sounds Canadian. But she's still a dyed-in-the-wool, born-and-bred, flag-waving American. This is never clearer than on the hockey field. I think she gets off on yelling at us.

"I'm sorry?"

"Do. You. Think. I'm. An. Idiot."

"No. Why?"

"Well, that's music to my ears. The way you're pussyfooting around out there, it's like you think I haven't noticed how lazy you've been all morning." She adjusts her visor.

"Um . . . I'm sorry? I'm not sure why you're upset." I hate people yelling at me.

"You're not sure why I'm upset? How about your time around the track this morning? You added six seconds. Or the fact that you were late to practice?"

"I'm very sorry. Like I said, my alarm didn't go off this morning, and then I needed to run to Powers Hall to turn in a late paper—"

"Quit it with the excuses. There are no excuses in real life. Either you win or you fail. Do you want to be a winner or a failure?"

"A winner?"

"Exactly. You want to be a *winner*. That means you need to get your head in the game. We're never going to win anything this year if you're strolling around the field like my grandmother."

Sometimes I feel like Coach Wilkinson has seen too many sports movies.

"I'm sorry. I understand," I say firmly.

"Good." She gives me a curt nod. "Back to practice."

I push myself hard, determined to show Coach Wilkinson that I'm giving it my all. Sure enough, she claps me on the back as I'm heading to the locker room. It's not exactly praise, but I think it's as good as I can expect from her.

But while we're undressing, she comes into the locker room.

"Listen up! We're going to be having extra practice every day this week after classes. Five p.m. sharp."

The group erupts.

"What?"

"No!"

"But I have plans."

"You can't!"

Once everybody has stopped complaining, she says, "You got dinner plans? Cancel 'em. Our game in two weekends is against Norfolk, and we need the extra work. Badly. You're a hot mess out there. I'm not going to name names"—her eyes dart toward me—"but I need everybody on the team to step up. Don't like it?" She points toward the exit. "There's the door. You're welcome to get the hell out."

Silence.

"All in agreement? Good. Meet me in the weight room at five p.m."

I shoot Edward and Libby a group text message:

ME: Ugh. Have to practice late every day this week. Wilkinson sux. Don't bother rescheduling dinner. Have fun. Xxx

EDWARD: Damn. Ok.

LIBBY: Proud of you, Lotte! Should we bring back a takeaway?

ME: Rock star! Yes, pls.

At least they'll have some time to bond without me.

Later that night, after practice finally winds down, I go over to India's room, knocking on the door. Nobody answers, so I move on down the hall to Flossie's room, where the door is open.

She's leaning back on her bed, a sea of pillows behind her, writing something longhand.

"Hey," she says. "Come in. Want some wine?" There's a mug on the desk that I'd assumed was tea, surrounded by lit candles.

"Sure. Should I close the door?"

"Yeah."

I enter, closing the door behind me. Flossie sits up, swinging her long legs over the quilted blanket.

"So. Donatella," she says.

"Huh?"

"Your sister. She looked bloody fantastic."

"She did, didn't she?"

"You did a tremendous job. You should be proud." Flossie reaches into the nightstand and pulls out a pack of Camel Blues, popping one into her mouth and lighting it with one of the candles. "Want one?"

I lean over, plucking a cigarette from the pack. "Shouldn't we open the window?"

"Sure," she says. It's clear she's not going to do it, so I stand up and push open the panes, looking out onto the back forests of Sussex.

"What are we all doing this Saturday?"

But Flossie doesn't seem to hear me. She frowns into her phone.

"What? What's wrong?"

"Libby and Edward are in town without you."

"Yeah," I say, shrugging. "Hockey practice went long."

"So?"

"The three of us had dinner plans—so Libby and Edward could keep getting to know each other. We have late hockey practices the whole week now, so I told them to go without me."

Flossie nods. "I see. That makes sense, I suppose."

"What? You sound weird."

She takes a deep drag of her cigarette. All she needs is bloodred lipstick and a deep side part and she'd look like a film star from the thirties. "I don't know." She exhales slowly. Libby hates it when I smoke. But most kids at Sussex Park smoke at least a little bit—except Edward.

"I'm not sure I understand why you're *so* keen on Edward and Libby getting along," she says. "Explain it to me."

"She's my sister."

"We've established that."

"And he's my boyfriend."

"Aware of that, too . . ."

"I guess I just thought they would get along."

"Yes, but Charlotte, there's a world of difference between making sure your sister and your boyfriend get along, and setting them up on a romantic dinner. Sure you don't want to book them a hotel room and send a bottle of champagne while you're at it?"

Now it's my turn to frown. "You think it's too much? Maharajah is hardly *romantic*."

"How many options do we have in this town? We're not in London. It's a real restaurant with tablecloths. They don't serve burgers, pizza, or fish and chips. And it's your date spot with Edward. I'd say it qualifies as romantic."

"You're freaking me out. Should I worry? Ow!" My cigarette has burned down to the nub, burning my index finger. I toss it into the water-filled mug on the window ledge that she's using as an ashtray.

"I'm sure it's fine."

I look at her suspiciously. "Do you know something?"

She shakes her head. "I don't. But even if I did, I wouldn't get involved. Your love life, your problem."

I start picking at my cuticles. "Well, that's lame," I say sullenly. "I'd tell *you* if something were going on with your boyfriend."

"First of all, I don't have a boyfriend. Maybe this summer, we'll see what we can put together on the Mediterranean cruise"—Flossie's family charters a yacht off Sardinia every June—"but until then, I have zero interest in teenage boys. Secondly, if something were going on with my boyfriend, I'd *know*."

"Where is this coming from? Did somebody say something?"

Her eyes flick toward her phone.

"What? Who texted you? India? What did she say?" Any pretense of keeping my cool is gone.

"It wasn't India, it was Alice. She says she saw Edward and Libby in Maharajah. From behind, she thought it was you at first."

"Is that all? Jesus, you freaked me out. Libby and I look alike. Our hair's the same color—I think she's even wearing my clothes tonight. I lent her my favorite blazer."

Flossie doesn't look convinced.

"Did she say anything else?"

"That's all."

"So why are you so concerned?" I'm beginning to feel exasperated.

"Charlotte. Alice thought Edward was with *you*. Doesn't that imply something?"

"Like what?"

"Like . . . maybe they were too close. Maybe he was looking at her a certain way."

My stomach clenches.

"I don't know," she continues. "I don't want you believing something that's not true. But something feels off. Maybe you should have your guard up."

"My guard up against what?"

Flossie looks at me impassively. She waits several beats before lighting up another cigarette. "I'm sure it was nothing. I don't know what I was thinking. Edward and Libby . . . it would be laughable."

We move on to other subjects, working our way through a bottle of wine before I decide it's time for bed. But while washing my face, I can't help but turn Flossie's words over and over.

Back in my room, I text Libby:

ME: How's dinner going?

No response. I wait twenty minutes and text again:

ME: Come to my room when you're done, k?

It's another half hour before Libby knocks. I'm half asleep on top of the covers. I wipe a trickle of drool off my cheek and call, "Come in!"

"Hey! How was practice? Did you have a good night?"

"It was fine. So, tell me everything. How did it go?" I pat the bed next to me.

"I'm *knackered*. Mind if we chat in the morning? I'll give you the full scoop."

"No. Come. Sit."

She obeys, kicking her shoes off and sinking into the mattress.

"How'd it go?" I repeat.

"We had so much fun. He's a great guy! I completely understand what you see in him now."

"How was dinner?"

"Delicious! Maharajah was a good choice. I had the tandoori chicken. And their popadams are to die for."

"That's nice," I say distractedly. "What did you talk about?"

"Oh, everything. Honestly, it was kind of awkward at first: there was a lot of small talk about classes. He's really having issues in maths, so I told him I'd help tutor him."

"That's cool. He'll appreciate that."

"Eventually, I talked about how we grew up in Guildford, he talked about going back and forth between Cedar Hall and Kensington Palace as a kid, we both talked about how scared we were to go away for boarding school. But at one point I brought up Dad and how he's freaking out about my going to university, and that got him talking about *his* dad and university, and then the floodgates opened. He's stressing about all that Firm business. It seems like a lot for somebody our age to deal with alone."

This is news to me. "Firm business?"

"The Firm? Hasn't he said anything?"

"Um, *no*. I don't know what you're talking about."

"It's what they call the royal family. King Henry coined it."

"Huh. Can't say he's mentioned it."

Libby looks chastened. "I'm sorry, I thought you two had talked about it. I know this sounds silly, Lotte, but I'd better not say anything else. I don't want to betray his confidence."

"Are you serious?" I can feel my face getting red. "Libby, you've known him for like a week. I'm dating him."

"I know. It's just . . . if he hasn't told you, I don't want him thinking I blabbed. You know how I feel about discretion." Libby is like a vault when it comes to keeping secrets, which I've always admired—plus, it has served me well with our parents. But I don't care about any of that now. I'm annoyed.

"You're my sister!"

"Charlotte, I'm *sorry*. It just doesn't feel right. Wouldn't you feel bad if you told me something in confidence and then I blabbed it to Edward?"

"No," I say sullenly. "Plus, that's different. You should have loyalty to *me* over some guy."

"Now he's suddenly just some guy?" she says, smiling a little, as if she expects me to joke with her. I won't take the bait.

"I don't think it's right for my sister and my boyfriend to have secrets," I say, sitting up straight in bed and crossing my arms over my chest. "That's lame."

Libby sighs, her smile fading. "I'm sorry, Lotte. I'm not trying to be lame, and I don't want to hurt your feelings. But it has nothing to do with you *or* me. It's not my secret to share. Please understand."

"I don't know what to say to that."

"I'm sorry," she repeats.

"Stop saying that! I don't accept your apology."

She sits up on the bed. "I should probably go. It's late."

"Fine. Whatever."

She moves toward the door, beginning to close it and then peeking out from behind it. "Should I keep it open?"

I shrug. "Do what you want."

"Breakfast tomorrow morning?" she asks hopefully.

But I don't respond, not turning around until I hear her footsteps echoing down the hall.

It's been awkward since Libby wouldn't tell me what Edward said. I don't believe in holding grudges, but I sulk for a couple of days to let her know that her behavior was unacceptable.

"Want to get lunch?" she asks, stopping by my bedroom on Saturday for the second day in a row.

"No, thanks," I say, flipping through my maths textbook.

She stands there until I look up.

"Yes?"

"Are you still mad at me? Don't you think you're overreacting a *little* bit?"

"Gee, thanks."

"Charlotte, come on. You're being silly."

"Did you only stop by to insult me, or was there another reason, too? Do you want to tell me all about how terrible I am at maths while you're at it?"

Libby scratches her head and sighs. "I don't know why you're punishing *me*. He's the one you're dating. He's the one you should be annoyed at."

"And you're my sister."

"Charlotte, how many times do I have to say I'm sorry? You know how I feel about sharing other people's secrets. I would keep yours from anybody, no questions asked."

"Can't you just tell me a little bit of what he said?"

Libby groans. "You're insufferable. It's been four days. Haven't you talked to him about this yet?"

"No." In truth, I haven't even seen Edward since his dinner with Libby. Apparently, he's been skipping classes, and none of us has seen him for any meals. His mind is clearly somewhere else. And if I'm being honest, I haven't really been seeking him out, either. Libby's right—I'm upset with him for revealing something to her that he won't talk about with me.

"Why not? The hallmark of a good relationship is communication."

"What, because you know so much about relationships from the hundreds of boyfriends you've had? Have you ever even kissed a boy?"

Libby's face falls. "You're being mean. I'll see you later."

"Libby, wait." I push myself up off the bed. She's already halfway down the hall, walking quickly. "Libby. Libby!" I chase her in my bare feet. "I'm sorry."

Her eyes are wet. "It's not fair to drag me into the middle of this. I didn't ask to have dinner with him. *You* suggested it."

"You're right."

"I didn't want to leave Greene House—I liked it there."

"Of course." I'm surprised that she's bringing this up now.

"Having to switch schools in my last year was awful. I miss my friends, I miss feeling like I fit in, but at least I'm *trying*. It's not my fault that Edward is keeping secrets from you, but now you're punishing *me* for it instead of talking to *him* about it. Please don't put your relationship issues on me."

"Absolutely," I say soothingly. "You're right. Let me run back to my room and put some shoes on and we'll go down to lunch."

As we walk to the dining hall, Libby is quiet. Finally, she says, "I *am* sorry. I hate keeping secrets. Why can't you just talk to him about it? I'm sure he'd be happy to have your support."

"I will," I say, even though I'd rather swallow knives than ask Edward why he felt comfortable confiding in my sister but not in me.

"I haven't, you know," she says. Her voice is quiet as we walk outside onto the quad.

"You haven't what?"

"Kissed a boy. Not yet."

"Shut the front door—*what?* Libby, are you serious? I was only joking! How have you never kissed a boy?"

"Greene House . . . the opportunity never presented itself," she says, mumbling.

"Well, we're going to have to rectify that immediately. I'll organize a game of Truth or Dare this weekend. You can practice on . . .

damn. None of our guy friends are that appealing. I mean, Oliver's super cute, but I think he and Georgie are hooking up now. So that just leaves David and *Tarquin*."

She starts laughing. "Pass. But thanks, Lotte. It'll happen *someday*. Just waiting for the right guy, I guess."

"Prince Charming is around the corner. I know it." I look at her sidelong. "You look really nice today." She's wearing a pair of fitted jeans, a soft cream-colored jumper, and buttery black flats. It's a much more low-key outfit than I'd wear, but it looks both comfortable and stylish. Thank God for weekends, when we don't have to wear the uniform.

"Thank you. I've been working my way through back issues of *Elle* and saw a similar outfit. I spent twenty minutes trying to mimic it."

This practically breaks my heart. I change the subject.

"So, my birthday's in a fortnight," I say. "On a Saturday this time—finally."

"Come on, who are you talking to?" she says, poking me with her elbow. "Like I'd forget your birthday! Should I make plans for everybody? A Justin Bieber theme?" she teases, humming "Baby."

I shoot her a look. "That song was like a billion years ago."

She laughs. "I'm just messing with you. We all know your musical taste is way better than mine. Even if you secretly still like Justin Bieber."

"Ignoring you now. I can't remember the last time we spent my birthday together." Libby's birthday is in the spring, which means sometimes it falls over break. Last year, we both went back to Wisteria to celebrate with our family, and Libby brought a few friends home from Greene House with her. Since my birthday is in November, however, I've been stuck the last three years celebrating it at school. For my sixteenth birthday, I got a cupcake and candle from my lacrosse teammates in the dining hall. Lame.

"Flossie's offered to throw me something. It's going to be epic." Her parents have a country home near campus: a two-story farmhouse with huge polo fields that are perfect for an outdoor party.

"That should be fun!"

"I'm beyond excited." We enter the dining hall. It's early in the lunch hour so it hasn't started to fill up yet. "India says she goes *all* out for parties. Plus, it makes me feel like I'm finally a part of the group."

"Part of the group? Why wouldn't you be? You're besties with India. You're dating Edward. You've got nothing to worry about."

I snort. "Not with this crowd."

Libby looks apprehensive.

"I'm not taking anything for granted—but I think Flossie throwing me a party is kind of a big deal. It's like she accepts me for real."

"Friend politics are so weird," says Libby, nodding. I think back to my mother's comment about how things have always been harder for Libby socially. I didn't realize she was missing her friends from Greene House so much. Poor Libby. She's trying so hard.

"Tell me about it," I say.

We sit down at the table and say our hellos.

"Is that a new jumper?" Flossie asks Libby. "It looks gorge on you."

Libby looks pleased. "It is! Thank you!"

"Although you always look amazing in the uniform, too."

She flushes. "That's so kind. Thank you, Flossie. I like your hair like that." Flossie has arranged her long brown hair into braids and wrapped it around the crown of her head.

"Thanks."

"Should we leave you two alone?" Tarquin says. Flossie shoots him a dirty look.

"You do look very nice, Libby," says India. "Speaking of clothes, have you all decided what you're wearing to Charlotte's party in a couple weeks?"

"It's a fancy-dress party," I say, turning back toward Libby. "I think I forgot to mention that."

"That's a great idea!" Libby says, nodding. "My friend Savannah loved throwing those. I have the perfect costume at home—I'll call Mum and ask her to send it."

"What's your costume?" Alice asks.

"Ginger Spice," Libby says, grinning. "From the Spice Girls."

"What? I can't picture that at all," says Flossie.

"That's why it's fun!" I say. Although, in truth, I can't picture it, either.

"It's a throwback," says India, nodding. "I like it."

"What are you all going to wear?" Libby asks.

"I plan on going as a moon goddess," says India, as if that explains everything.

"I'm going as a clown," Tarquin says as he sits down.

Libby and I both look up in alarm. "No!" we say in unison.

"Jesus," says Flossie. "What's *that* all about?"

"We hate clowns," I say.

"Ever since that awful movie *It*," says Libby.

"Our babysitter let us watch it once when we were little and . . ." I shudder at the memory. "You can't go as a clown."

"Please," says Libby, looking at him.

"Okay, okay, jeez. No clowns," says Tarquin, rolling his eyes. "Don't get your knickers in a twist."

Libby and I exchange relieved looks.

"Oh, by the way, David," Libby says. "It took some time, but I found that article on the history of Robben Island I was talking about. I thought it might help with your history paper. If you still want it, I can email it to you later tonight."

"You're the best!"

At the other end of the table, Georgie and Oliver are murmuring to each other and laughing softly, clearly in their own little world.

"What are you wearing, Oliver?" I ask. He looks at me, startled. I notice that he seems to be growing his hair out—it must be Georgie's influence.

"Sorry to distract you away from the missus," I say.

Georgie giggles as Oliver smiles.

Finally, Edward shows up. His hair is wet and his fair cheeks are flushed red. "Hey, everybody. Rugby practice went long." He and David slap high fives. "Hiya," he says, planting a quick kiss on my lips. He smells like soap.

We haven't seen each other in four days—not since Libby and Edward had dinner together. I've been so irritated at Libby that I've barely thought about Edward—and she's right. He's the one I should be frustrated with.

"Hi, stranger. How was it?" I ask.

"It was fine." He pops a bit of bread roll in his mouth, holding up a taped finger and making an exaggerated frowny face. "Digby went hard on me again. He couldn't care less about the ball. He prefers trying to tackle me."

"Oh my God, that looks bad," Libby says. "Have you gone to the infirmary?"

"Nah. Nothing a little spit won't fix."

"It could be broken. You should probably go so they can at least look at it. They may need to set it."

"He said he's fine, Libs," I say.

She flushes. "Sorry. I was just trying to help. I took a first aid course a few summers ago. It never hurts to be prepared."

I smile at her. "I know. But Edward's tough," I say, slapping him on the back. "He can handle whatever's thrown at him." For some reason, I suddenly feel more like a teammate than a girlfriend.

As Libby eats her lunch, laughing at everybody's jokes, giving Edward study advice, and piping up here and there with supportive comments, my heart melts. She really is trying.

I resolve to put the Edward situation behind me. I'll be mature if it kills me.

ten

As promised, Edward takes Libby and me to a polo match in Windsor Great Park the next week. It's the annual Chairman's Cup, marking the end of the polo season, and Edward is playing.

"Where'd he say to meet him?" I frown, looking around anxiously as we drive up the long gravel driveway through the woods toward Guards Polo Club. Libby told me that she and Edward discussed it in maths class and so I left the planning to her.

It's been a full week since Edward and Libby had dinner together, and things haven't been sitting right for me ever since. I know I should probably gather up the courage and talk about it with Edward, but something's holding me back. Shouldn't he confide in *me*? Should I have to drag secrets out of him? Maybe I'm overthinking it, but all these little details are adding up to make me feel like Edward and I aren't a good fit. He and I barely see each other and always want to do different things when we *are* hanging out.

Right now, a tiny part of me doesn't even know why we're still dating.

I mean, he's hot. And he's a prince. And he's sweet most of the time . . . at least, when I actually see him. But is that enough? I'm not sure.

Libby scrolls through her phone. "He says to drive to the end and then turn left. There's a car park by the grandstands, and we're supposed to show the people our badges to get through. Are you wearing your badge?" She looks down at my lapel, continuing. "Okay, good. Then he says he's at the northeast end of the field, by the giant maroon-and-white tent."

Our taxi driver drops us off, and we tentatively make our way past the gates.

"Are you sure we're not underdressed? Shouldn't we be wearing dresses and hats?" I'm wearing a pair of skinny jeans, a flowy top, black leather booties, an oversized scarf, and a leather jacket to help combat the early November chill.

"We should be fine. Apparently, you're only supposed to get dressed up for the Gold Cup and the Queen's Cup—and that's mostly just for spectators. We're with Edward, so . . ." She's wearing her new skinny jeans and knee-high brown boots with a chunky knit jumper and her army jacket. She looks like she's about to go fishing at Balmoral, not watch polo at the most elite club in England.

"Are we allowed to walk on the field before the game?" I ask, looking around anxiously.

"I think so, yes."

We step onto the lush, manicured lawn, looking back and forth as if we're expecting security to come drag us away. Nobody does anything, so we keep walking. I look across the field and see a few other random people streaming across the field confidently.

"Edward's over there," Libby says, pointing to a maroon-and-white-striped awning. "By the giant *D*."

I feel out of place, but remind myself that it's important to act confident. If you fake social graces, even if you don't feel them, it puts other people at ease. Everybody's usually too busy focusing on how awkward *they* feel to notice your own discomfort. My mother sat me down and taught me that once my old friends ditched me—a lesson that's served me well at Sussex Park.

As we get closer, I wave toward Edward and call out, "Hi, babe!"

But he doesn't seem to hear me.

"He must be distracted," Libby says. "It's probably stressful right before a game."

"He's always distracted," I say, walking up to Edward and patting his bum. "Hey."

"Jesus, Charlotte! You scared me." He turns around, looking slightly irritated.

"I called out to you," I say, feeling rejected.

"Sorry," he says. He hugs me with one arm. He looks dead sexy in his polo uniform: a white polo shirt with a maroon stripe emblazoned on the front, white breeches, and dark brown riding boots. On his sleeve, there's a maroon "4," and the word "Doha" is on his chest in white, down the stripe.

"Hi, Edward. Good luck today," Libby says.

"Thanks, Libs."

Libs? They have one dinner together and a few study sessions and she's *Libs* to him now?

"Um, let's go over to the sidelines, I guess," I say, flustered. "We'll see you after the game?"

"Sounds good," he says distractedly, blowing me a kiss before turning away. He huddles together with one of his teammates, a short, balding man with ruddy cheeks and a substantial paunch.

Libby looks around. "Should we go over there?" she asks me, using her arm to shade her eyes as she points to a row of Land Rovers and Audis. Several blond thirtysomething women in aviators, jeans, flowy tops, and Barbour jackets are standing around, looking like professional girlfriends. I'm relieved to see that our outfits are right on point. Funny, relying on Libby for fashion advice.

"Okay." I shrug, letting her lead me. "I doubt it matters. This seems way more casual than I expected. Those girls are in jeans, too, thank God."

"I don't know," she says. "I get the feeling that it looks casual—but one slipup, and we're branded for life."

Maybe Libby understands more than I give her credit for.

"Here," she says, leading us to a patch of grass near a car and pulling a blue blanket out of her bag. "Sit."

"Look at you. All prepared."

"I did some research online yesterday. I was scared we would feel like outsiders—so I needed to arm myself. Knowledge is king."

"I'd make fun of you for being a nerd if I weren't so grateful. Explain this to me: I thought everybody in polo was supposed to be a hot Argentine. Why's *that* dude playing? He's like fifty years old."

"Ah!" Libby says, punctuating the air with her finger. "I read about this, too! He's probably the patron. Polo is a pro-am sport, so it's played by both professionals and amateurs. The patrons are the team owners, and they hire the professionals."

"The hot Argentines."

"Precisely."

"So the old dude owns the team."

"Yes. Likely."

I shake my head. "Why not just enjoy it from the sidelines like all the *other* rich men who own sport teams? Make your money and go home."

"Nobody makes money on polo. It's a million-dollar money pit. And he's not just any old guy. His family owns half of Qatar. Hence the team name: Doha."

"Oh. Well, that's something, at least," I say, looking at the patron with renewed interest before turning back to Libby. "Do you think any of these girls is his girlfriend?"

"Maybe," she says. "He's a billionaire. I'm sure there are at least a few women out there willing to play the part."

"Ugh," I say, shuddering. "Can you *imagine*? Gross. I could never be with a guy for the money—not for all the billions in the world."

"Not for a title, either—right?" she says, smiling at me impishly.

"I don't like what you're implying," I say haughtily, "but *no*. Not even for a title. I don't care if I marry a pauper or a prince, as long as he's hot and he gets me."

"Good," she says. "That's the spirit. I'd like somebody with a good sense of humor, who's kind and thoughtful—and who's taller than I am."

"Taller than you? *Tall* order, indeed."

She giggles at my pun. "Tell me about it. I'll settle for somebody my height who doesn't forget my birthday."

"Now we're talking. Aim high, Libs!" I still can't believe she's never kissed anybody. Scratch that—actually, I *can* believe it.

She's sitting on the blanket now, legs spread out in front of her just like the blond women on either side of us.

"So, are things better between the two of you?" she asks. "You talked it over?"

I pull a face, sitting down next to her and wrapping my scarf around me tighter for warmth. "No. What would I say, anyway?"

"Tell him the truth! Say that your feelings were hurt. Ask him to confide in you. Let him know that you care."

"Eh . . . thanks, but no thanks. Besides, why should it all be on me? I don't see *him* worrying about our relationship."

She nods. "That's true."

"I mean, we're so casual anyway—I rarely see him alone anymore. I might need to downshift our relationship after the new year." Even as I say it, I don't completely believe it, but somehow it makes me feel in control. Thinking about it makes me feel bad, so I change the subject. "Thank God I didn't wear a hat or a dress," I say. "I would have been completely out of place. How embarrassing would that have been?"

"Hats are for Ascot. Women in America wear them at those Veuve Clicquot polo matches in New York and LA—but that's not high goal. It's not *real* polo."

I burst out laughing. "You sound like a total snob."

Her cheeks glow pink. "Do I? I don't mean to sound like that. I'm just passing on what I learned."

"The advantage of approaching even fun activities like homework, I guess." I watch the men trotting across the field, their mallets slung over their shoulders. "It's weird we didn't go to more polo growing up."

"Dad hates horses, and Mum was always busy with the business."

"Yeah, but Cowdray Park is practically in our backyard. It's like the biggest polo mecca in the world. You'd think we would have gone more than only once, if only so we would be 'exposed,' to use Mum's language."

"Cowdray's the third biggest," she corrects me. "Argentina is where the real action is."

"And second?"

"Guards Polo Club. Right here."

Once the game starts, Libby begins explaining it to me. I try to follow along as she talks about the line of the ball, but I quickly start to get bored. I upload a few Snaps of the field, a selfie of me and Libby, and an Instagram of my leather booties. I'm relieved when India texts me.

INDIA: How's the polo?

ME: Boring.

INDIA: Sacrilege.

ME: Don't tell Edward.

INDIA: Don't tell Edward what? Xx

ME: Haha.

"Oh my God, you've been on that thing for the last twenty minutes," Libby says. "I swear, you'd die without your phone."

"Guilty." I put my phone on my lap. "Plus, you see one horse, you've seen them all."

She squints, taking in the action across the field as Edward swings his mallet.

"I think it's exciting! And in polo they call them ponies."

I shrug. "I'm remembering why I never go to polo matches at home. I'd rather be riding the horses—ponies, whatever—not watching them!"

Every few minutes, Edward gallops back to our corner of the field and switches out his horse, which Libby explains is to keep the mounts from getting overtired. Near the end of the game, when he's hopping from one pony to another like he's playing a game of musical chairs, he looks over at us and whoops. He swings his mallet over his head like in a war chant before kicking his pony and setting back off down the field at full speed.

The girls around us, who have mostly been ignoring us, suddenly start looking at us with interest after it becomes apparent we're with Edward.

"Are you with Doha?" one of them says, a leggy blonde with faint wrinkles around her pretty eyes.

"Yes," I say, smiling sweetly. "You?"

"I'm Pablo's wife," she says. Two small boys with beautiful long blond curls toddle around her. "And these are our boys, Matias and Joaquin."

"Congratulations on the win at Tortugas," Libby says. "Pablo played spectacularly, I heard."

The woman smiles proudly. "Thank you. It was a nail-biter. Oh, excuse me—Matias, no!" She rushes after the younger boy, who's trying to climb over the boards and run onto the field with his own mini mallet.

"Tortugas? Pablo?" I whisper to Libby.

"You'd be amazed what you can pick up by doing a little bit of reading—and by just being quiet and watching. Paying attention goes a long way."

"Not my strong suit," I laugh. "Thank God I have you along for the ride."

Libby smiles, waving gaily at Pablo's wife as she heads back our way, little Matias scooped up in her arms. "Thank God."

After the game is over, Libby and I walk back to the tents to congratulate a jubilant Edward on winning. He's filthy, his shirt soaked through with sweat and his boots and white trousers caked in mud.

"You were amazing!" I say brightly as we walk up.

In response, he picks me up and swings me around. "Did you see that last goal?"

"Oh, yeah, totally. It was awesome!" Actually, I missed it because I was watching Flossie's Story on Snapchat. She's in Copenhagen for the weekend with her family.

"I can't believe you made that penalty shot," Libby says. "And from fifty yards out! Seriously impressive."

He beams.

"So, listen," I say. "We were thinking of going out to celebrate. What do you think? Our treat."

"I wish I could. The patron is throwing an *asado* for all the players tonight."

I look at Libby quizzically. "It's a barbecue," she whispers to me. Her primary school Spanish is way better than my rusty French.

"Oh. Okay."

"Sorry," he says. "I'd much rather hang out with the two of you."

"No, that's cool. I get it. You have responsibilities."

"Unfortunately," he says, pulling a face.

"Are you back on campus tonight?"

"Not until Monday morning. Since we're near Windsor, I told my parents I'd spend some time with them."

I want to tell him that I miss him. I want to tell him that I'm feeling neglected. I want to tell him that I'm not okay with barely seeing the guy I'm dating. I want to tell him things need to change.

Instead, I say, "Cool. See you Monday," giving him a quick kiss and a hug before turning and walking with Libby back toward the car park.

The following week, I wake up and lie in bed, stretching my arms over my head and trying to shake the sleep off me.

Seventeen years old.

Now that I'm seventeen, I should finally feel like I'm becoming a woman. It's when people come out of their shells, moths turn into butterflies, and girls embrace their true selves, right? I've always heard that you stop caring what people think when you're older. You do what you want. You say what you want. You give zero fucks.

However, this morning, I feel exactly the same.

I still have all the fucks to give.

If I were Libby, I'd probably be methodical and solemn about it: write in my journal, take a long, contemplative walk through the windy November woods, make a bucket list of things I want to do before I turn eighteen.

Instead, I sleep in—it's a Saturday and there's no field hockey practice, thank God—and then spend a full hour leisurely getting ready. This morning I spend time on the little details—body bronzer, a few passes of the curling iron, the special mascara that makes my lashes look a mile long—enjoying the feeling of making myself look glamorous. I know the cool thing is to pretend I don't care what I look like and just roll out of bed—like India and Flossie—but I like makeup, damn it, and if I want to spend twenty minutes applying bronzer, I'm going to spend twenty minutes applying bronzer.

I hate being a cliché—the girl upset over her neglectful boyfriend—but everything with Edward is only getting worse, and it has me in a funk.

It's not normal to have your boyfriend ignore you like this, right? *Is* he my boyfriend? We never said anything to make it official.

I don't know what to think. I don't like feeling so out of control.

As I get ready, the texts roll in:

LIBBY: HAPPY BIRTHDAY!!! Love you so much. Proud of you.

Tonight's going to be fun! Xoxoxoxo

LIBBY: By the way, I have a little surprise for you . . . ☺

INDIA: Happy birthday! It's going to be a great year. Xxx

FLOSSIE: Happy bday! Don't forget 2 bring red wig for 2nite. Meet at gates at 12. X

ALICE: It's SO real now, RIGHTTT?

TARQUIN: HB, yo.

EDWARD: Sending u big kisses. Can't wait for 2nite. Happy birthday! Xx

eleven

The piercing, happy voices of drunk teenagers echo throughout Flossie's country house, past the barn onto the polo fields and the forests beyond.

Flossie's place is only five minutes from campus, a two-story farmhouse surrounded by tall hedges and shrubs so that it's not visible from the main road. With five bedrooms, it's relatively small, considering how much money her family has—but apparently they have about seven houses, so it's not like they have anything to prove or need the extra space.

The group met at the front gates this afternoon to share cabs to Flossie's house. I split a cab with Libby and Edward, and the two of them spent the entire ride talking about homework and upcoming assignments and their shared history professor. I guess their study sessions are, like, a regular *thing* now.

Libby and I are sharing a room on the driveway side of the house. Flossie has invited India to share her bedroom, giving the boys prime real estate overlooking the property's polo fields. Edward gets his own room in the back of the house, as always—his security team doesn't like him sharing rooms. They needed to do a sweep of Flossie's house before he arrived and put Simon the bodyguard next to Edward's room. Edward's security team is on strict orders to protect him from security threats, but that's all, so they're not allowed to interfere when they see him doing things like drinking.

The whole barn has been turned into a disco, with the doors flung open onto the polo field. Bales of hay are scattered everywhere, there's a vinyl dance floor in the center of the barn, and an actual disco ball has been affixed to the barn ceiling. Flossie's gone all out: she's rented speakers, she's gotten a DJ and a bartender, there's a taco truck in the driveway leading to the polo fields, and there's even a photo booth. The lights are turned down, the beer is flowing, and Rihanna is blaring. The perimeter of the barn is surrounded by heating lamps, so that we don't all freeze to death in our flimsy costumes.

Libby and I walk together to the bar.

"Two glasses of wine, please," I say.

"Just don't drink too much," she says. "You have the big game tomorrow."

"Whatever, I'll be fine. I won't have more than a couple glasses."

"I wish Flossie hadn't scheduled this for today," Libby says, looking worried.

"Yeah, but it's my actual birthday—it's the first Saturday birthday I've had in years!"

Libby doesn't look convinced.

Flossie's by the speakers, her hands waving animatedly as she talks to the DJ. Her costume is amazing—she's dressed as the supervillain Poison Ivy, wearing a green corset with green leaves affixed to the bodice, a green mask, and the fire-engine-red wig I lent her.

"I said *no* reggae," she complains to the DJ as "Could You Be Loved" floats from the loudspeakers. "Not *only* reggae."

"Floss, you look incredible," I say as we walk up to her. The DJ shoots me a wounded look. "That corset is bananas."

Her face immediately brightens. "You think? You don't think it's too much?"

"No way. It's genius. The leaves are a nice touch."

"Thank you," she says, practically purring. "I like your outfits, too." I'm dressed as Wonder Woman and Libby is, as promised, Ginger Spice.

"Oh, this old thing?" I joke. "The barn looks incredible. Thanks again for throwing this."

"Any excuse for a party, right?" She smiles at both of us, leaning in quickly for cheek kisses before turning back to the DJ. "Do I need to send you the approved music list *again*?"

Libby and I turn and face the crowd. Tarquin and David wear suits and oversized Batman and Robin masks, running around the perimeter of the dance floor like lunatics, waving their arms. India's lounging on a hay bale, wearing a flowy white tunic and a long red braided wig—I'm not sure who she is—while talking to a girl in a

Russian fur cap. Alice stands next to them, wearing a white flapper costume and enough pearls to anchor a ship. Georgie and Oliver—who are now totally dating—are dressed as Bonnie and Clyde. Edward is a pirate, with a long, curly black wig, a thick black mustache, and a magnificent red-and-black costume threaded with gold. At his waist, a sword hangs from a golden belt.

I poke Libby. "Do you think the sword and the belt are real?"

She considers the question. "He does have access to lots of historical knickknacks. You never know! Hey, I need to go do something quickly. Do you mind?"

"Oh. Okay. Sure."

I lean against the bar at the far corner of the barn with my drink, watching the action as people approach me every few seconds to say hello and wish me a happy birthday. Surprisingly, I don't know most of the crowd—word must have gotten out.

I'm seventeen, all my best friends are here, we have *zero* adult supervision—even less than we did at Huntshire—and I'm the guest of honor. Tonight is all about me. It should be one of the best days of my life.

But my dark mood is only getting worse.

Edward comes up behind me, hugging me.

"Hey," I say, turning and melting into him. I know that things aren't perfect between us—but right now, it just feels nice to have his arms around me. "I've kinda missed you."

"Oh, yeah? I've kinda missed you, too," he says. "Sorry I've been MIA. It's been a stressful month. Dealing with family stuff. And December is bound to be worse, what with exams and the holidays."

"So I've heard. Libby told me *all* about it," I say, exaggerating. Edward frowns slightly, releasing his hold on me. "Oh, yeah?"

"Yeah. She said all the Firm stuff was really getting to you."

Edward looks annoyed. "Oh. I see."

I look at him expectantly.

He takes a sip of his beer.

"But it's all okay?" I ask.

He nods. "Yeah." He changes the subject. "So, how mad are you going to be at me if I *didn't* buy you that bracelet you kept hinting about?"

I'm disappointed—not about the bracelet, which I couldn't care less about, but about Edward being so tight-lipped with me. Now I feel ten times worse than I did two minutes ago.

"Whatever you get me will be perfect," I say, with a brightness I don't really feel.

After the barn has filled to capacity, hobbits partying alongside scuba divers alongside samurai, the lights go down. Flossie appears, holding a cake with seventeen flickering candles. Everybody sings "Happy Birthday" to me, and I plaster a smile on my face, blowing out the candles as everybody claps.

"Thank you for coming—I love you all!" I say. "Now have some cake!"

"Yum!" Libby says, tucking into her piece. She's reappeared after her mysterious errand. "Did you make this, Flossie? It's delicious."

She snorts. "Hardly. I ordered it."

I turn toward Libby. "Do you remember when you made that strawberry short—" I stop when I see that she and Edward have their

153

heads together, whispering about something. He's nodding enthusi-astically.

She catches me looking at her and clams up.

"What's that?" I ask them suspiciously.

"Nothing," Edward says, looking amused.

I definitely woke up on the wrong side of the bed today, because suddenly the sight of my boyfriend and my sister with their heads together irritates me beyond belief.

"I'm going to the loo," I say to nobody in particular, walking away.

I walk out of the barn and head inside Flossie's house to the powder room on the first floor. It's a grand bathroom: the sort self-consciously designed to impress visitors. Inside, I stare at my reflection in the gilt-edged mirror, the low light flickering around the corners of my face.

Why were Libby and Edward whispering together like that?

He and I haven't spent any significant time together in weeks. Meanwhile, he and Libby are now regular study partners. As soon as he started hanging out with her, he *stopped* hanging out with me. Are they more than friends? Is that why he was confiding in her? Was Flossie right?

Or am I just being paranoid?

I fix my wig, use my pinkie fingers to smooth out the eyeliner under my eyes, and blot my T-zone with a piece of tissue before head-ing back into the barn.

India is still lounging on a bale of hay, drinking a martini from a real glass, her wig slightly askew. As I start to make my way over, I'm stopped by Robert, the prefect from Stuart Hall.

"Happy birthday," he says, stepping forward to give me a hug. We embrace awkwardly, his Sonny Bono wig caught in my lip gloss.

"Sorry," I say. "Occupational hazard. I'm a wig killer tonight." I reach up to straighten his wig. "There. Much better."

"Have you had a good birthday so far?"

"Not bad. How are you doing?"

"Better now." He smiles at me, little dimples visible in his cheeks, and then looks around. "Where are all your friends? No crowd of admirers?"

I frown. Suddenly, I feel like being honest. "I don't know. I'm having an awful day."

He looks genuinely sorry. "Can I help?"

"You can help me find my bloody sister and my bloody boyfriend. They seem to have snuck off. Again." Robert raises an eyebrow, and I realize I might be a little tipsy.

"Again?"

"I'm probably just imagining it," I say, shrugging as I look around the crowded barn. One of Grandmother Nana's mantras is something she claims Elizabeth Taylor said: *Never complain, never explain.* "Sorry, I'm just in a funk." A waiter walks by with a tray of wine and I pluck a cup off it, downing it.

I need to be alone.

"See you later?" I say to Robert.

"Absolutely." He holds up his glass, clinking it with my almost-empty wine cup. "To you. Here's hoping this year makes all your dreams come true."

"You are *so* sweet," I say. "I needed that tonight. Thank you." I stand on my tiptoes, leaning up to give him a kiss on the cheek. He blushes.

I snake through the throng of laughing students to the fields surrounding Flossie's house. With each step I take away from the barn and the flickering heat lamps, it gets colder and colder. I'm shivering by the fields, trying to clear my head, when Flossie and Tarquin appear.

"How are you?" Flossie asks. She's thrown an old jacket over her Poison Ivy costume.

"Fine," I say morosely.

"You don't seem fine," Tarquin says, holding a beer as he gives me the once-over. "You should probably drink more."

Flossie reaches over and wipes something off my cheek. "Is it Libby and Edward?"

I frown. "What do you mean?"

"Look, I know everybody's drinking tonight—but I just want you to know that I think it's *rude*," Flossie says. "Especially since you've done so much for Libby since she arrived. You've gone out of your way for her."

"What's rude?"

I want my suspicions confirmed.

I want proof that I'm not crazy.

Flossie and Tarquin look at each other.

"It may have been my imagination," Flossie says, verbally backtracking.

"Is something going on between them?"

Suddenly, she's coy.

"You *assume* when you see things," Flossie says, "but maybe that's all it is. Assumption."

I look at Tarquin.

He shrugs, taking a swig of his beer. "Damned if I know."

I turn and look back into the barn, where Libby and Edward are now sitting on a bale of hay, their heads together as they talk to each other. Their body language is intimate, unmistakable. Libby seems happier and more confident than I've ever seen her.

"Give me that," I say, grabbing the cigarette out of Flossie's hand and taking a long drag. I hand it back to her grimly. "Thanks. Do you mind? I need a moment."

"You okay?" Flossie asks.

"Yeah. Just had a little too much to drink."

I'm out there facing the field, my arms crossed around my body as much for warmth as for emotional protection, for what feels like hours. I hear Libby's voice behind me.

"It's freezing out here!"

I don't say anything.

"Wait. Are you okay?"

I shrug, my back still to her.

"Charlotte? Are you okay?" It takes me several seconds to turn around.

"I don't know what to say."

"What's going on?" she says, looking concerned. She has a small, wrapped present in her hand. "Can I help?"

"Yeah, by backing off."

Libby steps back. "I . . . I'm confused. You're not *angry* with me, are you?"

"Oh, is it that obvious?"

She puts her arm around my shoulders, partly as a gesture of affection and partly to stop me from dying of hypothermia. "Come on, Lotte. Let's go back inside and talk. You're going to catch a cold. I have a little surprise for you."

"I don't want to go inside, and I don't want any surprises." I pause, gathering my courage. Finally, I say it. "I want you to stop talking to Edward."

"Huh? I thought you wanted us to be friends."

"Yeah—but *only* friends."

"Okay, now I'm seriously confused."

"Please. I have eyes." The wine has definitely gone to my head. I'm sure there must be a more nuanced way to express my frustration and confusion, but it's not coming out right now.

"Charlotte, I'm lost."

"He's mine, so you'd better not cross the line."

Libby's eyes widen. "Do you think I'm putting the moves on Edward?"

"Ten thousand points to the brilliant Libby Weston."

"Bug, we really should go inside," she says. "You're not making a ton of sense. I think you've had too much to drink, okay? You have the big game tomorrow. I *knew* it was a mistake for Flossie to throw you a party the night before, but I didn't want to take the wind out of everybody's sails."

"Stop acting like Mum and leave me alone." I turn on my heel, heading back into the party.

I storm inside the barn, making a beeline for the bar. The bartender hands me a cup full of wine and I down it like a dehydrated rugby player. Too much to drink? How dare she?

Edward's now standing in a corner of the barn, surrounded by our friends.

I sidle up to him. "Hi."

He puts his arm around me. "Hi!"

"It was cold outside," I say. "Thought you might like to warm me up." I peer at him. Things are starting to become a blur.

He touches my elbow. "Let's go sit?"

I look down and realize I'm swaying slightly. I giggle. "Whoops! A bit tough standing in these heels."

I slide my arm through Edward's. "Psst," I whisper. "Come with me. I want to tell you something."

We walk arm in arm onto the makeshift dance floor, and I notice Libby looking at me from the other side of the room. She looks concerned. Screw her and her concerned looks. I shoot her back a *See? You were wrong* look.

"Everything all right?" Edward asks.

"I just missed you, that's all." I throw my other arm around his neck, pulling his face close to mine. We make out.

The room is spinning. I'm feeling dizzy.

He squeezes me tightly, looking at me with concern. "Are you okay?"

"I'm fine, honestly," I say. "Just a little dizzy." I clap my hand over my mouth to block an escaping hiccup, but I'm too late. "I might have had a little too much to drink."

"I think it's time to get you to bed."

"No, I don't want to go to bed! I'm having too much fun here."

"I know, I know," he says. "But I couldn't live with myself if I didn't take care of you."

Edward beckons Libby over to help as I stumble.

"What can I do, Lotte? Are you okay? Can I bring you something?" she asks.

"I don't feel well, Libs. I want to go to bed. Edward is going to take me upstairs."

"That sounds like a perfect plan. Let's go. Here, put your arm around me."

Libby and Edward hoist me up, and together the three of us make our way through the crowd and out of the barn toward the house.

I focus on my breath, trying to keep it together until we make it back inside the house and upstairs. Libby and Edward are talking about me, but I don't care anymore. I have a singular goal: bed.

We're almost at the room when a wave of nausea overtakes me and I throw up in a crystal vase.

After that, everything goes black.

I wake up with a start. *Where the hell am I?*

There are framed herb prints on the wall and gold curtains with too much light streaming through.

I'm at Flossie's country house.

Last night's events come flooding back: flirting with Robert;

Flossie confiding her concerns about Libby and Edward; fighting with Libby on the back lawn; downing glass after glass of wine and drunkenly slobbering all over Edward.

I try to remember how I got upstairs and have a vague memory of kneeling outside my room puking in a vase while Libby held my hair back. Was Edward there?

He *was*. I can't believe he saw the whole thing.

I find a note next to my bed on top of a wrapped box. I think it must be the same box from last night.

Hope you're feeling better, Lots. Sorry about last night, and sorry I didn't have a chance to give this to you then. It was meant to be a surprise. Edward and I both chipped in and bought it together.

There's water and paracetamol on the table. Come find me in the kitchen when you're ready. I'm making a fry-up.

Love you. L

The clock says eight fifteen a.m. Libby no doubt bounced out of bed at dawn feeling like a new woman and decided to go for a five-mile run. No hangovers for the perfect sister.

I open the box: it's the bracelet I've been coveting.

Well, now I feel like a total jerk.

I scrape myself out of bed and stare at my reflection in the mirror. My brown eyes are bloodshot and I have mascara and eyeliner smeared all the way down to my cheeks. My pillowcase is caked with foundation and eye makeup. I cringe. I must have been *plastered*.

The game is at three p.m. I have plenty of time to sober up and get my head on straight. I pull my hair into a bun on top of my head and make my way downstairs. The smell of sizzling bacon and onions makes my empty stomach grumble.

Flossie's farmhouse kitchen is small and cozy—half the size of my own kitchen at home. Behind the stove, Libby stands, wearing an apron and wielding a pair of tongs. Everybody else sits at the table, wearing T-shirts and blearily holding mugs of coffee and cups of tea. India is wearing oversized black sunglasses.

"Morning!" Libby chirps. She turns and pours me a fresh cup of coffee, handing it to me as if she's been waiting all morning for this very moment. "Two sugars, just the way you like."

"Thanks," I say, looking around warily.

Edward sits on the far side of the table. He holds open his arms for a hug.

"How are you feeling?" he murmurs. "You went pretty hard last night."

"I feel like a bag of rubbish," I say, looking at everybody. Only Flossie and Libby look clear-eyed. India looks like she might be asleep behind her glasses. Georgie and Oliver are leaning on each other in the corner, looking like zombies. Tarquin and David are too busy shoveling food into their mouths to notice me.

"Sorry," Edward says, patting me on the back. "Libby made a delicious breakfast. It should make you feel better."

Libby putters around the kitchen, turning sizzling bacon and sausages, frying bread, chopping tomatoes, and opening a can of baked beans.

"You're a brilliant cook, Libby," David says, stuffing his mouth with omelets. "This is better than our cook at home."

"It really is tremendously good," says Flossie.

She blushes. "Thanks. I like cooking. It's relaxing."

"The only thing I make are reservations," I say, wincing as everybody's laughter triggers my headache. I look at Flossie. "How are you not hungover?"

"I only had two beers," she says. "I didn't want to be wrecked before the game today."

Libby's face tightens, but she doesn't say anything.

"I pounded some ginseng before bed," Alice says. "Although you know what also works? Beetroot juice."

"Beetlejuice?" Tarquin says, laughing.

Libby piles a huge stack of pancakes in front of me. "I made them just for you: with strawberries and blueberries mixed in with the batter. I hope it makes you feel better." She learned how to make pancakes from an American cooking show when we were home on break a couple of years ago. They've been one of my favorite things in the world ever since.

"Thanks." I spear a huge stack and am about to take a giant bite when I remember that Edward is watching me. I take a smaller, socially acceptable bite. "God, these are delicious. What time did you wake up?"

She must have four things sizzling on different burners, but she looks as calm and composed as if she were a professional chef. "Probably six thirty. You know it's hard for me to sleep in." Libby has struggled with insomnia since we were kids.

"What I wouldn't give for a lie-in," I yawn, rubbing my eyes. "I hate waking up early for field hockey. After I graduate university, I'm never waking up before noon again."

Edward laughs. "Noon? That's a bit excessive, even for me."

"Okay, then, ten a.m. But that's the earliest I'll do it."

"Let's hope your kids get the memo," says Flossie, standing up to pour more coffee. Libby reaches over and refills her mug.

I wrinkle my nose. "I'm not sure if I want children. Ask me in fifteen years."

"Fifteen years!" Libby exclaims, putting down her spatula and looking shocked. "Does Mum know that you don't want kids?"

I'm so hungry that I finish all the pancakes on my plate in about five seconds flat. I'm too hungover to care anymore about table etiquette. "Probably not. She and I don't exactly spend time talking about my future children. I've only been seventeen for about eight hours."

"I know it's kind of cheesy, but I want two—a girl and a boy," Libby says.

"*You* want kids?" Edward asks her. "That surprises me."

"Really? Why?" She wipes her hands on a tea towel.

"You're so smart. And feminist. I guess I figured you'd go that career-gal path."

"Career gal?" Libby snorts. She crumples up the tea towel and throws it at his face. "You sound like my grandmother. Let me know when you've time traveled back from the 1930s. These days, women can have kids *and* a career."

He laughs good-naturedly, tossing the tea towel back to Libby. It slides off her head and lands on the floor.

"I don't know," Flossie says, looking doubtfully at my sister. "Libby's *literally* barefoot in my kitchen cooking right now. I'd say she's pretty maternal."

"Maternal, a great chef, and smart: she saved my arse in history," David says, shoveling eggs into his mouth. "You're the perfect woman, Libs."

She turns away, busying herself cracking more eggs, but not before I see the pleased expression on her face.

"What, so the perfect woman needs to cook? And be a mum? That's pretty sexist," I say, thoroughly annoyed. "Should she greet her husband with a foot rub every night after work, too?"

"Hear, hear," Libby says, sliding more food onto my plate. "Feminism is all about choices."

"Well," I say, "I choose more coffee. And seconds of those pancakes."

twelve

I bite my tongue as my shoulder slams into the ground, a metallic taste filling my mouth. I curl into a ball to protect my body.

The crowd gasps at my tumble. Above me, the player from Norfolk who bodychecked me laughs and runs down the field.

It's been a rough game to cap a rough weekend. The group took cabs back to campus after breakfast, and I've been downing coffee ever since to sober up. It's not working—I'm still exhausted and have missed goals and passes at every turn, stumbling over routine plays and fumbling with my stick as if I'm a rookie. It's not normally so difficult for me to snap my head back into the game. Then again, I've never played hungover before.

My stomach churns. I feel like I might vomit.

"What's with you?" Flossie hisses to me. She points the butt of her stick at me accusingly. "You're a mess out there."

I look at my stick doubtfully—as if it's the problem, not me. "My head is killing me."

"So?"

"I think I'm going to be sick."

"Don't. Snap out of it. You're a disaster out there." Flossie is wildly competitive.

"I know," I say, irritated. "You don't need to tell me."

Wilkinson blows her whistle. "Weston!" she bellows.

As soon as I see the look on her face, I want to sink into the ground. I jog over to the sidelines.

"Are you hungover?" she demands.

"No."

"One of the girls told me you got wasted last night."

"Who said that?"

"So it's true."

"It's not."

"I can smell the booze on you. You're a walking distillery."

"Not sure why. I wasn't drinking," I lie.

She narrows her eyes, leaning in so close I can see the freckles on her weathered cheeks. "Look. I'm not your mommy. You and I both know you're not allowed to drink, but I don't care what you do in your spare time. You wanna get wasted on wine coolers and warm beer? Be my guest."

I'm not in the mood for a lecture. I just want to get back out there and make this right.

"But I've got a problem when *your* after-hours shenanigans start affecting *my* game." She leans closer. The crow's-feet around her eyes make her look like a shriveled lemon. "I don't wake up at five a.m. for fun. I'm out here with you day in and day out, and the least you could do is show some respect—for me and for yourself. You've missed four passes. You've cost us several points. You got in Corrie's way when she was lining up that shot. Is this your idea of a good time?"

"No."

"What? I can't hear you."

"No," I say more loudly.

"You want to screw up things for yourself—go nuts. But when you put my team on the line, I get pissed."

I sigh. "Okay, Coach."

"I don't like your attitude!" she yells.

"Okay. Sorry."

She looks at me sourly. Finally, after a pause of several seconds, she nods curtly. "Get it together."

I race back to the center of the field. Everybody is standing in a circle waiting for me.

"Coach wants to make me the team punching bag."

I expect sympathetic looks, but everybody glares at me.

"What?"

Flossie rolls her eyes. "Seriously? You're all over the place, you're still hungover, *and* you were late to the game. Don't expect us to give you a free pass because it was your birthday yesterday."

"You're the one who threw me a party last night!"

"And you're the one who chose to get plastered."

"You were also late to practice twice last week," one of the girls, a tall senior named Megan, pipes up.

I look at her hard, hoping my stare will make her flinch. It doesn't. "You *all* feel this way? You're all annoyed?"

They look back and forth between one another, but nobody says anything.

I set my jaw, massively irritated. "Well, none of *you* are scoring, either."

More looks.

"Okay. Whatever. Let's just start scoring."

We break the circle as the ref throws the ball in. I launch myself after it, dashing around the players from Norfolk, trying to play the hurt and anger away.

I run down the field, catching my cleat on a mound of grass and tripping. My head is seriously killing me. Behind me I hear somebody mutter, "Looks like Her Royal Highness is blowing it."

"If she's not careful, she might smear her makeup," somebody else says.

I whip around, glaring. "What?"

I try to figure out who said it, but everybody looks at the ground innocently as we line up again for the ball.

"If you have something to say to me, then say it to my face," I say, throwing my shoulders back and jutting out my chin. I look from person to person, but nobody says a word. One of the Norfolk players smirks at me.

I look up in the stands, where Libby, Edward, and India are all watching the game. Edward looks dismayed.

Flossie snaps her fingers at me. "C'mon, Charlotte. Shake it off."

I run back on the pitch without responding to her.

The referee throws the ball in and I race across the field. I'm determined to take all this energy and channel it. I try my hardest to score, hoping to salvage the game, but all my passes miss, all my shots go wide.

"Weston!" Wilkinson screams at me again.

I run over to the sidelines, pulling out my mouth guard and bending over, placing my hands on my knees as I struggle to catch my breath.

"Get it together!" she yells. "You're a disgrace out there!"

"Okay! God, I *get* it. Stop *yelling* at me!" I shout back. "I'm *trying*!"

"WHAT DID YOU SAY TO ME?"

I open my mouth to protest, and Wilkinson yells, "Get off my field! You're out!"

Up in the stands, everybody's whispering and giving me disappointed looks. Libby's face is concerned, but Edward's face is blank. I notice a few people nearby turning and looking at him, as if to see his reaction to my temper. India puts her hand on his arm but he shakes it off.

The referee blows his whistle as my teammates run back onto the field without me. Game on.

In the locker room after the match, I stand under the hot water, letting it run off my shoulders. I stand there for what feels like hours, thinking back on the day.

My team lost. The final score was 0–5.

What's worse, I completely lost my cool—and everybody saw it.

"What is *with* Charlotte? She's a complete wreck."

My back stiffens as I try to make out the whispered voices.

"She hasn't been herself recently. I think Edward might be cheating on her with her sister." That's Flossie.

"With that new girl Libby? You think?" I can't place the voice—maybe Megan.

"Wouldn't you be humiliated? You land Edward and then he only wants to hang out with your sister? Cringe. How embarrassing."

My bottle of shower gel falls from my hands and lands with a thud against the tiles. I freeze.

Neither of the girls seems fazed.

"Whatever's going on with her, she needs to figure it out. She was wasted on the field today. And the way she yelled at Coach? It's going to *ruin* her reputation. I thought she was smarter than that." Flossie again.

"I don't know. I feel sorry for her," says the other girl. "It's got to be tough." A locker slams and the voices begin to fade.

"Tough or not, she . . ."

They exit the locker room and I can't hear them anymore.

I stand in the shower, water pooling around my feet, looking dumbly at the opposite wall.

After I'm done getting dressed, I swallow my pride and text Edward while walking back to my residence hall. He left immediately following the game, and I didn't have a chance to talk to him.

ME: Having the worst day. Still totally hungover. Wanna stop by

Colvin? Could really use a hug after that game.

I stare at the phone, feeling a rush of relief as the ellipses start. He's responding.

But then the ellipses stop.

After dinner, Colvin Hall comes alive. The halls hum with the sound of laughter and iPhones blaring dance music. Officially, Sussex Park has a mandatory study period from seven to nine p.m., but only the underclassmen get held to it. Instead of staying in our rooms, the girls of Colvin slide in and out of friends' rooms and the common room, dressed down in yoga leggings and with hair messily tied in topknots.

Usually, India's room is the hub. Tonight, my room's the designated hangout. India left campus after the game, doing something that none of us was able to piece together. I think she might have a new girlfriend.

She's as mysterious as Edward sometimes.

He wasn't at dinner, and he still hasn't responded to my text. But while I previously felt sad and confused about the past couple of weeks, being ignored by him gives me clarity.

I'm not sad anymore. Now I'm angry.

I open a bottle of white wine, hiding it in a cabinet in case Arabella or McGuire makes a surprise appearance—unlikely, but always possible. I've also put a pack of Camel Blues and an ashtray under the bed and have placed a fan near the door blowing toward the open window. Libby is stuck in the library, finishing up an English assignment due tomorrow.

I change out of my day clothes into something suitably loungy: a pair of black leggings and a Rolling Stones concert T-shirt I bought in London last year at a posh thrift shop. Everything was so expensive it might as well have been brand-new.

Flossie and Alice are the first to stop by, wearing shrunken Sussex Park sweatpants and T-shirts that show off their bums and tummies.

"What a weekend!" Alice says, pouring herself a huge glass of wine and sinking onto my bed. "I'm knackered!" She resembles a small hummingbird.

"What have *you* got to be tired about?" Flossie asks. "You're not the one who has to wake up at the crack every day for field hockey." She shoots me a glance but doesn't say anything else.

"Yes, but I've decided to give up coffee. It's got too many toxins, apparently."

"That's stupid," Flossie says. "Coffee is good for you."

"Coffee is not good for you. That's a fact. Right, Charlotte?"

"I couldn't survive without at least three cups a day. But, yeah, you may be right. It's probably not that good for you." I shrug. "Life's too short to worry about that, don't you think?"

"Besides, if you're really worried about toxins, you should give up wine, too," Flossie points out.

"Now *that's* stupid," Alice says.

"Whatever. How are you feeling now?" Flossie asks me. "Better?"

I frown. "I'm fine. Nothing a handful of paracetamol and some water couldn't cure."

"Coach went pretty hard on you."

"Yeah." I pause, debating whether to complain or apologize. "But I deserved it." Flossie nods, and I see a hint of respect on her face.

"How's Edward?" Flossie asks. "He seemed annoyed after the game."

"I haven't seen him. I texted him, but he hasn't texted back."

"Hmm. That's odd. What about Libby? Have you spoken since last night?" she asks, lowering her voice. "She has a lot of nerve, if you ask me."

"What do you mean?"

Flossie and Alice exchange looks.

"The party?" Flossie says. "Weren't you upset by the way she was hanging on Edward?"

"She wasn't *hanging* on him—they were just talking. I was drunk and wasn't seeing clearly."

They look at each other meaningfully.

"If you've got something to say, just say it."

"It's not really our place . . . ," Flossie says.

"We're just looking out for you . . . ," Alice says.

"It's the kind of thing I'd like to know . . ."

"But I'm sure we're wrong . . ."

My heart starts pounding. "Let me get this straight. You think there's something going on between the two of them—for real?"

They exchange another look.

"What do I know?" Flossie says, shrugging. "*I* wouldn't be comfortable with it, but . . . I could be totally off base." She doesn't look convinced.

The room gets more crowded as other girls stop by, but I barely hear the chitchat about classes and other students.

"Did you see Marcy Lawrence in chapel last week?" Alice says. "I think she was stoned."

Sara Gibson looks around as if the room is bugged. "I heard she's not just smoking weed. I heard she's doing *real* drugs."

"What—like cocaine?" Flossie says. "That's so naff. Nobody does coke anymore."

"Other things, too, though," Sara says, nodding and sipping her wine. "Like Molly."

As everybody slips into a conversation about party drugs, I'm completely zoned out. I feel humiliated—clearly everybody's been talking about Edward and Libby behind my back.

My mind is racing through all the possibilities.

If Libby and Edward are hooking up behind my back, I will never forgive them.

"And don't even get me started on heroin," says Sara as Libby comes in the room. "It's trendy now, if you can believe it."

Libby looks shocked. "What kind of conversation am I walking into? Heroin at Sussex Park?"

"Don't be stupid," I say, frowning at her. "Sara's talking about teenagers in bad towns. Nobody here is doing heroin."

"How was I supposed to know what you were talking about? I just got here."

I roll my eyes. "Have some wine," I say, thrusting the bottle toward her.

Flossie and Alice exchange another look.

"So, Libby, where were you?" Flossie says.

"I was doing homework—I'm drowning in it."

"Alone?" I ask, studying her face carefully.

She looks confused. "Yeah. Why?"

"Have you seen Edward?" Flossie asks. "He hasn't texted Charlotte back all day."

"Oh." She flushes, turning to me. "I saw him in the library when you texted. He had to go to Windsor at the last minute, but I wouldn't take it personally, Lotte—he seemed really stressed about everything."

My heart sinks as my face burns, too—blushing deeply during tense situations is a family trait we share. Libby and Edward? It *can't* be true. Can it? "Okay," I say coldly.

"Are you feeling better?" Sara asks. "I heard you were a wreck on the hockey field. *Everybody's* talking about it."

"I'm fine, thank you," I snap.

Sara turns to Libby. "I love your dress!" I glare at her. She's clueless.

"Oh, thank you so much." Libby fans out the black-and-white polka-dot skirt.

"I don't recognize it," Flossie says. "Where'd you get it?"

"I bought it online. Do you like it?" she asks anxiously. "I probably should have asked Charlotte before I purchased. I was taking a risk. It looked like a dress I saw in *Elle*."

"Cute."

"Good." She looks pleased. "Fashion doesn't come as naturally to me as it does to all of you."

"I don't know," Flossie says, taking a sip of her wine and

exchanging a look with me. "This all seems to be coming rather naturally to you, indeed."

After everybody leaves, I try to get some maths homework done, but I can't bring myself to concentrate. I keep looking at my phone to see if Edward has replied.

Nothing. He's never gone this long without responding. I'm clearly not a priority.

And what is this nonsense about him rushing off campus but still having time for a cozy chat with Libby? It takes two seconds to respond to a text.

How *dare* he ignore me?

The fury inside me is coming to a boil. Sooner or later, I'm bound to explode.

thirteen

Every Monday morning, the entire school congregates in the chapel for mandatory convocation. Teachers make announcements. Clubs put on skits to bring attention to their fund-raisers or to drum up membership. Students make impassioned pleas for the social justice cause of the moment.

Once again, I'm running late, so I text Libby to go on without me. I'm so hurried that I barely have time to apply makeup, swiping an eye-shadow brush back and forth across my lids and making a quick slash with my eyeliner. Before I enter the chapel, I remind myself to calm down and take a breath. I run my fingers under my eyes to make sure there's no smeared eyeliner or goop in my inner corners, and then smooth my damp hair back, slicking it into a neat ponytail.

My humiliating performance on the field against Norfolk feels like a distant memory. Instead, I'm laser focused on one thing: confronting Edward. I don't know what's going on, but I'm determined to talk to him today. He should be comforting me and making sure I'm okay after yesterday—not ignoring me. We never spend any time together anymore and I'm sick of this hot and cold.

No guy treats me this way. I don't care if he's a prince.

I sneak into the chapel, finding a seat in the back. Master Kent walks to the front of the lectern, jabbing the air with his pointer finger as he addresses the student body.

"This year," he booms in his plummy tones, "we'll be taking up the theme of giving back. It's critical to think of your fellow humans—less a responsibility and more of a privilege for most in this room." He gives a rousing speech about the importance of charity, both in our local community and the world at large. He flashes his megawatt smile throughout the speech.

As Master Kent talks, I scour the room for my friends. They're all seated together a few rows up. Edward is next to Libby.

Libby leans over to Edward and whispers something in his ear. He whispers something back. She responds, nodding emphatically.

I study my boyfriend and my sister with narrowed eyes. This ends now.

Suddenly, my phone pings with a text.

EDWARD: hi! So sorry for radio silence yesterday, had a busy night with family stuff. really sorry you were having a bad day—hope you're feeling better now? See you after chapel? Xxx

Is he pity-texting me because Libby told him to?

Oh, *hell*, no.

After the assembly, I wait outside for my friends to exit. Flossie walks out first, a bored look on her face.

"Four years at this school and I'll never understand the point of those things," she says. "As if I care about the dance team and its bloody bake sale." She stops when she sees the look on my face. "What's wrong with *you?*"

"Nothing."

"You look constipated."

"I need to talk to Edward," I say, clenching my jaw and mentally preparing for battle.

When Edward exits—surprise, surprise—he's deep in conversation with Libby. I march right up, interrupting him.

"Why didn't you text me?" I demand.

"What?" he asks, sounding taken aback.

"You didn't text me all day. What the hell?"

He blinks, looking around to see if anybody else is paying attention. Libby takes a step back, looking uncomfortable. Edward's bodyguard is exiting the chapel, looking at me doubtfully but keeping his distance. "I *did* text you. Just now."

"Not for, like, eighteen whole hours. I had a horrible day and you completely ignored me."

India, Alice, Georgie, and Oliver exit the chapel, looking at me in alarm. I know I'm drawing attention—a cardinal sin—but I can't help it.

Edward frowns. "Stop making a scene."

"Well, then stop ignoring me."

"Charlotte, you're being rude."

I start laughing. "That's hilarious. I don't think you quite understand the meaning of the word. Calling out somebody you're dating on their BS isn't rude. Rude is ignoring your girlfriend for an entire day, with no explanation. Rude is not comforting your girlfriend after she loses a huge game. Rude is suddenly spending all your free time with your girlfriend's sister. Why don't we talk about how rude *you* are?"

"This is a pretty big conversation," says India quietly. "Why don't you two go somewhere more private?" I ignore her.

"I'm sick of everybody walking on eggshells around you. Blessed Prince Edward, who can do no bloody wrong. Poor Prince Edward, who needs his privacy. Nobody calls you out—ever."

His eye twitches. He inhales sharply before speaking. "Is that so?"

"Yes. That *is* so."

He takes another deep breath. He seems to be struggling to control himself. "Charlotte. You don't seem yourself right now. Why don't we take a pause and talk about this later?"

"I don't need more pauses from you. That's all our bloody relationship has been lately—one giant pause."

"Look," he says through gritted teeth. "There are things you don't understand."

"Educate me."

"I'm sorry if I've been distant recently, but I'm dealing with some family things—and *I really don't want to talk about it here and now*." If I weren't so worked up, the force of his voice might cause me to

181

take a step back. But that thing inside me I'm constantly trying to keep together has snapped—I'm beyond the point of no return.

"You don't get a pass just because you're royal," I say. "You're always banging on about how busy your family keeps you, but then you don't confide in me and explain *why*. I'm totally in the dark—and what's worse, you confided in Libby about it!"

I glance at her. She looks apprehensive.

"Relationships are give and take," I say. "If you can't hold up your end, then you shouldn't be in a relationship at all."

"I'm *busy*!" he says. "God, can't you cut me some slack?"

"Kids. Somewhere else. Come on," says India.

"Are you and Libby hooking up behind my back?"

Libby recoils as if I've slapped her. "What?"

Edward snorts. "You've got to be kidding me."

"Charlotte, c'mon," Georgie whispers, drawing her fingers across her throat and making a slitting sound. "This is bananas."

"Why don't you just calm down, Bug," Libby says soothingly. "Nothing is going on."

"God, back *off*!" I shout. "You're so irritating!"

She looks wounded. "You're just as irritating."

"I'm irritating *you*? That's hilarious." I swivel back to face Edward. "And I'm through being ignored. You and me are *done*."

India stands off to the side, her head buried in her iPhone, now pretending as if nothing's going on. Georgie has her hand over her mouth, looking at me in horror. Flossie and Alice watch everything unfold with barely disguised glee. All they need is a tub of popcorn.

"Wait, what?" Edward says in disbelief. "You're breaking up with me?"

"You're damn right I am. Maybe next time you'll think twice before taking your girlfriend for granted."

As he stands there looking stunned, I spin on my heel and flounce off.

I feel a heady mix of panic and elation, the thoughts tumbling around my brain as I have a silent conversation with myself.

Did I really just dump Edward?

That'll teach him.

Has he ever been dumped before? I bet I'm the first.

Crap, I can't believe I lost it on him.

Whatever, he deserves it.

I'm halfway down the lawn back toward Colvin when I hear Libby yelling my name.

"What is *with* you?" she asks, her chest rising and falling from running after me. "You're acting bonkers. There's nothing going on between me and Edward."

"I wish you'd never come here," I say coldly.

Her face falls. She stares at me, her eyes filling with tears, and I know I've gone too far.

She turns around and walks away.

"Can you *believe* them? The nerve. They deserve each other."

India pours a cup of white wine, wordlessly handing it to me as I pace back and forth across her room. Flossie, Alice, and Georgie are sitting on the bed, eyes wide, watching me as if I might snap. The door is closed—and India never closes the door.

I suppose it's only fair that they're all treating me with kid gloves. They've never really seen this side of me.

India takes a sip of wine, not saying anything. The look she's giving me is enough.

"I know," I say. "You don't have to tell me. I made a fool of myself."

She shakes her head as if to say that she's not getting involved.

"I shouldn't have done that in public—but I reached a breaking point!"

"You broke, all right," Flossie says. Georgie shoots her a look.

They stare back at me from the other side of the room.

"You've *seen* them!" I continue. "They're always together. And he's telling her all his secrets? He should be telling *me*. I'm his girl-friend, not her!"

"I don't blame you for that part," says Flossie. "Libby's in the wrong there. You shouldn't go after your sister's boyfriend. It's totally tacky."

"Why is it Libby's fault?" says Georgie. "That's messed up. If anybody's to blame, it's Edward."

India raises her hand slightly, as if calling for silence.

"Well, it takes two," Georgie mutters quietly, chastened.

My shoulders fall. All the fight has gone out of me.

"I shouldn't have lost it in public," I say. "I couldn't help myself."

India nods. "Nobody's perfect."

"How bad was it?"

"Bad."

I remember the shocked look on Edward's face. "I don't think anybody's ever spoken to him like that."

"It may have been a first," India says.

"Are you going to text him or go over there?" Flossie asks.

"Huh?"

"Edward."

"I have no idea what you're talking about."

"When you apologize to him," she says slowly, as if talking to a five-year-old.

"Um, I'm not apologizing to him."

Flossie's eyebrows nearly fly off her face. "Are you insane? But what if he cuts you out?"

"Then he bloody cuts me out. He should be apologizing to me. I wouldn't have needed to lose it on him if he'd just treated me like a human being in the first place."

Flossie nods slowly. "Actually . . . you may be right. He's been totally ignoring you in favor of Libby. Screw it. Why should you apologize to him?"

"My mother never apologized to my father," says Alice. "Of course, they're divorced now."

India shakes her head, rubbing her hand across her eyes as if she's exhausted by this turn of events. "You've got balls, Charlotte. I'll say that much for you."

"What about Libby?" Georgie asks me.

My sister's stricken face flashes in my head, and I feel ashamed. "I think I really hurt her feelings."

"I'm sure she'll understand, right?" says Alice. "She's so dependable. She's *Libby*."

"Maybe," I say, pulling out my phone. I start to craft an "I'm sorry" text, but India puts her hand on my arm.

"Nothing has happened between them."

"How do you know?"

"I just know. You should apologize to her in person."

I leave my cup of wine and stand up, dusting off my bum as I make my way to the door. "If I'm not back in an hour, send a search team after me," I joke.

I walk upstairs one flight, knocking on Libby's wooden door. There's no answer, so I knock again.

"Libby? It's Charlotte."

"Go away," she says, her voice teary.

I ignore her, opening the door. She's curled up in a ball on the bed.

"Go away," she repeats.

She looks so vulnerable, her thin body shrunken into itself. Her face is pressed into the pillow, her glossy brown hair billowing around her head as if to protect her from insults and hurt.

"I'm sorry," I say, sitting next to her and putting my hand on her back.

She flips over, turning to face me. Her cheeks are red and her nose is puffy. Her white pillowcase has streaks of black mascara on it. For a second, I think about how this means she's wearing mascara now. "I didn't *do* anything," she says, sniffling. "Edward and I are just friends. You must know that."

"I know," I say soothingly.

"I would *never* go after your boyfriend, Charlotte."

"I shouldn't have accused you. I was jealous. I snapped. You've been spending time together, and he and I aren't, and this year is really starting to get to me. I'm mad at him, not you."

"The last thing I'd want to do is make you uncomfortable or overstep boundaries, Lotte," she says, sitting up. "I wish you'd talked to me about it first so I could have taken a step back. I'm sorry."

"It's got nothing to do with you. I'm just being a cow."

"Maybe a little bit," she says, smiling through her tears. "Tiny cow. Baby cow."

"I wanted us to have the best year ever, and now look at us. Me single, with everybody thinking I'm a crazy person, and you collapsed in tears looking like a hot mess. We're a pair."

Libby laughs, crying a little bit at the same time.

I reach out to play with her hair like when we were kids, plaiting a braid on the side of her temple. It's thick and strong between my fingers. "I was a jerk."

"No, you weren't," she says. "It breaks my heart to think that you were suffering in silence because of me."

"It really threw me for a loop—him confiding in you and not me."

Libby looks sad. "I'm sorry, Bug. I should have tried harder to see it your way. I get why it was hurtful."

"Thanks, Button." I almost ask her yet again to tell me what Edward said, but I decide to let it go. It's beside the point.

We're both silent for a minute. "So, what are you going to do about him?" she asks.

I sigh. "I don't know. What do you think I should do?"

"Did you really want to break up? Were you serious?"

I consider the question. "You know what? Yes. I was serious—I *am* serious. We barely saw each other. We're not into the same things. And apparently he doesn't even feel comfortable enough to confide in me—" I put my hand up as Libby starts to say something. "I'm not saying that to make you feel guilty. It's just the truth. I can't be in that kind of relationship. I guess I've realized I'm not built like that."

She nods. "You have to be true to yourself."

"Exactly."

"It's just . . ."

"What?"

"Look," she says. "You have a good thing going this year. Your friends love you. But everything revolves around Edward—he's like the sun to them. It would be a shame to throw it all away because of your pride."

I fiddle with her hair, taking it out of the plait and then rebraiding it. I see Libby's point. Even if I don't want to get back together with Edward romantically, I should still try to smooth things over. I've spent all this time building foundations and creating new friendships.

"Have I ever told you how smart you are?" I say, leaning on her for a hug.

"You sure you're okay?" she asks. "You seem really calm considering you guys just broke up."

"Honestly . . . he's *boring*. I know I kept saying it wasn't about him being a prince . . . but that's not true. If he'd just been any old hot guy, I probably would have lost interest after three weeks.

Although he *is* a dynamite kisser, so maybe not."

She blushes.

"I'll be fine," I say, patting her arm. "Next! Who've you got for me, Sussex Park?"

I'm putting on a good show: of course my pride is wounded. Of course I'm a little sad about breaking up with Edward. But it's not like the two of us were going to get married.

We'll just be friends, and I'm sure everything will be fine.

I pull my jacket around my body as I walk across campus to Stuart Hall. The weather has changed and it's seemingly dropped fifteen degrees overnight. Winter is in the air.

As I stand outside Stuart Hall, I look up at the dormitory. There are only a few lights on in the dark: most students are probably still at the dining hall, or maybe at the library. I'll get in trouble if I'm spotted in the boys' dormitory, but it's a risk I'm willing to take.

I push open the door, looking both ways down the corridor to make sure the coast is clear before dashing up the marble steps toward the rooms. The carpet is red and well-worn, faded in the middle from years of footsteps.

Edward's room is on the third floor. It's nondescript—just like every other door from the outside. Nothing visible that says the future king of England lives here.

I knock on the door twice.

Immediately, the door across the hallway from Edward's swings open.

"Everything all right?" It's Simon, Edward's personal protection officer. He frowns upon seeing me. "You shouldn't be here."

"Sorry, Simon. I just really needed to talk to Edward."

When I turn back, Edward's standing in his own doorway, looking at me warily. "Yeah?"

"Sorry. Can we . . . ? Can I . . . ?" I hear footsteps on the stairs, and instead of waiting for Edward to invite me inside, I step through the door into his room. I'm half expecting something magical to happen: heroic rays of sunshine streaming through the window, a Gregorian choir chanting melodically.

"It's okay, Simon," Edward says. Simon looks at me suspiciously as Edward closes his door.

"So," I say, looking around the room. It's my first time inside. Edward always insisted we go to my residence hall. I wasn't sure if it was chivalry on his part—he'd rather get in trouble than me—or a desire to protect his privacy. Now that I know better, I suspect the latter.

I try to look casual while my eyes sweep the small room. It looks like a normal guy's room. The only hint of his royal status: a silver-framed photo of Edward with his father, King Henry, and mother, Queen Madeline. "So," he replies. "What's up?"

"Can I sit down?" I point to the chair next to his desk. It has stacks of jumpers on it, but I'd rather sit there than the bed.

He shrugs, so I move the jumpers to the floor before sitting down.

"Look," I say. "I guess I should apologize."

Edward walks over to the bed and sits down opposite me. "Okay."

"I didn't handle it well."

"No, you didn't."

"Well, that's why I'm *here*," I say, my temper flaring. But the whole point of coming here is to apologize, not to get into another fight. For a moment I focus on the wall behind him, trying to buy time while calming myself down. On the notice board above his dresser, I'm surprised to see photos tacked up of the two of us at Huntshire, wearing our swimming costumes and acting silly by India's pool. I point to them. "That was the best night."

He nods. "Yeah, it was."

"I was so nervous in the maze with you."

"You were nervous?" He looks surprised.

"Of course!"

"I didn't think anything made you nervous."

"You said the same thing that night. Plenty of things make me nervous: My mum's temper. Getting into university. Letting my family down. Coming here tonight."

He cracks a tiny smile. "Thanks for coming."

"I *am* sorry, Edward."

"Thanks. I'm sorry, too."

"You are?"

"Yeah. I ignored you too much."

I flush, feeling a sense of validation. "We should have talked more."

He nods. "Well . . . no use crying over spilled milk, as my dad says." He's silent for a few moments. "I guess I should have told you what's been going on with me, rather than just disappearing. I don't like to bother people with my family stuff."

"But you talked to Libby about it," I point out.

Irritation flickers briefly across his face. "I'm sorry," he says. "She's easy to talk to. And I barely scratched the surface."

I don't say anything, letting him continue.

"It's just . . . a lot of things will change when I turn eighteen in a few months. They're teaching me the ropes now. Letting me in on things I always wondered about but never knew. It's like a brain dump—and I'm not supposed to talk about it. It's a lot to take in."

"I get it." Of course, I don't, really.

"I wasn't trying to ignore you or avoid you. But I think you were right. We probably weren't that well suited for each other, personality-wise. Plus, you deserve somebody who can give you loads of time."

"It's okay. Thank you."

We smile at each other and, for a moment, I feel a wave of sadness. He really is a decent guy. I stand up. "I should go. Better sneak out before they do dorm check."

"This was nice," he says, smiling.

"Friends?" I ask.

"Friends."

I look again at the photos of the two of us on his notice board, and he follows my gaze. "Do you want them?" he asks.

"Oh! Do you mind? I know how you are with pictures and privacy—but they *are* cute."

He walks over and untacks the three pictures from the wall, handing them to me. "I trust you—they're yours." Somehow, the moment feels symbolic in more ways than one.

We give each other an awkward hug. When I exit Edward's

room, I say, "Bye, Simon!" to the closed door across the hall. I know he's snooping.

As I hurry down the steps toward the front doors of Stuart Hall, I run into Robert coming out of the common room. He looks surprised to find me coming down from the rooms.

"Charlotte? What were you doing upstairs?"

"Crap."

"That bad to see me, huh?"

"No." I laugh. "It's just—don't you have to report me now?"

He looks around, making sure the coast is clear. "Come on." I walk down the steps toward him and he takes me by the elbow, hurrying me out of the front door until we're standing outside Stuart. "What's to report?" he asks. "I saw you coming from the common areas. No big deal."

"You're the best."

He grins and gives me a small bow before returning inside.

As I walk back to my residence hall, I'm relieved that Edward and I are on friendly terms. It'll make things much more convenient for our friends. What a disaster if we pitted everybody against each other. So much more mature this way.

I head back to my dorm to give Libby the full scoop.

fourteen

Winter is my favorite time of year at Sussex Park. Once the snow starts falling in early December, it sticks to the bare tree branches and coats the rolling lawns. The main quad looks like something out of a postcard, the student center sets up a hot cocoa station, and students roast chestnuts by the fire. It gets dark by three thirty p.m, and the whole campus has a romantic feeling, as if it's a Christmas poem come to life. Snow fell early this year, so I'm shivering in the flakes, holding my books against my coat for warmth while scurrying to the library after dinner.

The Sussex Park library was modeled after the Bodleian at Oxford. It's all mahogany wood and high, vaulted ceilings, with stained-glass windows depicting key scenes from the Bible. The main chamber features row upon row of long wooden tables for communal studying, with several smaller rooms for private studying in cubicles.

I look for a quiet nook in one of the smaller rooms, away from the hustle and bustle of the students stage-whispering to each other at the long tables. Every year, I tell myself that *this* is going to be the year I buckle down and focus on my studies . . . and every year, I find myself in early December panicking about my low marks. This year is particularly bad: I've lost the plot in several classes and am coming dangerously close to failing maths. History and graphic design are the only classes where my marks are decent.

I find a quiet space in the back corner of a room by the stacks. A few minutes after I sit down, I hear laughing.

It's Libby's voice. And she's not alone.

I stand up, peering over the cubicle.

Libby sits at a cubicle across the room. She's visible in profile, but I can't see the guy she's with. She looks up at him through her lashes, giggling flirtatiously. The guy puts his hand on her arm.

"Stop it," she says. "We're supposed to be studying."

I push my chair back before I can help myself and walk over to them.

"What do we have here?" I ask.

Libby and David look up at me, both surprised.

"Hey, Charlotte," David says.

"*David?* But I thought you were . . ." For some reason, I expected to find Edward.

"Devastatingly handsome? The most charming bloke you've ever met? Brilliant like a Nobel Prize winner? Don't stop now."

"Nothing," I say, chastened.

"Do you want to sit with us?" Libby asks, pulling up a chair. "It might be boring for you. We're going over our history homework."

"No," I say, pointing back to my cubicle. "I'm drowning in assignments. I heard your voices and wanted to come say hi. Just a little break."

"Okay, well, hi and bye!" David says.

"Should I stop by your room after we're done here?" she asks.

"Sure," I say. I go back to my cubicle and try to work, but my brain is racing a million miles a minute.

Libby and *David*?

A couple of hours later, after finishing an assignment for English, India and I are lounging in her room when I bring it up.

"Are you sure you weren't confused? She's been helping him with his homework all term. She's *everybody's* resident tutor, apparently. She should start charging tuition."

"I saw it with my own two eyes! He was flirting with her—but that's nothing new. What's crazy is she was flirting back."

"Maybe she's getting her footing," India says. "You say she's never had a boyfriend?"

"Right."

"Everybody has to start somewhere, I suppose. Huh. I thought she had better taste than that."

"I don't know," I say. "They could be kind of cute together. He's silly and sweet. At least he's not Tarquin."

India looks at me as if I've grown a third eyeball. "But David? I thought *you* had better taste than that."

India's not smoking, but I stand up and rummage through her goodie drawer, pulling out a pack of cigarettes and lighting up. Weirdly, I feel like celebrating.

"Do you mind?" I ask after I've already lit the cigarette.

She shrugs.

I walk on my knees over to the window, pushing the panes out and letting the blast of cold air stab me in the face. Strains of old-school Radiohead play on her music dock.

"Libby and David. You know—it could work. He'll loosen her up, bring out her silly side."

"I don't think Libby needs much prodding," India says. "It's hard for you to see it because you're her sister. But she's already done a one-eighty from when she arrived on campus."

"Yeah?"

"Abso-*lutely*. Do you remember how shy she was those first few weeks? She barely spoke. She's so much more relaxed—much more comfortable in her own skin. She even makes jokes! Thank God for that wardrobe revamp, too. She doesn't look like some refugee from a Nirvana video anymore."

"She's pretty, right?"

India raises an eyebrow. "You're joking if you have to ask. She's bloody gorgeous."

"That's what I thought." I take another drag, satisfied. "Good. Looks like all's well that ends well."

"Kind of funny," India says. "Reversal of fortune."

"What do you mean?"

"I mean: the second you stop dating Edward, Libby gets a guy."

I shrug. "Good for her! I'm swearing off dating for at least a few months. I need a little 'me' time, you know?"

India nods. "Story of my life."

"Even now?" I ask. "I thought you might be seeing somebody. Who's the lucky girl?"

She looks at me, smiling enigmatically. "What makes you think there's somebody?"

"Oh, *please*," I say. "You think you're all mysterious but I see right through you."

"A lady never tells," she says, brushing her hair from side to side over her shoulders in mock snootiness.

"Well, *I'm* no lady," I say.

"And that's exactly why I love you."

"Seriously? Not a peep? I can tell you're hiding something!"

But India just smiles again, pulling out a bottle of sauvignon blanc from her drawer. "More wine?"

The following weekend, after our house Christmas parties, the group meets at Donatella for the last dinner before break. The last week of school is all about nose-to-the-grindstone studying, so we arrange our farewell get-together for the weekend before. Most of us are scheduled to leave campus to go home the second our last exam is finished.

I'm sitting between Edward and India at one end of the table in Donatella's small private room. Apologizing to Edward seems to have made all the difference in the world—he and I are on great terms now. Everything feels easy again, like at the beginning of the year when Libby first arrived on campus.

Speaking of Libby: she's tipsy. Like, *really* tipsy.

We've all been into the wine tonight, excited to let off steam before diving into the madness of final exams. But where Libby normally stops after one, maybe two glasses, tonight she's refilling her glass over and over.

Earlier, I threw on a casual but cute outfit—skinny jeans, a boxy blouse, and a chunky jeweled necklace, plus a leather jacket—and went by Libby's room early, thinking maybe I could help her pick out an outfit. No need: she was all ready to go. Her blue-and-white patterned pleated dress is so cute *I* want to borrow it, and she's paired it with sheer black tights, her trusty army jacket, and short black booties. It strikes the right note of sexy and self-assured.

The duckling has turned into a swan.

I lean over to Edward, poking him. "Get a load of Libby and David."

"What about them?" he asks, stopping mid-sip and putting his glass of wine down.

"I think they're going to pull."

At this, Edward starts laughing. "You're mental. There's no way Libby would get with him in a million years. Never."

"That's what I thought, too," I say. "But then I saw them in the library last week."

"The library? What was David doing in the library?"

Across from me, India glances up from her phone and shoots me a look. It seems like she wants me to stop talking, but I can't begin to understand why.

"Right? But they were totally flirting. I *know*!" I say in response to the shocked expression on his face. "I didn't believe it, either. But I heard them before I saw them—and trust me, she was chatting him up right back."

"That's surprising," says Edward. He takes another sip of wine, and I follow suit, refilling his glass, then India's, and finally mine.

"Totally. But, you know, Libby's never had a boyfriend. I'm sure she's told you that."

If he knows, his face doesn't betray anything.

"I bet he's a harmless diversion. A way to get a snog in, but nothing serious," I continue.

We all look down the table at Libby and David. She's leaning into him, he's touching her, and the two of them are laughing at each other's jokes.

Edward bristles. "I don't think they're a good idea together."

India shoots me another look. This one is easier to read. It says: *I told you so.*

"Why not?" I ask tentatively. "They're just having fun. What's the big deal?"

"He's not good enough for her."

"He's good enough for us to be friends with," I point out.

"Yeah, but being friends is different. He's too much of an idiot for her to actually date."

My feminist instincts start to prickle. "It's not your place to decide who Libby should and shouldn't get with. And what's the big deal if she wants to hook up with David? At least it's not *Tarquin*. She's a big girl. She can take care of herself."

Edward looks visibly frustrated.

"Anyhow," I say, irritated that this conversation has taken a weird turn, "it's not a big deal. She's rat-arsed. They'll probably snog for five seconds and won't even remember it tomorrow."

"I don't like it," Edward says, still fixated. "She'll get hurt."

"She'll be fine."

"They're not a good fit. I could see you with him, but not her."

I'm beyond offended. "Weren't you *just* telling me how he's not good enough for her? But he's good enough for *me*? Oh, gee. Thanks a bunch."

He rolls his eyes. "That's not what I meant."

"It sounded like *exactly* what you meant."

"I meant that you'd know how to handle him. Libby's never even kissed a guy. She needs somebody who respects her."

I look at him sourly.

"David's bound to try something with her. She needs somebody looking after her right now, not cheering on some drunken hookup. I don't like it."

"You're not her dad. And, frankly, this entire conversation is irritating me."

"Well, anyhow, I think—" Edward starts to say, but I push my chair back with a scrape, interrupting him.

"I'm going to the loo."

In the ladies' room, I wash my hands, staring at my reflection in the mirror. Why can't Edward get a clue? Saying that David is good enough for me but not good enough for Libby? That was rude. And implying that I'm not looking after my sister? I stalk back out of the ladies', ready to give him another piece of my mind, when India intercepts me.

"Take it down a notch," she says. "Let's go outside and have a ciggie."

We go on the back porch and share a cigarette while I vent.

"He's so full of himself. And I don't appreciate him mansplaining my sister's love life!"

India nods.

"It's like we never even dated!"

"Isn't that what you wanted?" India asks. "It's the only way we can all hang out with no awkwardness."

"Yeah, but when Edward starts insulting me, it *is* awkward."

"It wasn't like that," India says soothingly. "That's not what he meant. He wasn't thinking straight."

"Why are you sticking up for him? And what was with all those bloody looks you kept shooting me?"

India shakes her head. "You're a smart girl, Charlotte, but sometimes you are *shockingly* obtuse."

"Whatever." I shrug, plucking the cigarette from her fingers and taking a deep drag. "I can't wait for Christmas. I'm sick of this place. I need a break from Sussex Park."

"Let's go back inside," she says, patting me on the back.

But when we go back inside, Libby and Edward are both gone.

"Where are they?" I ask David, sinking into Libby's former seat. Flossie and Tarquin look over at me with interest.

"Who?" David asks, looking unsteady. He's plastered.

"Libby. Edward. Where'd they go?"

"Outside," says Flossie, leaning over. "They were in the corner whispering, and then they got up and left."

David shrugs. "What Flossie said."

I stand up again. "Be right back."

"Are you going after them?" Tarquin asks.

Flossie shoots him a look. "Butt out."

"I'm just going to check on Libby and make sure she's okay. She's had a lot to drink."

I walk through the restaurant, weaving my way through the crowded tables and doing my best not to collide with the waiters. For some reason, I have a panicked feeling in the pit of my stomach—like if I don't make it to Libby in time, something will happen.

I reach the entry vestibule, about to push through the doors and step outside, when I see Libby and Edward through the window. They're standing together on the pavement in front of the restaurant, the moonlight reflecting off their faces.

When Edward and I were dating, he was so much taller than I was that I had to stand on my tiptoes just to kiss him. But his height matches Libby's perfectly—they look like two halves of a matched set.

I'm about to go outside and crack a self-deprecating joke about being a Peeping Tom when Edward reaches out and brushes Libby's hand with his.

What the HELL?

She looks surprised, her eyebrows raised, her arms by her sides. He's murmuring something indecipherable. He puts his other hand on the small of Libby's back. As they talk, she reaches up and puts her hand on his face. He leans down, kissing her gently. Libby stands still. She seems paralyzed.

I feel paralyzed, too.

But after a few seconds of Edward leaning down into her, she throws her arms around his neck and kisses him back.

A cold wave of shock pours over my body.

"What the hell is going on?" I say, bursting through the door.

The two of them jump back, startled.

"Charlotte," Libby says. "It was just . . . we just . . ." She looks terrified. "Are you okay?"

"How could you two do this?"

Edward looks guilty, stuffing his hands into his jeans. "Um . . ."

My heart is pounding. I feel oddly vindicated—obviously everything they told me these past few months has been nothing but lies. "So you two *were* hooking up behind my back."

"No!" says Libby. "It wasn't like that, I swear! Edward and I came out here to talk, and . . ." Her words are coming out all in a rush and her voice is an octave higher than usual. "I'm so sorry, Charlotte. Please don't be mad."

I look back and forth between the two of them. I can't decide if I want to cry or scream, but all I know is I have to get out of here.

I push through them, marching down the road back to campus, ignoring Libby's calls of "Charlotte! Please!"

It's not until I'm back in the safety of my dorm room that I collapse onto my bed, unleashing the betrayal and confusion in a flood of tears.

Nothing will ever be the same.

fifteen

Every year, our family throws a lavish dinner on Christmas Eve. Sometimes extended family will drive in, but this year our only visitor will be Nana, my mum's mum and our only living grandparent. She's taking the train down from York.

I'm particularly excited to see her because Nana is hilarious. She can be exhausting, and the most revolting things occasionally come spilling out of her mouth—but I still love her to bits. Even though I disagree with the majority of what she says, I have a feeling her politically incorrect bombs will distract everybody from the fact that I'm still not speaking to Libby. Catching Libby and Edward in the act was like a dagger through my heart. I've turned the moment over and over in my head since last weekend, sleepwalking through my final exams because I was so distracted and confused and hurt. Libby has tried to apologize, but I refuse to hear some half-baked apology. What if I *hadn't* caught them? Would they have spent months sneaking around behind my back? I still don't understand it. How *could* they?

I would never steal my sister's boyfriend. And I would never get together with my ex-boyfriend's brother. I don't know who to be angrier at.

In my more charitable moments, I remind myself that Edward and I were broken up. Libby and Edward are friends, they got drunk, and Edward couldn't help kissing her. Libby's beautiful and kind. What guy wouldn't be attracted to that? She probably didn't mean for it to happen. It just did.

But then my heart tightens again, and I think: *That's no excuse. She's my sister. She should have known better.* Edward's face pops into my head, and I get even angrier: *What a piece of shit. Swapping one sister for another? Who does that? Of all the entitled, manipulative, arrogant guys, he takes the cake. Prince Charming, my arse.*

On the train back to Midhurst, Libby sat next to me, but I got up and moved to a different seat. We gave each other a wide berth for the rest of the ride home. We've managed to ignore each other for almost a week now.

Mum and Dad refuse to take sides, although I suspect my mother agrees with me.

Meanwhile, I feel like a volcano. I'm trying to ignore Libby for my parents' sake, but if I don't let off some steam, eventually, I'll explode.

I decide to take a walk into town and buy some Christmas decorations. Doing things that require concentration always calms me down—and I take my party planning very seriously.

Our house is on the outskirts of town: a good twenty-minute walk from the high street. Although we didn't move to Midhurst until I was a bit older, I consider it my hometown. Sure, I'm biased— but I think it's the prettiest town in England.

I turn out of our front gates, walking up Selham Road and then making a right toward town. The Spread Eagle, one of the best hotels in town, is dusted with a light coat of snow, making it look like a gingerbread house. The car park is full, crammed with visiting relatives and families out for a Sunday roast, no doubt.

All the Tudor architecture around Market Square is one of my favorite parts of town. It makes me think of Queen Elizabeth I and King Henry VIII, both visitors to Midhurst back in the 1500s. The fact that Edward is descended from them, however distantly, blows my mind. Will history remember *him* someday?

Elizabeth I was one of my childhood heroes. She seemed so fierce: fighting her way to the throne, refusing to get married, standing up to the men who were trying to tell her what to do. But even though I've turned her into this mythical creature in my head, in reality, she was an actual person born into a very surreal set of circumstances— just like Edward. She probably cried. She used the bathroom. She got hungry. She felt fear. Someday, students like me will be reading history books, and Edward's name will come up, and he'll just be a photograph and a bunch of old, irrelevant stories to them. They won't know how he chews his nails, or has a weird laugh, or has the worst taste in music of all time.

They won't know that he was *real*.

As I continue farther up the narrow country lane, passing St. Mary Magdalene & St. Denys Church, my spirits darken again. I try focusing on the shop windows, turning left down Knockhundred Row, but every restaurant, every shop, every brick reminds me of Libby and the thousands of times we've walked these streets together.

Is this what happens when you get older? Is it inevitable that your sister stops being your best friend—and, worse, eventually becomes a stranger to you?

The thought makes me want to cry.

I turn right onto the high street, nearly breaking my neck as I slip on a patch of ice. I have to breathe deeply as I stand back up, fighting the urge to burst into overwhelmed tears. The decorations store is just ahead, and I step inside carefully, closing the door tightly behind me to keep the heat in. Inside, the tiny shop smells like cinnamon and holly.

"Heya, Charlotte," says Mrs. Cooper when I walk inside. This is both the blessing and the curse of growing up in a small town. It's comforting having everybody know your name—but on days like today, I'd rather be anonymous. I just want to get from point A to point B without having to pretend everything's okay.

I take a deep breath. "Hi, Mrs. Cooper. How are you?"

"Oh, fine, dear, just fine. I hear you're back at Sussex Park. I haven't seen you around town."

"This is my first time home since school started. Haven't had a chance to come back for a visit this term."

"And how is Libby? Greene House is a beautiful school."

"She's switched to Sussex Park. She loves it." I pick up some holly decorated with fairy lights. Libby and I always used to fight over colored lights versus white lights when we were kids. She preferred the elegance and simplicity of the white. I liked the colors. More fun.

"Oh, how wonderful! And Prince Edward goes to school there, too, doesn't he? That must be terribly exciting. Have you met him?"

"Yeah. A few times." I put the holly on the counter, changing the subject. "I think I'll just take these."

Later that afternoon, I stand at the kitchen sink, tearing off pieces of lettuce for a salad while I stare mindlessly at the falling flakes. It's been snowing on and off all day, and normally I'd be thrilled, but today I'm just annoyed at the weather for being so pretty and cheerful. I'd rather a thunderous rainstorm to match my mood.

Nana is due to arrive soon from York. Dad is at the train station now picking her up, and Libby volunteered to go with him—presumably to get out of the house and away from me.

Libby spent all morning cooking. Cooking has never been my thing—like my mother, I'm the takeaway queen—but every year I make precisely one dish. It's walnut and cranberry salad.

I survey the kitchen counter. Libby has made three different types of stuffing, including one with sausage and green apples that the whole family is gaga for. My salad is almost done. And the turkey that Libby spent half an hour butter-basting with herbs is roasting in the oven, scenting the house pleasantly with sage and making my mouth water. She might be a Judas of a sister, but she definitely can cook.

"Charlotte?" Mum calls from upstairs.

"Yeah?"

"Can you come here for a second?"

I lope up the stairs to Mum and Dad's bedroom. Our stairway is lined with photos in mismatching but complementary frames. Mum saw the design in a photo spread in *Hello!* when I was a kid and decided to replicate it, immediately replacing all the matching brown wooden frames we had with silver, gold, checkered, and decorated ones. At the top of the stairs is one of my favorite photos: a picture of Libby and me when I was eleven and she was thirteen, the day before she left for Greene House. We have our arms around each other and are standing on our tennis court, sweaty after a heated match. Our faces are so open and happy; our grins are from ear to ear.

It's been only five years, but it feels like a lifetime ago.

My parents' bedroom door is open. It's a huge rectangular room with a sitting room attached. Mum got really into equestrian-themed decor after we moved to Midhurst because of all the polo here—despite never going to matches—so she hired a designer and made the bedroom look like something from a Ralph Lauren catalog. The walls have framed oversized equestrian prints from the late 1800s, and there's a giant potted plant threatening to take over the far corner of the sitting room, a vintage telescope, and an old Louis Vuitton steamer trunk at the foot of the bed. The walls were painted red last year, which Mum thought matched the wood furniture and wood paneling nicely, but this year she decided it all looked like a bordello and redid everything in shades of green and cream. The massive wooden sleigh bed is blanketed in outfits.

"Mum?"

"I'm in the closet," she calls.

I walk into her enormous closet to find Mum sitting cross-legged on the circular sofa in the center, looking panicked. Her shoulder-length brown hair is blown out and her makeup is immaculately applied. If she weren't wearing only a white satin slip, she could be heading to a dinner party.

"I have literally nothing to wear." Around her, there are probably one thousand outfits, plus wall-to-wall racks of shoes arranged by color in the shelves she had custom-built.

"I'm not sure you know what the word 'literally' means, Mum. You have more clothes than Harrods."

"Your grandmother will be here in fifteen minutes. I can't have her seeing me like this."

"You're still freaking out over what Nana thinks of you?"

She regards me with a sour look on her face, her eyebrow arched. "I know, it must be a novel concept for you: worrying about what your mother thinks."

"Ooh. Burn." I walk in the closet, running my fingers through the clothes. Mum loves silky blouses, the more expensive the better. I think she's always trying to make up for wearing hand-me-downs from Aunt Kat as a kid. The blouses feel like butter slipping through my fingers. "What about this one?" I pull out a long-sleeved purple silk blouse with a bow at the collar. "You look adorable in this."

"I don't want to look adorable, I want to look Christmas-appropriate."

"You could always wear an ugly jumper."

She shoots me another look. "Charlotte. Be serious."

I laugh.

"Why are you laughing?"

"Because this conversation is silly. I feel like I'm *your* mum right now."

"I don't appreciate that," she pouts. "You and Libby were very lucky to grow up with a mother like me. You have no *idea* what a nightmare it was with her."

I frown at the mention of my sister's name but let it go.

"I have an idea, all right. You do know I've met my grandmother before?" I pull out another blouse—a red-and-green paisley print—and Mum shakes her head.

She sighs. "I still don't know what to tell her about Edward. She's been pumping the well dry for months. This latest development . . . oof."

I thrust a white blouse at her. "Just tell her that Libby stole him from me. I'm sure she'll be fine with it. Who cares *which* sister, right?"

Mum groans. "Can you two please try to keep it civil?"

"I'm not the one you need to worry about," I say. "I play by the rules. Apparently, Libby doesn't."

"Charlotte, I wish you'd give your sister a chance to apologize to you properly. She's beside herself about it."

"Good. She should be." I grab another blouse to distract her. "What about this one? The cream looks elegant. And wasn't this a gift from Nana?"

"It was—personally, I think it's hideous, but that doesn't matter. She'll be thrilled I'm wearing it. Or, at least, she won't criticize me *quite* as much as normal. Well done, Charlotte."

I beam.

"Now what about you?"

"What about me?"

"What are you going to wear?"

"Mum. Please. I have it covered."

"Thank goodness I never have to worry about you," she says, putting the blouse on over her slip. She opens a drawer and pulls out a pair of opaque stockings, sitting back down and carefully rolling them up her slender legs. "You always know just what to do."

"Hardly," I say. "But thanks, Mum. I'd better go change before they get back from the train station. Love you."

An hour later, I've showered, blown out my hair, and painstakingly applied sparkly holiday makeup. I debate about which dress to wear, but finally settle on a printed wrap that Nana bought me for Christmas two years ago.

Back in the kitchen, I pull some homemade nonalcoholic wassail from the fridge. It's full of spices like cinnamon, nutmeg, and ginger, and Libby makes it every year. Both Nana and I are addicted to it—although Nana takes hers with booze.

I'm peering through the glass oven door at the turkey, wondering if I'm supposed to do something to it, when I hear a hubbub in the hallway. Dad and Libby are back from the train station. I dry my hands on a tea towel before plastering a smile on my face and walking into the foyer. Mum is already waiting, looking as picture perfect as a *Vogue* fashion spread.

"Nana!" We hug. She smells like amber and mint, a combination

I remember from my childhood.

"Let me look at you, dear," she says, holding me firmly at arm's length. She looks me up and down, her eyes narrowed, as if searching for something—anything—to criticize. Finally, after several seconds of scanning, her face relaxes. "You look wonderful. School is treating you well." She pulls me in again for a hug, this time patting me on the back crisply. Libby stands awkwardly behind her, watching the two of us.

She turns toward Mum. "Jane, my darling. Have you been watching your figure? You look well."

"Hi, Mum. Thank you. I'm so busy recently with Soles," Mum says, looking flustered. "But I do Pilates when I can."

"Well done. You should keep it up," she says, nodding.

Nana's been here for five seconds, and she's already off to the races. Libby and I exchange an exasperated look before I remember I'm angry at her.

My dad comes in the house, weighed down with Nana's luggage.

She waves her hand in the general direction of the bedrooms. "Just put them upstairs, Matthew," Nana says without looking at him.

Mum looks at my dad, a pleading expression on her face, and he sighs, carrying Nana's trunks up the stairs wordlessly. He glances down at me as he turns the stairs toward one of the guest bedrooms. I roll my eyes at him, smiling in solidarity, and he nods in agreement.

Despite coming from a working-class background, my grandmother married way above her station. My grandfather was a banker in Leeds but fell in love with my grandmother the day he laid eyes on her behind the till at the local grocer's. She spent the rest of her life trying to get my grandfather to make as much money as possible, insisting every decade or two that they upgrade their house and upgrade their life.

As a result, my mother was born into nice, comfortable, middle-class surroundings. Her childhood in Leeds wasn't remotely what you could describe as entitled, but she never wanted for the basics, and they lived in a respectable town in a small but cute house.

The same striving that caused Nana to put years of pressure on my grandfather also led to pressure on my mum. When Mum met Dad, rather than being excited about her choice in mate, my grandmother was disappointed that he wasn't grander. And so my father—from a well-off family in Berkshire, educated at St. Andrews, with a decent-paying job at BP—found himself in the strange position of forever having to defend his station to my grandmother, who was born above a fishmonger and didn't finish secondary school.

There's no love lost between Dad and Nana.

But my grandmother loves Libby and me fiercely, even if she's too critical of my parents. I think she simply can't help herself.

As Dad busies himself upstairs—he doesn't come back down after finishing with my grandmother's bags—we girls head into the kitchen with Nana.

"Do you want some tea, Mum?" my mother asks.

"Or how about something stronger?" I say, wiggling my eyebrows up and down. "Brandy?"

"That's my girl," she says, holding her hand out. A designer gold bracelet shimmers against the translucent skin on her bony wrist; I saw the same one last week in a magazine.

"Nana!" I gasp. "This is beautiful! When did you get this?"

"Oh, this?" she says, looking kittenish as she pulls it to her chest and looks at it lovingly. "My boyfriend surprised me with it yesterday. Isn't he a dish?"

My mother looks suspicious. "He surprised you with it, or you nagged him until he bought it for you?"

Nana looks wounded.

My mother turns away, and I see another flash of frustration across her face.

Nana continues, "I may have suggested it to him, but Gary makes up his own mind."

I shoot Mum a look that says, *Be nice.*

"Well," says Mum, clearing her throat, "it's a beautiful piece of jewelry. Gary sounds very lovely."

Nana smiles. "Thank you, darling. Now, Charlotte, how is school treating you? Your mother says you're running with quite a smart crowd now. Of course, I'd expected you would be. I told her from day one that sending you to Sussex Park was the right move. A girl like you—so beautiful, so outgoing, so sunny—you were bound to align yourself with the right people."

"Thanks, Nana."

"And Prince Edward! What a coup! My friends are dying to know everything. Cousin Betsy—you remember her, the tall one who never married? She insists I'm making it up. It's remarkably insulting. I told her if she kept it up she wouldn't be invited to the wedding."

"Nana! We're not getting married!" Now I wish Mum had

already told Nana the news.

"No? Why on earth not?"

Libby opens her mouth to speak, but Mum cuts her off.

"They're only seventeen, Mother. It's just puppy love. In any case, I think you should know something—"

"Listen to me, my dears. If you play your cards right and always keep him guessing, you'll see it through. Just don't go to bed with him. Men won't buy the cow if the milk is free."

I can feel Libby's eyes on me. I take another sip of wassail and avoid looking at her. Why should I be feeling awkward? *She's* the one who should worry what Nana will say.

"Mother! That's enough! They've only been dating for a few months. Stop filling their heads with this rubbish. It's too much pressure. And nobody's going to bed with anybody."

"Um, Nana?" says Libby. "I have to tell you something." She and Mum exchange nervous looks.

But Nana stands up, saying, "Let's talk later, dears. I need to take a quick nap before dinner."

"Okay," Libby says, looking defeated.

Nana turns to me. "You *haven't* gone to bed with him, have you?"

"Nana! No! We're done talking about this!"

"Good girl." She downs her brandy-spiked wassail and holds her glass out. "I'll have a quick refill, thanks."

INDIA: How's home? You surviving?
ME: Barely. I'm still not speaking to Libby, and my grandmother is like a bull in a china shop

INDIA: At least you don't have 4 rowdy brothers yelling over each other around the clock

ME: My nana versus your brothers: fight to the death

INDIA: Based on what I've heard about your gran, it sounds like an even match

INDIA: Have you told her?

ME: No.

ME: Libby just tried to.

INDIA: What happened?

ME: Mum panicked and changed the subject

INDIA: What's the worst that can happen?

ME: My sister steals my ex and drives a permanent wedge between us, and my grandmother finds out and spends years moaning about how we lost a royal wedding, and nobody's on my side and Wisteria turns into World War Three. Oh . . . wait a minute . . .

INDIA: Ha. Hang in there. Xxx

I put my phone on the dining table as I finish setting it. Our dining room just might be my favorite room in the house. The long mahogany table seats up to twenty, and when the lights are turned down and the candles are blazing—like now—the room feels like a medieval banquet hall. The walls are lined with hunting tableaus that my mother bought on Portobello Road, and I've done the table decorations based off something I found from my favorite home-decorating app, putting a long red-and-green runner down the table, lining it with pinecones, holly, garlands, and winter squash, and tall candleholders filled with berries and cinnamon twigs. I spent hours yesterday in the woods behind our house gathering the decorations, topped off with this morning's trip into town for the candleholders, cinnamon, and squash.

I place a Christmas cracker in front of each place setting and then sigh, looking around the table. Everything looks perfect. Too bad I can't enjoy it.

"Dinner!" I call.

Everybody comes in from the sitting room and the kitchen, sitting down at the ornately decorated table. My father sits at the head, with Nana to his right. She's changed into a beaded dress and smells heavily of perfume. Her long silver hair is arranged into a beautiful Gibson girl chignon on top of her head.

"You look like you wandered off the set of *Downton Abbey*," Mum says.

"Is looking smart a crime? I can't stand this terrible trend of 'dressing down.' Everybody appears as if they've just come back from the gym," Nana counters.

Libby and I catch each other's eyes and exchange a smile. Damn it. I keep forgetting I'm angry at her. I pick up the Christmas cracker, fiddling with it.

She clears her throat. "Charlotte? Wassail?" She offers me the jar sitting in front of me.

"No. Thank you."

Mum leaves the kitchen and comes back into the room holding the turkey. Dad stands at the end of the table and brandishes the carving knife with a flourish.

"Wait!" Mum says. She places the bird on the table and comes back in with a white apron.

"Oh, not this old thing," Dad says.

"Matthew, you must." Mum cackles as she drapes the tatty apron over his button-down shirt and navy blazer. She stands back and regards him in a mock-pensive pose, as if appraising art. The apron reads "Kiss the Cook" and has a naked torso of a Roman statue printed on the front. It's shockingly tacky.

The two of them giggle as Dad pretends to jab Mum with the carving knife. I look over at Nana, who is exasperated. She doesn't appreciate this sort of display.

"When you're quite ready, Matthew," Nana says frostily. "I was rather hoping to eat *this* year."

"Of course," he says, back to all-business as he tucks into the bird.

I love this about my parents. Even though they're both fairly serious people, they bring out the silly side of each other. They've been married for two decades and yet they seem like giddy newlyweds. I hope I can find that for myself someday.

I remember Edward and Libby kissing and my stomach sinks. I still just don't understand. How *could* they?

Libby is picking at the food on her plate, barely eating. I realize that she's lost weight. Even though she's a traitor, I should throw her a bone. It's Christmas.

"I like your dress, Libby," I say.

Everybody looks at me, and I realize that I must have interrupted my grandmother.

"No, no," she says drily. "*You* go ahead, please."

"Sorry, Nana."

"Libby's dress does look very nice. Makes your eyes look special, instead of that boring brown. I do wish you had inherited my blue eyes. Did I pick it out?"

"You did, Nana," Libby says. She looks at me gratefully.

"Quite right. Thought so." Nana looks pleased as she sips champagne that my mother bought specially for her. "And what about you, Charlotte? We've been circling around the topic at hand for hours and I'm tired of ducking it. How is your relationship? How is His Royal Highness?" She relishes these words, letting them roll off her tongue slowly. She's shimmering with pleasure. I wait a few seconds. Finally, I come out with it:

"We broke up."

"No! What happened?"

I look at Libby. She looks like a deer caught in headlights.

I take a sip of the half glass of red wine my parents allow Libby and me to have every Christmas.

"Well. I don't really know what to say."

"Something must have happened," Nana says. "You were so excited!"

"I dumped him."

"Oh, Charlotte! Why?"

"He never had any time for me. And he was spending too much time with *other* girls," I say, shooting a passive-aggressive look at Libby.

Nana frowns. "I see. That won't do."

I look at her in surprise. "You're not upset?"

She takes a sip of her champagne, disappointment etched into her face. "I'd hoped for more from him. He's a *prince*. But the only person I'm upset for is you, my dear. Maybe you can forgive something like that after you're married—and only once, mind you!—but this early in your relationship? No. Once a cheater, always a cheater. Prince be damned."

"That's what I said! I don't know if he was cheating, but he wasn't treating me well. I didn't care that he was a prince."

She nods, looking satisfied. "That's my girl. Kick that deadbeat to the curb."

Mum's face registers shock, while Dad looks impressed. Clearly, Nana's reaction has surprised us all.

"Besides, there was plenty of other stuff, too," I say. "We just weren't the right fit. He's kind of boring."

Libby shuffles in her seat.

I'm in the kitchen washing dishes while Dad takes out the garbage and Mum and Nana huddle over brandies in the living room.

"Charlotte?" Libby asks timidly at my back.

I don't turn around. "Yeah?"

"Can we talk?"

"Go for it," I say, shrugging.

"How are you?"

"Fine."

She clears her throat. "I just wanted you to know: the night you saw us—it was the first time we kissed."

"Congratulations." I finish wiping a serving platter dry and set it back in the cupboard. I can see her reflection in the window behind the sink. Like me, she's still wearing her paper crown from the Christmas cracker.

"We were both really drunk."

I don't say anything.

She continues, clearing her throat again. "Um . . . after he kissed me, I realized I *did* have feelings for him, but I'd been pushing them away because of you. I feel awful."

"You should. And being drunk is a pretty lame excuse."

"I'm so sorry."

"Here's what I want to know," I say, swiveling around and throwing the tea towel on the counter. "What if I hadn't caught you? Would you have let it go on for days? Weeks? When were you going to come to me and say, 'You know how you've been paranoid for weeks? Turns out you were right to be'?"

"Charlotte, I promise you that nothing happened while you two were dating. I didn't even *realize* I thought of him like that until the night you saw us kissing. I swear it to you."

"How can I believe a single word you say after you were so quick to betray me?"

She's quiet for a second. "I understand. But . . ."

"Oh, there's a 'but'?"

"Never mind."

"No. Please share. I'm riveted."

"I mean, you two only casually dated for a couple months," she says in a rush. "You said yourself that you didn't even like him that much."

"Are you serious? *That's* your defense?"

Her cheeks are bright pink.

"Look, here's the reality of the situation. You're a boyfriend stealer. You're selfish. You're two-faced and clearly only out for yourself. I would *never* do this to you."

Libby's back stiffens.

"You threw me under the bus at the first opportunity to be with him. How low can you get? You betrayed me."

"Now wait a minute," Libby says. "You're not being fair."

"I'm not being fair? How is my sister making out with my boyfriend *fair*?"

"Ex-boyfriend."

"We're still quibbling about word choice?"

"The two of you had nothing in common! You had nothing to talk about! And you broke up almost two months ago!"

"We had plenty to talk about."

"That's not what he says. He seems to think you were pretty boring, too." As soon as she says it, she looks ashamed. "I'm sorry, I shouldn't have said that."

I reel back as if I've been slapped. "Screw. You. I knew you were trying to steal him from me."

"I didn't steal him! You broke up!"

Mum comes into the kitchen, her face anguished.

"Please," Mum says, putting her hands out. "Stop."

"I hate you," I say to Libby, throwing my paper crown on the floor at her feet.

I run upstairs, slamming my bedroom door so hard the walls shake.

✿ ✿ ✿

Several hours later, I go downstairs to make a cup of tea. There are voices in the sitting room: it's Mum, Dad, and Nana, all talking in hushed tones.

I tiptoe down the stairs.

"I'm confused," he says. "She's . . ."

I can't quite make out what he's saying, so I inch down the stairs quietly, poking my head around the corner and trying to hear without being seen.

". . . it's going to derail her studies. She's only been at Sussex Park for a few months. What happens if he gets bored of her the way he did of Charlotte?"

"It still doesn't make any sense to me," says Nana. "Libby is so focused on her studies. When she'd even find the time for man-snatching is beyond me."

"For once, we're in agreement," Dad says. "It doesn't make sense to me, either. Edward was suitable for Charlotte. She cares more about boys and sport than university. At least dating a prince would have forced her to grow up and find some direction. And she's socially equipped to navigate that world."

"You think Libby's too good for him?" Mum asks.

"Not exactly. But she's too ambitious to be stuck on the arm of a prince, waving from a balcony and opening hospitals."

"Well," says Nana. "Thank heavens for small favors. At least he kept it in the family."

While my father and I have a decent relationship, I've never been as close to him as Libby is. I know he's proud of my athleticism, but my academic failures always bothered him. Libby's perfect marks were comforting: something he could set his clock by.

But still: to hear my father say that Libby's too good for Edward but that *I'd* be okay for him—because what else will I do with my life? It's like a dagger through the heart. It feels like I'm doomed to be second best in the eyes of everybody I admire—always in perfect Libby's shadow.

I sneak back up the stairs to my room. I'm no longer in the mood for tea.

A few minutes later, there's a soft knock at my door.

"Charlotte?"

It's Libby, tentatively calling my name.

She knocks again three more times, each time calling my name.

"I'm sorry," she finally says through the door. "Please forgive me. I didn't want it to be like this."

"Leave me alone," I say. "I don't want to see you. I don't want to talk to you. Just leave me alone."

Screw her. In fact, screw them all.

sixteen

Most girls don't realize that you need to prune your makeup regularly.

If you don't do a big cleaning twice a year, mascara grows bacteria, brushes accumulate gunk, and your makeup bag starts to develop a grimy layer of filth. The whole thing is one giant cesspool of gross.

Generally, I'll replace two or three items, buying a couple of lipsticks and a new mascara and foundation, and simply dust off the rest.

Not this year. Back at school after Christmas, I decide to throw away the whole lot, dumping my entire bag into the bathroom rubbish bin and heading to the Boots in town to rebuild from scratch.

I need a fresh start.

Libby and I didn't speak to each other the rest of Christmas break, which made for a super-awkward week. Even though I told her to leave me alone, I'm surprised that she's stopped trying. It's not that I wanted her to keep groveling for forgiveness, but . . . okay, yeah, I wanted her to keep groveling for forgiveness.

Now that we've been back on campus for twenty-four hours, both she and Edward seem to be going out of their way to avoid me. They're never at the dining hall, and I could have sworn she pulled an about-face and ducked behind a building when she saw me walking toward her yesterday. I don't know what any of this means. Are they hooking up now? Are they *dating*?

They would never. That would be a bridge too far, even for them.

The day after break is over, I'm in the Colvin bathroom on my floor, brushing my teeth after dinner. Edward and Libby weren't in the dining hall, and none of my friends seemed to notice that I had little to contribute to the conversation—I was too busy mulling over things.

The door opens and Libby walks in holding a shower caddy and carrying a towel. She stops when she sees me.

I give her a dirty look before turning back toward the mirror.

"Hi, Lotte," she says. She looks awkward, like she doesn't know what to do.

"Hi."

"I was just about to take a shower. Maintenance is fixing the ones on my floor—there's no hot water."

I shrug. "Okay."

She walks across the linoleum floor in her flip-flops, entering one of the shower cubicles and closing the plastic curtain. I debate saying something to her, but she turns the water on so I finish brushing my teeth and go back to my room.

Twenty minutes later, however, there's a knock on the open door. Libby stands there, wet hair braided, wearing her pajamas.

"Yes?"

"Can I come in?"

I'm feeling charitable. Maybe we can get things started back on the right foot this year. "Fine."

Libby steps through the doorway, holding a box of chocolates. "Want one? I saved all the white choc for you."

"Okay," I say, plucking a piece from the box. I take a bite, staring at her as I chew. She looks hopeful, which makes *me* feel hopeful— I think she's here to apologize one more time. It'll take some time to forgive her properly, but I know Libby—she'd never hurt me on purpose. I've just got to dig deep and find the strength to forgive. "Thanks," I say.

"So, uh . . . can I sit?"

I point to my desk chair. "Okay."

She sits and we stare at each other.

Finally, she talks. "I miss you, Lots."

I don't say anything, my mind racing. It's been two weeks since I caught them kissing; two weeks since my life felt like it turned upside down. We've never gone this long without speaking, not even with the two of us at different schools.

I do miss Libby—a lot. I can't count the number of times over the past couple of weeks I've wanted to tell her a joke or ask for her advice. But I still feel so hurt.

"Thanks," I say.

"I, uh, wanted to talk to you," she says, sounding nervous.

"Okay, we're talking. What's up?"

"Yes. Right. So . . ." She swallows, looking like she's about to pass out. "I need to ask you something."

"Okay . . ." I don't know where this is going, but suddenly I don't have a good feeling about it.

"I know things have been horrible the past couple of weeks."

"Right."

"The last thing I want to do is hurt you, Charlotte."

"Not *wanting* to hurt me and not *actually* hurting me are two different things."

She looks miserable. "True."

"So? What do you want to ask me?" I say, swallowing nervously.

"Um. Well . . . how would you feel . . . I mean, that is to say . . . would you be okay if . . . ugh." She groans. "If Edward and me . . . um . . ."

My eyes narrow. "Yes?"

She exhales sharply, all in a puff, as if gathering courage. "He's asked me if there's a chance for us."

"A chance for what?"

"Um. You know."

"A chance for winning the lottery? A chance for getting struck by lightning? A chance for *what*?"

"To . . . to be his girlfriend. I told him I'd need to talk to you first."

My heart sinks.

"Get out."

"But—"

"The fact that you would even have the *nerve* to ask me that."

I don't think I'd be this upset over Edward dating somebody else—it's not like I still have real feelings for him. But it's my sister. It's Libby.

And of all the people in the world, why did they have to choose each other?

"I haven't said yes! I told him if you weren't okay with it, we couldn't date. I would never choose a guy over you, Charlotte."

Something in Libby's voice makes me waver. If this were any other guy, I'd be thrilled for her. Am I being melodramatic? She's always been so supportive of me—my biggest cheerleader. But then an image of the two of them looking at each other tenderly and kissing flashes through my mind, and I feel betrayed all over again.

"Except clearly you *would*," I say. "Look, I don't care what the two of you do. You don't need my permission. Date him. Fall in love. Get married, for all I care. But if you think I'm going to hold your hand through it all, you're deluded."

She looks miserable. "Lotte, I'm a wreck."

"Guilt is a funny emotion."

"I love you. The last thing I want to do is hurt you. But I don't know what to do—I've never felt this way about anybody. I can't eat. I can't sleep. My stomach hurts. It's an awful feeling. I hate myself for liking him."

I pause. If she's trying to get through to me, it's working. I don't want her to suffer.

But I need more time. I can't let it go this easily. I just *can't*. "You two deserve each other."

She stands up, looking defeated. "I'm so sorry, Lotte."

Libby walks out the door, and I close it behind her, immediately pulling out my phone to send a group text.

ME: Are you free? Wine in my room. Five minutes.

A few minutes later, India, Flossie, Alice, and Georgie have all piled into my room. I want to deep-dive into the news that Libby and Edward are dating—I need some friend sympathy over being betrayed yet *again*—but everybody's too busy yammering on about skiing.

"We've started going to Zurs," Flossie says.

"Not St. Moritz?" Alice asks.

"Daddy says he's done with St. Moritz. Too many Russians."

"We only do Gstaad, of course," says India.

"But the skiing is better in Austria, I think," Flossie says.

"Really?" India says. "*Totally* disagree. Switzerland or nothing. *Maybe* Kitz, but that's it."

"You're all insane," says Georgie. "Deer Valley smokes all those towns—the snow is like powdered sugar. Besides, Europe is over-rated—unless you think skiing on ice is fun."

"Says the American," cracks Flossie.

"Says the *half* American who learned to ski when she was *two*," retorts Georgie.

As I silently pour everybody cups of wine, they get into a serious debate about the best ski resorts—whether "Verb" or "Val" has the best après-ski, whether Gryon or Klosters attracts more royals, whether Zermatt or St. Moritz is flashier. I cross my arms, wedging myself into the far corner of my bed near the wall and feeling incredibly left out of this conversation. My family didn't have enough money to take me skiing when I was a child, and if you don't learn to ski young, you might as well not even try. The couple of times I've tagged along with Sussex Park teammates on ski vacations, they'd be whooshing down the black runs while I struggled on the bunny slope. Sometimes a friend would take pity and ski with me, but they'd never last more than half an hour before coming up with a lame excuse for why they needed to dash. I'd eventually find myself hanging out alone in the chalet, downing cup after cup of hot chocolate while waiting for everybody else to finish their runs. Unlike other tracks I can cover, the fact that I can't ski well immediately marks me as an outsider in this world. It's just one more reminder that my family might have money, but unlike everybody else, ours is *very* new.

"I almost broke my leg on one of the black runs, but luckily the ski instructor called a snowmobile to take me back to the lodge," says Flossie. "Then he felt so sorry for me that we chatted by the fire for an hour."

"And . . . ?" Alice asks.

"We didn't pull, if that's what you're asking."

She looks disappointed. "Damn."

"It was still exciting. He was twenty-five!"

"Ew. Pass." Alice wrinkles her nose. "Personally, I think eighteen is the perfect age."

"Disagree," Flossie says, stretching her arms over her head. Her tanned tummy peeks out. "If anything, twenty-five is too young for you. Everybody knows men remain boys until they're at *least* forty."

Now *this* conversation I can contribute to. "Forty? Gross. That's my dad's age."

"I'm not saying you should date a forty-year-old. I'm saying age doesn't equal maturity. And I'm sure your father is totally older than forty. Speaking of family—how are things going with Libby after she snogged Edward? I haven't seen either of them since we've been back." She looks around the room, as if she's just recognizing my sister's absence. "Where *is* she, anyway?"

Finally.

"You guys aren't going to believe it, but . . ." I pause for maximum dramatic effect. "It wasn't just one snog. Libby and Edward are dating—like, for real."

They exchange looks.

"Um, yeah," Flossie says. "Obvs."

"Wait, you knew? How?"

Alice shifts uncomfortably on the floor. "More wine, anybody?"

"I *tried* to warn you," says Flossie. "I've been telling you for months."

I narrow my eyes. "So he *was* cheating on me with her."

"Obviously," says Flossie.

"*No*," India says, frowning at her. "He was *not* cheating on Charlotte."

I feel hot. "I'm so stupid."

"You're not stupid," says India. "I suspected, but I didn't know for certain. They must be trying to hide it."

"Whatever. Let them date. Let them get bloody married for all I care. They deserve each other."

Alice walks on her knees over to me, refilling my mug. "Here. You need this."

India sighs. "I don't like the way the whole thing went down. You're right to be upset, of course. But he and Libby *are* quite well matched."

I stare at her.

"I know that's hard to hear, but it's true," says India. "Besides—and I say this with all respect for her, Charlotte—but your sister is totally boring."

Even though I'm angry with Libby, I feel a knee-jerk desire to defend her.

"And . . . boring is good?"

"For Edward? Boring is great. I don't think *he'd* say that. He's still deluded enough to think that he has choices. But he needs to be the star, and he needs a steady girl who won't compete with him. His family couldn't have it any other way."

"You're acting like they'll get married," I say, thinking about my grandmother's prediction.

India shrugs. "You never know. Like I said, he thinks he has choices. But he doesn't, really. His life is totally mapped out."

"So won't his family choose for him?" Discussing the marital prospects of your seventeen-year-old ex-boyfriend is beyond surreal.

"Never," she says, frowning. "He'd die. He needs to have *some* say in the matter. He'll meet a new crop of girls at university."

"Fresher meat. Bigger boobs. Smaller brains," cracks Georgie. I shoot her an exasperated look.

"But he'll always return to the inner circle. We're the girls who knew him when. There are only a few people to choose from, really. Mummy says it was the same with his father, and his father before him. They never learn."

"Damn," says Georgie. "It's all written like a book, huh?"

Flossie nods. "It's comforting, in a way."

Only Alice looks depressed. "Comforting? It makes our world sound so small. So fated."

"It is fated. And if you think our world is *large*," says India, "then you haven't been paying attention."

"Well," I say, feeling wounded, "out with the old." I reach over to my desk and hold up the Polaroid photos. "Edward gave me these. One last parting souvenir from our time together, I guess." I open a drawer, jumbled with DIY accessories and loose-leaf papers, and toss the photos inside. "Souvenirs for my children's children to marvel at someday—Good-Time Granny and her princely conquest."

"That's the spirit," Flossie says. "You'll find a nice boy who's more *your* speed—I know it."

"Don't be glum," India says. "Boys are disposable. Even Edward."

I don't know what I was expecting from Libby after she came to see me. A public rejection of Edward out of loyalty to me? I'm not sure—but I'm surprised that she stops trying.

Maybe I just needed her to ask my forgiveness one last time.

Now it's like I can't escape the sight of them.

There they are, giggling at each other over a stack of history textbooks and Russian novels in a remote corner of the library during study period.

There they are, sitting dead center at our usual table in the dining hall, laughing with Flossie and Alice at David's lunchtime antics.

There they are, walking through the quad during the daily three p.m. break, hands clasped, arms swinging, sun shining bright and hard into their smiling faces.

After a week of awkward run-ins, stilted chapels, and pained silent breakfasts—I refuse to back down and she's stopped apologizing—we've silently settled on a joint-custody arrangement of our friends. I'm taking athletics this term and am always starving after practice, so I have India and Co. for breakfast. Lunches are theirs: while Libby and Edward hold court, I sneak into the dining hall like a thief, loading up my tray with food on paper plates, and then either taking it outside to eat by myself on the lawn or back to my room to stare blankly at my textbooks.

Dinner is the only minefield. India has become a begrudging Switzerland, fielding texts from each of us asking if it's safe to come and whether the other offending parties have left. ("You're all bloody exhausting," she complains one night over wine in her room, a rare moment of the mask falling. "I'm not your minder, and I wish you'd all buck up and be friends for the sake of the group. I feel like a child again, before my mother and father called off the divorce and came to their senses.")

We fall into a pattern of them eating on the earlier side, before eventually going back to Edward's room or Libby's room or wherever the hell the two of them go to giggle and paw at each other. I halfheartedly do homework in the common room or library until about seven p.m., when starvation takes over and I show up at the dining hall for my dinner. Only a few times have we tidily crossed paths: Edward and Libby walking out hand in hand at the exact moment I'm entering. When recognition dawns, their eyes slide to the floor, to the ceiling—anywhere but full-on to meet mine.

To be honest, I don't miss Edward at all. Now that we're broken up, it's become clearer than ever that the two of us didn't do much talking. Most of the time was spent either hanging with our friends, watching TV, or making out. And now that the word is out I'm single again, boys have been flirting with me. Just yesterday, Robert walked me back from chapel after I slipped in late (mostly to avoid sitting with my friends).

But the distance from Libby is hard. Every single time I pull out my phone to text somebody, I think of her. Even though I spent years at school without her by my side, we'd be texting daily—now, there's nothing, and it's lonely. India's doing a good job trying to fill the void, but it's not the same. We pass each other on the stairs of our dormitory or run into each other in the common room, and she'll give me a hopeful look. Sometimes, she says hi, and sometimes she looks grumpy and ignores me right back, which only serves to make me more irritated.

I miss her—but I can't bring myself to forgive her.

One night in late January, while I'm watching *Britain's Got Talent* alone in the Colvin common room, one of the contestants makes me think of my aunt Kat. For reasons I've never been able to pin down, Mum and Kat haven't spoken in over ten years. My mother used to tear up whenever Kat's name was mentioned—usually by Nana after a few too many brandies during the holidays—but these past few years, she's been stoic, not rising to the bait and eventually changing the subject altogether.

When I walk upstairs after the episode is over, feeling sorry for myself, I find a little stuffed E.T. sitting outside my room. There's a note attached to his pointer finger, and inside, written in Libby's loopy scrawl, are four words:

I'm sorry. Sisters forever.

The combination of the thoughtful gift and the reminder of my mother's falling out with Aunt Kat makes my chest tighten. I suddenly see their feud through new eyes.

I don't want to lose my sister.

I walk back down the hall, staring at the stuffed alien and smiling a little to myself as I climb the stairs. Libby's room is at the end of the hall, but when I get there, the door is closed. I'm about to knock when I hear voices.

My heart stops, and I press my ear to the door.

Edward's in there with Libby. She's snuck him into her room.

I should just knock on the door. I'm sure she'd be happy to let me in. I'm sure Edward would leave. I'm sure we could bring this whole thing to a close here and now and put it behind us, and laugh about it someday like the whole thing wasn't totally twisted. Like: "Pass the peas. Hey, remember that crazy time we boyfriend-swapped?!"

But hearing Edward's voice, plus the realization that Libby has changed enough to be sneaking boys into her room, snaps me right back into that awful, confused, hurt place where I've been living for the past few weeks.

I walk back to my room, still clutching the stuffed alien.

Mum and I talk each Sunday, and every week she asks if Libby and I have made up yet.

Week after week, the answer is the same: no.

seventeen

"Valentine's Day is the best holiday when you're in a relationship, and the absolute bloody worst when you're single," says India.

We're sitting on a bench outside the student center waiting for Flossie to meet us.

Valentine's Day decorations have taken over campus—paper hearts on the walls, little stuffed Cupids decorating the dessert station in the dining hall, the annual Cutest Couple list in the student center. (Big shocker: Libby and Edward win. Vomit.)

"Cosign," I say. "They're all so smug. Even Georgie and Oliver are insufferable—I wish they would quit it with all those goo-goo eyes. I've had it up to here with everybody being so . . . *cute.*" I say the word like it smells awful.

At the far end of the quad, Libby and Edward are walking hand in hand. Edward doesn't look in our direction—he's probably pretending he doesn't see us—but Libby gives me a pained, awkward look.

"I can't stand them," I say.

India nods. "I get it."

"They don't even *try* to make peace anymore," I say. "Libby was apologizing to me twenty-four seven for weeks, and now—nothing. Glad she was willing to throw her sister under the bus at the first sign of a guy showing interest in her."

India sighs. "Didn't she leave that stuffed animal thing outside your door? You never said thank you. Libby's nice, but she's not Mother Teresa."

"It was a stuffed alien."

"Look, you're all my friends. I don't want to pick sides."

"Okay, but forget the peace offering for a second. Don't you agree that them dating is a little bit shitty?"

She puts her arm around me. "Yes. It *is* shitty."

"Thank you," I say, feeling gratified. "That's all."

"You're handling it well. Better than I would be."

"Better than you? I can't imagine you giving two flying figs if your girlfriend suddenly took up with one of your brothers. You'd just shrug and be like, 'Such is life,' and then order a glass of champagne and light a cigarette or something."

India bursts into laughter. "So, basically, what you're saying is that I'm a cliché from a foreign film?"

I laugh. "Sorry."

"Let's get the hell out of Dodge," she says. "I need off this bloody campus."

I give her a sidelong look. "What's up with you?"

She sighs. "I don't want to bore you with the details."

"Girl trouble? Family stuff? Failing classes? I'm all ears. Misery loves company!"

"Classes?" She pulls a face. "Definitely not."

"Okay, well, I'm here if you want to talk."

"Thanks," she says, glancing at her wrist as her Apple watch lights up. "Do you want to go into London this weekend? We could spend the night at my parents' flat and get away from all these bloody lovestruck twits."

"That sounds perfect." It'll be a good distraction: the thought of seeing Edward and Libby mooning at each other around campus makes me want to throw myself off a building.

I groan looking at the price tag: nine hundred pounds.

"India, I can't. My parents will throw a fit." We're in Harvey Nichols, just off Brompton Road in London.

First we hit up Bond Street—India buying a new pair of shoes, three jackets, and a pair of cream-colored trousers—before walking several blocks to Harvey Nicks, as everybody calls it.

India frowns into a mirror, staring at her reflection as she tries on a pair of gold sunglasses. "Why?" she asks, swapping out the pair resting on her thin nose for black aviators.

I clutch the blue dress. "They hate it when I shop too much with their credit card."

She sets the sunglasses down on a display case. "But your parents aren't here now."

"It's too much." Sometimes I think India, Flossie, and the rest think my family has more money than we do. We're not poor anymore, but we don't have generational money the way they do; India's great-grandkids, for example, will never have to work a day in their lives. We have a nice house, go on expensive trips around Europe, and Soles is actually so successful that Mum and Dad are talking IPO. But when you've grown up worrying about money, it's hard to shake that deep-seated financial insecurity.

And when you're new money, you're always jealous of those who are old.

"Fine, let's go downstairs; this entire floor is overpriced anyway. We'll hit the high street and get new dresses on the cheap for tonight. Nobody'll know the difference, and even your parents can't complain about one bloody dress from H&M."

"Tonight? Where are we going?" We walk through the department store and get on a downstairs escalator.

"Alpine Haus. It's brand-new, across from KP. Let's stop by the flat, dress, run by Il Carpaccio for a bite, and then it's up to High Street Ken."

"Thanks for this. I needed a girls' night desperately."

She looks at me full in the face, patting me on the shoulder. "You've had a tough run these past couple of months. But you'll figure it out. Now let's find you something to wear and show those London boys what you're made of."

✿　✿　✿

244

Four hours later, our arms are laden with shopping bags as we turn off the King's Road in Chelsea, stepping around the slushy puddles of ice and melting snow pooling on the street.

I got carried away—between the dresses, the blouses, a new winter coat, several wool skirts, and a couple of pairs of shoes, I guess that I've spent at least two thousand pounds today. I try not to think about what my parents' reaction will be when they open the credit card bill.

Oh, well. It's not like they don't actually have the money.

I follow India upstairs to the fifth-floor penthouse, the two of us scraping our Wellington boots against the mat outside her front door before stepping inside. The flat is cavernous and full of light.

The hardwood floor is covered with faded Oriental rugs. Three large floral sofas anchor the sitting room, which connects to an open kitchen opposite the front door and a hallway to the left. The right side of the sitting room has sliding glass doors leading to a wraparound balcony with views of leafy Onslow Square below. I know I shouldn't be surprised that India has a place in Chelsea—and clearly renovated, to boot—but I'm still impressed. Most families we know have been priced out to Fulham.

"Should I take my boots off?" I ask, looking for a slipper bin near the door.

She shrugs, leaving her wellies on as she walks over the rugs to the kitchen. "Only if you want to."

Another one of those invisible little class markers: my mother would be having a heart attack at the idea of mud tracking around her expensive carpets. Old money *likes* it when toys lose their shine.

"This place is awesome." I walk around the apartment inspecting everything. Libby would love it here—she's always dreamed of a flat in Chelsea. I pick up a wooden frame displaying a photo of the extended Fraser family, gazing at the tanned, smiling faces. "How often do you come here?"

India tosses her bags on a sofa and walks to a wooden cabinet in the far corner. She opens a bottle of Tanqueray and pours two generous glasses.

"Not often enough. Whenever I go out in London. Once every couple of months? My older brother uses it when he's visiting from New York."

She hands me a glass and we cheers, knocking the drinks back. The metallic-tasting liquid trickles down the back of my throat, making my insides glow.

India gives me a quick tour of the four-bedroom flat. Her parents are usually traveling or in residence at Huntshire, her older brother works at a fund in New York, and her younger brothers are all at Harrow, so India often has the whole place to herself when she's in London. Her bedroom is cold and surprisingly modern, decorated in shades of silver and blue, with a renovated walk-in closet and adjacent, state-of-the-art bathroom cluttered with designer perfume bottles.

"Make yourself at home," India says. "I'm taking a quick shower. We have a reservation at Il Carpaccio at eight thirty—you'll love it. It's just Italian, nothing to write home about, but you don't go to a restaurant in London for the *food*, do you?" she laughs.

After a hearty—and despite India's description, delicious—Italian dinner, we're holed up at a table at Alpine Haus, drinking spiked fruit punch from giant jugs. I'm wearing a skintight red minidress over tights; India's in a more demure blue-and-white printed silk dress that falls to her knees, one of her newly acquired goodies. Despite the cold, we each wore a single black peacoat over our dresses—the alcohol and the dancing will keep us warm.

"Are we here all night?" I ask, my eyes darting from person to person as I check out the scene. The bar is full of pretty, well-dressed people: the type of social pioneers whose coolness christens a place and makes it an official hot spot.

"I had been thinking Maggie's after," India says, leaning back against the leather seats and surveying the crowd. "But I heard this is the new place to be. And Maggie's has gotten really strict with IDs. So many places in London are a drag about underage drinking now." She rolls her eyes and sighs wearily. It doesn't take much imagination to picture India in middle age, ruing estate taxes.

"So, tell me," she says. "Now that we're alone, just you and me and all these strangers: How are you?"

"Not bad." I've barely thought of Libby all day. I've been too consumed with the brilliance of London: Hyde Park, Big Ben, the King's Road—the whole charming, gorgeous, frantic city mine for the taking. It's so different from the quiet sameness of Sussex Park, where it's impossible to forget your problems.

"Good. You're handling it well. Someday we'll all look back and laugh."

"I don't know about *that*." A waitress walks by with a bevy of shots on a tray, designed to look like chemistry experiments. "What do you think? Shots?"

India smiles. "You read my mind."

We knock back several shots of something yellow, and then switch to tequila on a dare by India.

"Whew!" India looks unsteady in her seat and already a bit worse for the wear. She always goes from sober to drunk instantly, which is disconcerting. I'm not in the mood to babysit tonight. She bops her head around. "Dance?" We bounce up and elbow our way onto the tiny dance floor.

I'm dancing, losing myself in the music, when I hear my name. I look up to see Robert.

His eyes are wide. "Hi. You look bloody amazing," he says in his distinctive northern accent.

"Robert!" I throw my arms around his neck. He smells delicious, and I nestle myself in the crook of his neck for a second. "Your cologne is yummy. You smell divine."

"Oh, thanks," he says, blushing and looking pleased. "What are you girls doing here?"

"We fled Sussex Park for Valentine's Day. Thought we could have some adventures in town. What about you?"

"Same. Some of my friends and I came down for the weekend, and this place is supposed to be the cool spot."

"Ooh, a prefect sneaking off campus for some underage drinking. I like it." I lean in. "I won't tell if you don't."

Robert blushes. "Deal."

We spend the next couple of songs dancing, wheeling each other around the dance floor in a blur of laughter. He's good fun and, judging by the puppy-dog looks he keeps sending my way, has a bit of a crush on me. It's very flattering. He's not a bad-looking guy at all.

"How'd you hear about this place?" I ask, standing with him at the bar after we take a break from dancing.

"My dad," he says, blushing again. "Is that a lame answer? He's friends with the owner."

"What does your father do?" My right foot is starting to feel slightly pinched in my heels, so I lean on Robert's arm for balance.

"He owns one or two restaurants in London. The Dominion?"

"Your dad owns the Dominion? My parents love that place. They go there for their anniversary every year."

"Yeah, I basically grew up at the restaurant."

"Don't they own a few other places?"

"Yeah. L'Espace, Warden, Sui Generis, All Spice, Matisse, a few others . . ."

"So one or two places isn't quite accurate. He's major."

Robert laughs. "I suppose he is."

"Color me impressed. I had no idea."

"Well, it's not *me*," he says. "It's just my parents."

"That's not a very English attitude," I joke. "Especially at our school. You're *completely* defined by what your parents do."

"But it shouldn't be like that. I spent summers in the States as a kid—my mum's sister is married to an American in San Diego. Nobody cares what your parents do. They care about what *you're* doing. My brother is the perfect example of that."

"Oh, yeah? What's he do?"

"He's an angel investor. Like a venture capitalist—those guys who invest in Facebook and stuff like that. He does small tech start-ups."

"He must be loaded."

Robert shrugs. "He does all right. He's always looking for the next big thing. He's obsessed with the idea of finding another Zuckerberg."

"That's funny. Well, you'd better get a *major* finder's fee if you lead him to Snapchat 2.0."

"Tell me about it. But the point is—he's done it on his own, no money from Dad. It might seem like the cards are stacked against us because we're not aristocrats, but it's not like that anymore. *Anybody can rise to the top.*"

"Yeah, well, you'd think we robbed a bank and crashed society the way my mother gets treated sometimes."

"She grew up poor?"

"She grew up okay, actually, but her family was originally working-class—totally bottom of the barrel," I confess. "But my father came from a good enough family."

"Why should you feel embarrassed because of that?" He looks at me sidelong. "I think you've been hanging out with the wrong crowd for too long."

"You mean India and her lot?"

"Yeah. And Prince Edward, too."

I flush. "I'm not hanging out with him anymore."

"I heard about him and your sister. I'm sorry. That must have sucked."

My face falls. "You have no idea."

"I'd be lying if I said I wasn't happy."

"Oh, yeah?"

"Yeah. You broke all our hearts when you were off the market." He laughs self-consciously.

"Well, I'm back *on* the market now," I say flirtatiously, putting Libby out of my mind again.

I feel a tug on my elbow. It's India. Her makeup is starting to slide down her face. "Come with me," she demands.

"Girl talk," I say apologetically. "See you later?" I race off hand in hand with India.

"Where have you been?" she asks. "I've been looking for you everywhere."

"I've been talking to Robert," I say.

She shrugs. "Anyhow. Guess who's here?"

"Who?"

"Clemmie Dubonnet!"

Clemmie Dubonnet is *the* hottest supermodel in the world right now. She's only eighteen years old, but she's already been on all the big magazine covers. She just broke up with her girlfriend, an American TV actress.

"Oh, yeah? That's cool."

"She hasn't seen me yet. How do I look? Is my makeup okay?"

It's not like India to get so excited over a celebrity. I look at her strangely. Is she saying what I think she's saying? Is Clemmie the reason she's been so mysterious?

I look her up and down. She's beautiful as ever, but the alcohol is taking a toll on her fair complexion. Her eyes look bloodshot and her long, thin hair is appearing a bit stringy.

"You're looking a little worse for wear," I say honestly. "Can I help?"

I reach into my handbag, pulling out some makeup blotting wipes, lip gloss, and a comb. I spend a couple of minutes freshening India up, and when I'm done, she looks much better.

"Thanks," she says, giving me a big, long hug. "You're amazing, Charlotte. I knew you'd have a few tricks."

It occurs to me that India, who barely wears makeup and just rolls out of bed looking fabulous, probably doesn't know what to do the .01 percent of the time when she appears anything less than perfect.

"Good luck with Clemmie," I say.

She looks startled for a minute, like she's been caught out, but then she laughs. "Thanks. I'll need it."

We go back out into the club from the bathroom and I look for Robert. I find him standing by the DJ, dancing spastically. He's thrusting his forearms and closed fists in the air, one at a time, which has the result of looking like he's pantomiming being locked in a box.

"Oh my God," I say. "You are the *worst* dancer."

He laughs. "I know. Careful, I might infect you."

The DJ throws on old-school Madonna and a roar goes up from the crowd.

It's only when India reappears that I realize Robert and I have been dancing and laughing for hours. It's nearly three a.m.

"I'm getting a cab with Clemmie," she says. Her hair looks like a rat's nest.

"Where the hell are you two going at three in the morning?"

"She says there's an after-party?" She points vaguely off into the distance, swaying.

"I don't see her. Where?"

"Over there," India says, looking irritated. Clemmie stands by the bar, frowning into her phone and shooting us little looks.

"And where am *I* supposed to go? I'm staying at yours, remember?"

India sways a little. "With Robert?"

"India looks smashed," Robert whispers into my ear.

"Tell me about it. She wants to go home with Clemmie Dubonnet. I don't think it's a good idea—she's wasted."

"Isn't Clemmie a lesbian?"

I shrug. "So's India."

"You should take her back—it's late. Can I help?"

"Agreed, and thanks. Let's go." I turn to India. "Come on. You can text Clemmie from the cab and say you'll see her tomorrow. But right now, you're coming with us."

Together, we take India upstairs, each one of us holding an arm. Robert helps her maneuver the steps, and he hails us a cab once we're upstairs and outside on the street.

"Where are you headed?" he asks me.

"Chelsea. Onslow Square."

"Take them to Onslow Square," Robert says to the cabbie, handing him a wad of cash. "What's your number?" he asks me. "I'll text you so you have mine. Let me know when you're back home safely."

We exchange numbers, and I wave at Robert as the cab turns around the corner.

I look at India, who's giggling in the seat next to me as she jabs at her phone.

"How are you feeling?" I ask.

She puts her phone in her lap. "Fine. You and that boy were *so* dramatic about it."

"You're wasted!"

"I'll be fine."

"What did you say to Clemmie?"

"I just texted her that you were jealous and I had to take you home." She starts giggling again. "Gotta keep her on her toes. So, did tonight take your mind off things?"

"Yes."

As the cab drives through the circular around Buckingham Palace, the gold windows blazing with light, I think of Libby yet again. I wonder what she's doing right now. It's been a month since we've had a proper conversation. Suddenly, I have an impulse to be truthful.

"Can I be honest?" I ask.

India looks at me, her eyes a little bloodshot but her gaze steady. "Yeah. Everything okay?"

"I'm lonely."

"Oh."

"I miss Libby."

"Well, obviously."

"Plus, our group is all weird now. I miss half of our meals. I was betrayed, but I feel like nobody *gets* it or really gives a crap about it.

It's just like, 'Oh, well, Edward and Libby are dating now! That's life!' None of them text me to check in. Nobody ever really asks how I'm doing with it. I just sort of feel . . . forgotten." The drinks must have gone to my head more than I realized. India and I don't usually deep-dive on our feelings like this.

She gives my hand two quick pats. "I don't like to hear that."

I turn back toward the window, feeling lonelier than ever. India's great, but she's not Libby.

We're driving through Victoria now, the Thames ahead of us and Big Ben and the Houses of Parliament visible in the distance. The cab turns right, heading toward Chelsea. "It's fine. I get it. Everybody has their own things going on. I'm just complaining." *Never complain, never explain.*

"I'm sorry you feel that way. I thought I *was* checking in on you." India seems slightly offended. I'm reminded of the fact that she's not as emotional as I am. I don't know if that's a class thing or just an *India* thing, but it makes me feel distant from her.

"No, you are, thank you. This weekend was huge. It's just . . ." I exhale in a puff of frustration. "Like I said—this year has been really shitty so far."

"Well, buck up, buttercup," she says, giving my hand another pat. "Good days are just around the corner."

"I hope so," I say. "I don't think I can take much more of this."

Monday morning, I wake with a start.

Shit. It's six fifty-five. My alarm was set for six thirty and I completely missed it. I look at my iPhone and the volume is turned almost all the way down. My alarm has been going off for the past twenty-five minutes and I didn't hear a thing.

I jump out of bed, grabbing my toothbrush and toothpaste and racing down the hall to the bathroom. No time to apply makeup or even wash my face—I throw my hair into a ponytail and run back to my room. There's a note pinned to my wooden door in shaky, loopy handwriting.

Charlotte,
    You weren't in your room Friday night for dorm check. Neither were you there Saturday night. We did not have a parental permission slip on file for you to be off campus. I shall be forced to report you to Master Kent. Please be in your room tonight (and every night) for checks.
Mistress McGuire

Damn it. Now McGuire is doing surprise dorm checks?

I change into my practice clothes and then book it down to the field.

Despite hurrying as quickly as I can, it's still already past seven when I get there: seven oh three, to be precise. The locker room is already empty, and I run onto the track, trying to fall in line behind the other girls.

"I *see* you, Weston," bellows Wilkinson. "Don't think you're fooling me by sneaking in with the other girls."

"Sorry, Coach," I call, putting on a big show of running even faster to try to overtake the pack. After a few minutes of full-throttle running, I have to stop, standing on the sidelines to try to catch my breath.

Wilkinson glares at me. "Weston, I'll deal with you after practice. Get back out there."

It's a rather uneventful practice, although I almost trip once or twice from tiredness. Once we're done running, I wait on the sidelines for her to come talk to me, but she's ignoring me, talking to the assistant coach and going over their clipboard. I walk back into the locker room with the rest of the girls and hope maybe it'll blow over.

No luck. As I'm wrapping tape around my knee, Coach Wilkinson comes barreling into the locker room. "Weston," she barks. "Come with me."

I set the tape down in my locker, looking warily at the other runners. They're all averting their eyes. I follow Wilkinson into her office and close the door. It's just my luck that she's my coach again this term for track.

"Are you kidding me with this?" she asks.

"I'm sorry?"

"This morning was the fifth time you've been late to practice this year. Five times!"

"But I've only been late once," I protest.

"Are you delusional? You don't get a clean slate after the holidays. No way. I'm still paying attention. I don't give a damn which sport you're playing. You've been late for *me* five times since school began. That's unacceptable. It's disrespectful and demonstrates a complete disregard for not just me but for your fellow athletes. Do you think your time is more valuable than ours?"

"No."

"I'm sorry, what?"

"*No*," I say, this time louder.

"'No, *Coach*.' And I don't believe you. That's not what your actions tell me. Your actions tell me that you don't give a good goddamn about anybody's time but your own. Seven a.m. doesn't mean seven a.m. It means being in the locker room at six forty-five, ready to go, suiting up, taping your knee, or doing whatever it is you need to do to run. Showing up at seven oh five means you're not on the track and ready to go until seven oh eight, and then we're all having to stand around with our thumbs up our asses waiting for Lady Charlotte to grace us with her beloved presence. It ends today."

I'm not used to being on the receiving end of this type of rant, even when my parents are at their angriest. The difference between my parents and Mistress Wilkinson, obviously, is that my parents love me. Wilkinson is looking at me like I'm a cockroach on the bottom of her shoe.

"I'm sorry."

"I don't believe you. You were sorry the last four times you were late. This is it, Weston. I'm done."

I look at her blankly.

"If you're late one more time, and I mean fifteen seconds late, you're off the team."

"But that's not fair!" I protest.

"It is the very definition of fair. You're not the only athlete out there, and it's not *fair* to hold up fifteen other girls just because one of them can't tell time. I need you to step up, and I mean pronto, or you're done."

I slink out of her office feeling a pressure in my chest. I want to scream or cry or throw something, but instead I head directly to the showers, hoping a hot one will calm me down.

I'm sudsing up, fuming about Mistress Wilkinson, when I hear two girls talking by the lockers in low voices.

"She really needs to get her shit together," says one girl with a Scottish accent. It sounds like Sasha, one of the distance runners. "I'm sick of her waltzing into practice ten minutes late and acting like it's no big deal. The rest of us manage to get there on time."

"I'm not even a morning person and I'm there five minutes early," says another. Sounds like Katherine, a sprinter.

"Charlotte's put her foot in it this time."

The voices are getting louder as the two girls walk into the shower. They freeze when they see me.

"Oh. Charlotte. Hiya . . . ," says Sasha.

"Um, did you just . . . we were just . . . ," says Katherine.

I grab my towel with as much dignity as I can muster and pick up my shower caddy, sailing past them without a word.

Once I'm back in the locker room, however, I start crying. I wipe the hot tears away from my cheeks, trying to pull myself together as I slide into my school uniform. I catch a glimpse of myself in the mirror by the door as I'm about to exit onto the quad—my nose is red and my cheeks are blotchy.

After classes, I go to the dining hall to grab a furtive lunch. It's a typical slushy, freezing February day. I promise myself I won't look, but I can't help but sneak a peek at my old table. They're all there: India, Alice, Flossie, Tarquin, David, Oliver, Georgie, Libby, and Edward. They're laughing as David pounds his fists on the table, bellowing something unintelligible from across the room. Even Libby is in stitches, wiping the tears away from her eyes, and looking perfectly at home with all of them as they laugh at David's usual antics.

Libby looks over at me, as if sensing my presence. We lock eyes for several seconds, and she raises her hand as if to say hi. I'm about to take a step forward, to finally go talk to her and clear the air, when I see Edward put his hand on her arm, still laughing at David. My stomach clenches at the intimacy between them. I wonder what their relationship is like. Have they slept together yet? What do they do when they hang out? Does he like her weird sense of humor? It makes me sad that Libby has a boyfriend now and I haven't even talked to her about it.

I turn and walk away.

Over the weekend, things get even worse. I'm exiting the library on Saturday night, lost in my thoughts, when I run into my friends. They're all laughing and chatting away.

"Charlotte!" Libby says.

Georgie looks guilty.

I look back and forth between everybody. India looks particularly embarrassed, as if she's been caught with the enemy.

"Hi," she says. "We were just . . ."

"Donatella," I say. "I get it. No worries." I remember mentioning to India this morning that I'd be skipping dinner tonight to study. They must have put it together last minute, since we've been eating our dinners together in the dining hall on Saturday night this term. Libby and Edward are almost always off campus together on the weekend.

"Sorry," Edward says, in a quieter voice.

"We should have invited you," India says.

Libby and I are staring at each other. Is this what it's come to? My friends sneaking around behind my back? Even *India* letting it happen?

My chest tightens. "Gotta go," I say. "Later."

I push past them, holding my books close to my chest for warmth. As I walk away, I realize that Libby's birthday is coming up in April, and for the first time in forever, I don't know how she's spending it. It presses heavily on my heart. I hurry away from them so they won't see the tears welling up in my eyes.

"Wait!" Libby says.

I turn around. "Yes?"

"Do you want to come with us? We're going over to Snog Point. Maybe we can all have some wine together?"

As I look at everybody, I've never felt like more of an outsider.

"That's okay," I say. "Don't want to crowd you all."

A few days later, I get a note in my mailbox. It's from Master Kent. He wants to meet with me today at three p.m. in his office, during my free period.

As soon as I sit down, I know I'm in trouble.

His office both looks and smells expensive. The walls are a kelly green with rugby photos on the walls. Behind a large oak desk, he sits, wearing a navy blazer. His cheeks are pink, his wavy hair is brown and deeply parted, and I catch my reflection in the unrimmed glasses framing his blue eyes. There's a gold signet ring on the pinkie finger of his left hand.

"Charlotte," he says, his white teeth glinting in the spring sunlight. "How are things?"

"Fine, sir."

"Are they? I've been hearing troubling reports. Professor Dark said you failed your most recent maths exam."

"I did."

"And Professor Carle indicated that you've been having trouble in literature recently."

"I wouldn't call it trouble," I mutter.

"Mistress Wilkinson says you've been late to practice several times."

"Only a minute or two." I wish I could sink into the ground.

"And finally, Mistress McGuire has reported you for sneaking out during bed checks. Arabella Whiteley came to her and has seen you running through the campus grounds late at night on several occasions and has reported you for drinking wine."

I don't say anything.

He rests his chin on his knuckles, looking like Rodin's *The Thinker*.

"What's going on, Charlotte?"

"Nothing, sir."

"I'm not sure I believe you," he says kindly.

"Well, there's not anything. Sir."

"Everybody stumbles on occasion, and I'm aware that the academic environment at Sussex Park is extremely competitive. It can lead to difficulties for even the most gifted student. I've spoken with your teachers, and they all report differences in your behavior. Not only have you repeatedly been late to class, you've been failing exams and have had a sharp decline in participation. You've always been an enthusiastic participant in student life, and your change in behavior has been noticed."

My cheeks feel hot. "And?"

"It's perplexing."

I fold my arms.

"Between your field hockey performance last term and your declining marks this term, you're jeopardizing your chances of getting into a good university."

"I'm having a rough patch."

"If it were just one class, it wouldn't be ideal, but I'd understand. But you're demonstrating a drop in participation and preparedness across the board. You're one of our most promising bright lights, Charlotte."

As we look at each other, I feel like he's trying to burrow inside my soul. I stiffen in defense, narrowing my eyes.

He continues, "With your athletic promise, a scholarship has always been your best chance for a place at a top-tier university. Several of your professors have remarked on your previous desire to attend Exeter or Durham—or maybe even St. Andrews, like your father. I think those are commendable goals, but only achievable if you buckle down." He leans in, placing his hands on the table. "It's almost March and we have only a few months left in the year. I'm going to be quite blunt: if you don't turn things around, and quickly, your chances at getting into a good university are in jeopardy. You must right the ship for the sake of your future. Otherwise, you'll be looking back on this moment fifteen years from now with deep regret."

He waits for me to respond. My chest feels tight and my heart is pounding.

"I'll try to do better, sir."

He leans back in his chair, exhaling sharply. Disappointment is etched into his face.

"I see." He's quiet for several seconds, looking at me over the rims of his glasses. Finally, he says, "We'll have to call home to your parents to keep them abreast of the situation."

I close my eyes.

"I understand it's distressing," he says, "but we must get you back on track."

"Do you have to call my parents?" I ask. "Isn't there another way?"

"You're a shining star, Charlotte. It would be a shame to see you burn out." He dismisses me, and I walk back into the waiting room in a daze.

eighteen

The following day, my mother shows up on campus. I'm shocked to see her—I was expecting a screaming phone call, not her arriving in person. She must have cleared her schedule to come down.

Which means I'm in serious trouble.

"What is the meaning of all this?" she demands once we're settled in the small, heated back garden of a tea shop on the high street. Even though it's freezing, she takes off her woolen coat, as if preparing for battle.

"Mum, it's nothing. They're just blowing things out of proportion. It's really not that big of a deal."

"Master Kent emailed me your transcripts, as well as reports from all your professors. These are going in your permanent file,

Charlotte. Stop downplaying. It's an *enormous* deal."

I look away, taking a sip of my tea. It burns the roof of my mouth, and I make a huge show of it. "Ow! I burned myself!"

My mother ignores me. "I had to reschedule five meetings to come down here. We're in the middle of shipping our autumn inventory. Do you understand what that means?"

"Sorry to ruin your busy day."

"Enough. What's gotten into you? They tell me you've been skipping class left and right, sneaking off campus, playing hockey drunk, screaming at your teachers—my God, the list goes on."

"It was the hockey coach, not a teacher," I say quietly.

"And what's worse, you don't seem to care. Do you understand that this will affect your chances of getting into a good university?"

"Well, at least you have Libby to fall back on. *Her* future is set."

My mother regards me with narrow eyes. "Is this about Libby and Edward?"

"I don't give a shit about Libby and Edward."

"Language!"

"Thank God you have one perfect child. Too bad I'm messing up all your plans for the future."

"Stop it!" Mum says, looking horrified. "Why are you saying that?"

"Because it's true. I heard Dad over Christmas, talking to you and Nana about how much smarter Libby is than me. How you aren't worried for Libby's future but you're worried for mine. I get it—I'm a dummy, and my only shot at a good future is getting into a good university through sport."

Mum scoots her chair so close that I can smell her perfume, the same one she's worn since I was a kid. "You're breaking my heart. Nobody thinks you're a dummy. I'm so proud of you—I always have been. We've *never* needed to worry about you."

"Not till now, right? I've messed up my year, and now it seems I'm messing up my whole life. Did you know that my friends have basically ditched me? I get stabbed in the back, and yet somehow *I'm* the pariah."

Mum looks bothered. "I know I can't make you forgive Libby for what she did to you. But she's your sister, darling. You can't ignore her forever."

"Wouldn't *you*?" I say. "You cut out Aunt Kat. What'd she do that was so much worse?"

Mum looks away. "There are things you don't understand, Charlotte. My relationship with your aunt is complicated."

"So is my relationship with Libby."

Mum sighs. "I wish you would forgive her. It was a regrettable thing and Libby didn't handle it well. I agree with you. But by trying to punish her, you're only hurting yourself."

I fold my arms across my chest. "It is what it is."

"Fine," Mum says, reaching into her handbag and pulling out a sheaf of papers. "That brings us to the other matter at hand. Can you explain these?" They're credit card statements.

I take the stack of papers, my heart pounding as I leaf through them. "Credit card statements?"

"Here," Mum says, taking them back. She runs a manicured finger down a page, stopping on a highlighted line. "Selfridges: two thousand pounds. And another one." Down the page her finger goes, stopping on another item highlighted with yellow marker. "Il Carpaccio: one hundred pounds." She looks stern. "First of all, you know you're not allowed to go into London without asking me and your father."

"Sorry."

"And secondly—two thousand pounds on clothes? One hundred pounds on dinner? This is unacceptable, Charlotte."

"It's not like you don't have the money," I say, feeling sullen.

"That is not the point. Your father and I have tried to instill good values in you, but you're acting as if having a credit card is a right, not a privilege."

I shrug.

"Unfortunately, until you start taking some responsibility for your actions, we're going to have to cancel your credit cards."

I stare at her. "What? But that's not fair! How will I eat?"

"We pay for the school meal plan. You can get everything you need from the dining hall. You'll be just fine."

"But what about coffees? What about going into town?"

Mum looks at me, her expression sour. "What about it? You're going to have to stop until you get your grades up and demonstrate to your father and me that you can handle it."

"You can't do that!"

"We can and we already have. Your cards are cut off."

I stand up, my chair scraping loudly against the cement patio. "Why isn't anybody on my side?"

"Darling, it's not about sides. Your father and I love you, but it's time to start acting like an adult."

"Well, what do I need to do to get the cards back?"

Mum is silent for a second, pondering. "You can get a job this summer."

"A *job*? Like, at a coffee shop?"

"No, like an internship. Summer's nearly here, and I don't want you to spend another two months lying by the pool and shopping, like last year."

"And if I get a job, you'll turn my credit cards back on?"

"We'll see."

Even though it's only March, I swallow my pride and start applying for jobs online immediately: temp positions, the front desk girl at the Spread Eagle in Midhurst, a boat hand on a day cruise off Portsmouth. After a week of trying, however, nobody has bothered to get back to me. It seems there's not a booming job market for seventeen-year-old girls with no quantifiable skills.

I wish I could text Libby. Job hunting is right up her alley: she'd know just what to do. She'd probably even tweak my CV and take me into London to pound the pavement.

But I feel embarrassed. Too much time has passed, and my reaction to her and Edward now feels a little like an overreaction. I don't know how to make things normal again. The joke is: the one person I'd normally ask for advice about the entire situation is Libby herself.

After yet another round of email applications sent into the ether on a Saturday morning, I'm starving. I slide on a pair of wellies, grab an umbrella, and head downstairs to brave the rain on the way to the dining hall.

It's been raining for the better part of the winter, almost nonstop since we've returned from break. Unlike Libby, I can't stand the rain. Normally it would put me even deeper in a funk—however, for some reason, it cheers me up. It's like the weather is on my side by matching my mood.

Inside the dining hall, I'm loading up my plate with food, about to head back to my room—lunches belong to Libby and Edward, of course—when India appears next to me.

"Hey. Come sit with us."

"What about Libby and Edward?"

"They're not coming today. Come sit!" she repeats. They must be off campus—the weekend lunch invitations are getting more and more frequent.

I follow her to the table, where everybody makes a big show of seeming happy to see me.

"Hi, Charlotte!" says Alice.

"Hey!" Flossie says, smiling.

"Lunch together like old times—yay!" says Georgie. She elbows Oliver, who plasters a smile onto his face.

I look at them suspiciously. They're all acting really weird.

Tarquin just grunts at me, stuffing a sandwich into his mouth. At least he's being the same idiot as always.

"So, are you going to come to Donatella this weekend, Charlotte?" asks Flossie.

India looks at her weirdly.

"Oh, I'm invited this time? Thanks."

They seem to shift in their seats. Finally, Georgie speaks. "Sorry about that."

"Can't we all be big boys and girls?" says Flossie. "I'm sick of everybody tiptoeing around the elephant in the room. Libby and Edward are throwing a joint birthday party next month, Charlotte. We just got a text that we're invited."

"You mean, *you're* all invited."

"Well, yeah. Exactly."

"So that's why you're all being weird?"

Georgie looks miserable. "We didn't want you to feel left out. We feel awful about the Donatella thing. You told India you were doing homework that night, and it just kind of . . . happened."

I shrug. "Whatever. I'm getting used to it." I take a bite of my pasta. "So, where is this big shindig? Don't tell me *you're* throwing it for them and not inviting me, Floss."

She shakes her head. "Of course not."

Tarquin pipes up. "They're throwing a big bash at Windsor Castle. It's going to be epic."

Now this is a low blow.

I've been fascinated by Windsor Castle since I was a kid. It was the one place I always fantasized about having a behind-the-scenes tour. And not only am I not invited, but all my friends are going without me—to celebrate Libby and Edward.

I'd almost start crying if the entire thing wasn't so ludicrous. Fun joke, universe. You win.

"Why am I not surprised? Enjoy."

India looks nervous. "You're okay with it?"

"What else can I do but laugh?" I say, my mood dark.

After finishing lunch, we girls walk back to Colvin.

"Ugh," says Flossie.

"What?"

"Nothing." Her eyes dart behind me.

I turn around to see what she's talking about. In the car park across from the student center, a driver is loading Libby's and Edward's bags into the boot of a Mercedes sedan. They're standing hand in hand, and then Edward helps Libby into the car, the driver closing the door behind the two of them.

I've taken to studying in the library. Colvin's unofficial open-door policy means that I feel exposed at all times. When my friends pop in, I've started to feel on edge. I know it's probably not fair, but I've started associating them with all the drama—even India.

On the rare occasions when Libby walks by my door, glancing in and then looking away, it only makes me feel sad.

I have a massive midterm assignment due Monday for my graphic design class, and I'm only halfway done. Instead of buckling down and focusing, however, I can't stop watching YouTube beauty tutorials. My favorite, Kyla Buzz, is an American girl from Texas who talks as slow as molasses and has a dreamy-techno soundtrack playing while she applies her makeup. I heard she gets millions in advertising, so she's started doing travel videos, putting on makeup in cool foreign destinations like the Great Wall of China, on safari in South Africa, and the top of the Eiffel Tower. To be honest, she slightly irritates me, and yet I can't stop watching her videos. They're mesmerizing.

Part of me feels grumpy at times that I didn't hop on the You-Tube tutorials train a few years ago like Libby kept suggesting—I can do makeup *way* better than half these girls—but whatever. That ship has sailed, and now it's too late to make my mark in the space.

"Hey, you."

I look up to see Robert. "Hi!" I say, taking off my headphones.

He leans against my cubicle, gesturing to my computer screen and grinning. "Hard at work?" On screen, Kyla is now applying her mascara on a dragon boat in Hong Kong, with the harbor lights and skyscrapers behind her.

I flush. "I'm super busy, actually. Just taking a homework break."

He smiles. "I'm only teasing. You should see how much time I waste when I have an English paper due. Suddenly, I find myself on Wikipedia *needing* to know what's the national dish of Jamaica, or why Bonnie Prince Charlie's rebellion failed."

"I can answer that one!" I say, clicking out of YouTube. My graphic design project is now the only thing left on the screen.

"That's right—I forgot you were a history buff." He looks back at my computer. "Wireframes?"

"Yeah, I'm taking a graphic design course. Last term was learning how to code, and this term is all about apps and mobile design."

"A whiz at history, a pro at coding—is there anything you can't do?" he says, looking impressed. "I wish I knew how to code, but I hate maths."

I sit up a little straighter, feeling proud. "I mean, it *is* difficult, but you'd be surprised—there isn't a lot of maths in coding."

"No?"

"It's more like being diligent. It's a lot of checking your work. I shouldn't like it, but I do. It's cool when you're done and you've actually created something."

He pulls a chair out, sitting down next to me. "So what's this? You made it?"

"Yeah," I say, clicking around the screen to show him details. "It's kind of like Instagram, but for beauty."

"That sounds like a million-pound idea."

"Ha! I wish."

"Tell me more."

I pull out my phone, showing him Viewty. "Well, I'm obsessed with this app, which kind of does the same thing. Girls upload their makeup photos, hair photos, stuff like that. But the search functionality is terrible."

"It's hard to search?"

"Yeah. And they need more categories—they just have like hair and makeup and skincare, but it should go by brand and by style inspiration, too. Sometimes I want to do a mod sixties look. Sometimes I want to see cool steampunk nail art. There are *so* many good beauty looks people have uploaded on here, but it's impossible to find them. You have to spend like *minutes* scrolling and scrolling and scrolling."

"Interesting."

"And this one," I say, opening a home-decorating app. "I love it for DIY bedroom inspiration, but I have to scroll through all the boring stuff for old people's sitting rooms and back gardens—stuff I don't care about. I want to see bedrooms girls *my* age have done."

His eyes light up. "Okay. Tell me more."

"I want an app that's like a cross between these two—like a DIY Instagram. So not just people uploading their crafts, but also their beauty tutorials, their style hacks, stuff they've made for their bedrooms. And I think just for teenage girls. I don't care about a lot of the home improvement stuff I see on there, or the furniture renovation stuff, and I *seriously* don't care about nursery decorations and baby showers and wedding decor, which is like all over Pinterest. I just want stuff for beauty and fashion and maybe my bedroom. I think a lot of other girls would, too."

"So that's what this is?"

"Well, no, not exactly. That's what I *want* to do, but that's a ton of work. I'd need to be coding for years before I could do that—if ever. So I'm just trying to do a baby version of it for my midterm project."

"But if you could really do it, you think there would be a market for it?"

"Oh, yeah, definitely. Those apps are huge."

"May I?" He takes my phone back, scrolling through the app and looking interested. "I see what you mean about these other apps. The UI isn't very clean, either."

"What's UI?"

"User interface. It's like how the app looks and works—as opposed to UX, which is all about the user experience."

"How do *you* know all that? Oh, right—your brother." An idea

275

pops into my head. "Do you think he'd be interested in checking out a mock-up?"

"Of your app idea?" Robert looks down at the phone, scrolling through each app for a few more seconds. He looks back up at me. "Yeah—could you put one together?"

"Of course. I could do some sketches of what the home screen would look like, the feed, the user profiles, all that stuff."

"That would be great."

"And I'll do a few paragraphs about the idea, too. Like the names of the other apps that are kind of similar, but why I don't like them."

He grins. "You never know. Doesn't hurt to try, right?"

"Exactly. There's always room for competition—look at Facebook after MySpace, or Lyft after Uber. You don't have to be the first. You just have to be the best."

"I'll take fifteen percent as your agent, please," he jokes.

Libby's been pushing me to do this for ages. Even though we're not speaking right now, I still feel her presence. She'd be proud.

My stomach flutters. I haven't been so excited about something in forever.

I blow off studying for my exams and spend all weekend sketching out concepts instead. Late Sunday night, I've finally finished putting together my idea: a comprehensive DIY lifestyle app for teens. A few hours of internet research in the library helps me find templates for business plans, so I even write up a five-page document explaining the basics: the concept, who'd use it, similar apps, and a few sentences on how I might make money off it down the road. I found an article in *Inc.* magazine about my favorite existing DIY app, and they mentioned that they make money by forming partnerships with brands and using affiliate links. I don't know if that would work for me, but I put it in the plan just in case, adding the idea of letting people sell their crafts through the site, like Etsy.

I email the proposal to Robert on Monday morning, who passes it to his brother, Bill. In between the madness of exams, we exchange a few back-and-forth emails that week. It certainly seems like Bill is interested, but I'm not exactly holding my breath, either.

I mean, I'm a seventeen-year-old girl. Is some investor I've never met *really* going to fund my app? Dream on.

nineteen

ROBERT: FREEDOM!!!

ME: I know—I'm SO relieved midterms are finally over. How'd you do?

ROBERT: Okay, I think. U?

ME: Decent. I hope.

ROBERT: So, listen, crazy news. Are you free tomorrow?

ME: Yeah, why? Was planning to veg—first Saturday without homework in forever.

ROBERT: Wanna go to Paris?

ME: WHAT?!?!

ROBERT: My brother wants to meet you.

ME: OMG, seriously?

ROBERT: Super serious.

ME: YES!!!

ME: Paris in the springtime!!!

ME: Shit. I don't have any money. My parents cut off my credit cards

ROBERT: He'll fly you out. The flight is like twenty quid

ROBERT: It'll be in and out, just there for the day

ME: I don't care if I'm only there for an hour. Paris!!! Aaah!!

Saturday morning, Robert arranges for a car to pick us up and take us to Gatwick Airport. We land in Paris after a quick hour-long flight, where another car is waiting at Charles de Gaulle for us. I press my nose against the glass as we make our way into the city, craning my neck for glimpses of the Eiffel Tower and Sacré-Coeur in the distance.

"You're acting like you've never seen buildings before," Robert says, smiling at me as our car makes its way up through the southern end of the city into Paris. The wide boulevards are lined with buildings that look like cream-colored Lego blocks. Everything is uniform, elegant, picture perfect.

"Never *these* buildings. It's my first time in Paris." A few of my friends took a weekend trip to Paris with their parents when I was younger, but we just never had the money. And after Mum hit it big, we started taking yearly beach vacations to exotic, faraway places like the Maldives. Paris is in our European backyard, and yet I've still never been—like people who have lived in London their whole lives and never been inside Westminster Abbey.

I take in the tree-lined streets, the packs of teenage boys with skinny jeans and messy hair, the bicycles and mopeds whizzing by. Something about this place makes me feel at home.

"You didn't tell me it was your first time!"

"You didn't ask," I say, smiling at him.

We make our way farther into the heart of Paris, the Eiffel Tower so close I feel like I could reach out and touch it, finally pulling up to the George V, a grand hotel just off the Champs-Élysées. "My brother's Paris office is just around the corner, so he has all his meetings here," Robert says.

We walk into the lobby, where a floral arrangement as tall as I am is majestically displayed on a marble coffee table in the center of the room.

"*Le bar, s'il vous plaît,*" Robert says

"You didn't tell me you spoke French!" I say.

He grins. "*You* didn't ask."

The bar is charming, with soft yellow up-lighting and a total Moulin Rouge vibe. The tables have black marble tops, and the chairs are wood-paneled with maroon upholstery. His brother sits at one of the corner tables. He's younger and more normal-looking than I expected—dressed more like a university kid than a businessman, in a hoodie and jeans. He stands when Robert walks over, throwing his arms around him and engulfing Robert in a big hug.

"You look like shit!" he says. They have the same northern accent.

"You smell like poo," Robert replies.

Brothers are weird.

"Bill, this is Charlotte Weston," Robert says, introducing me.

Bill and I shake hands; he pumps my hand vigorously up and down. "Great to finally meet you! I loved your proposal—it's a great idea! The DIY market is incredibly hot, and of course beauty—well, that's a multibillion-pound operation. I think there's a market for this. It's just a matter of getting the word out! I have some thoughts."

Unlike Robert, who's a great listener, Bill loves to hear himself talk. I barely say a word during the hour-long meeting, but it doesn't seem to matter—Bill clearly has it down to a science, and I've already answered a lot of his questions in our back-and-forth email exchanges. By the time Bill dismisses himself, downing a double espresso, smothering us both in hugs, and then literally running out of the room to his next meeting, we have a deal. Bill's going to fund the app and set me up with his designer and developers. In exchange, he'll help me create a company and will get 50 percent of it. I'll be sole founder. My parents will have to review the paperwork, but I'm sure they'll be thrilled.

During the meeting, I try to keep it together and seem professional. But once Bill leaves, I lose it. "Holy crap!" I say. "Is this real?"

Robert high-fives me. "I told you he moves fast. When he sees something he wants, he pounces. But you sure you're okay with fifty percent?"

"Definitely. He's putting up all the money. And I don't know the first thing about apps. This is what he does."

"That's not true. You put the business plan together. You did the sketches, you know the DIY marketplace, you explained the competition to him. You're selling yourself short."

"Thank you," I say. "But it seems like a fair deal. Fifty would be too much if I were a *real* company, but he's only investing in an idea. It doesn't cost me anything but time. He might lose money. And I'm just a seventeen-year-old kid. He's like an actual businessman."

Robert looks impressed. "You *have* done your homework. Okay, then, we need to celebrate. Oh, *pardon*," he says, flagging down a waiter. "*Deux verres de champagne, s'il vous plaît. Perrier Jouet rosé.*"

"I hope you just ordered something super expensive," I say, joking.

"To you and your new app. What are you going to call it, anyway? You never said."

"I was thinking about Selfsy," I say shyly. "Like do it yourself, plus selfie, plus Etsy? What do you think?"

"It's perfect. To Selfsy." He grins at me as we clink glasses.

It feels so good to have somebody say they believe in me again. It makes me feel like a whole new world of possibilities is unfolding before me—and now it's just up to me to grab them. It's a great reminder that you can't control what happens to you—but you *can* control how you react to it.

And I'm done feeling sorry for myself—it's time to take charge of my life.

"Okay, down your champagne," I say to him. "We have four hours before our flight home and I am *dying* to see the Eiffel Tower. Let's go."

A few weeks later, just before Libby's birthday, India texts me after lunch. I'm walking through campus, leaving my graphic design class and heading back toward Colvin. Even though I've already submitted my graphic design project to high marks, I'm obviously still devoted to the app it spawned. Bill and I have daily phone calls or Skype sessions, moving forward at breakneck speed. He wants to release the app by June, to take advantage of the beginning of summer and people making a fresh start.

INDIA: Have you seen the Sun??

ME: No, why?

INDIA: Read this.

The headline of the link she sends me reads: "The Girl Dating Eds." I dust some dirt and rainwater off a bench on the quad, sitting down as I begin to scroll:

> She turns nineteen this weekend, a public schoolgirl who loves tennis, photography, and reading, and doesn't know how to ride horses. He turns eighteen soon, a public schoolboy who enjoys skiing, water polo, and rugby, and is never happier than when on a polo pony.

The article includes paparazzi photos of Libby and Edward, and describes Libby as "beautiful but also extremely introverted. Unlike the flashier girls in Edward's set, Libby has her feet solidly on the ground."

> The *Sun* can exclusively report that before Edward dated Libby, he did briefly date one of those flashier girls—Libby's little sister, Charlotte! A source on campus tells us that Edward and Charlotte were "never a real relationship," and that it was merely "a few drunken snogs, sitting together in the dining hall, stuff like that." By contrast, says the source, "He and Libby are the real deal."

Watch this space. Rumors around campus are swirling that pretty Libby Weston has captured Prince Edward's heart for good. Could this be your future queen, Britain?

ME: Are you in your room?

INDIA: Yeah.

ME: Be right there

Inside India's room, we sit on the bed, talking about the article. "How did they *get* this information?" I ask.

India looks around, as if the campus might be crawling with spies. "Somebody talked, of course."

I reread the article, my eyes catching on the line about me. "And what the hell does this mean? 'A few drunken snogs'? Piss off." I feel grumpy.

"What would you have rather it said? 'Edward dated Libby's sister, Charlotte, first. Theirs was a torrid romance—one for the ages—which ended in tears and heartbreak when our fearless heroine Charlotte brutally dumped Prince Edward and nearly ruined him for all other women. It was only in the sloppy-seconds embrace of the lesser Weston sister that Edward's broken heart was mended.'" She raises an eyebrow. "Something like that?"

"*Exactly.* Thank you for translating."

India smiles, shaking her head at me. As she scrolls through the article again, her face turns serious. "It's bad news for them."

"Who, Libby and Edward? Why?"

"Now that it's public, all bets are off."

I don't know much about the press, but I do know that they

love nothing more than royal gossip. Libby's fair game now. Maybe I am, too. I'm silent for a few moments, weighing the information. "I should reach out to her."

"Are you ready to?"

These past three months must have been as awful for Libby as they've been for me. I think back to my mother's prophetic warning to me that, by punishing Libby, I'd only be punishing myself. I think of Mum's confusing, mysterious estrangement from her own sister. I think of all the wasted conversations and missed giggles between Libby and me. I think of these glamorous new friendships I coveted for so long—none of which will ever measure up to my sister's.

Enough is enough.

"Yes," I say, nodding. "I should have done it a long time ago."

I go back to my room, pulling the E.T. stuffed alien out of the closet, along with my DIY supplies, some red fabric, and a little sewing kit. I measure the alien and the red fabric and then cut into the cloth, slowly and methodically turning it into something that resembles a jacket.

It takes me three hours, working all the way through dinner. I munch on some crackers in my drawer to sustain me.

Finally, I step back, admiring my handiwork.

The E.T. is now clothed in a little red hoodie, with a tiny white heart emblazoned on its chest.

I spend another twenty minutes trying to figure out what to write on a notecard. Eventually, I decide simple and direct is best:

I'm sorry, too. Sisters forever.

I rummage through my supplies until I find some balloons and decorative paper straws, blowing up the balloon until it's the size of an egg, tying it and cutting off the tip, before stuffing it in the end of the straw and taping it for security. I attach the mini balloon to E.T.'s arm with some twine, taking the stuffed alien, notecard, and balloon upstairs and knocking on her door. Nobody's there, so I leave them leaning against the door frame.

Not long after, I get a text.

LIBBY: Hi, you. How's it going?

ME: Hi . . . things are okay. How are you?

LIBBY: Same. Just okay.

LIBBY: Thank you for the card. It was adorable.

ME: ♥

LIBBY: I'm not on campus right now, so I still haven't seen it in person, but India found it and sent me a photo. It's in her room for safekeeping.

ME: Ah, cool

ME: So . . . I miss you

LIBBY: I miss you, too!

ME: ♥

ME: Can we meet up when you're back? You're at Windsor for your birthday, right?

LIBBY: Yes! I wanted to invite you, but I thought you'd say no. Please come.

ME: ARE YOU KIDDING ME? YES.

I look up from my phone, goose bumps running down my arms. Finally. I'm going inside Windsor Castle.

twenty

The long, narrow driveway to Windsor Castle stretches on seemingly for miles. As our caravan of cars inches through the manicured forest toward the hulking medieval fortress, the lights flickering in the distance slowly blaze brighter and brighter. Edward must have invited hundreds of people tonight, because the traffic jam is immense—each and every car needs to go through security to confirm they're all on the list.

Everybody decided to rent a fleet of chauffeured cars—taking trains the forty-five minutes from Sussex Park to Windsor in our evening gowns wasn't an option. My stomach clenched when I learned the cost per person—how would I come up with that kind of money?—but India sensed my hesitation. Before I even had time to say anything, she quietly let me know she'd cover my portion.

Now India and I are sitting in the back of a chauffeured black car, dressed in evening gowns. My gown is a slinky, floor-length gold number, with a cut-out back and chiffon sleeves. I didn't have the money to buy a new dress so I had to borrow it off India, who had her mother's personal assistant send her dresses from home. Apparently, India has an entire closet full of glittering gowns back at Huntshire. (You know, as you do.)

Alice and Flossie, Georgie and Oliver, and David and Tarquin are in three cars behind us, our group making a caravan trip all the way from campus for the occasion.

Tonight should be huge. Not only am I finally getting to see behind the scenes of Windsor Castle, I'm reconciling with Libby, too.

The long driveway is thronged with cars, so it takes forever before we arrive at the entry checkpoint. There's a small gate on the right with two guards standing watch, and directly opposite, a crowd of photographers. When our car stops at the gate, our driver turns down the radio and gives our names to a skinny man with a clipboard. The photographers go crazy.

"Bloody hell," I say, wincing and squinting as the flashbulbs pop. "They're going to blind us!"

"Don't look at them," says India, her face stony. "Just ignore them so they can't get a good shot through the windows."

The guard consults a list and then opens the gates, waving us through and safely beyond the reach of the paparazzi. Once we're past the gates, we're inside the inner quadrangle of the royal palace, where the Queen's private apartments are. I know because my family and I did the public castle tour a few times in my childhood, but we were ants scuttling around, not personal guests of the future king. Looking up at the stone archways and turrets, I feel the thousands of years of history pressing down on me. It's like a dream. It doesn't feel real.

Our car skirts a circular green lawn inside the courtyard, coming to stop by an archway leading to the back entrance. I smooth down my dress, looking around anxiously as a footman opens the door for us.

"Are you all right?" India asks. Not for the first time, I think how lucky I am to have her as a friend.

"I think I'm going to vomit."

She pats me on the arm. "You'll be fine."

"I hope so."

"But if you must be sick, don't you dare vomit on my dress." She's wearing a strapless crushed-velvet black dress that's cinched at the waist.

"Oh, gee, thanks."

We wait in front of the stone courtyard for all our friends to pile out of their cars.

Georgie and Oliver step out of their vehicle, Oliver exiting first and offering his hand to Georgie to help her out smoothly. He looks especially handsome, his increasingly long hair slicked back and combed to the side, setting off his thick eyebrows and dark blue eyes. Georgie is wearing a slinky sequined dusty-rose gown that she got from an online couture rental website. She threads her arm through his and looks up at the castle, her face shining like a child's on Christmas.

"I'm dying," Georgie says. "*Dying*. I can't believe we're here. Think I can get a selfie with the Queen?"

Flossie and Alice exit their car in time to roll their eyes at Georgie's question. Flossie wears a long black lace dress with a boat-cut neckline and sheer lace sleeves all the way to her wrists. Meanwhile, Alice's canary-yellow satin dress, chignon, and fire-engine-red lipstick make her look like a dead ringer for Emma Stone.

We only have to wait for the rest of the boys now; Tarquin steps out of his car and dusts off his tuxedo. It pains me to entertain the thought, but he looks fantastic—as if he were born to wear white tie. David exits, looking ill at ease, like he's wearing his father's suit.

The eight of us stand in the courtyard in a circle.

"I'm shitting myself," says Georgie.

"That makes two of us," I say.

"Be strong and courageous, soldiers," says India. "Onward."

We pass through a courtyard, our heels clicking on the cobblestones. Butlers in white tie flank each side of the entrance, nodding gravely at us as we enter. "Welcome to Windsor Castle."

"The greeting committee is out in full force," I whisper as we step inside the vestibule.

"Do you think they do that for all the parties?" Georgie whispers back. "I bet this is special because of Edward."

"You know we don't have to whisper," Flossie says loudly from behind. "We're not sneaking in. They *have* actually invited us."

We walk up a grand staircase, laid with bloodred carpet and flanked by two giant statues of knights in armor riding horses. At the top of the steps, there's a marble statue of Queen Victoria. We turn a corner, passing through a wide hallway and another series of grand rooms—I vaguely remember these as the State Apartments—and suddenly we're in the most magnificent room I've ever seen.

"Je-*sus*," says Georgie, whistling.

"St. George's Hall," says Flossie approvingly.

St. George's Hall is spectacular: a long, rectangular room, easily wide enough to house a jumbo jet. It's laid with a red carpet that runs the entire length of the hall. On one side of the room, there are gigantic portraits of monarchs in stately robes, and every few feet, a marble bust sits on an intricately carved base. The wood-beamed ceiling is dotted with crests in reds and blues and greens and blacks. The walls are up-lit in a soft peach, suffusing the entire room with an otherworldly glow.

"Just so you know," Georgie says to me, "your skin looks amazing."

"Even the beauty lighting is better for royals," I joke.

My eyes do a quick sweep of the grand hall, trying to take it all in. Everybody is dressed to kill, with the women in glittering ball gowns and the men in bespoke tuxedos. There's the prime minister in the middle of the room, holding court and sipping a martini. I spot the queen of the Netherlands talking to the crown princess of Denmark. Prince Michael and Princess Verena, Edward's aunt and uncle, look gorgeous as always, laughing with a group of admirers surrounding them. And is that . . . ?

"*Stop. Everything*," says Georgie. "David and Victoria. Three o'clock."

Sure enough, David and Victoria Beckham are in the corner of the room, their heads together in conversation.

God, I wish I could Snapchat this. Instead, I pull out my phone to take a photo of the room, texting it to Robert.

ME: I've died and gone to heaven

ME: P.S. Windsor Castle smells like money and blind ambition

Almost immediately, the ellipses go as he texts back.

ROBERT: Steal a painting and let's pawn it on the black market. One of the Stuarts. Nobody cares about them.

I giggle at his response, putting my phone away. I'll text him more later. Suddenly, the crowd in front of us parts and there stand the guests of honor, Edward and Libby, ready to greet the arriving guests.

When I see Libby, I'm stunned into silence.

Gone is the dowdy sister I grew up with. In her place is a glamorous, perfectly groomed bombshell.

Libby's hair is straight, long, and glossy, cascading over her shoulders in fetching sheets. Her smoky eyes are expertly rimmed with kohl. Her lips look fuller, glossed to a pink shine, and when she talks and smiles, her teeth are a dazzling shade of Hollywood white that could only have been achieved artificially. I peer at her skin: Is Libby wearing *foundation*?

I don't know what's more stunning: her hair and makeup or her dress. It's a teal chiffon gown with a plunging neckline, bejeweled ribbon belt, and lace cap sleeves. She looks almost as tall as Edward—she must be wearing heels. This fact alone nearly sends me into shock.

I take in the waxed brows, the manicured nails, the Oscars-red-carpet-worthy outfit, and the high heels, and my head spins. I can't believe the towering girl standing in front of me is the same shy, nerdy sister I've known my entire life.

But what really amazes me is her poise. Libby holds court as if she's to the manor born. Her shoulders are down, her back is straight, her smile genuine as she greets a parade of guests.

When I've seen her around campus the past few months, she's looked like normal old Libby. Tonight is different—it's not just her appearance, but her demeanor. She appears literally transformed.

She looks every inch a princess.

As we enter the room, the people ahead of us approach Edward to pay their birthday respects. India, Georgie, and the rest of us follow the crowd, making our way toward the couple one step at a time.

Georgie grabs my arm in a panic. "We're not supposed to curtsy to him, are we?"

"No. Crap. I don't know." I turn to India. "Do we need to curtsy?"

Flossie stifles a giggle.

"Not if you don't want to, no," says India.

"But by all means, curtsy away," says Flossie. "I beg you."

When India and Flossie go up to Edward and Libby, they hug them each in turn. Thank God I wasn't first. How humiliating would it have been if I'd curtsied after all?

Finally, it's my turn to greet them.

"Happy birthday, Edward," I say. We lean in for a stiff hug, giving each other a quick pat on the back like we're rugby teammates.

"Hi, Charlotte. Thank you for coming."

"Charlotte!" Libby says. "You made it!"

"Hey, Libs. Thanks for the invite."

We stare at each other awkwardly.

"Oh, come here," she says, giggling.

We collapse into each other's arms, hugging tightly in the middle of the room for several long seconds.

I pull back but she grabs my hands, clinging to me.

"You look amazing," I say.

"*You* look amazing."

"I love that color on you."

"Your dress is gorgeous!"

"Did you do your makeup yourself?"

"I did!" She beams. "I've learned a few tricks."

"Your hair . . ." I reach out, running my fingers through it. It's shiny and silky.

"A gloss treatment, a Japanese treatment, and an arsenal of styling products." She touches it self-consciously. "I had it professionally blown out earlier today in Windsor. There's no way I could have done this myself."

"We have *so* much to catch up on," I say.

Edward clears his throat. The two of us look at him, startled.

"Thank you so much for coming, Charlotte," Edward repeats, sounding shy. He gives me a little smile. "I'm sorry to be rude, but we need to keep the line going. Otherwise my PA, Helen, will have my head." I wonder if that's the old woman with the owl eyes standing off to the side, shooting us dirty looks. "Can we catch up later by the drinks?"

"Sure, no problem. And, um, again, happy birthday to you."

"Thank you. I appreciate that." He smiles at me again, and then turns to the right of me, slipping back into HRH mode. "Davina! Hello!"

"I should probably . . . ," Libby says, gesturing toward the long line of people behind us waiting to greet Edward.

"Oh. Okay. Yeah. Cool. I'll just be over there."

I walk back toward my friends, Libby's polite laughs echoing behind me as she strikes up a new conversation with one of Edward's guests.

Flossie hands me a glass of champagne. "Here. You look like you need this."

"Yeah, that was intense. Thanks, Floss."

"What did he say to you?" asks Alice. She suddenly seems several inches shorter. I look down to see that she's in bare feet.

"Alice! Where are your shoes?"

"Eh." She swats her hand through the air as if batting away an insect. "I can't stand heels."

"She kicked them off underneath a table," says David, jerking his thumb toward a white tablecloth nestled into an alcove against the wall. He looks jealous, like he wishes he could do the same with his monkey suit.

"But what did he *say*?" repeats Alice.

"Not much. We just said hi to each other, and he said thanks for coming."

"So everything's back to normal?" asks Flossie.

"It seems so. Normal-ish. At least we're on speaking terms again."

Flossie nods. "At least."

"And Libby?" Alice asks. "You're all good?"

"We're all good."

"Oh, Cousin Mary is here!" says Flossie, spying the Danish crown princess. "I haven't seen her in months." She walks over to the princess, who looks excited to see Flossie and embraces her warmly.

"*Cousin Mary*," mutters Georgie while looking at me, her eyes comically wide. "We're not in Kansas anymore."

"Don't you see famous people all the time with your dad?"

"Are you kidding me? He won't let me *near* a red carpet. He thinks Hollywood is corrosive—that's why he shipped me off to boarding school. The only celebrity I know is Alan Alda."

"Who?"

"Exactly."

"Plus your mum," I point out.

"Ha! Yeah, like she counts."

"She's famous! She totally counts!"

Georgie shrugs. "It's not like she's Meryl Streep. But *this*," she says, waving her arm around to indicate the room, "now *this* is real glamour."

India joins us, linking her arm through mine. "Come with me." As she propels me down the red carpet toward the far side of the room, we pass David and Victoria Beckham standing underneath a portrait of George I. They look as out of place as the rest of us.

"So," she says. "You. Edward. Libby. That wasn't so bad, was it?"

"No," I say. "Definitely a little awkward. But mostly fine."

"I'll admit it. I'm surprised," she says.

"By what?"

"Greeting guests with Libby by his side: talk about a bold

statement. His parents won't be chuffed about that."

"They don't like Libby?"

India shrugs. "That I don't know. But I do know his family is big on tradition. Having your new girlfriend standing by your side for a receiving line . . . that is *not* tradition."

Flossie comes up behind us. "Are you talking about Libby?"

"Obviously," I say. We all look back toward my sister, who is now shaking hands with an old guy I'm pretty sure is the Duke of Wellington. Behind her, one of her former classmates from Greene House waits to greet her.

Flossie shakes her head. "I can't even *explain* how absolutely bizarre that is."

"Speaking of bizarre," I say, "what the hell is Alice doing?"

We all look over at Alice, who is flirting with a waiter who seems desperate to ignore her.

The three of us are still laughing when Flossie lets out a sharp gasp. "They're here."

"Who's here?" I ask, turning around and looking behind us.

India stands up a little straighter. "The King and Queen."

My eyes widen. Edward's parents enter the room from the far end, several guards holding open the doors to escort them from their private apartments. I'd always imagined them entering every room to the strains of "God Save the King," but the musicians in the corner continue softly playing classical music, switching to a song I don't know. The Queen is resplendent in a floor-length silver beaded gown with a blue sash draped over her shoulders. She's dripping in jewels, wearing a diamond-and-sapphire tiara and a matching diamond-and-sapphire necklace. Golf ball–sized sapphire earrings hang from her long earlobes, so enormous that they're visible all the way across the room. The King wears a black tuxedo and white tie, also with a blue sash slung across his shoulders. He has a slew of multicolored medals pinned in a row above his heart, with a cross-shaped medal hanging from his neck under the tie.

I look around to see if everybody is as enthralled as I am. In the center of the room, Edward's aunt and uncle formally greet the King and Queen, bowing and curtsying as if they're visiting dignitaries and not their brother- and sister-in-law.

"Prince Michael and Princess Verena are here, too," I say, pointing at them.

"Oh, I've met them loads of times," Flossie says, looking unimpressed.

We watch as the King and Queen approach Edward, who gives them both a quick bow before the King claps him on the back and hugs him.

I'm watching warily, waiting to see if Edward will introduce Libby to his parents.

"There's no way," says Flossie, as if reading my mind. "It's just not done."

But we all gasp as Edward turns to Libby, taking her by the hand and leading her a few inches closer to the King and Queen. We're too far away to hear their conversation, but every eye in the room is trained on them as Libby makes two deep curtsies in rapid succession. The Queen nods, the slightest hint of a smile turning up the corners of her mouth. Libby looks enchanted, her face lighting up.

My sister has just been introduced to the King and Queen as their son's girlfriend.

I realize that Flossie's thin fingers are clasping my own hand, her beautiful face registering shock. "I've never seen anything like it," she murmurs, her hand still glued to mine. Her mouth is slightly agape. "Blimey. It's absolutely unprecedented."

"So what does it mean?"

India answers, looking strangely impressed. "It means Edward has just thrown hundreds of years of tradition out the window."

"So Libby's special."

India looks at me, eyes wide. She nods. "Libby is *very* special."

I feel proud of my sister—she's clearly being treated with respect, and she's breaking down barriers in a family not exactly known for change. I'm so impressed by her.

And when I realize that I'm not jealous anymore, not even a little bit, it feels like a huge weight has lifted off my shoulders.

A waiter glides by with a tray of champagne and Flossie grabs two glasses, thrusting one into India's hand and then motioning for another for me.

"Cheers," Flossie says, clinking her glass against ours. "To Libby. It's quite a coup."

After an hour of drinking, dancing, and stuffing our faces with canapés, Edward materializes at the far end of the room, making a speech to thank everybody for coming. He's been working the room all night, with Libby never more than a couple of feet away from him.

"I especially want to thank my parents for hosting this party. Thank you, Mum and Dad, for allowing us to throw this very quiet shindig here." Everybody laughs and raises their glasses to the King and the Queen, who smile and incline their heads in acknowledgment.

"I'd also like to thank my girlfriend, Libby," Edward continues. "Her own birthday is in two days, so it was gracious of her to let me steal her spotlight—as usual. I'm a lucky guy to be celebrating with her by my side."

Everybody in the room raises their glasses again.

"You okay with all this?" Flossie asks me.

"I'm good. I'm great."

"I think it's wild," Alice says. "Who could have predicted *this* when Libby transferred here?"

"I predicted it," Tarquin pipes up. "I told you all Libby was smoking."

"So you've got eyes," Flossie says. "Congratu-bloody-lations."

"Do you think the castle is haunted?" Alice asks, staring at the ceiling.

We're all studying a painting near the State Apartments—a scowling monarch in a curly black wig and knee breeches—when I hear Libby's quiet voice behind me. "Charlotte."

I turn and she reaches out, squeezing my hand.

"I'm *beyond* pleased you made it," she says.

I open my mouth to speak, but am interrupted by a tall girl with protruding eyes and long dirty-blond hair who's suddenly appeared to chat. Libby makes small talk with her for a few moments. I'm impressed with her calm demeanor. The skittish, nervous edges seem to have been smoothed and polished away. This more mature, less self-conscious version of my sister is going to take some getting used to.

As she dismisses the blond girl, she turns back to me.

"Sorry. Guys, do you mind if I steal my sister away for a minute?"

"Go for it," India says.

"Not at all! By all means!" says Georgie, flourishing her arms to make a path for us.

Libby grabs me by the hand and leads me down the hall and around the corner.

"There's a room over here."

"I think Georgie was prepared to curtsy to you back there," I giggle. "Should I start calling you Your Highness *now*, or . . . ?"

"Oh, stop."

We enter into a huge drawing room with a majestic chandelier hanging from the gilded ceiling. The room is decorated in shades of red and gold, all the sofas and chairs in the same crimson that decorates St. George's Hall, and the heavy red curtains featuring gold tassels and trim. The lamps are off, the only light visible through the windows from the courtyard below.

Libby walks over to a wood-and-gold table, turning on a small lamp. "Edward brought me here earlier," she says by way of explanation.

"Okay." I look around warily, expecting guards to burst into the room and haul us off to the dungeons. Clearly I've watched too much TV. "Did you guys stay at the castle last night?"

"Yes! How weird is that? He has a set of apartments, just off his parents' private quarters. The rooms are beautiful, but really musty. It feels like being in an old hotel that hasn't been renovated."

"That's. So. Weird."

"Tell me about it," she says. "There's so much to catch up on. I've missed you so much."

"Oh. Have you?"

"*Yes!* Are you serious?"

"I don't know," I say, shrugging. "It seems like things have been going pretty well. I'm not surprised you and I haven't spoken, what with your smart new life."

She looks hurt. "I know I deserve that."

I pick up a small golden box on the table, pretending to study it while I wait for her to continue. Of course I'm finally going to forgive her—but I want to make her work for it.

"I know I've apologized over and over again, but I'll keep doing it until you forgive me. I was a jerk. I was insensitive and I didn't handle things at all well."

"Mmm," I say.

"I didn't want you to think I was *trying* to steal Edward. I really wasn't, Charlotte—I didn't set out to get with him. I hope you know that by now."

"Mmm," I say again. "Yes. I think so." I pause, hoping she'll keep apologizing.

"I completely went against all my principles and I put my relationship with Edward before my relationship with you. I can't apologize enough. You're blood. You should come first, and I'm so sorry."

"Thank you," I say, feeling relief. "That means a lot."

"The past three months have been bizarre. I'm so happy with Edward. It's nice to be with somebody who *gets* me. But I've been missing you desperately. So much has happened and it's killed me I couldn't share it with you. I've been racked with guilt."

"I feel a little guilty, too," I say.

"*You* feel guilty? Why?"

"You know how Mum and Aunt Kat haven't spoken in years?"

Libby nods.

"I keep thinking about them. I don't want that to be us."

"Me, neither."

"Mum refuses to tell me what happened, but I feel like—it takes two to tango, you know? You know Mum. Even if Aunt Kat was awful to her, it's never one-sided. And I was kind of a brat at times."

"I wish I could go back in time and do it differently," Libby says. "I knew I might be starting to have feelings for Edward, but I didn't want to hurt you. I pushed them away, and then it all blew up in my face when we kissed and you got ten times as hurt."

"It *did* hurt," I say. "I know that's silly, since he and I only dated for a couple of months, and we barely ever saw each other. But"—I shrug—"it made me feel silly. I felt like a fool."

She nods as if telling me to go on.

"And then it was awful. Everybody was like, 'Buck up! Get over it!' like nothing had ever happened, but I'm not a *robot*. It felt like I was being pushed out of the group to make room for *your* relationship with Edward. It was lonely. It sucked."

Libby takes my hands in hers. "I am so, so sorry, Charlotte. For everything."

I nod. "Thank you."

"Now can I be honest?"

303

"Sure."

"I know it's not fair"—she pauses—"but my feelings were hurt, too. I kept reaching out to you, and you kept shooting me down."

"Is it weird that you saying that makes me feel better?"

"Yes." She laughs.

"Well, I'm sorry, too. I punished you for too long. As usual, I took things too far."

"Don't say that! You felt betrayed. Your reaction makes sense."

"Well, it's water under the bridge now. I'm over it."

"Are you sure?" she asks.

"Moving on. I'm already bored by this conversation. Catch me up to speed on you. I want to hear *everything*."

"Well," she says, "things are going great. I've narrowed my university choices down—I'm leaning toward Edinburgh. I have the summer to decide, but my application is due in September."

"Wait, Edinburgh? You've always talked about St. Andrews, like Dad."

"I know." She looks embarrassed. "But Edinburgh has an amazing history-of-art program."

"Edward's going there, isn't he?" I say, realization dawning.

She blushes. "Yes."

"And he wants you to come."

She nods. "That's not all."

"What else?"

She pauses. Her face has turned scarlet. "We, um. We're . . . we've . . ."

"Oh my God, Libby, just say it already!" I laugh.

"We've slept together."

"Eiii!" I squeal, grabbing her hands. "How was it? I can't believe it. Where were you? When did it happen? How did it happen? Tell me *everything*!"

She laughs, squeezing my hands. "To answer your questions: nerve-racking but amazing, although Helen *almost* walked in on us. At Kensington Palace last month after dinner. And I told him I'd never wanted anything more."

I'm beside myself with excitement. "I can't believe it. I mean, I can believe it, but . . . wow. This means you've had sex before me!"

"Well, it's not a race," she says, smiling.

"Okay, so: hot sex life with a gorgeous prince. Check. How's everything else going with him?"

"Well." She bites her lip. "I think I'm falling in love. No—I know. I *am* falling in love. I love him."

"That's huge!"

"Yes. Except . . ."

"Except what?"

"It's hard. Being with him."

I frown, the wind leaking out of my sails. "Hard? How?"

"I don't know if you—" She stops, blushing.

"If I what?"

"I was going to say, I don't know you if went through this when the two of you . . ."

I nod. "When we were deeply, madly, *passionately* in love and banging like rabbits twenty-four seven. You can say it."

She laughs. "When you were dating."

"At least *I* didn't sleep with him."

"Small favors. But you're really not mad at me any longer?"

"I'm not mad!"

"Okay. Good," she says. She exhales, looking visibly relieved. "Thank you. That means a lot to me."

"But don't stop—tell me more. You don't know if I went through *what* when the two of us were dating?"

"The family stuff. The pressure. It's constant. I feel like we're a team, so when he's stressed because his dad is getting on his case for some reason or another, I'm stressed. But he has *me* to talk to about it, and I have nobody. Sometimes I feel like I'm going to be crushed under the weight of it all. You must have seen that piece in the *Sun* this week."

I nod. "India showed me."

"They haven't run a new photo yet, but it's only a matter of time. Edward is hugely private—*much* more than I realized—and he's terrified of me being hounded by the paparazzi. They've already been following us, and I feel like I'm being hunted every time I turn a corner."

"Vultures."

"I don't mean to complain."

"You're allowed! God knows you've heard me go on and on in the past."

She looks tentative, fiddling with a tassel on a sofa pillow. "It's just . . . I have to juggle him with schoolwork and with applying to university. He's always got a crisis at home. His father is an absolute handful. We have an event to attend every weekend, and I have to act appropriately so I reflect well on him. It might sound fun, but it's not—it's bloody exhausting. I feel like I've stepped into the lion's den: there are all these unspoken rules and codes and it's impossible to navigate."

"He doesn't make you feel bad about it, does he?"

"No! He's incredibly supportive. But I can tell Helen can't stand me. She's always making snide little comments when he's not around about 'new money' and 'suitable girls.' Nothing I can report back to him without sounding paranoid, but she's clearly being passive-aggressive. Edward's a dream, and his cousins are fairly down-to-earth, all things considered. But the people who work for them are nightmares."

"Like *Downton Abbey*? Carson the butler being snobbier than Lord Grantham?"

"Exactly. And I have nobody to talk with. Not speaking to you was torture. India tries to be supportive, but she and I don't get on the way you two do. She's so . . . remote. Flossie scares me—I can't explain it, but I don't really trust her. And everybody else is nice enough, but their allegiance is to Edward, not to me."

"Yeah, that's smart," I say, thinking of how I felt ditched by the group after Edward and I broke up. "India and Flossie aren't about the warm fuzzies."

"I'm so happy with Edward. He's so wonderful, and I know it sounds daft, Charlotte, but I think . . . I think he could be the one. We get on so well, and we understand each other, and we have the best chemistry." She blushes. "Not that it matters, but—"

"Of course it matters! Otherwise you're only friends. Chemistry is crucial."

"And he's introduced me to so many interesting people, and I've already had so many opportunities. I'm volunteering with a great charity, and I'm learning all about polo and horses, and I'm finally taking photography lessons."

"You are? Yay! Finally!"

"I thought about you when I signed up," she says, smiling.

"As you should."

"He and I have so much in common. He gets me. He makes me feel safe."

"Huge."

"Yes. But—"

"I was waiting for the 'but.'"

"It's still hard. I worry at times I'm betraying myself by being with him—that I'm betraying *womanhood*, as cheesy as that sounds. I'm happy to let him shine in public. But I'm not cool with always walking two steps behind my partner, literally *and* figuratively."

"Nor should you! Because he's a man?"

"Because he'll be king."

The simplicity with which Libby says this takes my breath away. My protective instincts kick in. "Let me help you. What can I do?"

She shrugs helplessly. "This helps. I missed you so much. I desperately needed somebody to talk to. My life consists of precisely two things right now: studying and Edward."

"That won't do. What are you doing this weekend? Wanna hang out? I'd say let's take the shuttle into London, but Mum and Dad cut off my credit cards. Maybe we can walk into town?"

"Mum mentioned they froze your cards," Libby says. "Sorry."

"I'm managing."

"Unfortunately, we have a lunch with his cousin," she says apologetically. "I'm booked the next five weekends in a row."

"Five?"

"The royals schedule out. What's funny is he doesn't even like going out. We'd both rather be vegging in front of the telly with a takeaway."

"Then you're perfect for each other," I say, thinking back to all the stir-crazy nights I spent with Edward in front of the television. "We don't need to get wild. What about lunch in the dining hall? Whenever you're free. I want to be there for you, Libs."

"I'd love that," she says, looking pleased. "And I want to be there for you. I've missed you. Even if everything else is going right, it's like part of me is missing if you're not there. I don't feel whole."

We smile at each other, and I feel a calmness settle over me. Something clicks back into place in my heart.

"Enough about me," she says. "What's been going on in your life?"

"Well," I say, "kind of a whole hell of a lot." I get Libby up to speed with the app. "Bill is like totally intense and so we're moving forward at this breakneck pace. I have a phone call on Monday with his designers, and they're going to turn things around pretty fast, I think. Then Bill will send everything to the coders, and we should have a working app in the next two months, by June."

"That's amazing!"

"I wasn't sure if India told you. I'm surprised Flossie didn't say anything."

"I don't hang out with Flossie very much, and it's always awkward when I do. The only thing we talk about is horses. I get the impression she's waiting for us to break up. She makes me a little uneasy."

"Eh, that's Floss. She's nice enough, when you get past literally everything that comes out of her mouth."

"I suppose," she says, shaking her head. I realize that she's taken on some of Edward's and India's mannerisms and phrases.

"Your voice sounds different," I say.

She looks embarrassed. "Helen made a few cracks about my accent, so I felt insecure about it. Edward thought I was being silly, but he arranged for a friend to give me elocution lessons. Just as a favor. Somebody comes twice a week to campus and gives me private lessons in my room."

"Elocution lessons? Get you! Soon you're going to be *way* too posh to hang out with little old me."

"It's mental, isn't it?"

"Libby, that is the bloody understatement of the year."

We burst into laughter, doubling over and giggling so hard we both have to wipe tears from our eyes.

"Mum must be having a coronary. Did she know you were meeting the King and the Queen?"

"I told her it might be a possibility," Libby admits. "But I swore her to secrecy."

"I understand." I look around the room again, trying to soak up this moment. Me and my sister, alone in a grand chamber at Windsor Castle.

The door to the room opens and we both look up in alarm.

"Oh, thank God," says Libby. "It's just you."

Edward walks in, looking confused. "I've been looking for you everywhere. What are you doing in here?"

"Charlotte and I needed a moment alone."

Edward doesn't hesitate, and looks over at me with a small smile. "Of course. Take your time. When you're done, come find me. Perry's just arrived, and I want you two to meet."

"Finally," Libby says. "His friend Perry Kent flew in from Kenya just for Edward's birthday."

I nod, recognizing the name from the society pages. Peregrine, the Marquess of Kent. He's set to become a duke when his father dies.

"Maybe we should introduce him to Charlotte?" Libby says teasingly.

I look at them in alarm. "Let's not with the setups, shall we? I have enough on my plate without adding a guy to the mix."

Edward laughs, and for a moment, I feel like we're friends again. "I'll leave you to it." He blows Libby a kiss and then closes the door shut behind him.

We're quiet for a moment after Edward exits. His presence is so powerful that it's like he's still in the room, even though now it's only the two of us sitting in the dusk.

"He's a good dude," I say.

"He is. Thank you, Charlotte."

"He takes care of you? Treats you well?"

"He does. He tries."

"Then that's all I can ask. When are you bringing him home?"

Obviously, I'd fantasized a few times about triumphantly bringing Edward home to Wisteria myself, but it was more like a girlish fantasy than an actual reality.

Libby's eyes bug out. "Never? How does never sound?"

"Libby!" I laugh. "He's got to meet them *sometime.*"

"Cringe," she says. "Mum keeps asking me to bring him around, but I don't want to ruin it. We've only been dating a few months."

"People have gotten married in less time."

"Not when they're only eighteen!"

"Tell that to his grandma. Wasn't she eighteen when she married the crown prince? And besides: *you're* nineteen now."

Libby laughs. "I don't want to freak him out. It's a bit soon to bring him home, don't you think?"

"Look, if you've already met the damn King and Queen, I think it's okay to ask him to Wisteria for a bite with Mum and Dad."

"I guess," she says reluctantly. "I just don't want anything to ruin it."

"Libby, he's head over heels for you. What could possibly ruin it?"

twenty-one

"So, Edward, tell me," Nana says. "What are your intentions with my granddaughter?"

It's a Saturday in early May, and the family has gathered in our sitting room at home in Midhurst. Edward takes a long sip of his water, trading a glance with Libby. The rest of us look at each other in alarm while Nana sits calmly in Dad's favorite lounger. Her legs are crossed, arms resting on the chair. She reminds me of a scene from *The Godfather*.

When Libby decided to invite Edward home to Wisteria, it was meant to be a casual, low-key meeting—just the immediate family, and nothing special. Libby begged Mum not to tell Nana.

Mum couldn't help herself. She's always trying to impress her.

The morning of Edward's visit, Nana showed up unannounced. She missed the country air! She wanted to stay for a day or two to spend time with us! What? Prince Edward was coming? What a lark!

The timing was purely coincidental, *of course.*

Now it's me, Nana, Libby and Edward, and Mum and Dad. I took the train last night, but Libby and Edward had a car drive them from campus this afternoon. They're heading back to campus tonight, while I'm planning to stay the full weekend.

I've snuck some sips of Mum's white wine from the fridge while nobody was looking. Dutch courage.

Edward looks at Libby again in response to the question. She makes the tiniest motion with her eyebrows, as if to say, *I told you my family was nutters.*

"Well," Edward says, clearing his throat. "I'm crazy for Libby, ma'am. That's why I've introduced her to several members of my family—including my parents."

"And why he was keen on coming here to meet you today," Libby adds.

"So when she was introduced to the King and the Queen, it was as your girlfriend?"

Libby squirms in her chair, but Edward looks Nana full in the face and smiles politely. "Yes, ma'am." We should have known better than to worry about Edward dealing with Nana. He's clearly been trained for worse.

"That's wonderful. Good boy." Nana sits up higher in her chair, looking satisfied. She turns to my father. "Matthew, dear, would you get me a cup of tea?"

"Just tea? Not your usual double gin, Mother?"

"Just tea will be fine, thank you," she snaps.

"I'll get it," Mum says, standing up. "Edward? Tea?"

"Yes, please. Thanks, Mrs. Weston."

I push my chair back. "Here, let me help you."

Once we're in the kitchen, Mum turns to me. "Thank you, honey. Don't think your father and I haven't noticed the effort you're making. You should be working on your app right now, not having to babysit us all. We're incredibly proud of you."

"Thanks, Mum. I am working, don't worry. Bill is texting me nonstop, and I'm sending him back some wireframe sketches tomorrow. And, no, this isn't my preferred way to spend a Saturday—but only because I'm worried Nana's going to say something ridiculous and send Edward running for the hills."

Mum laughs, brewing the tea and pouring it into a floral china pot. "It's a miracle your father ever married me."

"Don't you forget it," Dad says, coming into the kitchen. "Throw the scones on there, too, Jane."

"You left the two of them alone with Nana?" I gasp. "Dad! What were you thinking?"

He shrugs. "The boy'll have to learn sometime. We can't hide the crazy lady in the attic forever."

Mum shoots Dad a look. "Watch it, Weston. Regardless of how she acts, she's still my mother."

"You *guys*," I say, stressed out, "I don't think you're taking this seriously enough."

"Oh, relax, Charlotte," Mum says. "Edward's not fragile. That young man is capable of much more than people give him credit for. He knows how excited people like us get over royalty."

"People like us?"

"Nonroyals. Commoners."

"Peasants," Dad adds helpfully.

She takes a plate of perfectly cut rectangular mini tea sandwiches out of the fridge: watercress and cucumber, smoked salmon and cream cheese, and egg salad.

I motion to the sandwiches. "You didn't make those yourself, did you?"

"Of course not." Mum snorts. "I picked them up this morning from the Village Eatery. We're trying to impress him, not poison him."

As she exits the kitchen back into the sitting room, Dad smacks her on the bum.

"Dad!" I say.

"What *will* the in-laws think?" he says. "We'd better get back in there, otherwise Nana will scare him off and he'll never return."

After tea and thankfully uneventful conversation, we move into the dining room.

Dad brings in the roast he's prepared, while Mum uncorks the wine. She pours glasses for Dad, Nana, and herself.

"Aren't you going to let Edward and the girls have some, Jane?" Nana asks.

Mum looks startled. "I wasn't planning on it, no."

"Of course the children must have wine. Let's not be provincial." She turns to Edward, who's sitting on her right. "Isn't it terribly common how some people fret about these things? Libby and Edward are of age. And nobody's driving tonight, are they?"

"We're leaving tonight, Nana," Libby says. "But we're not driving—Edward has a car waiting to take us back to campus."

"Absolutely not. You must stay here. We can play Scrabble after dinner and then watch *Big Brother*. Tonight's the premiere, of course."

"He doesn't want to watch *Big Brother* and play Scrabble," Mum says, sounding exasperated.

"Actually . . . that sounds like a perfect evening to me," Edward says, looking at Mum hopefully. Nana beams. "But we haven't brought any bags with us."

"Not to worry," says Nana. "You're just Matthew's size, isn't he, Matthew?" My father looks Edward up and down, nodding.

"Probably just about. Size thirty-two waist?"

"That's right." Next to Edward, Libby looks panicked.

Nana continues, "And, of course, Libby already has clothes here. Edward can sleep in the guest bedroom across the hall from me. That way I can keep an eye on him to make sure he's not sneaking off to Libby's room late at night." Nana winks at Edward.

"Oh, you don't think we should put them up in the same room?" my father asks. "Isn't it a bit *provincial* to separate them?"

"I might be a progressive old lady, but even I have my limits," Nana sniffs.

"The guest bedroom sounds lovely, thank you," Edward says. "But I really don't want to be an imposition. You're sure it would be all right?"

My mother opens her mouth, but Nana beats her to the punch.

"Perfectly all right. We'd be delighted to have you."

"Um, what about Simon?" Libby asks. Edward's personal protection officer has been sitting outside in the waiting car for the past few hours.

"We have enough bedrooms," says Nana. "He's welcome, too."

"Glad that's settled," my father says, suppressing a smile.

After dinner, the conversation turns to Dad's Triumph motorbike renovation.

"I love motorbikes!" Edward says. "But my parents are paranoid. I've been forbidden to ride them—too dangerous, apparently."

"Really?" Dad says. "That surprises me. Don't you play polo?"

"I do."

"That's hugely dangerous. Isn't it?"

"Yes, it is. But I guess my family is a bunch of hypocrites. My dad's comfortable with what he knows."

"You wanna go out back and check it out?" Dad asks. I'm struck by how excited he seems to be having Edward around. Knowing Dad, it has nothing to do with Edward's status, or even the fact that he's dating Libby. I think he's simply happy to have another guy in the house.

"Yeah!" Edward's face lights up.

"So long, Edward," my mum says. "It's been nice knowing you."

"Mum," I hiss. "Stop it."

My parents dissolve into giggles as Nana looks at them with disapproval. Libby rolls her eyes.

"Sorry, Moose," she says. "You knew what you were signing up for."

Nana and I look at each other, our eyebrows nearly flying off our faces. *Moose?*

As my father takes Edward into the back shed, we girls pick up the dishes and ferry them into the kitchen.

"How do you think it's going?" I ask.

"Fine, I think," Libby says before lowering her voice. "There have been a few choice moments, of course. For somebody so obsessed with royals and propriety, Nana certainly knows how to put her foot in it."

"I might be old, Elizabeth, but I am certainly not deaf," Nana calls from the sitting room. "I can *hear* you."

"Sorry, Nana," Libby calls back, chastened.

"So, how *are* things going?" Nana asks, coming into the kitchen holding a snifter of brandy. "It certainly seems you two have a connection."

"I think we do, too," she says, smiling.

Nana takes a sip of her brandy as my mother begins washing up. "Is he a good kisser?"

"Mother!" Mum says, scandalized. "You don't have to answer that, Libby."

Libby turns bright red.

"Okay, then Charlotte can tell me," Nana says, turning toward me.

Now it's my turn to blush.

"Oh, honestly, the lot of you." Nana looks grumpy. "Is *nobody* going to give me the dish?"

"Sorry, Nana," I say.

"Just take care not to give too much of yourself away," Nana says.

"Boys don't like running around with fast girls."

I snort.

"Oh, *Mother*," Mum says. "It's not the 1950s."

"It doesn't matter. You lot make the mistake of thinking women's lib has changed things when it simply hasn't. Boys are boys. Girls are girls. No amount of wishing it away will stop girls from wanting to be courted and boys from wanting to conquer. It's Darwinian. It's the nature of the beast."

"So, what's next? Can we expect virginity tests from the palace? Is our Libby going to be subject to a rigorous physical from the physician of the King's choice?" Mum shakes her head. "Honestly."

"Don't get mad at *me*. I don't make the rules. It's helpful to be aware of what's expected from you."

"Enough of this," Mum says. "I don't want you filling Libby's head with rubbish. She's dating a nice boy, and that's that. Everything else is just noise."

Nana rolls her eyes, looking grumpy. She takes another sip of brandy, changing the subject. "What kind of things do you do together? Date nights?"

"We go to our favorite Indian restaurant for fish curry and tandoori chicken. Sometimes I watch him play polo. I'm teaching him how to use my DSLR camera. And his marks are a bit low in history and biology, so we spend time together revising in the library every night."

"Sounds like you're building something very real," Mum says, smiling.

"Sounds a bit dull, if you ask me," Nana says.

"Well, thank goodness nobody's asking you, Mother," Mum says, frowning at her before turning back to Libby. "He seems like a *lovely* boy."

"I'm so happy you like him."

"And you're fine with all this, Charlotte?" Nana asks.

"Oh, I'm totally over it. Edward and I dated for like half a second. Anyone could see their connection. I just want Libby to be happy."

My sister smiles at me. "I am," she says. "Thanks in no small part to you."

After a lengthy, competitive Scrabble competition—surprise, surprise, Libby wins—Mum, Dad, and Nana head to bed, leaving me, Edward, and Libby alone in the sitting room.

"Well, I guess I should go to bed." I want to review the wireframes Bill's coders have sent me. We've been lobbing emails and texts back and forth all week.

"Oh, no, don't!" says Libby. "Stay with us and watch *Big Brother*."

I look back and forth between the two of them. "Are you sure? Wouldn't you rather be alone?"

"Alone with *this* girl?" He pulls a face and jerks a thumb in Libby's direction. "The horror!"

Libby giggles. "Stay. Please. I've barely seen you in months."

"Okay," I say, settling down on the sofa and pulling a blanket over me. "Twist my arm."

I get a text from Robert.

ROBERT: How's tricks? You surviving?

ME: Ha! No, it's all good. Everybody's getting along

ROBERT: How're the wireframes going? You giving Zuckerberg a run yet?

ME: Patience, young Jedi. The force is strong.

I giggle to myself at my *Star Wars* reference. Robert will think it's cute.

Libby and Edward look over at me. "Is that Robert?" she asks.

"Yeah. We're texting about *Star Wars*."

Edward's eyes widen. "*You* are texting with a guy about *Star Wars . . . voluntarily*? Who is this bloke?"

"You know him—Robert. Your prefect."

"You and Robert?" A smile spreads slowly across Edward's face. He nods. "I like it."

I blush. "Me and Robert nothing. We're just friends."

He and Libby exchange a look. Libby grins. "Whatever you say, Lots."

Every once in a while, I look up from the wireframes on my phone to peek at Libby and Edward. It's nice watching them together. There's a sweetness between them I wasn't expecting: the way she offers him popcorn and feeds it to him, the way he gazes at her and reaches over to brush her hair from her eyes. They're curled up together on the other sofa, the light from the screen reflected on their faces, and I think about how they seem to just *fit*.

Edward seems more relaxed around her, too. I don't know if he's like this all the time, or if it's the coziness and relaxed atmosphere of my parents' house, but he seems in his element. It's not hard to imagine him sliding right in and becoming a member of the family. Judging by tonight, Dad is ready to sign adoption papers.

Of course, if he does become a member of the family, it means this is the new normal. No longer will I have my sister all to myself. I'll have to share her.

At one point, he looks down at his phone and starts laughing a little.

"What's that?" asks Libby.

"My mum is checking in. She wants to make sure everything is going okay."

"First time meeting the parents?" Libby asks, poking him with her elbow.

"No, I make this a regular habit. The houses of Midhurst are littered with remnants of my overnight visits. I'm staying at your neighbors' next." He pokes her back, grinning cutely. "Of course this is my first time meeting the parents."

Libby burrows deeper into his arms, looking cozy.

"Tell your mum you have a new father now. I don't think Dad's going to let you leave," I say, giggling.

It's only awkward when Libby gets up to make more popcorn, leaving Edward and me alone during the adverts. We stare at each other from opposing sofas, each reclining and buried under blankets.

"So," I say.

"Um."

"Well, this is awkward." We both laugh nervously.

"Thanks for . . . uh . . . for being cool with the whole thing," he says.

"Cool is my middle name."

"I thought it was trouble."

"I'm a woman of many colors."

"I guess I've never really said it to you, but I'm sorry. I didn't handle everything so well . . . you know, back then."

I don't feel the need for a big apology from Edward. Just knowing he treats Libby well is enough.

"That means a lot—thank you. But it's all good. I like seeing you with Libby. It makes sense."

"She gets me."

"Well, she actually listens. Instead of, you know, banging around like a lunatic. Like *some* people," I joke self-deprecatingly.

He chuckles. "You weren't a lunatic."

"Uh-huh."

"But seriously," he says. "I know how much your relationship means to Libby. She's been miserable these past few months without you. Not because of *me*, obviously—"

"Obviously."

"But she just, you know, needs somebody to confide in, I guess. It's a lot to take on."

"It . . . or you?"

"Oh, I'm perfect," he quips. "Surely you remember that. No—the pressures, the expectations, my family."

"The Firm."

He frowns. "Right. The Firm."

"I'm always going to be there for Libby—she's my sister. You don't need to worry."

"It's just . . ." He looks embarrassed, his voice a bit shaky. "I've been sold out by people close to me before. I've never let anybody from outside my family get as close to me as Libby. I've never been able to let my guard down like that. She knows everything, and I'm okay with it. I *like* it. I trust her."

"Okay . . ."

"I need to know I can trust you, too," he says in a rush, his speech faster than normal. "If Libby tells you private details. Now that the press has wind of the relationship—not to mention the fact that you and I . . . you know . . . first—they're already poking around. A call from a reporter is an inevitability."

"Edward, I would *never*."

"You don't know how they can be, Charlotte. They'll promise you everything—that's what they do. They'll find your weakness and they'll exploit it. If you have a secret, they'll blackmail you. If you have a wish, they'll make it come true. Anything, as long as you give them the scoop on me." His face is a slideshow of shifting emotions: hurt, anger, anxiety, hope. "I have a zero-tolerance policy for people talking to the press about me. *Zero*. I need to know that you understand that. I need to know I can trust you," he repeats.

"You can trust me. I'm a vault. Your secrets are safe with me."

His face relaxes. "Thank you."

"Unless they offer me the cover of *Entrepreneur* magazine. Then I'm totally selling you both out and moving to Silicon Valley."

He laughs. "Noted."

"What's so funny?" Libby asks, coming back into the room with two large bowls full of freshly popped popcorn. She hands one to me and then slides back under the covers with Edward, giving him a little peck.

"Oh, Edward and I are just plotting out all the ways I plan to exploit you both for fame and success. First I'm going to hold a press conference talking about your terrible taste in television. Then I'm going to live-tweet all of Edward's disastrous attempts at making legitimate Scrabble combinations—'omg' is not a word—and then finally I'm going to take all of my zillions of dollars and move to San Francisco, where I plan to date Elon Musk and become queen of Silicon Valley."

"Elon Musk is married," says Libby.

"Nah, I think he's divorced again. Who can keep up?"

"Not Liam Hemsworth?" asks Edward, laughing and twisting as Libby tries to tickle him under the covers.

"Hollywood is *out*. Tech is where it's at," I say.

Libby looks over at me, grinning. My heart explodes. She deserves every second of happiness.

And, honestly, so do I.

twenty-two

It's been a long, hard spring. We've been blanketed with months of gray, rainy weather that make me want to curl into a ball and never leave my dorm room.

But not long after Edward visits our house and meets our parents, the clouds that have become a permanent fixture the past five months are suddenly gone. The damp starts to dry out. The sun makes fleeting appearances. Warmer days are finally around the corner.

As the big track meet approaches, I throw myself into my sprints with an intensity I've been lacking all year. My time on the track has increased—not substantially. Just by a few tenths of a second.

But sometimes, a tenth of a second is all it takes for everything to change.

Six intense weeks of juggling schoolwork, track practice, and app paperwork have left me feeling physically exhausted—but emotionally, I've never felt more energized. Selfsy is now in beta mode. Bill and I have gone from once-weekly phone calls to daily Skype sessions. There's still a snag with the Facebook login, and we're getting close to missing our proposed May 15 deadline to submit it to the app store—but I have faith. I know we're going to crush it.

My friends can't believe it.

"So, you're going to be like an app mogul?" asks Flossie one night in May over wine in India's room, looking impressed.

"I don't know about *mogul*, but we'll see," I say. "If all goes well with Apple and they approve it when we submit on the thirtieth—assuming we make our deadline—it should go live in mid June. Then it's all about marketing and publicity—getting the word out and hopefully getting downloads. According to Bill, that's the hardest part. But if we get enough active users, then we release the Android version, and then web. And then maybe we'll localize it—you know, release it in other languages."

"And how do you plan to do all that?" India asks.

"I mean, obviously it would be nice if you all shared and 'grammed it to help get the word out."

"Of course," Flossie says. "We wouldn't dream of not supporting." She smiles at me.

"Thanks, Floss. Every little bit helps. Bill has some marketing team who he uses for all his launches. I guess he wants to do a big social-media campaign and was thinking of running Facebook ads and doing something through Pinterest. He said after we get fifty thousand downloads—*if* we get fifty thousand—we can talk about hiring a PR firm."

"I am *super* impressed," says India. "This is beyond legit, Charlotte."

"Let's hope."

"I can't believe how fast it all happened," Georgie says. "Where's *my* fairy godmother?"

"Has your mum turned your credit cards back on?" Alice asks me.

"I've been so busy with the app that I forgot to ask. I'm sure she will soon enough. And if not, maybe soon enough I won't need their cards anyway."

"Your parents must be really proud," says India.

"I hope so. I think so."

"Whatever," says Flossie. "Parents are easier to please than you think. What's important is whether you're proud of yourself." She holds out a bottle. "More wine?"

The following week, it's the day of the big meet. We're running against the girls at Marlborough, and I'm determined to prove to Coach Wilkinson—and myself—that I have what it takes.

I feel like I've really whipped my life into shape. The app's beta is in great condition and we're on track to be approved. Libby and I have a standing lunch date. I've been heading to the library a few nights a week to get my grades back up. I've put in good time at the gym working out, trying to get my strength up. I even find time for an extra half-hour run every morning, making sure my speed is up to snuff. I've shaved that extra tenth of a second back down—but now I want to push myself further.

Coach Wilkinson thinks I have a chance of breaking the school's 200-meter record—but I don't want to jinx it. I carbo-load the day before the match and promise myself that I won't be disappointed, no matter the outcome. After all, it's not about how fast you run—it's whether you muster the courage to run, period.

Clearly, Coach Wilkinson's mumbo-jumbo affirmations have been rubbing off on me.

In the locker room before the game, I tape my bad knee, rubbing my wrists anxiously.

"You okay there?" Flossie asks at her locker.

"All good. Excited."

"Excited enough to break the record?" she says, raising an eyebrow.

"I won't," I say. "There's no way."

"I don't know." She shrugs. "I've seen you running the past couple of weeks. You're not looking bad out there."

My stomach is a mass of butterflies. "What about you?" I ask, changing the subject. "You're doing the sixteen-hundred meter, right?"

She nods, bouncing up and down on the balls of her feet. Flossie is a yoga devotee, something clearly visible in her long, sinewy limbs. There's a fluidity to her movements I don't think I'll ever possess. Sometimes I wonder if it's because of who she is—there must be a certain security in knowing the world will always open its arms to you, no matter how you act or what you do.

"I'm so impressed by distance running," I say. "I don't have it in me."

"Sure you do. It's all about maintaining your pace, but keeping a little something in your back pocket for the last minute. You reserve it, bide your time, and then just when your opponent thinks they've won—*bam*. You unleash it. Strategy," she says, smiling.

I slap her a high five. "Well, good luck," I say. "We'll celebrate after the meet either way." I'm happy that Flossie and I are now on decent terms. I don't think the two of us will ever be BFFs, so our recent détente is probably the best I can hope for.

We head out onto the field. The weather is hot by May standards. The afternoon sun beats down, hard and unyielding.

I grab a paper cup from the water cooler by the track and pour myself a cup of Powerade, chugging it. I already feel warm. I'll have to make sure I don't get dehydrated out there today.

The stands are packed on both sides, with a few Marlborough fans sprinkled among the Sussex Park supporters. Our friends are all there to lend support. Georgie's running the 400 meter and hopes that she might place. Libby jumps up and down, holding a Sussex Park banner and brandishing it enthusiastically. Next to her, Edward gives me the thumbs-up.

"Gooooo, Charlotte!" I hear her call, waving the banner back and forth and grinning. India and Alice wave at me from the stands. The support from my friends calms the butterflies in my stomach.

My event isn't for half an hour, so I put on my headphones and crank up my inspirational playlist, finding a place in the shade to watch the events. The girls' 4x100 relay is up first, followed by the boys'. Then the girls' 1600 meter, and so on, down the list.

I take off my headphones to cheer for both Georgie's and Flossie's races. Georgie runs well, coming in third, while Flossie places second. I think I know them well enough by now to guess that Georgie will be thrilled, while Flossie will be gutted.

Finally, it's my event.

I take my position on the track, the din of the crowd fading into the background as I concentrate.

Run your own race, Charlotte, I tell myself. *It's just you and the track. Nothing else matters.*

I'm in the fourth lane, in between a tall brunette runner from Marlborough and a Sussex Park first-year. I take my mark. The starting gun blows and I push off, giving it everything I've got.

I pump my arms and legs as fast as I can, keeping my head down so that the only thing I see is the track. The race is a blur. I'm neck and neck with the brunette from Marlborough. Every time I think I've outrun her, I catch the faintest glimpse of her in the corner of my eye. My feet start tingling as they slap against the pavement in rapid succession, and my lungs are burning. As the finish line looms, I dig deep inside myself, trying to unfurl whatever secret reserves of strength I might have. I can do this. I have to.

I cross the line, my chest thrust out, only slowing down once I'm well beyond the finish.

The first thing I see is Libby jumping up and down, looking ecstatic. I bend over and lean my hands on my knees to catch my breath, looking up at the scoreboard: I've broken the school record by point two seconds.

"Atta girl!" says Wilkinson, jogging over to the finish. She slaps me on the back so hard I feel like my teeth might fly out. "You see? I knew you could do it. The only person you were competing against was yourself." She gives my back another few thrusting pats of encouragement and then rushes away to oversee the last couple of races.

Libby hops down from the stands, engulfing me in a hug. Edward waits off to the side. India, Alice, Oliver, Tarquin, and David are across the field, consoling Flossie and hugging an elated-looking Georgie. Tarquin throws his arm around Flossie, but she shrugs it off. Only India can get through to her, it seems. India puts her hands on either side of Flossie's face and says something. Flossie seems to visibly relax.

"I'm so proud of you!" Libby says to me. "You were like a blur!"

"Thank you." I beam, wiping the sweat away from my forehead. "I feel amazing. I'm having a total runner's high right now. Where should we celebrate? Dinner at Maharajah, then maybe drinks at the White Horse?"

Libby's face falls. "I can't tonight. We have plans with Edward's cousin Isla. We have a car coming in an hour. We simply can't cancel on her."

"Oh. Of course. That's okay." How many bloody cousins does Edward socialize with?

"I'm so sorry, Charlotte."

"No, I get it. It's totally cool."

I turn away so that Libby won't see the disappointment on my face.

She puts her hand back on my arm. "Wait."

As I look back, Libby trots over to Edward. I watch them

carefully, Edward nodding as Libby waves her arms animatedly to explain something. She has so much more energy than she used to have—even with the stresses Edward's position brings to her life, it's as if he's her battery-charging station.

She throws her arms around Edward. When she pulls away, he leans down and gives her a series of cute little kisses all over her face, like he's a puppy dog.

"Edward said it was cool if we rescheduled with his cousin!" Libby says, returning triumphantly.

"He did? That's brilliant! We're going to have so much fun tonight."

"What time should we meet you?" she asks.

"We?"

"Well, yeah. Me and Edward."

"Oh. Right." For some reason, the realization that Edward is coming along takes some of the fun out of it. Even though tonight was supposed to be a group outing, I'd hoped to have Libby there without Edward. Just the two of us—like it used to be. I hurry to cover up my disappointment, so I don't hurt Libby's feelings. "Let me talk to Georgie and Flossie, but maybe seven?"

"Okay, cool!" Her face is shining with excitement. "I'm so proud of you, Lotte. We have a lot to celebrate tonight." She gives me a big hug and then practically skips back over to Edward, the two walking off down the lawn hand in hand. They're even wearing similar outfits—jeans and powder-blue jumpers. From behind, they look like an old married couple.

I feel a twinge of jealousy in the pit of my stomach watching them go. It has nothing to do with Edward—I've long since realized that he and I were completely incompatible. Rather, all my complicated emotions are focused on Libby: this messy coil of envy and sadness and irritation, layered with a nobler mix of pride and satisfaction and approval.

I'm so happy for Libby that she's found a great boyfriend. Edward seems to calm her insecurities. He bolsters her confidence and channels her nurturing side. He understands her—or, at least, it seems like he does.

I just miss her. I know things between the two of us will never be the same. Even if she and Edward break up—which, let's face it, will probably happen at *some* point—this little magical moment in time will soon be gone forever. Libby graduates in a few weeks, and then in a year she'll be off to university. Time has a way of slipping away, and before I know it, we'll be adults with jobs and kids and mortgages and horrible taste in music.

Sometimes I wish we could go back in time to when we were little: the two of us together 24/7 in our tiny little house in Guildford, sharing a bedroom and staying up late into the night swapping stories. But we're not little anymore: we're all grown up now.

It's like that cheesy meme that everybody was sharing on Instagram a while back: The days go slowly. It's the years that go fast.

twenty-three

After showering and changing into party clothes, I'm too exhausted to do anything more than slap on a coat of mascara and some red lipstick and call it a day. When I show up at the front gates, Georgie is already waiting, along with a couple of other girls from the team, Corrie and Kate.

"Hiya!" I say. "Where's Flossie?"

Georgie raises an eyebrow. "Is she actually coming?"

I shrug. "I don't know. She seemed like she could use cheering up."

"Today and every other day of the year."

I pull out my phone to text her only to find a message from Flossie waiting.

FLOSSIE: Can't muster up the energy. Going to drown my sorrows in mint choc. Have fun.

"She's not coming," I say.

Georgie has no such qualms. "Praise the Lord. I *can't* with her acting like second place is something to cry about."

"Well, she has high standards, you know . . . ," I say lamely.

"You don't need to defend her," Georgie says. "We'll still think you're nice."

"Hiya!" says Libby, coming up behind us with Edward. They give everybody hugs, and Edward congratulates me again.

Corrie and Kate giggle nervously after Edward says hi to them. It's funny to see how excited they are about hanging out with him— was it really only the beginning of this school year that I felt the same way?

We make the ten-minute walk to the outskirts of town, passing by all the shops on the high street. It's just before dinner, and the narrow street is crammed with cars making the commute back from London.

When a Sussex Park graduate bought the White Horse pub on the outskirts of town two years ago, all the students were thrilled— mostly because the owner turned a blind eye toward underage drinking. As long as we're on our best behavior, students can order drinks, no questions asked. A couple of years ago, one of the waitresses told me that Elizabeth I once stayed there. After all, it's not an English country pub if it doesn't claim to have hosted distant royalty at least *once*.

The main room downstairs is for beer and pub fare, like fish and chips. The side rooms have deep sofas and a strong Wi-Fi signal: during the day, it's not uncommon to see students doing their homework over coffee, heads buried in laptops. At night, students and locals cram the sofas and the tall bar stools around wooden tables, sipping wine and G&Ts. Upstairs is where the action is, with a nighttime DJ who spins everything from old-school nineties music to brand-new Top 40.

We settle into one of the sofas downstairs, ordering burgers and pasta and laughing as we go back over the day.

"I still can't get over the fact that teenagers can hang out in pubs here," Georgie says. "I can't even walk *into* a bar in California."

"But what if you're hungry?" Edward asks.

"Then you go to a restaurant. Restaurants are for eating, bars are for drinking, and never the twain shall meet."

"Do you think you'll apply to university back in America or here in the UK?" I ask.

Georgie groans. "Ask me next year. We still have at least six months before we have to grow up and start thinking about the future, right?"

"You and Charlotte are lucky," says Edward. "You don't have to worry about anything until next year. Libby and I get thrown into the gap year soon."

"Have you decided what you're going to do for gap year yet, Libs?" I ask.

"There's this photography course in Florence I'm kind of interested in," she says, her voice trailing off. She and Edward exchange glances. "But maybe I won't do it." She clears her throat.

I look at the two of them, alarmed. Libby's not turning into a Stepford Wife, is she? This is exactly why I wanted to have it be just the two of us tonight—so we could deep-dive and gossip and catch up on everything. I make a mental note to ask her about it later. I don't want her giving up on something she loves just because of Edward.

How the tables have turned.

Everybody is starving after the meet, so once our food comes, we all attack it.

Just as I'm about to take my first bite, I look up and see Tarquin walking into the pub.

"Ugh." I poke Georgie, nodding discreetly in Tarquin's direction. "Ten o'clock."

"Oh, great," she says. "Lord McDouchey. Maybe he won't see us."

"Fat chance."

"If it isn't my favorite runners!" Tarquin calls from across the pub, walking toward us. He plops down at an open seat on the couch, slapping hands with Edward and giving Libby a kiss on the cheek. "Charlotte, please allow me to be the first to congratulate you on your stellar victory. I always knew you were more than just a banging bod."

I roll my eyes. "Gentlemanly as always. Do you know our teammates Corrie and Kate? This is Tarquin. I apologize in advance."

Tarquin looks at the coffee table in front of our sofa. "What's this? Nothing to drink?"

"We have drinks," says Georgie, holding up a tall glass of Diet Coke. "See?"

"I'm not talking about *those* kind of drinks. I'm talking about *real* drinks. You all just ran for your lives, and you're celebrating like you're a bunch of ninety-year-olds." He motions for the server. "We'll have a bottle of prosecco." He grins at us. "My treat."

I raise an eyebrow. "Why are you being so nice, Tark? You must want something."

He looks wounded. "Why must I want something? Can't I just want to help you celebrate your victory?"

"No."

"I need a favor."

"I knew it. What do you want?"

"No, no, no. Not until after I've plied you with alcohol."

"Come on."

"Fine. This girl I'm trying to pull wants an internship at your mother's shoe company. Apparently, she's a 'big fan.'" He uses air quotes as he says it, looking unimpressed.

"Of me?"

He rolls his eyes. "No. Of your mother."

"Oh."

"So, can you help?"

"What's that word we're always talking about? The p-word?" Edward says to Tarquin. It takes me a second before I realize he's being a little sarcastic. "P . . . puh . . . puh . . . pleeeeease?"

Tarquin sighs. "*Please* can you help?"

"That's my boy," says Edward.

I shrug. "Maybe."

"Thanks, Lotte." He throws an arm around me.

"I didn't say yes!" I say, shaking off his arm.

"Yes, you did." The prosecco arrives in a silver bucket with seven flutes. "I got it," he says to the server, taking the bottle and smoothly uncorking it without a sound. "Keep 'em coming. We'll need more than one."

After another hour of eating and drinking, we head upstairs, where a small crowd of locals and students has gathered for the DJ. The room is dark and smells like stale beer, but I'm feeling tipsy from the prosecco and don't care. The DJ plays the latest Zayn single and we rush the dance floor. Tarquin returns from the bar with shots for each of us, and even Libby and Edward start dancing, whirling around the dance floor and laughing as they crash into each other.

I text India:

ME: Party at the White Horse! U should b here!!

The next time I look at my phone, I see a reply text.

INDIA: Having a quiet one in. Drink all the bubbly for me xxxxx

Tarquin comes over, grabbing me by the hand and swinging me in a circle.

"Having fun?" he shouts into my ear, his breath hot.

"Get off," I say, pushing him away.

He responds by breaking into a spastic dance. "Okay, if you don't wanna dance with me, I'll just have a party over here by myself."

Despite myself, I laugh. I must really be drunk. "Tonight has been so fun. I really needed a night like this."

"Good." He pulls out his phone and then frowns. "Ugh. It's late. I'll leave you to it. I have to get up early tomorrow."

Libby and Edward dance their way over to us. Libby has always had a surprising amount of rhythm, but Edward is quite possibly the worst dancer I've ever seen. He pumps his arms back and forth over his head, slightly off the beat, looking like he's slapping invisible high fives in the sky. It makes me think of Robert and *his* terrible dancing, and suddenly I wish he were here.

"You leaving?" Libby asks.

"What?" Tarquin shouts.

"I said, are you leaving?" she repeats loudly over the music.

"Yeah. Gotta get up early."

Edward starts rubbing his eyes, looking like a tired little kid.

"I think that's our cue, too," Libby says, leaning in to give me a hug.

The second Kate and Corrie see Edward leaving, they come over to Georgie and me to say good-bye. They look exhausted, and it's my bet they simply wanted to hang out near Edward as long as possible. I hug them, feeling the euphoria that only two glasses of prosecco and a lemon-drop shot can bring.

"Looks like it's just you and me, kid," says Georgie. "More shots?"

As Georgie and I dance to Rihanna, I realize that I feel good for the first time in months. I feel like myself.

I've gotten my life in order. I'm creating a cool app that might actually succeed. I broke a school record and am back on track for an athletic scholarship, assuming I keep it up next year. And Libby and I are speaking again. Hell, even Edward and I are speaking again.

Sure, Libby's replaced me with Edward—but that's just part of growing up, isn't it?

We're not little girls anymore.

✿ ✿ ✿

On the Monday morning after my track race, I wake to my phone ringing at seven a.m. The only person who would call me this early is Bill—I hope everything's okay with the app. We're supposed to submit to Apple next week.

It's Libby.

"This better be good," I groan.

On the other end, all I hear is crying.

"Libs? Are you okay?"

More sniffles.

"Libby, *what's wrong*? Why are you crying?"

Through choked sobs, she manages to speak. "Edward and I broke up."

"*What?* You're in your room, right?"

She sniffles. "Yeah."

"Don't move. I'll be up in ten seconds."

I bolt from my room without even changing my clothes, running up the stairs and down the hall to Libby's room.

Clothes are strewn across the floor. In the far corner of the room, Libby lies faceup on the bed, eyes open. She's staring up at the ceiling, not blinking. Her nose is red and her eyes are puffy. It looks like she's been crying for hours.

I slowly approach, like I've seen people do with skittish horses.

"Libby?" I say soothingly

Libby sits up, her face crumpling when she sees me. I sit on the bed next to her and give her a hug as she cries into my shoulder. Soon, my shirt is soaked from her tears.

343

After a few minutes of crying and clinging to me, Libby pulls away, rubbing her hands back and forth over her eyes.

"What happened?" I ask tentatively.

She reaches over and picks up her phone from the bedside table. "Here," she says, handing it to me.

It's an article in the *Sun*—and I'm in it. Three photos are blown up on the front page: the half-naked Polaroids of Edward and me from Huntshire, the ones he gave me after we broke up. Alarm bells sound in my head. How did they get those photos? I'm the only one who should have had them.

The screaming headline makes my stomach twist:

"Charlotte the Tech Wiz: Prince Ed's Ex-Girlfriend Taking Tech World by Storm."

What the hell?

I scroll through and read as quickly as I can:

Launching soon, and poised to be the hottest app launch in ages, Selfsy was created by Charlotte Weston, a seventeen-year-old classmate of Prince Edward, and sister to Edward's girlfriend, Libby Weston . . .

. . . now constantly seen with his demure girlfriend, Libby—but he dated her gorgeous sister, Charlotte, first!

. . . naughty schoolboy Prince Edward was involved in a love triangle between the Weston sisters, as the *Sun* previously revealed . . .

A source close to the Weston sisters reveals . . .

. . . Libby was Edward's special guest at his eighteenth

birthday party last month . . .

. . . Charlotte's following in the footsteps of her
entrepreneurial middle-class mother. Jane Weston yanked
herself up by the bootstraps, literally—her online shoe
company, Soles, is rumored to be worth over 100 million
pounds . . .

. . . suddenly, the family found themselves swimming in
money, but despite hobnobbing with royalty and millionaires,
they haven't lost their middle-class touch and pride
themselves on remaining humble . . .

. . . Selfsy eliminates the search troubles of other DIY apps . . .

. . . only proves that clever, popular Charlotte was more
suited to being a royal girlfriend than shy wallflower Libby . . .

. . . can exclusively reveal their pet names: Bumble (that's
Libby) and Moose (that's Edward) . . .

. . . our insider tells us Edward is worried about becoming
king, spending hours each weekend in London holed up in
secret meetings at Buckingham Palace . . .

. . . sexy Charlotte's Instagram account is addictive—click
here to follow!

. . . sign up at SelfsyApp.com to get on the mailing list and be
alerted when the app launches.

Other photos in the piece include a long-lens paparazzi shot of
the three of us in town holding ice cream cones, Libby and Edward
sitting on a bale of hay at my birthday party, a photo from my Instagram of me mugging for the camera at Donatella one night last

fall, and a paparazzi shot of me in the car outside Windsor Castle before Edward's birthday, wearing India's gold gown and displaying a stunned, deer-in-the-headlights expression.

How the *hell* did they get all these?

I scroll back to look at the three Polaroids again. Seen through a public lens, they look really bad. Edward and I were just being silly that night, but if I were a stranger looking at them, they suddenly don't seem so innocent. I still think the one of me on Edward's back is cute, although Edward's eyes are a little blurry, so he looks wasted. The one of us hugging isn't terrible. But our photo with the beer bottles is especially bad: I look like I'm giving the rim a blow job while Edward grabs me from behind and pulls my bum into his torso. I'm in a bikini and he's in swim trunks, so there's a ton of skin showing. It's beyond suggestive—suddenly our playing around almost looks pornographic. He's all about controlling his public image, so he must be furious these were leaked.

But maybe the worst part is that the piece spends several paragraphs praising how beautiful and smart I am, talking up Mum's company, and complaining about how Edward was stupid to let me go. I feel a twinge of pride when I read the part about how the app works and why it's poised to be the next big thing, but then immediately feel guilty.

"'An intimate source close to Charlotte Weston,'" Libby says, her voice trembling. "Who could it be?"

My stomach sinks. All the positive press in the article totally makes it look like I traded private photos and insider information about Libby and Edward's relationship in exchange for app publicity.

It makes it look like *I* was the source.

twenty-four

"Libby," I say. "You have to believe me. I'm not behind this, I swear. I promised Edward I would never talk to the press, and I meant it—not even for publicity."

Libby starts chewing on a cuticle. I reach over and slap her hand away from her mouth.

"I know you would never sell me out."

Relief washes over me. "Oh, thank God," I say. "Thank you for believing me."

"But Edward *does* think you sold us out to help launch your app," she says. "He was beside himself: I'd never heard him like that. He kept saying over and over that trust is the most important thing, and if he can't trust you, then he can't trust me."

I stare at her. "And that's why he broke up with you?"

She looks down, picking at her cuticle. "His mum was having a fit about it. You know how close they are." I can at least understand that. After marrying Edward's dad, Queen Madeline spent years dealing with people selling her out from all sides—her own brother even wrote a book about her.

"Right."

"He said that if you were willing to publish photos of us just to get publicity for your business, then he can't have you in his life." Libby crosses her arms against her chest, looking embarrassed. "He wanted me to choose. He said if I wanted him in *my* life, there was no place for you, too."

My heart sinks. "Oh, Libby," I whisper. "I'm so sorry."

A fresh wave of tears wells up in her eyes, a thin trail snaking down her cheek.

"I can't believe he dumped you over this. You had nothing to do with it, obviously. It's temporary insanity. He's not thinking straight."

"He didn't dump me," she says. "I dumped him."

I'm so shocked that I drop her phone on the carpet.

"I told him"—she breaks into tears again—"I told him that there was no way you'd ever speak to a reporter, and if he couldn't trust my word, then there were bigger issues in our relationship. And if he was going to make me choose between him and you, I'll choose you every time. You're my sister." She sniffles and wipes her nose. I reach over to the Kleenex box on her bedside table and pluck one out, handing it to her.

"You chose me over him?" I ask, my voice sounding small.

"Of course I did, silly." She puts her index finger to her lips, kissing it twice, and then holds her finger out toward mine. "Sisters forever, right?"

I repeat the gesture, feeling like I might explode with love and gratitude. "Sisters forever."

I pull her back into my arms for another hug.

"He's an idiot," I say. "If he's willing to be without you for a single second, he's an idiot."

"I didn't think he'd take me up on it," she says. "I thought he would believe me."

"Boys are stupid."

"He's not stupid, though. He's smart, and kind, and funny, and . . ." She stops, taking a deep breath to compose herself. "But it's in the past. He was going to break my heart eventually, right? It's not like we were going to live happily ever after. We're too young." Libby's brave tone doesn't match her hurt face.

I hear a phone vibrating. "Is that yours or mine?" I say, searching on the floor for her dropped phone. I find it in a pile of uncharacteristically unfolded clothes and I glance at the screen.

"It's from Edward! It says, 'Please, Libby.'"

"He won't stop texting," she says sadly.

"So text him back! It's not over!"

"It *is* over. Read them."

I enter her passcode—our childhood dog Leonardo DiCaprio's birthday—and scroll through the text exchange from this morning.

EDWARD: I can't believe u threw me out.

LIBBY: I can't believe you wouldn't listen to me, so we're even.

EDWARD: She sold us out. Doesn't that mean anything to u???

LIBBY: I told you ten times already that Charlotte would NEVER sell me out. It had to be somebody else.

EDWARD: She needs publicity for her business. She's the only person who had those photos.

LIBBY: Then somebody stole them. I don't know what to tell you.

EDWARD: Please don't do this.

LIBBY: I'm not DOING anything! You're the one who wants me to choose! It's not fair.

LIBBY: I can't believe you don't know me better than that. She's my sister. You can't make me choose.

EDWARD: Looks like u chose already

LIBBY: Guess so.

EDWARD: Please, Libby

It's hurtful reading Edward's texts. I thought he knew *both* of us better than that.

"So, you see?" Libby says. "What am I supposed to say to that? I'm not dating a guy who asks me to choose between him and my family. That's seriously messed up."

I nod. "Yeah. But that doesn't make it any easier."

She looks sad. "No, it doesn't."

"I'm proud of you. And I'm really sorry, Libs."

"It's not your fault," she says, gnawing on a cuticle again. For once, I don't bother trying to correct her.

The two of us sit in silence. I think back to my conversation with Edward in my room the night I discovered Libby was transferring to Sussex Park. When we started talking about privacy and photos, his entire demeanor changed. I realize I've never told Libby that story.

"Something happened with me and Edward right before you got here in the fall."

She looks wary. "Okay . . ."

"We were in my room, hanging out or whatever"—obviously, I gloss over this part—"and I tried to take a selfie of the two of us. He freaked out and got really cold—almost rude. It was like he became a totally different person."

"He's over-the-top when it comes to the press and his privacy."

"No, I know. I'm just saying—clearly somebody set me up. If we can find out who it was, he'll have to believe you and then he'll know we didn't betray his privacy, right?"

"Yeah, but what then? So he apologizes? We get back together— and then he loses it the *next* time a story appears in the press about him? When does it end?"

"It can't be over," I say, feeling a flash of frustration as my competitive juices kick in. "Somebody set us up. We can't take this sitting down. You and Edward are perfect for each other."

"The perfect guy wouldn't ask his girlfriend to reject her family."

"Okay, true. But the perfect girl wouldn't dump her boyfriend without showing empathy. She should at least try to understand where he's coming from. Right?"

Libby looks unconvinced. "Empathy's a two-way street."

"Look, Edward thought you were the *one* person in the world he could be safe with. You're, like, in on all the state secrets—he's breaking all the rules for you, right? So, he feels betrayed and he's not handling it perfectly. But it doesn't mean you should end it forever. If it's a solid relationship—a real relationship—you fight and you fix it and you become stronger. It doesn't mean running away."

She looks out the window. "Maybe it does."

I throw up my hands in frustration. "What do I know? The only two people who are in this relationship are you and Edward. I can't read his mind—even if I can kind of read yours." At this, she smiles a little bit. "But it seems like you make each other better. You guys just *fit*. I think you have two options. You can just walk away and be sad and say, 'Boo hoo, oh, well, I guess it just wasn't meant to be,' and cry into your Weetabix. Or you can say, 'Hey, idiot. You're wrong and here's why. I'm the best thing that ever happened to you. Wise up and stop feeling so damn sorry for yourself. And, by the way, my sister is awesome.'"

Libby starts laughing. "Is that a direct quote? Should I take notes?"

"Something *like* that," I say. "Use your Libby words. Make it pretty."

I skip my classes, spending the entire morning with Libby huddled together in her bed under the covers and watching old episodes of *The Vampire Diaries* on Netflix. I can't pay attention to Elena and Damon, though—I'm too busy trying to figure out who's behind that article.

At lunchtime, I drag myself out of bed.

"I'd stay here with you all day, but I'm starving. If I don't have a sandwich, I might literally die. Do you want to come with?"

"I'm not hungry," she says. "Wait, actually—bring me some fruit?"

"I'll bring you an entire bucket."

I stop by my room to change quickly into the uniform and then walk out of the building clutching my phone.

"Smile, Charlotte! How does it feel to sell out everybody close to you for fame?"

I turn around and see the camera lens, long and menacing, before I see the tiny man behind it hiding in the bushes. The clicks come fast and furious—*click, click, click, click, click, click, click*—the lens rapid-fire snapping before I have time to move.

"What are you . . . ? Stop!"

I look around wildly for protection, but there's nobody in sight. Nobody but me, and a short, wiry man with a ponytail who seems hell-bent on getting a photo of me looking upset. He steps out from behind a tree, still hiding behind the camera, *click, click, click, click, click.*

"Did it hurt when Edward dumped you for your sister?" he calls.

I've watched enough Sky TV documentaries about celebrities like the Kardashians to realize that he's trying to coax me into a reaction for a dramatic, high-paying photo. Adrenaline rushes through me—what a low-life scumbag, preying on a teenage girl for a photo paycheck. I want to sneer back, "Does it hurt when you wake up in the morning and you're still you?" but I know the worst thing to do would be to show any emotion at all. Instead, I plaster a stony look on my face, throw my shoulders back, and march forward, my head held high. I ball my hands into fists so that he won't see they're shaking. As soon as I get to the dining hall, I'll report him. When I leave, I'll sneak out the back.

As furious and panicky as it makes me, it also gives me a little insight into what Edward must have been dealing with his entire life. No wonder he's so paranoid about his privacy.

The sound of the camera fades into the distance—the photographer no doubt hiding to score another photo later—and I finally feel safe enough to look down at my phone, turning the ringer on.

Oh, shit.

I have forty-seven text messages, fifteen Kiks, six WhatsApp messages, a voice mail from Bill, and three missed calls from my mother. One of the texts is from Robert.

ROBERT: Bill just called me. I saw the article. You okay?

I shoot him a quick text back.

ME: Yeah. Paparazzi just found me but I survived. Can we meet up later?

ROBERT: Absolutely. Just tell me when and where. Whatever you need.

ME: Thanks x

I open Instagram. I've gained more than twenty thousand new followers *in a single morning*. There are so many comments on my last photo—a random selfie of me before track practice—that they blur together. They're all from strangers:

@EmmaBlaineSmith Ohhhh shiiiit ur sis is gonna b sooooo mad!!!!!

@kittykatzmeow1294 @yellowjackfever93 did u see this? this is the article from sun today I was talking about. She dated prince Edward before her Sister

354

@Planet_Ging_Love Is this article 4 real? U sold out your
sister for publicity?

@bdkanon6807 Hii Charlotte!!!! Signed up for ur mailing list!!
Can't wait 2 download ur app it sounds so cool!!!

@MadisonGreen99 Never seen a person more self-absorbed
than her. And her family is no better. Social climbing
trash. Prince Edward had better run.

@apps4u76969 Want to gain more followers? Follow us here!
You're guaranteed to get one hundred new followers PER
DAY!

@Minimeeee she is gorgeous and ur all just jealous

@Minimeeee u wish u could all be with a prince like charlotte
n b so smart her app is dope charlote i love u pls follow
me back pleeease

@Lollipop21marine Seriously, you are disgusting. It's people
like you who make Prince Edward and the other royals
feel like they're living in a cage.

@tm_marie22 Lb first

@kraykke You're a pathetic social climber. Hope you enjoy all
your new Instagram followers, because you will never be
queen.

If the comments weren't so horrendous, I might laugh. Who *are* these people?

But even though I know that they don't know me, don't know the truth, and obviously don't know what the hell they're talking about, finding myself as the target of a social-media firestorm hurts. I should still be riding high from the triumph of my track win. Instead, I feel sick to my stomach reading all the hate and anger directed at me through my phone. It's like somebody has scraped the bottom of the Internet barrel and dumped the sludge on my photo feed.

I've been tagged in an Instagram post. I know I'm probably going to regret it, but I can't stop myself from clicking on it.

It's a screen grab of a tweet. The tweet says, "A little birdie told me that Charlotte Weston is the 'secret' source behind @theSUN article about her new app." The person who screen grabbed it and then tagged me on Instagram has posted only one word of commentary: #Obviously.

I open the Twitter app and search for the tweet.

It has 418 likes and has been retweeted 793 times.

My head is pounding. Mum calls again, but I press divert. I need sustenance before I can deal with her—before I can deal with any of this.

She leaves a message. I don't listen to it.

I walk into the dining hall apprehensively. I'm expecting heads to swivel, glares darting in my direction. But nobody really looks up. Everybody is too busy focusing on their food, their friends, their own personal dramas to pay me any attention as I load up my tray. I'll report the photographer later.

But then I arrive at my table, and it's a very different story.

"What are you doing here?" Flossie asks, her eyes narrowing.

"Um, I'm here to eat . . . ," I say, looking from person to person to gauge their reactions. Oliver and David are avoiding my eyes, while

Georgie and Alice have sad looks on their faces—like they're disappointed.

Tarquin shakes his head. "Is anybody *actually* surprised?" he says. "You're all daft if you didn't expect this." He crumples his napkin into a ball and throws it onto the table.

"What are you talking about? You were like my best friend two days ago. You practically begged me to help you with that girl."

"Your services are no longer required."

I stand at the edge of the table, not sure what to do.

I can't read India's expression. What's worse, Edward refuses to look at me.

"You think your shit doesn't stink," Flossie says. "We know it was you."

"Except it wasn't."

Georgie looks at me hopefully, like she wants to believe me.

"Says you. Who else could it be? It was like a publicist planted that article for you. I looked at your Instagram—you've gained like fifty thousand followers today." I don't think it would help matters much to correct her by saying it was only twenty thousand.

"It wasn't—"

"Bye," says Flossie. "Leave."

"Are you serious?"

"And are you deaf? There's no room for you in Edward's life. We'll stand behind him—his *real* friends."

"But—"

"Get. Out." Flossie stands up. "If you don't leave, we will. Right, Edward?"

He doesn't say a word. It's as if the conversation isn't happening. His head is to the side, his eyes averted. I am, so it seems, dead to him.

"Okay, forget it." I put the tray on the table, removing my sandwich and an apple for Libby. "Whatever."

When I hear people talk about how they wish they could trade places with somebody else, I never get it. My life, up until this point, has been pretty bloody great. But now, for the first time, I understand. I would give almost anything in the world to not have to deal with the fallout from this stupid tabloid gossip.

"Good riddance," I hear Flossie say as I walk away.

twenty-five

I'm on the floor of my room later that afternoon, surrounded by Apple paperwork I've printed out in the library for the app, when there's a knock at the door. At first I assume that it's Libby, finally rousing herself from bed and looking for some distraction. Or maybe it's Robert, since he seems to be one of the few people who don't hate me.

I called Bill back after lunch, and needless to say, the article thrilled him. Apparently, we had thousands of people sign up for the Selfsy mailing list to be alerted when the app drops. He said, "You can't buy that kind of publicity!" about five times and told me he's been fielding phone calls from PR firms dying for Selfsy's business.

"I'm coming in, so you better be dressed." It's India.

The door swings open. She stands there, looking concerned.

"You're still talking to me?" I ask warily.

She doesn't respond, shoving her hands into the long cashmere cardigan topping her uniform. Instead, she nudges the papers with the tip of her ankle bootie. "What's all this?"

"Stuff for the app. It has to be completed in order for us to submit for the App Store. I thought I'd work on it to calm me down. Take my mind off everything."

"And this?" she asks, sitting down on the floor next to me, picking up a notebook.

"More of the same. An analysis of competitive apps I did last month for Bill."

"You sound like an econ major."

"Ha. I just tell him what I find, and then he's the one who dolls it up and makes it all business-y and professional. But I *am* learning a lot about projections and all that stuff. Even if the app fails, it'll be useful for university."

"You're thinking of majoring in graphic design?"

"Business."

"I see." She pops right back up again, climbing onto my bed and swiping the open curtains shut. "There are photographers everywhere. Arabella says the headmaster hired special staff for the day to patrol the campus perimeter."

"I know. I reported one outside the dorm after lunch. Another one followed me to Stuart Hall. All because of that stupid article."

"All because of *you*, according to Twitter."

Something in India's voice makes me pause. I stop, putting my phone down and looking her full in the face.

"I didn't have anything to do with it, India."

She doesn't hesitate. "I know. I believe you."

"Flossie hates me now. And Edward wouldn't even look at me. Seems like I've been axed for good."

She leans over, picking up a sheet of paper off the floor. It's a loose-leaf page from Bill's business plan. I pulled it out to read while writing down stuff about the apps that inspired me. India rolls the paper into a tube and then starts absentmindedly tapping it against her palm. "Seems so."

"And? What are you thinking?"

She keeps tapping the paper against her hand, finally tossing it back onto the floor. "I've never seen Edward so upset."

"God, he's such a stubborn asshat. How could he possibly blame Libby for this?"

"He's not angry. He's hurt. And he doesn't blame Libby."

The silence between us is deafening.

Finally, I speak. "When Libby told me, I went off on this dumb speech about how she and Edward are perfect for each other. But I'm starting to feel like: screw it. If Edward's so determined to blame me, if Libby is miserable, if the two of them are so damn busy throwing pity parties that they can't *communicate* with each other—then why should *I* fix it for them? I'm sick of feeling like collateral damage."

India bites her lip.

"And you guys know me—how could any of you possibly think I'd do that? It really hurt." Now that I'm letting it out, I realize how bothered I am by my friends not giving me the benefit of the doubt.

I expect India to roll her eyes at me for being dramatic, but instead, she's looking at me like she really, desperately wants to say something. It's not like India to hold her tongue. I pause, giving her a chance to speak. When she doesn't say anything, I launch right back into my critique.

"I know what everybody thinks—that neither of us had any business dating him in the first place. Two middle-class sisters from Midhurst dating the future king? What a joke. We were stupid enough to think we could play the game at all, let alone win it."

India's eye twitches.

"Obviously Edward just needs to be with somebody who sang nursery songs with him in Gloucestershire, who used to run around with him in diapers on the lawn at Cedar Hall, whose parents own zillions of acres and go to all the same boring charity luncheons as the Queen. Clearly, the only thing that matters in your world is being born into the right family. Screw the rest of us, right?"

"You need to get over that. Nobody cares about where you were born," India says softly.

"Everybody cares."

"Okay, *some* people care. But those people are dinosaurs. Morons. The world isn't like that anymore."

"Yes, it is. Flossie and Tarquin, and Oliver, and even David—the whole lot—they all play like they're so egalitarian—hanging with us poor little Weston sisters, letting an American into the group—but when you really get down to it, they'll always see us as outsiders."

"Yeah, but Edward's not like that. He doesn't give a toss where Libby came from—or Georgie, or you, for that matter." India's voice becomes more impassioned. She seems to be waking up from whatever daze she's been in for the past few minutes. "He just wants to surround himself with good people. He wants to have a group of friends he can trust—and *it doesn't bloody matter* where they came from."

I look at India in surprise. In the year we've been close friends, I think that's the first time I've heard her raise her voice.

"What's got *you* all riled up?"

"Believe it or not, I'm annoyed, too. Flossie came to lunch today and said she *knew* it was you, and everybody automatically believed her, just like that. They're sheep."

"You're only realizing that now?" I say. "Edward's the shepherd. You're all just the flock."

"Except Edward's sleepwalking on the job. He's miserable over Libby."

"He should be."

"I was trying to get Flossie to see reason, but she wouldn't."

"I'll go talk to her," I say. "Flossie's loyal. I'll get through to her."

She nods. "I'm starting to realize that maybe our friends aren't as loyal as I'd thought. There's a traitor somewhere in our midst. Good luck rooting them out."

"What do you want?" Flossie asks, crossing her arms. I've knocked on her door and am standing outside her room a few hours after our showdown in the dining hall.

"I want to talk, Floss."

"I don't think there's much to say."

"Come on," I say. "You *know* me. You know I would never do that."
We stare each other down.

"Fine," she says, opening the door wide. "You've got five minutes."
I walk inside, sitting down on her bed.

"So," she says, looking at me like I'm a bug. "How's the app? Seems like your social media following has shot through the roof. That's quite the coincidence."

"It. Wasn't. Me. You think that's my MO? Selling out my sister? Getting on Edward's bad side? How dumb do you think I am? I thought you knew me a little better than that."

Her face darkens. "Well, I'm sure you've had thousands of downloads, no?" I nod. Bill's been sending me a flurry of texts all day—we now have more than sixty thousand people on our mailing list.

"You're right. Nobody knew who I was before today, and now the entire damn country knows me and Selfsy."

"Lucky girl," she says. "Going straight to the top—isn't that what you really wanted all along?"

"By throwing my sister under the bus? By betraying my friend? No."

"I thought you came here to apologize, not to argue."

"But I didn't *do* anything. I don't have anything to apologize for!" I feel like I'm talking in circles. Why is Flossie refusing to believe me?

She sighs. "I don't think we have much more to say here, Charlotte. I wish you luck with the app. Really, I do. But I think this is all for the best. Our group doesn't respect traitors."

"Ugh!" I feel like stomping my foot in frustration. "I need a cigarette," I say, as much to myself as to her.

"Denial isn't very becoming of you," she says. She opens the drawer next to her bed and pulls out a pack of cigarettes, handing me one. "But, here. Knock yourself out."

"Libby doesn't smoke, you know," I say, trying to make small talk while I figure out how to get through to Flossie.

Flossie rolls her eyes as she places a cigarette between her own lips. "It's so irritating."

"I think it's smart. We're all going to quit *someday*—like, I'm not going to be thirty and smoking—but for Libby, that someday never has to come."

"Okay," Flossie says, shrugging. "That's nice. Whatever."

When she goes back into the drawer for a lighter, I catch a glimpse of something at the bottom of her drawer. It's a small stack of square photos, piled on top of one another.

They're Polaroids.

Oh. My. God.

Suddenly, everything becomes clear.

It's Flossie. She's the leak.

"What are those?" I ask.

"What?"

"In your goody drawer. Are those Polaroids?"

Flossie slams the drawer shut. She takes the unlit cigarette out of her mouth and tosses it on the table. "I don't know. Probably. Look, Charlotte, this is getting old. You should go."

My eyes narrow.

"I want to see them."

"You're acting crazy. I want you out of my room, *now*."

"Show. Me. The. Photos."

Flossie takes a step toward me, as if trying to scare me into backing down. "If you don't get out of here, I'll call campus security."

I stand my ground.

She pulls out her phone, shaking it menacingly. "If you don't get out of here, *I'll call the press*."

It couldn't be Flossie. It doesn't make any sense. She would have absolutely nothing to gain by selling Edward out.

And yet I know with every fiber of my being that she's the leak.

I have only one shot to get this right. I pull my phone out of my pocket and start jabbing at it with both my thumbs, pretending to send a text. In actuality, I'm opening my voice memos app. I press record, praying this works, and shove the phone back into my bag.

"What are you doing?" she asks, sounding panicked.

"I texted India to come over. We're sorting this out here and now."

Flossie takes a step back uneasily, as if she's not sure what to do.

I'm not sure what to do, either. I need to get Flossie talking—something I can play to Edward as proof of her betrayal.

"India will be here any second," I say. "One word from me and she'll see the photos in your drawer herself. India's smart. She'll know that it was you, not me."

Flossie's eyes narrow. She licks her lips. Finally, she says, "It's your word against mine. I'll tell India you planted them to set me up."

"So it *was* you."

She seems to be regaining her confidence. She reaches back for the cigarette on the desk, actually lighting it this time. "Congratulations. We have a winner."

"But why, Flossie? Why throw me under the bus like that? I thought we were friends."

She shrugs. "It's not personal."

"It's entirely personal." Now that we're talking plainly, I decide to go for broke. "You contacted the *Sun* about me. How is that not personal?"

"I didn't. They contacted me. I said no, at first. *Obviously.* I'd never talk to the press about Edward. But then I thought about it. The more I considered it, the more I realized I would be doing Edward the biggest favor of his life."

"I'm sorry, you considered this doing Edward a favor?"

"Oh, please. He was making a fool of himself. First you, then Libby? What's next—he's going to take up with the gardener's daughter at university?"

"You're a snob."

"I'm not a snob. I just understand how the world works. People like *us* don't end up with people like *you*."

I'm shocked. I've always thought Flossie was wary of me, but she seemed to thaw eventually. Now it's clear that she was harboring a secret grudge the whole time.

"Except they do," I say. "First me, then Libby . . . but never you, unfortunately."

She glowers at me. "Whatever. Eventually, it became plain that I *had* to act. I asked Tarquin what he thought, and he agreed."

"Tarquin?"

Flossie smiles.

"Oh. Right. All the drinks at the White Horse. You needed a

decoy to make sure I wasn't in my room."

"Nobody ever said you weren't clever."

"Why make it look like I planted the story?" Keep her talking.

She takes a deep drag of her cigarette. I want to reach over and smack it out of her smug little mouth. "You should be thanking me. I gave you ten thousand pounds of public relations in a single article. Plus, obviously, Edward thinks you can't be trusted now. And since he's realized Libby isn't good enough for him, he's free to date someone better."

"Someone like you."

She rolls her eyes, not responding.

"Mmm," I say, satisfied. "Cool. But you probably should have thought it through. Libby and I have never been closer, and you're about to bring Libby and Edward closer, too."

She snorts. "There's no way he'll take her back."

"Oh, didn't you hear? She dumped him. Not the other way around. He's been begging *her* to take *him* back." The shocked look on her face is immensely satisfying. "If you didn't have your head so far up your arse, you'd see that Edward is *lucky* to have Libby—and he knows it. Once he hears what you've had to say"—I pull out the phone from my pocket, still recording—"I have no doubt they'll reconcile and be back on by tonight."

Flossie's eyes widen as she sees the phone. She lunges for me, swiping at my hand. "Give it to me."

"No."

"Give it!"

"Screw you, Flossie."

"That's illegal. You can't use it as evidence. I didn't know you were recording me."

"Well, thank God we're not in court. I'm not suing you. I'm just taking it to Edward so he knows who he can trust. Whether he decides to keep you and Tarquin around is up to him. I don't give a toss about that."

She looks stunned. "It's illegal," she repeats weakly. "I'm calling my lawyer."

"Go for it. I bet he'll tell you stealing is illegal, too. And I'm sure your parents will be thrilled when we're all in court. They don't mind having your family's name dragged through the mud, right?"

"How *dare* you," she says with all the force she can muster.

I shrug. "If you weren't such a snob, maybe you'd see that I only wanted to be your friend. You can't treat people like you do. It doesn't matter who your family is."

"You can't go up against me. You're *nobody*," she says passionately.

"You're wrong, but whatever. I don't care what you think anymore," I say. "Have a nice life, Floss. Good luck on the way down."

I stub my unsmoked cigarette in Flossie's ashtray and then walk out.

On my way to Stuart Hall to find Edward, I pull out my phone, texting Robert.

ME: I'm heading your way. Need to tie up some loose ends first, but when I'm done, I'd love to see you . . .

ROBERT: Can't wait. I'm in my room whenever you're ready.

I climb the steps of Stuart, my heart pounding as I walk down the hallway toward Edward's room.

I knock. Across the hallway, Simon swings open his own door.

"Hi, Simon."

If menacing looks were an Olympic sport, Simon would win gold.

"Edward's going to want to hear this, trust me."

He crosses his arms but doesn't say anything.

Edward opens the door. When he sees it's me, his face falls.

"Oh. You."

He has dark circles under his eyes, as if he hasn't slept. He scratches his chin, which has a slight layer of stubble, and I think: he's just a guy. To the rest of the world, he's Prince Edward, who appears on the cover of magazines and lives in palaces and is the son of the King. But in reality, he's just an eighteen-year-old guy who is heartbroken because a friend has sold him out and his girlfriend has dumped him.

I think back to the beginning of the year, when the two of us were at the edge of the field, sneaking kisses and laughing at each other's jokes. I remember how he took my hand in his and called me sexy. How we stood outside Colvin Hall kissing until our noses were red and our lips were chapped. How I felt like the luckiest girl on the planet, because not only was I dating somebody, that somebody was Prince Edward.

And now we're here.

"Before you slam the door in my face," I say, holding up my phone, "I have something you need to hear."

I press play.

twenty-six

Can I be honest?

My happiness over Libby and Edward reconciling is nothing compared with the jubilation I feel heading to the splashy London launch party for my app. Because of all the PR Selfsy got following the article, Bill hired one of the top PR firms in London, who insisted we capitalize on the press with a launch party. Bill has rented out Beaufort House in Chelsea, a members-only club popular with aristocrats like India. He's all about "making noise" and "being disruptive"—two phrases he majorly overuses—so he's spared no expense with the party and has invited an army of press.

After I played Flossie's confession for Edward, he was stunned. He asked for my forgiveness and begged me to convince Libby to give him another chance. In the past, I might have felt satisfaction at Edward begging me to do anything. This time, I was simply happy to help my sister.

Libby and I spent a couple of weeks together at Wisteria after the school year ended, but now she's at Cedar Hall in Gloucestershire to visit Edward. She texts me happy updates, sending photos of the two of them riding horses and fishing behind the house, and keeps a running tally of surreal dinner conversations with Edward's parents. (You know: the King and Queen.)

So, things are going *very* well.

Mum, Dad, and I take a black cab from Victoria Station to Beaufort House, pulling up outside the four-story brick venue and stepping out into a hail of flashbulbs.

"Charlotte, this way!"

"Charlotte, look over here!"

"Charlotte, Charlotte!"

The flashes are blinding. There are so many photographers crowded outside on the pavement that it's hard to make my way to the door. I still can't believe they all know my name.

"Take your mum's hand," Dad says.

Dad grabs me by my other hand, firmly weaving his way through the throng of photographers and escorting the two of us safely inside.

The space is gorgeous: the main room is dominated by a massive circular wooden and marble bar underneath a giant crystal chandelier, surrounded by wooden stools with red leather seats and opposite a mirrored display of all the alcohol bottles. The decor has been completely redone for the party. The artwork lining the cream-colored walls has been taken down, instead replaced with giant blown-up images of the app's landing page, user screen grabs, and DIY details like a bouquet of flowers made from strings of candy and a chandelier made of ribbons. The wooden tables lining the perimeter of the room feature paper inserts depicting beauty-shot screen grabs from the app's beta users, with giant floral bouquets artfully placed behind the bar and on a few tables.

Once we're inside, I realize I've been holding my breath. I exhale in a puff. "Jesus! How do people deal with that?"

"You'd better get used to it!" says Bill, coming over from the bar. He engulfs me in a big hug. "Hi, you!" He turns to my parents. "And you must be Charlotte's mum and dad. I'm Bill!" He pumps their hands enthusiastically, flagging down one of the roving waiters and offering my parents glasses of champagne.

"So you're the young man who bet big on our Charlotte," Dad says, looking him up and down.

"I believe in taking chances—that's how I got here. When I see someone with potential, I pounce. Most people have it wrong. You're not just betting on an idea; you're betting on a person. And the second my brother, Robert, told me about Charlotte, I knew she was going straight to the top."

"Robert?" my mother asks, turning toward me and smiling.

I blush.

"I've never had so many journalists beg for an invite!" continues Bill. "Selfsy is all people can talk about. I've already had calls from prospective investors letting me know they're paying attention. We're on track for a million downloads by the end of the month—one *million*!"

"Is he always this intense?" Mum whispers to me as Dad and Bill discuss my business plan.

"Worse. He's practically comatose right now. But, hey, it works."

"Oh, believe me," Mum says, "I'm not complaining." Even though we're only fifteen minutes late—for *this*, you'd better believe I spent two hours getting ready—the room is already packed. I look around, not recognizing anybody.

"So, who are all these people?" I ask Bill.

"Come and find out." He takes me around the room, introducing me to tech journalists from the *Guardian*, the *Independent*, *The Times*, the *Daily Mail*, and all the other top papers. Online writers from magazines I wouldn't expect, like *Cosmo*, *Tatler*, and *Vogue*, are there, too, plus a mixture of tech bloggers, style bloggers, and society writers from places like *Grazia* and *Heat*. I spot party fixtures like Spencer Matthews from *Made in Chelsea*, Marissa Hermer from *Ladies of London*, Poppy Delevingne, and even Kate Moss, who looks shorter in person than I expected and has her daughter, Lila Grace, in tow. If I could get her to use the app, that would be a huge coup. There are only a few photographers allowed inside—the rest wait outside on the pavement, shouting at each new celebrity who arrives.

As we glide from reporter to reporter, giving quotes and answering questions about the app, I look around the room, soaking it all up. The longer I'm here, the less overwhelmed I feel.

I'm in my element. I belong.

Bill was right. It really does feel like all of London has shown up for the party.

"Now," says Bill, taking me to a corner of the room, "I have somebody you'll want to meet."

Sitting on a red leather chair away from the bustle is a blond woman. I look at Bill, confused. Am I supposed to recognize her?

"This is Tabitha Reynolds," says Bill. "From the *Sun*."

Now I know who she is.

"You wrote the piece on me," I say.

She stands up, extending an arm. "It's nice to meet you, Charlotte. Congratulations."

"Thanks." I look warily back and forth between her and Bill.

"You two have a lot to talk about," says Bill. "Come find me when you're done."

Tabitha sips a cup of tea. Next to her saucer sit a reporter's notebook, pen, and an iPhone.

"Do you mind if I record this?" she asks.

"I'd really rather you not."

"Okay, then—off the record?"

"Off the record."

"My editor is very interested in you—she loved your story. Ex-girlfriend of Prince Edward, sister to Edward's *new* girlfriend, app entrepreneur at the tender age of seventeen, and gorgeous, to boot. It writes itself."

"As we all saw," I say warily.

"We could create a good working relationship moving forward, you and me. You're still young; you're building your reputation. If your sister goes the distance with Edward, you'll want a friendly reporter on your side. And if she doesn't—you'll want to make sure somebody still cares about you. And about the app, of course. Future apps, too."

I have a sense of where this is going. I put my hands up. "Let me stop you right there. I don't want any part of some insider situation. If you want to write about the app again, that would be brilliant. But I'm not trading information about Libby or Edward to get it."

She nods. "I thought you'd say that."

"Good."

"I respect it."

"Thank you."

"But you can't blame a reporter for trying."

"I guess not."

"Will you tell Edward that my offer stands? He knows how it works: he needs a friend to help get his messages across. Now that he's eighteen, he's fair game—he'll have to pick a reporter at some point, and I'd like it to be me."

"I don't think he'll be interested."

"You'd be surprised," she says, standing up. "Look at his mum. The *Daily Mail* wasn't getting all those exclusives by accident, you know."

"Are you saying *the Queen* was feeding stories to the press? To the *Daily Mail*, of all places? I find that a little hard to believe."

A smile plays on her lips. "You've entered a strange world. It's *all* hard to believe." She reaches out her hand, shaking mine. "I wish you much luck. You're a clever one. I admire that."

She starts to walk away, heading back toward the party.

"Wait!" I say.

She turns. "Yes?"

"We're still off the record, right?"

"Yes."

"How did you get those photos of me? And the article. Who talked?" I'm curious to hear her side of it. As far as I know, Flossie and Tarquin fled campus immediately following their final exams, and nobody's seen or heard from them since. Alice and Flossie were so close for so long—I'm sure I could text her to find out the latest, but I can't help but remember how everybody but India was so quick to disbelieve me. I'm not Edward—I'm not going to cut people out willy-nilly.

But I won't forget, either.

"You know I can't tell you that. A reporter never reveals her sources."

"Oh."

"But based on my intel, you know exactly who it was. She's back in Denmark. Now that she's fallen out of royal favor, I don't expect we'll be seeing her on these shores anytime soon."

"Wait, how do you know that *I* know?"

A little smile plays at her lips. "Welcome to public life, Charlotte."

Back downstairs, I mingle with guests, sipping a celebratory glass of champagne and doing my best to remember every single moment. Time flies, but at some point, India shows up with Clemmie Dubonnet in tow.

"You made it!" I say, giving her a hug. I look at Clemmie expectantly, waiting to be officially introduced.

"Um, Charlotte, this is Clemmie," India says, sounding nervous. She flips her long blond hair back and forth.

"Hiya!" Clemmie says, leaning in to give me a single cheek kiss. "Congrats! This is major." She looks around the room. "Oh, Poppy's here! Be right back."

India and I look at each other. She's totally blushing.

"So?" I ask.

She clears her throat. "I . . . uh . . . that is . . ."

"Are you dating now? Like, for real?"

India blushes again. "Maybe. I think so. I'm not sure."

I can't help myself. "I'm never seen you like this!"

She shrugs, laughing a little.

"Even the great India Fraser is human, it seems," I say teasingly.

"Sadly," she responds.

"I'm proud of you. It's kind of a big deal, coming here with Clemmie. All the photographers and everything." Even though India hasn't been in the closet per se, magazines like *Tatler*—who are obviously obsessed with her—have never gotten wind of her sexual orientation. Knowing the press, I expect all the society blogs will be abuzz tomorrow with photos of India and Clemmie hand in hand.

"I know," India says, nodding. "Believe me."

"But who cares what other people think, right?" I say, raising my chin in defiance. "Isn't that the big lesson?"

"Wise words," she says, smiling.

"Speaking of caring what everybody thinks, have you talked to Flossie or Tarquin? I want the dirt."

India rolls her eyes. "Last time I saw Flossie was when she came to my room and yelled at me. Or she tried to—I slammed the door in her face. Oliver told Georgie that Tarquin didn't even sit for his last exam—he just slunk away like a thief in the night."

"Will he still graduate? Or will his daddy fix it for him, as always?"

India shrugs. "Who cares? Good riddance to them both."

"Charlotte? Excuse me, do you have a minute?"

It's another reporter. I look at India apologetically and she waves me off, going to find Clemmie.

An hour later, after I think my hand is going to fall off from getting pumped so many times and my voice is going to go hoarse from all the interviews, there's a commotion at the door. Photographers are shouting over one another. There are so many flashes it looks like a lightning storm outside.

"What on earth . . . ?" the reporter I'm talking to says, turning her head. She gasps. "Oh my God."

Libby and Edward walk into the room hand in hand. Libby looks around until she spots me, her face lighting up. The crowd parts, and Libby and Edward make their way to me, every eye in the room on the three of us. Through the window, the photographers jostle one another, faces and lenses pressed up against the glass.

"I can't believe you guys actually came," I say, allowing them both to hug me.

"Are you mad? I'd *never* miss this," says Libby. "We wanted to support you."

"But all the reporters. They're going to be on you like vultures."

He and Libby exchange a glance, some sort of telepathic conversation seemingly transmitting back and forth between the two of them. Edward nods. "Now that I'm eighteen, I plan to embrace public life, not run away from it. But on my terms."

Libby squeezes his hand.

"Besides," he says, "it was the least we could do for you."

"This is *major*. The party is guaranteed to be front-page news now."

"That's the idea," he says firmly. "I'll go get us some drinks. You two catch up."

"We'll be in the corner," says Libby.

"Even better, we can go upstairs," I say, pointing to the stairwell that leads to the members-only club. We walk up to the dimly lit room, settling in on a sofa so we can talk in private.

"So," I say. "I want to hear the latest details. Tell me *everything*."

Her eyes fill with happy tears. "He said he loves me."

"Yay!" I clap my hands together. "What did you say?"

"That I love him, too, of course," she laughs. "I've been wanting to say it for ages. But I didn't want to say it first."

"Of course. Nana would have a coronary. Were all her lessons for *nothing*?" I joke.

"Well, I broke the cow rule," Libby says. "And yet, magically, mysteriously, we're still a couple." We giggle.

"More importantly, we laid down some ground rules."

"Such as?"

"Family comes first—which means you, Mum, and Dad. I don't have to hold his hand at every bloody event. I can tell you whatever I want. He has to come to my events, not just me to his. *And* I'm applying to the photography program in Florence for my gap year."

"Was that an issue?"

"He wanted me to go to Chile with him—but I'm not that into it. If we're going to work, everything can't be on his terms. We have to be equal partners, which means what I want is just as important."

"Good for you!"

"We talked a lot about how much pressure it is, and how I don't have anybody to confide in. And I promised him that you would be a vault and that you could be the *one* person I'd tell things to, and he said he would never doubt you again."

"Atta boy. It's baby steps, but it's something."

"Agreed—I think it's going to make us so much stronger. We're setting a real foundation to go the distance."

"I'm so happy for you, Libs. And I'm proud of you for sticking up for yourself." Libby's sweet, but when push comes to shove, she's made of steel. I have no doubt she has what it takes to navigate the choppy waters of being Edward's girlfriend publicly.

She tucks a piece of hair behind her ear and looks at me steadily. "I'm hoping it can be a new leaf for you and me, too. All our conversations this year have been about Edward. And then we spent half the year barely speaking to each other. I'm sorry."

"Yeah, this year *has* been pretty Edward-centric."

"We would never pass the Bechdel test."

"Huh?"

"It's a movie thing. Anyhow, next year will be different. I'll be home this summer before going on my gap year, and we'll spend loads of time together. I'll even let you beat me at tennis."

"Oh, *please*," I say. "You wish."

"I need to do a better job being there for you. Sisters before misters, right?"

"You did not just say that," I groan. "You and Edward are perfect for each other. The two of you are so cheesy." We giggle. "But yes," I say, hugging her. "We *both* need to do a better job of making sure nobody comes between us ever again. Not boyfriends, not husbands, not kids—nobody."

I have a special place in my heart for the cheesy music my parents listen to: old singer-songwriter stuff like Bruce Springsteen and Sting. Whenever I hear that song "Glory Days," or the Bryan Adams song "Summer of '69," I think about how *right now* is supposed to be the prime of my life. I try to stop and take a mental snapshot of the moment, filing it away for when I'm old and gray as a reminder that you only live once and I really did try to make the most of every minute.

Libby is off for her gap year soon, and then she'll leave England for university in Scotland. I still have another full year of school, and somehow need to juggle schoolwork and university applications and Selfsy simultaneously. Next up is my gap year, then university—and then the great unknown. I can't imagine what the next year—hell, the next five years—have in store for us. But whatever comes our way, I believe with every fiber of my being that we'll look back on this time in our lives and we'll cherish it.

"Sisters forever," she says.

"Sisters forever," I agree.

We clasp hands and head back downstairs.

"Did you see?" I say, pointing with my free hand to the middle of the room. "Kate Moss is here!"

"Who's that?"

"Come *on*! You've got to be kidding me."

She laughs. "Of course I am. Jeez, Charlotte—I'm not *that* out of it."

Edward brings us each a drink, and then Mum and Dad join, the five of us talking about summer plans. Edward promises he'll make several trips to Wisteria, and I don't know who looks more elated—Libby or my father.

Right around when the party reaches max capacity—there's actually a line outside the door—I feel a little tap on my shoulder.

"Congratulations, Charlotte." It's Robert, looking edible. He's wearing a navy blazer over a white button-down shirt and fitted jeans. It's the perfect combination of smart and casual.

"Robert! You're here!"

"I got here a while ago," he says, "but you were so busy that I didn't want to bother you. Bill made me promise I wouldn't monopolize your time."

"Monopolize away," I say, giggling. "I'm really happy to see you."

"I'm happy you're happy." He pauses, looking like he's debating saying something. Finally, he says, "I kind of missed you these past few weeks. Texting isn't the same."

"*Did* you?"

"Yeah," he says. "You look great."

"You, too," I say, blushing a little as I give him the once-over again. He looks bloody hot, in fact. I've always been a sucker for sharply dressed guys.

After I exposed Flossie and Tarquin to Edward, Robert met me downstairs in the Stuart Hall common room, where I told him everything. We spent only a few minutes talking before I went back to find Libby, but just a few minutes was all the time I needed to catch him up.

"I'm sure you have loads of plans this summer, but I'd love to see you," he says.

"Well, you only live twenty minutes from me. You're practically in my back garden."

"Exactly." He grins, his dimples popping. "It would be a crime not to hang out. So maybe we could get dinner, or lunch, or whatever."

"Or whatever," I repeat. "I'd love that. Option C. All of the above." I lean up to give him an impromptu kiss on the cheek, and he turns his head in surprise. Our lips meet, and then we pull away quickly, smiling.

"Whoops," he says.

"Sorry."

"Didn't mean to do that."

"That's a shame," I say coyly.

We stare at each other, and I feel the heat rising into my chest. I want a real kiss. I stand on my tiptoes, pulling gently on his shirt until our lips meet again. We lean into each other, my heart running away like a freight train. He puts his hand on my lower back, pulling me closer into him. His lips are so soft I feel dizzy.

"Get a room!" I hear India whisper laughingly somewhere behind me.

Robert and I break apart, still staring at each other. We're both smiling.

"I've been wanting to do that forever," he says.

All I want to do is drag Robert into the back room and snog his face off, but I manage to compose myself. "Good things come to those who wait," I say, grinning.

Finally, the party begins to wind down a little bit. The reporters start to leave, India and Clemmie hug me good-bye and then make their way hand in hand past the braying photographers, and even Bill dashes, promising to call me tomorrow to powwow over the press clippings. Robert leaves with him, giving me another quick but intense kiss that leaves me spinning.

I don't want this night to end.

"Can we get a picture?" one of the photographers asks.

"All of us?" I ask, gesturing at my family and Edward.

"Yeah."

I look at Edward quizzically and he nods. "Let's."

The five of us stand in a line: me, Libby, Edward, and my parents.

"Can I rearrange you?" the photographer says. "Charlotte in the middle." He looks at the group as I move in between Libby and Edward. "And then one parent on each side. Thanks."

We smile for the camera, Libby and Edward each throwing an arm around me in support, my parents flanking them. I pull myself up to my full height, tilting my head the way I practiced in the mirror at home before the event.

"Thanks," the photographer says as we all break apart. "Now, one of just you, Charlotte."

My parents, Libby, and Edward move out of the way, but not before my father squeezes my shoulder. "I'm proud of you, nugget," he says.

"Thanks, Daddy." I feel so happy right now that I want to cry.

"Woman of the hour," says Edward.

I turn this way and that for the cameras, thrilling as a few other photographers rush over to snap my photo.

"She's a star," Libby says proudly.

"And don't you forget it," I joke, smiling at her and winking as the flashbulbs pop.

epilogue

TEN YEARS LATER

Outside St. Paul's Cathedral, Edward and Elizabeth, the newly minted Duke and Duchess of Oxford, glide in a hail of flashbulbs past the waving, cheering crowds.

While getting ready this morning in our suite at the Dorchester, I heard a commentator on Radio 1 say that one million people were expected to turn up in London today. And apparently almost one billion people planned to watch the wedding on TV. *One billion people.*

Edward takes Libby's hand—she'll always be Libby to me, anyway—and helps her up the steps of the gilded state carriage, gleaming in the bright May sunlight. She holds up the long white train of her dress, gingerly arranging the lace around her as she settles in the carriage. Finally, she looks up at the crowds in the square and waves.

The people cheer, with banners and signs and UK flags waving and undulating all the way down the road, as far as the eye can see.

I walk several steps behind them. As maid of honor, my primary official duty today was making sure that Libby made it safely down the aisle, not tripping on her gorgeous gown along the way, and then taking her flowers from her when she and Edward exchanged rings at the altar in front of the Archbishop of Canterbury.

Unofficially, I'm simply here for moral support on my sister's wedding day. She wasn't nervous about marrying Edward, or about officially shouldering the burden of public life as a royal. She was simply nervous about the crowds—even now, after ten years in the spotlight, Libby is shy sometimes. We shared a bed in the Harlequin Suite at the Dorchester last night, me drawing a bath and bringing a glass of red wine to steady her nerves before giving her an Ambien for a good night's sleep. I had to field a few emergency phone calls while doing it. Selfsy went public a few years ago, and even though I stepped down as CEO to start another beauty tech company almost five full years ago, I'm still on their board. This means constant check-ins from other members, royal wedding be damned.

After all, despite the pomp, the crowds, the magazine covers, and the sense of history pressing down on us—it *is* just a wedding.

I walk through the doors of the cathedral, exiting into the bright sunshine and momentarily shielding my eyes. As everything comes into focus again, I look around, taking in the photographers, the grandstands with news commentators, the minor members of the royal family ahead of us waving at the camera, and the massive crowds, stretching seemingly for miles.

Libby waves and smiles, holding her shoulders back and her head high: years of intensive behind-the-scenes training, all leading up to this one moment.

She turns in the carriage to face St. Paul's, and our eyes lock.

In this moment, a wave of love and understanding washes between us.

She puts her index finger to her lips, giving it the most imperceptible of double taps as she purses her lips before holding out her hand as if in a subtle wave. I repeat the gesture, tapping my finger to my lips twice and putting my hand to my heart, as if trapping the kiss there, before waving at her in return. We stare at each other for a moment, smiling, and then I nod as if to say, "Go." I'll see her in two weeks, anyway. After they get back from their honeymoon in the Maldives, and I return from Austin—I'm giving a talk at South by Southwest on the future of the beauty sphere online—we have a standing weekly tennis and lunch date. Every Sunday afternoon, without fail.

Libby turns back to face the adoring crowds again, adopting a royal wave as the carriage pushes off slowly toward Buckingham Palace. Next to her, Edward smiles at me, giving me a thumbs-up. It feels nice to have a brother.

All eyes swivel to me as the photographers begin screaming my name:

"Charlotte! Over here!"

"Charlotte! You look bloody gorgeous!"

"Charlotte! Smile for us!"

"Charlotte!"

"Charlotte!"

"Charlotte!"

I turn my head modestly to the right, angling my body so the photographers can get a wide shot of my best side. Libby isn't the only one who's learned how to play the game. I've had ten years of practice, too.

I turn back to face the cathedral as my mother and father exit, my mother looking like perfection in a long-sleeved royal-blue shift dress and blue hat with black plumes. Dad is as handsome as I've ever seen him, wearing a black suit and top hat—he's had the cutest little smile on his face all day. He and Edward became BFFs long ago. My dad is clearly a father to Edward in a way the King could never be.

My parents seem like they might die of happiness, walking contentedly arm in arm as if there aren't a million photographers screaming their names. They're nothing compared with Nana, however, who brings up the rear, dressed to the nines in her finest beaded dress and a hat she had specially commissioned for the day from the Queen's own milliner in Bond Street.

"Isn't this lovely?" Nana says, leaning on her cane and beaming as my family walks past the screaming crowds toward our waiting chauffeured car. "My hips might give way, but there's still some life in the old girl yet. I can't wait to get up on that balcony and be photographed next to the Queen. Everybody at home will be mad with jealousy."

"Nana," I say, laughing. "I think you have everybody at home beat, forever."

She looks me up and down. For a second, I think she's going

to scold me for being cheeky. Instead, she smiles, joy creasing her face. She walks toward the car, only wincing slightly as she shifts the weight. "I do think you're right."

My heel catches slightly on the pavement, so I pause, gingerly extricating it while smiling charmingly at the cameras. They're always there. I never forget.

Behind me, the royal family exits, Prince Michael and Princess Verena chattering away, and behind them, the King and the Queen.

"Are you all right there, Charlotte?" the Queen asks. She's dressed head to toe in canary yellow, a small handbag nestled in the crook of her arm. Up close, she's surprisingly pretty, with charming little crinkles at the corners of her blue eyes and a wicked grin.

My heart skips a beat. I still can't believe she knows my name. Even though I've been on the cover of scores of magazines over the years for Selfsy's runaway success, something tells me the Queen doesn't read *Wired*. I grew up with images of her on tea towels— and now we're in-laws. Of course, it's only been a year since we were formally introduced, when the King and Queen invited our whole family to Sandringham following the engagement. That may have been the happiest day of Nana's life—until now.

"Yes, ma'am," I say. "My heel was stuck. I was trying to avoid toppling in front of all the photographers."

My brain reels—wait, am I supposed to curtsy again? No, I curtsied to them already this morning. I'm set for the rest of the day. God, it's all so confusing. No matter how well the rest of my life is going, no matter how frequently our families come together, I don't think I'll ever get used to hanging out with the King and the Queen.

I mean, would you?

"Oh, they'd love that," she mutters drily in her high-pitched voice. "The *headlines*."

"Are we done here?" the King asks, looking from side to side. Even though his father and grandfather were kings before him, too, I've noticed in person that he always looks slightly bewildered, like he wandered into the wrong life.

"You know we're not, Bingo," the Queen says, using her nickname for him. "We have the wedding breakfast, followed by the diplomats' tea, and the reception." Like Libby, she's long since kept her partner in check—the true power behind the throne.

He sighs heavily. "I know, I know. Wishful thinking. Come on, then."

The Queen looks over at me, her eyes full of amusement. "Back to the palace—off we go. Let's give them a good show."

I follow the King and the Queen toward the royal carriages, toward my waiting family, toward whatever the rest of today might bring.

And so the next chapter begins.

acknowledgments

Is this the part where I get to practice my Academy Award acceptance speech? I have so many people to thank!

Thank you to Erik—my soulmate, my partner, the Han to my Leia—for being endlessly supportive. When I stop believing in myself, you tell me I can do it. When I stumble, you give me strength. Writing with a wee one is no easy feat, and there have been many moments when I've been full of doubt, creatively blocked, or just plain exhausted. You always give me the space and the encouragement to keep going, even when *you're* plain exhausted, so thank you for that. Plus, you take half of the mornings so Mama can regularly sleep in—if that's not true love, I don't know what is.

Thanks to Aurelia, for being the world's best inspiration and motivation (when you're not making me chase you around the living room with a comb). You are perfect.

Big thanks to my dream editor, Alex Arnold, whose patience and guidance resulted in me having way too much fun writing this book. You never made me feel silly for really, really, *really* caring about the details of life as a royally adjacent person, and for that I am endlessly grateful.

To everybody at Katherine Tegen Books and HarperCollins who worked on *Romancing the Throne*, a GIGANTIC THANK-YOU! I heart you all!

A huge thank-you to my patient readers (and wonderful friends) Dara Smith, Jerramy Fine, and Katherine Longhi, who never once were anything less than supportive (even during those scary early drafts).

Special thanks to Anica Rissi, Mollie Glick, my awesome agent, Jess Regel, and Melissa Harris.

To my friends and family, who lived through the years of ups and downs on the way to publication, thank you, and I love you. Thanks especially to my dad for teaching me to be brave, and to my mom for teaching me to be kind. I wish you could have read this book, Mama. I inherited my love of all things royal from you, and I think you would have gotten a kick out of it. I miss you.